DARK
HOLLOW
ROAD

Nov. 2019

Dark Hollow Road

Pamela Morris

Denise —
This one is particulary
dark and disturbing!
Hope you like it :)

Pamela Morris

Ardent
Creations

Special Thanks & Dedication To
Monster Man, Hunter Shea.

Your words of encouragement over the past few years have made a world of difference. Thank you for everything you've said and done on behalf of my writing. I will be forever grateful.

The Listeners

'Is there anybody there?' said the Traveler,
knocking on the moonlit door;
And his horse in the silence champed the grasses
Of the forest's ferny floor:
And a bird flew up out of the turret,
Above the Traveler's head
And he smote upon the door again a second time;
'Is there anybody there?' he said.
But no one descended to the Traveler;
No head from the leaf-fringed sill
Leaned over and looked into his grey eyes,
Where he stood perplexed and still.
But only a host of phantom listeners
That dwelt in the lone house then
Stood listening in the quiet of the moonlight
To that voice from the world of men:
Stood thronging the faint moonbeams on the dark stair,
That goes down to the empty hall,
Hearkening in an air stirred and shaken
By the lonely Traveler's call.
And he felt in his heart their strangeness,
Their stillness answering his cry,
While his horse moved, cropping the dark turf,
'Neath the starred and leafy sky;
For he suddenly smote on the door, even
Louder, and lifted his head:—
'Tell them I came, and no one answered,
That I kept my word,' he said.
Never the least stir made the listeners,
Though every word he spake
Fell echoing through the shadowiness of the still house
From the one man left awake:
Ay, they heard his foot upon the stirrup,
And the sound of iron on stone,
And how the silence surged softly backward,
When the plunging hoofs were gone.

Walter De La Mare

Dark Hollow Road

Chapter 1

I was eight years old in 1948 the night Daddy Clay came into my room and pulled the blankets down for the first time.

He told me to be real quiet 'cuz he didn't want to wake Mama or the new baby. Baby Kate was just shy of being a week old. Daddy reckoned being as I'd been taking such good care of him and my two brothers, Nigel was six and two-year-old Seth, while Mama was healing the past week, that I was a lady now. He said ladies took care of their menfolk and it made me real proud he thought I was so grown up.

Daddy said sometimes the lady of the house had to do things she didn't like doing. I knew that for certain. I'd heard Mama saying how much she hated doing up them dishes, but she done them all the same. He reckoned I wouldn't like doing what he needed me to do, but it was my duty until Mama was feeling better.

He was right. I didn't like it at all. It hurt and Daddy put his big hand that smelled of coal and dirt over my mouth. I almost couldn't breathe. Daddy said I mustn't tell nobody about it because it was a private thing. Daddy Clay was all about keeping things private, that's why we lived where we did, some three miles from the nearest town. We had five acres of

1

land butted right up next to one of the creeks that fed the Mighty Susquehanna or the Suck-A-Banana as Daddy called it. Two of it was on the same side of the road as the house and the other three was a big open field across the way. It kept folks from building too close, plus we needed it for our livestock, a few dairy cows and every spring Daddy would buy a few head of cattle for butchering in the fall. We kept six pigs and some chickens, too.

Daddy didn't like the idea of me going to school, but Mama insisted. She wanted all of us kids to learn to read and write properly. There was more to the world than our little farm, lumber mills, and coal mines, she said. She even had the notion we'd all graduate high school like her big brother, Uncle Eli, had done. Mama was real proud of her brother and how he'd made a good life for himself over in Scranton. He'd visit every year and always brought us presents. Daddy Clay said Uncle Eli was a good for nothing city slicker and was just trying to buy us off. I didn't know what that all meant at the time. I just liked the toys and sweets he gave us.

Anyway, back to that night. Daddy did what he called this Man Business while I did what he called a Lady's Duty. All I had to do was lay there with my nightgown pulled up, close my eyes, and hold onto the iron frame of my headboard and put my legs apart. I had to be real quiet, too. Not a peep, he said. Not a word, no protesting, and no crying no matter what. Daddy said the midwife told Mama she couldn't do her Lady's Duty for six weeks. That meant I had to do it for her all that time. I hated it, but I supposed it weren't no worse than shoveling out the animal stalls or working in the fields on those sluggish August days. I knew hard work and of all the chores I had, taking care

2

of Daddy's Man Business during them six weeks wasn't the most difficult thing I'd ever done. You did what you had to do and that was that.

After those six weeks, Daddy Clay didn't visit me for another three years. I sure didn't miss it, but I felt bad for Mama, knowing what she had to go through nearly every night. I could hear them, too. I supposed I'd heard them before, but I didn't know what it was they were doing until I'd done it, too. Sometimes it sounded like Mama enjoyed it, but I couldn't be sure. I kept my mouth shut about the whole thing for a long time 'cuz it was private business.

When I was eleven, the midwife, Mrs. Yagar, came to the house just like she done before for all us kids to help Mama bring another baby into the world. Things was going along alright for a while. I was downstairs finishing up tomato soup and grilled cheese sandwiches for everyone, when Daddy come down. I never seen him look so miserable. His face and eyes was all red and puffy. He was carrying Mama's old carpet bag.

"You kids go up and say good-bye to your Mama," he said. He didn't even stop. He just kept walking right through the kitchen, pushed the creaky screen door open with his free hand, and walked off the back porch like it were nothing.

"Is she going to the hospital?" I called out, but Daddy must not have heard, or more likely, just didn't want to answer.

Us kids looked at each other confused, 'cept for Kate. She was only three so it didn't mean anything to her. Seth and Nigel headed up the stairs while I hoisted Kate onto my hip.

I knew right away there wasn't going to be any trip to the hospital. Mama was the same waxy white color as the pillow her head lay on. Her hair hung in long, wet tangles of sweat and her skin had a weird waxy sheen to it. It reminded me of when we went to Great Gramma May's funeral. There was a weird smell to the room, too, like when we butchered chickens in the summer. It wasn't quite that bad, but the fine sour-sweet smell of that kind of work was hiding a little too close for comfort.

"Make it quick, children," the midwife told us in her hushed and gravelly voice. As she bent over to gather up an armful of blood stained blankets, sheets, and towels, a long strand of her gray hair fell down from the bun gathered on the back of her very round head. She paid it no mind and waddled out the door towards the bathroom at the other end of the hall. A few minutes later the rusted spigot on the tub let out a squawk as it was turned on.

At Mama's bedside, I gave Kate a heft onto my hip. The little thing still held half her toasted cheese in one grubby hand. Seth and Nigel were standing next to each other on one side of Mama and Daddy's bed. Mama hadn't moved that I could see. I began to wonder if she weren't already dead until she blinked.

"Where's my Mary Alice?" her voice was breathless and weak.

I inched a little closer. "I'm right here, Mama."

"Where?"

I reckoned she didn't have the strength to turn her head to see me, so I moved up even more, swallowing down the lump that rose up in my throat and trying hard not to breathe in the odor any more than I had to. "Here, Mama," I repeated and touched the back of her rugged tanned hand.

4

"You're in charge now," she said. It was all I could do to hear her over the hard thumping of my heart in my ears.

"Yes, ma'am."

"You keep the house nice, you hear? You tend to that garden like I taught you. All my recipes are in Gramma Fran's book, folded up neat. There's two pair of dungarees and one of your Daddy's flannels that need mending down by the sewing machine. Be sure and keep an eye on the coffee can over the sink, too. And Mary Alice, do as your Daddy tells you. You're the lady of the house now."

Tears were burning down my face and Kate had started in on a restless, whiny squirm in my arms. "Yes, Mama. I will."

"Tell your daddy her name is Virginia," she said in what seemed like a breathless sigh before adding, "Boys?"

They didn't say nothing, but their eyes was as big around as moon pies.

"They're right here, Mama. They can hear you."

"Boys," she went on in a voice more of air than sound at this point. "Help your daddy with anything he asks and you mind what Mary Alice tells you. She's going to be like your mama from now on."

I swallowed harder than ever. I didn't want to be like their mama. I didn't want to be the lady of the house and who was Virginia?

"We will, Mama," the boys muttered half together. Seth snuffed his nose and wiped one cheek with the heel of his hand. "Yeah, we will."

Mama closed her eyes then. We stood there watching her breathe until Mrs. Yagar come in and coaxed us out. The boys were the first into the hallway.

Seth took little Kate with him and headed back downstairs. I stood in the doorway, nibbling on my nails and scared to pieces at what was to become of us. My whole insides was trembling as the midwife lay the palm of her hand gently onto Mama's chest, then leaned over to put her ear only an inch or so from Mama's parted lips. "Bring me your mama's hand mirror, Mary Alice," she said.

I stepped back into the room, afraid to make even the slightest sound. Mama's comb, brush and mirror had been a wedding present from Daddy. Mama used them every day and night. I supposed they were mine now or would be soon. They were made of ivory, Mama had told me once, and were very expensive.

I passed the mirror over to the midwife who lowered the glass close to Mama's lips and watched. She took up Mama's limp wrist. "She's passed," Mrs. Yagar said with a frown even deeper than my own. "What time is it, Mary?"

A little wind up clock stood over on Daddy's dresser ticking away the seconds. "Almost quarter 'til one," I said.

"Twelve forty-five," she said stepping away. Real gentle-like she lifted the edge of the sheet, tucked both of Mama's arms under it then pulled it over Mama's face. All the hairs on both my arms stood up straight with goose bumps. The room was dreadful cold. "I'll call into town for you," she said, knowing we didn't have a phone. "Someone should be out before dark to take care of things."

"No," Daddy Clay's deep bass voice thudded into me from behind. "We take care of our own here, Ruth. You know that."

"Of course, but I just thought..."

6

"We'll take care of it. Thank you for your help," he reached into his front shirt pocket and pulled out a five dollar bill.

"Clay, you know I can't take that, not under the circumstances."

He stepped around me and held out the money. "You done us a service, Ruth, no matter how it turned out. You take it and head on home. Me and the kids will tend to the rest."

Ruth sighed, taking the five. "I'll at least call the coroner for you when I get home to get the death certificates done up. I can give him all the information he'll need for the public records."

Was then I looked around the room from where I stood. There wasn't any sign of a baby and Mama's belly weren't big no more, either. The lump started to rise and choke at my throat again. The carpet bag. My hand covered my mouth. I couldn't stand it no more and ran down the stairs.

"Mary Alice, where you going?" my brother Nigel hollered as I busted through the screen door, making it slam against the woodpile like Mama hated.

I didn't answer. I couldn't. My brain was on fire. The hard, dusty ground pounded under my bare feet. All I could think to do was run. Run and run and run as far and as fast and as hard as my skinny legs would take me. And I was crying all the while. Crying so hard and running and knowing I sure must have looked like a crazy person. I reckon I probably was. Temporary insanity, that's what I'd learn they called it some years later.

I scrambled down the river bank. There was a spot under the bridge where we all went to hide. I wasn't going to stop there at first. It was too obvious. They'd find me for sure and right then I didn't want anyone to know where I was but the Good Lord.

My thoughts choked on that idea, too. Weren't no Good Lord who let mamas with little kids and innocent babies bleed to death and die for no reason at all. No Good Lord would make me the lady of the house and take on all of the duties of that lady. No Good Lord would make it so I couldn't go to school no more and maybe even move away and live in Scranton with Uncle Eli. I crumpled to the ground, sitting in the moist dirt under the bridge and sobbed. He was a No Good Lord and I didn't want any part of Him.

I let the grief, hatred, and pain hold me in an iron fist until I could hardly breathe. Eventually, my senses started to trickle back to me one strangled sob at a time. Hugging my drawn up knees to my chest, I sat and watched the river float by. Mama's dead. My head kept driving that home. Seems I'd just get my eyes dry and those words would cold blast me to the core and I'd start in again. Mama's dead. I started thinking about what Daddy Clay meant by we'd take care of things. Did he mean he'd call on the funeral home himself? Or did he mean something I didn't even want to think about? It was August and steaming hot and humid. It wasn't anything pleasant to consider, the fact Mama was upstairs draped over with a sheet and, on account of the heat, would be drawing in the flies sooner rather than later. Mama's dead.

I sure hoped he was going to get someone soon. Real soon.

The crunch, tumble, and slide of gravel behind me let me know I wasn't alone.

"Daddy says you need to come help." It was Seth.

Dark Hollow Road

My whole insides shriveled up. Closing my eyes, I wished for this all to go away. It was time to wake up, Mary Alice. This ain't happening at all. It's a bad dream and nothing else.

"Mary Alice, Daddy says..."

"I heard you," I snapped without meaning to. I still didn't move, though.

Pebbles skittered down the embankment where Seth's voice had come from. That No Good Lord sure must have had it out for me that day. I don't know what I did to deserve this, but I didn't figure I had a choice but to take my punishment. Rising up, I gave the river one long, last look. Wasn't going to be the same, anymore. I'd left the house an eleven-year-old girl. I would be going back inside a woman, the lady of the house. I'd never find myself dreading anything so much for the rest of my natural-born days.

Daddy and Nigel was down in the barn banging together a coffin out of old boards when I came trudging back into the back yard. His beet-red face was dripping with sweat. He stopped pounding long enough to straighten up and level his blood-shot eyes at me. "Get your Mama cleaned up and put something pretty on her, Mary Alice," he instructed. "Seth's going to help you. He's inside with Kate."

Despite the sweltering sun, I shivered. "Yes, Daddy," I said. Mama's dead. She's dead and I'm going to have to touch her and see her poor naked body and try and get clothes on it. The tears started to come again. I didn't want Daddy to see me cry, so I ran towards the house.

Seth was sitting on the sofa in the front room watching Kate play when I walked in. He looked even worse than I felt. He'd never seen a woman's body, dead or alive. I'd seen Mama naked when it was bath

9

time, at least. God, I hoped Daddy didn't expect us to carry her to the tub. I wasn't about to go ask. We'd manage without doing that. Seth was only nine and Kate sure wouldn't be able to help at all.

"Let's get this over with," I said. "C'mon, Kate. You can help pick out a pretty dress for Mama."

My little sister looked up and smiled, "Mama 'wake now? We go town!"

I dug my nails deep into the palms of my hands to keep from falling apart all over again. "No. Mama ain't gonna wake up ever again. We need to make her pretty to meet Jesus."

"I want meet Jesus," Kate's smile grew as she let the dolls drop from her hands and stood up. "He coming supper?"

With a resigned sigh I took her little hand. "No, Mama's going to go visit him, instead. That's why she's taking her carpet bag. She's going to be gone a long, long time." What had Daddy done with that carpet bag anyway? I knew only one thing could be inside it and that both it and its contents should be buried with Mama.

With Kate in my arms, we trudged up the stairs. Seth dragged himself along. When we passed by the bathroom, I happened to see the sheets still soaking in the tub. The water was tinted deep pink. "Seth, why don't you take care of those, instead? Get the Borax and scrub the dickens out of them. You'll probably have to rinse them a couple times, but do the best you can." If we'd had more money, I'd have seen them sheets burned, but it wasn't like that.

My brother's shoulders sagged with relief. "Sure, Mary Alice. You can take care of Mama on your own?"

Dark Hollow Road

I looked down the long, gray hallway towards the open bedroom door. "I'll manage. It's best those linens don't sit too long, or we'll never get the stains out. Go on now, and if I get done quick enough, I'll help you hang them out to dry."

Seth seemed almost happy at the notion of washing blood-soaked sheets, but then I'd have jumped at the chance, too, had I been given the choice.

We buried Mama in the flower garden out back. Daddy made her a fine headstone out of wood and we done our best to make it pretty with flowers.

Daddy wasn't going to even send word to Uncle Eli, Mama's brother, but after a few days I convinced him to at least let me write a letter. He showed up unannounced a week after the burial, hopping mad and grief-stricken. This was his baby sister. How dare Clay Brown even consider not telling him she'd passed away?

There was no love lost between Daddy Clay and his in-laws, the Gundermans. It was a mutual dislike, if not a complete hatred on Daddy's part. I was surprised Daddy even let Uncle Eli onto the property to pay his respects, let alone into the house for the cup of coffee I offered. What Daddy did refuse was to remain with us in the kitchen for a visit. He stormed his way with swinging arms and a heavy, stomping gait to the barn.

In Daddy's absence, Uncle Eli gave me a sizable amount of cash with the words, "If you kids ever need anything else, Mary Alice, you just let me know, alright? Anything at all."

"Thank you, Uncle Eli. I will."

I'd grow to regret saying that.

Chapter 2

Orange. Orange was the perfect color for the leaves. Brandon selected a crayon from the line of them he'd placed on the living room floor. Left to right, nice and neat, all in order, light to dark starting with white and ending with black. Not just any orange would do. He picked the one in the middle of the three choices. Mommy called it Umber. Brandon just called it middle orange. He traced the inside edge of the leaf and drew hard over the skinny lines inside that looked like veins before coloring the rest of the first leaf. Once done, he studied the image of the tree in his coloring book and colored another leaf in the same way. Satisfied with the umber leaves, Brandon moved on to some dark yellow ones, or Ochre, as Mommy called it. He wasn't sure why she had all these funny names for his crayons.

Tap-tap-tap.

Brandon's head pivoted to look towards the sliding glass door. With the drapes wide open, sunlight streamed through the glass, warming the spot where Brandon lay on his belly, but the door itself was closed. Too cold for just the screen today now that it was fall time.

Tap-tap-tap.

With one finger, a lady tapped on the glass. Her hair hung in long, straight locks that shined a little in the sun and was streaked with gray. Over a thin blue-flowered dress, she wore a heavy knitted sweater. She smiled and waved when she saw Brandon looking at her. One of the neighbors. They hadn't lived here very long, so he didn't know everyone yet. He still remembered their little apartment in New Jersey. This place was better. Bigger. They had a big back yard and everything now.

Mommy, who was in the kitchen, must not have heard the lady knocking on the glass. Brandon sat up and smiled. "Hi," he said.

"Hello," the lady replied. "Is your Mommy home?"

The boy pulled himself to his feet and walked closer. "She's in the kitchen."

"Can you get her for me? I wondered if I could borrow a couple cups of sugar." She held up an empty canning jar. "I'm in the middle of making apple pies and here I am two cups of sugar short."

"Okay. You want to come in?"

She nodded. "If that's alright."

He didn't see any good reason for it not to be alright so pulled on the door as hard as he could, barely able to budge it at first. When it finally shifted, it slid with ease on the well-oiled track. A cool wind rustled the curtains and the hem of the lady's dress. Brandon crinkled his nose. "I'll go get her."

"Alright," the lady grinned again, stepped just inside the door frame, and looked around the inside of the room, her eyes lingering over the sight of the television where Doc McStuffins tended to the ouchie of a purple hippopotamus.

Brandon hurried into the kitchen. "Mommy, there's a lady here who wants some sugar." His nose scrunched as he whispered, "She smells funny."

Mommy paused and looked up from the bowl where she had just cracked an egg into a mixture of raw ground beef, bread crumbs, chopped onions and steak sauce. "Who?"

He shrugged. "I dunno. Some lady. She's in the living room. She wants to borrow some sugar. She came to the back door."

"Oh," his mommy's eyebrows arched a bit. "Let me clean up my hands," she said, then in a little louder voice, "Come on in. I just need to wash up a little here."

"We having meatloaf?" He liked meatloaf, meatloaf and mashed potatoes with lots and lots of gravy.

"Yep, your favorite. Green beans, peas, or carrots this time?"

His smile revealed he had two top teeth in the middle missing. "Corn!"

"You and your corn." She turned to the sink. "Just so long as you don't try to eat any of that corn in the field. It's for cows, you know?"

"I know. I like corn. It's my favorite, but not cow corn, human corn."

"Corn it is, now go tell the lady to come in. I don't think she heard me."

"Okay." Brandon spun around on the toes of one foot and skipped back to the living room. The lady was still there, still in the same spot, and still watching the television. "That's Doc McStuffins," Brandon announced.

"I see."

"Mommy says come into the kitchen. She's making meatloaf."

The stranger glanced towards her feet and shook her head, "Oh, I don't want to make a mess on your nice clean rug." Her shoes were pretty dirty and very old, like something Brandon thought his gramma might wear. You could tell she'd done a lot of walking in those shoes. "Maybe you can just get the sugar for me?" She held out the empty jar. "Two cups, that's all I need. I can repay your Mommy with some fresh eggs. I see you ain't got no chickens."

"Okay," he took the jar, trying hard not to breathe too much because it was getting stinkier in here every minute. "I'll tell her."

"Thank you."

Back to the kitchen he went again where Mommy was just wiping off her hands. "Did you tell her?"

"Her shoes are dirty. She doesn't want to mess up the rug. Here's the jar she brought."

Laughing a little, Mommy tossed the dish towel aside and took the canning jar. "Oh, it doesn't matter. That's why God invented the vacuum cleaner." She brushed past him and went into the living room. "Hello," the greeting fell on an empty room.

"Where'd she go?" Brandon ran to the sliding glass door that still stood open, and bounced out onto the back deck. "Hey, where'd you go?"

Mommy stepped out behind him. "Hello?" she called again, sliding the door shut behind her. "I'd be happy to lend you some sugar." She walked down the deck's few steps and into the large back yard enclosed in a four foot high chain link fence. Six feet beyond it stood the field of corn. Its husks and leaves had dried to a pale, rustling brown and each stalk was topped with a dark brown wad of corn hair. Mommy said it

15

was called a tassel of corn silk, but Brandon thought it looked more like messed up hair.

"Maybe she went to the front door," he said and headed towards the gate. He was just tall enough to unlatch it.

"Wait up, little man," Mommy warned.

Brandon sighed but waited anyway. "I'm not going to get hit by a car, Mommy. We're miles from the road!"

"We aren't miles from the road. Scoot," she gave him a playful pat on the butt. "Go see if she's out front then."

He took off like a shot, rounding the corner of the house and stopped. Nope. No lady. No anybody.

His mommy followed a few yards behind. "You sure there was a lady? I know how you like to make up stories."

He scowled. "There was a lady. I saw her. She gave me the jar."

Mommy seemed to have forgotten the jar still in her hand. She looked at it again. "Oh, right. The jar. Weird. I wonder why she left."

Brandon gasped. "Maybe she's hiding in the house!"

"That's just creepy, Brandon."

"But she could be. I bet she is."

"Dear lord, little man, your imagination," Mommy said and rolled her eyes. "Let's go look for her inside."

"Maybe she had to use the bathroom."

"That seems more likely."

With Brandon leading the way, they went into the house through the front door. Without an ounce of fear, Brandon raced down the hall towards the downstairs bathroom and laundry room. Both were empty. "Nope, not here."

Mommy was walking out of her home office when Brandon returned to the doorway between the kitchen and living room. "Nobody hiding in there," she said, setting the empty canning jar on the breakfast bar that separated the kitchen from the small area where the dining room table stood. "She must have changed her mind." Then Mommy stopped, turned her attention towards the sliding glass door again. The drawn curtains billowed against the cool, fall breeze. "Hello?" she said. Brandon could sense that something in her voice was different now. "I closed that door, didn't I?"

"I dunno," the child shrugged. "I think so."

Mommy pulled the curtains apart. "And these were open."

He nodded, remembering that part, the way the sun had shown down on his book and crayons and the tree he'd been making look like the ones outside. "Hey! Where's my coloring book?"

Mommy pulled the glass door shut, pushing down the little tab lock on it this time. "Where did you leave it?"

He pointed to the obvious empty space below the soldier straight row of crayons. "Right there." Now he was mad. "That lady stole my coloring book."

Mommy looked angry, too. "Are you sure you didn't take it outside with you?"

Brandon put his hands on his hips. "Mommy, you know I never color outside."

"I mean when we went looking for the lady. Did she tell you her name?"

He continued to give her that are-you-crazy look. "No," he said.

Mommy had that worried frowny expression on her face. "What did she look like?"

He shrugged again, "Just a lady. She had long hair with gray lines in it and brown shoes and she smelled funny."

"How did she smell funny?"

"I don't know, Mommy. It was just funny. Like old stuff, like the back of Gramma's closet."

"Mothballs?"

Brandon didn't really care what the lady smelled like and he didn't know what a mothball even was, he just wanted his coloring book back. "I guess. She stole my book," his eyes narrowed as he fumed, glaring at the back yard and the cornfield beyond through the closed window.

"Stay down here. I'm going to go look upstairs."

Dread prickled his skin. "No, I want to go with you." What if she came back? What if she was hiding out in that corn field watching? What if she started tapping on the door again like before, her and her stupid sugar jar. He bet she was lying so she could sneak in and steal his book.

Mommy must have seen how scared he was, because she held out her hand and didn't insist he wait alone. "C'mon. Let's look together." Then, as if reading his mind, "We can get you another coloring book if the missing one doesn't show up."

Brandon squeezed her hand and nodded. "Okay."

It was just as empty and quiet upstairs as it had been down. Whoever the lady had been, she was sure gone now. Brandon and his mommy stood in the middle of his bedroom. "Check the closet," he insisted.

She did. It was empty. No monsters. No weird, old lady.

Mommy took his hand again. "Grab another book if you want and you can sit at the table to color. I need to get that meatloaf finished and in the oven."

Dark Hollow Road

Brandon's mood brightened, "Can I squish the egg in?"

His mommy laughed, "Of course you can squish the egg in."

When Mama Sam heard about it, she didn't think it was funny at all. "She did what? What a stupid bitch."

"She took my coloring book, too!" Brandon piped up, releasing a bit of mashed potato back onto his plate from an overstuffed mouth.

"Don't talk with your mouth full," Mommy frowned. "And must you say that kind of thing in front of Brandon?"

"Oh, he's heard it a million times before. Relax."

"No thanks to you." Mommy looked over at Brandon and smiled. "Anyway, Brandon said she came to the back door, had this jar for some sugar then just left before I could even meet her."

"With my book."

"Pipe down, Bee. It was just a cheap coloring book. We can get you another." Sam cut off a generous bite of the meatloaf and chewed it slowly. "So you didn't even see her and she came waltzing onto the back deck and into the fenced in yard? What a nut job."

Mommy shook her head. "I know. She must have run like hell wherever she went to, though. We went outside and everything looking for her. Nothing."

"I think she went into the corn field."

Mama Sam grinned. "Actually, that makes the most sense, but what's the point? Why come begging for sugar then leave without it? And where did she come from? Our nearest neighbor is like two miles up the road."

"I told you it was weird."

19

Sam set down her fork in favor of the glass of ice water and took a sip. "Unless there's someone living in that other house."

"Oh, there can't possibly be anyone there. Can there?"

Mama Sam chuckled, "Why not? Maybe there's some crazy squatter secretly living in the basement. It's not like we have a clear view from here what with all the damned corn on three sides."

The house they were talking about was way down at the end of the next road up. Its yard was full of weeds, one of the windows on the front had a piece of glass missing from it, and part of the porch roof was starting to cave in. Mommy didn't know it, but Mama Sam had taken him down there once, just to look. There was a big barn out back, too. They hadn't gone inside the buildings or anything, hadn't even gotten out of the car, but it had been pretty neat, in a scary kind of way.

They'd taken Mama Sam's Jeep to the end of the road but couldn't get across the stream. Instead, they met with a big rusty sign with holes shot through it. "Dead End," Sam had read out loud to Brandon. "Bridge Out." They'd turned around and come home after that. Mama Sam had figured that sign had been there a really long time.

"We'd have seen something, don't you think? Lights upstairs, maybe. Or a car or something coming and going."

"Do you stand up in the spare room with binoculars watching the place all day and night?"

"Well, no."

"There you go. My point is made."

Dark Hollow Road

Mommy let out a sigh. "All I know is it was freaky. The doors will be locked from now on even when we're home."

"Ah, just like New Jersey. I'm glad we moved up here to Bummfuck, Pennsylvania where it's safer," Sam chuckled.

Brandon knew they were joking. He'd heard them talking about how their new town was a whole lot safer than where they'd been living. Mama Sam had gotten a job at a restaurant as head chef. She cooked for rich people and Mommy had been able to stay home with Brandon all summer long! She was looking for something else to do. Now that he was in school all day, she got bored. She wanted a store where they sold old things, ant eeks, Mommy called them. He'd been in a lot of ant eek stores with Mommy and Mama Sam. They weren't much fun. He never got to touch anything, not even the toys. Mama Sam was always telling him that if he touched it, he bought it and to keep his hands in his pockets, plus he'd never seen a single ant in any of them.

"She smelled like an ant eek," he said, busting into the middle of their conversation.

"Well, maybe we'll have to head over there after dinner and see if anyone is home," Mama Sam suggested. She gave Brandon a wink and he smirked back.

Chapter 3

After Mama's dying, I had to quit school. I really liked school, but I was okay with staying home, too. I'd already graduated the seventh grade and that was more book learning than anyone else in the family had except for Uncle Eli.

Mama always kept a grand vegetable garden. Now it was my turn. There's not a time in my memory that I don't remember helping in the garden. As young as three I knew just when a tomato was ripe and ready for picking. By seven, I could scrape the corn off the cob and right into the canning jar along with the best of them. My nimble fingers shucked fresh peas and snapped beans like nobody's business until they was sore. I taught my little brothers and sister to do the same, just like Mama had taught me.

Nigel and Seth dug the potatoes and it was them that got to climb into the three gnarled apples trees that grew out back. On weekends, Daddy took the boys hunting or fishing. Sometimes they'd come back with a wagon full. Sometimes there wasn't nothing. It was up to Seth and Kate to fetch the eggs every day and feed the pigs we fattened up all year for butchering in the fall.

For a while Daddy Clay didn't do much but drink whiskey, sleep, and yell at us. He almost lost his job at the mine because of it. I'd heard Mama's tender voice over the years urging Daddy on his way, talking sweet to him as she packed his lunch and filled his thermos. Now that I was the lady of the house, it was my duty to do those things. As for the other duty, Daddy pretty much left me alone. I suspect he had a lady friend in town which suited me just fine.

It was 1953, that first time, and dog days hot in late August. I'd thought I had the swimming hole to myself. Nigel and Seth had gone into town. We were out of coffee and flour. Daddy Clay was to work. I'd left Katie napping on the front porch. I stripped down to my panties and cami and swam all the way across the river and back first, before stretching out onto my back to do the Dead Man's Float.

"You're fat, Mary," Kate's little voice snapped me upright. She was standing on the dried out earthen bank. Dirt and sweat had drawn lines down her thin arms and legs. Her hair was a mess.

"You hush your mouth, Katie Sue," I blurted out.

Her saucer-round blue eyes stared back at me. "But you are."

"No, I ain't," I told her. I hurried up out of the water to grab my dress, one that had been Mama's and was a little big, and pulled it over my head as fast as I could. I didn't need no one else seeing what she had, because Katie was right. I was getting shameful fat. "You don't say nothing to anyone about this, Katie Sue. This is girl business. You understand? Girl business." I'd done what Daddy told me never to do and now I was paying the price.

"Okay," Katie said, the little bud of her mouth turning down.

I took her hand and we started walking back to the house. "Not even Daddy. Especially not Daddy Clay."

Can't tell you the fear that run through during those months when Daddy came home. As long as he had his lady friend, I was safe, but how long would that last?

Katie never said a word, but it was only a matter of time before Daddy noticed. It was colder then, mid-December, and I'd been wearing Mama's big, old sweaters, hoping he'd not see. He wasn't so naive as Kate and he growled his rage when he knew what happened.

"Who you been kissing, Mary?"

I remember clamping my jaw real tight. I didn't want no hurt coming to Bobby. He was a boy from school, one I was sweet on and him on me. I tried to see him whenever I went into what passed for the nearest town. Daddy Clay didn't know nothing about Bobby and I meant to keep it that way, but that night while I was cleaning up the kitchen table and Daddy accidentally turned as I was going by and run his hand across my belly, he knew. He made me stand up straight. He put his hand flat on my stomach, round as a melon under the layers, and growled, "Who you been kissing, Mary?"

I'll never forget the way he said it. I did the only thing I could. I lied. "I ain't been kissing nobody, Daddy."

Daddy Clay's face turned tomato-red as he rose up, towering over me. He was a big man, a hard man. It wasn't smart of me to lie to him like that. "Don't lie to me. You got a baby in your belly, girl, and that come from kissing boys. Ain't that what I always taught you? You think I don't know how babies come to be made?"

"No, Daddy." I didn't mean to cry, but the tears came all the same. It had only been a little kiss, but

24

according to Daddy that's all it took. "I'm sorry, Daddy."

Nigel, Seth, and Katie stood there staring and gaping. Daddy spun around and they all took a half step backwards. Daddy Clay wasn't one to hit us too often, but when he did, you didn't forget it for a good long time. "You all keep your mouths shut about this, you hear?" he bellowed. "Mary won't be going into town anymore until we get this taken care of. Anyone asks, you say she hurt herself, tripped in a groundhog hole and done twisted her ankle, that's all. She'll be fine. Just can't be making the long walk into town for a while now. That understood?"

"Yes, Daddy," my brothers and sister chorused.

"But, Daddy," I didn't finish my protest. Daddy Clay made a sound that scared me, scared us. It was like the warning grunt of an angry buck. You didn't argue with that noise, never.

"You hurt your ankle in a chuck hole, Mary. Don't argue. Nigel and Seth can do what needs doing in town for a while, can't you boys?"

"Yes, Daddy," my brothers replied obediently.

"Good. Now, you get to your chores and homework."

They scattered like flies from a swatter. I finished cleaning the kitchen. Normally, Daddy Clay and we would have listened to the radio an hour or so before bed, but this wasn't a normal night. Daddy spent a good part of it pacing on the front porch muttering to himself.

Was a real cold night when the stomach ache started, but I'd banked the fire good because of what the radio had said about the weather heading our way. Daddy and Nigel had filled the kerosene heaters for our bedrooms, the kitchen porch was so loaded with split wood there weren't nothing but a three-foot-wide path from the door to the steps, and Kate and I set a low fire in the front room. We knew all about bad storms and from what they were saying, this was going to be a big one. The winter had been pretty uneventful up until then.

I woke up around three o'clock that morning. I had to pee. Seemed I barely get up from the toilet when the urge to pee would come again. Everything hurt. My feet and legs were swollen. My breasts had gotten bigger and heavier right along with my belly that now stuck out so far I couldn't pull my chair up no closer than a foot from the kitchen table. I waddled my way to the bathroom and closed the door. Before I even got sat down I knew this wasn't like all the other times. My back hurt real bad. The pain would move around to the front on both sides so it felt like someone had me squeezed into a tight belt.

I leaned back, trying to catch my breath, when this huge gush of water come out from between my legs. It wasn't pee. I didn't dare stand up.

"Kate," I managed to say after a few minutes. Our room was right across the hall from the bathroom. I don't think I said it very loud the first time. I didn't want my baby born here sitting on the toilet like I was and by now the dripping had pretty much stopped. I cleaned myself up and went back to wake my sister. "Katie," I shook her out of sleep. She looked at me with annoyance in the weak light of the lantern I'd set on the dresser. "I think it's time for the baby to come," I whispered.

Dark Hollow Road

She rolled over, eyes getting bigger. "You want me to wake Daddy Clay?"

I really didn't. I wanted this to be private, just between us girls, but there weren't no other houses, let alone girls, within five miles of our place on Dark Hollow Road. I started to think maybe I could do this without making too much noise. I could have the baby real quiet and not wake anyone and when morning came, I'd show everyone what me and Katie did all on our own. Then the next pain come and nearly dropped me to my knees. "Yeah," I consented, "get Daddy." Another pain came while I was alone. I had to sit down.

Outside, the storm was starting up. The misty drizzle that had been falling at dinner time was now a steady snow. I didn't like the looks of it. If something bad was to happen, we'd not be able to get into town. We didn't have a phone.

Daddy Clay came in looking all sorts of frazzled. "You sure?" he asked. I supposed I was, but having never done this before I wasn't one hundred percent. I told him what had happened in the bathroom and he nodded. "Katie's getting towels," he said. "How many pains you had?" He'd brought another kerosene lamp with him that he set on the little table I once used for doing homework.

"Three."

"When was the first?"

I told him. He was quiet, like he was figuring something in his head. Daddy couldn't read so well but he knew about arithmetic just fine and I'd seen that look on his face when he was concentrating about numbers. "How long will this take, Daddy?"

He gave me a stern look that wasn't at all reassuring. "If you're lucky, a few hours. Get your night dress off and come over here to the rug by the heater."

"On the floor?" Weren't babies supposed to be born in beds?

He took my hand a little rougher than I'd expected and yanked me to my feet. "You want your mattress and bedclothes ruined?"

"No, Daddy." I did like he said. I didn't like how he stood there watching me undress, and I liked it even less when Katie came in with an armload of towels, leaving my brothers gawking by the open door at my huge, ugly belly and plumped breasts.

Daddy Clay didn't like them being there, either. "Boys, get the kitchen stove fire going good and heat up a bucket of water. Nigel, make a pot of coffee," he ordered. "Kate, close the door."

Pain after pain came. The invisible band grew wider and tighter, squeezing my waist all around harder and harder. Daddy kept making me open my legs wide so he could see what was happening. Hours ticked by. The sun rose before Daddy announced he figured it was almost time. All I could do was whimper, cry, and scream. My whole insides was being ripped apart and forced to come out the narrow passage of my girl parts. It burned and cramped. I threw up and when Daddy told me to, I pushed.

Oh, how I wanted it out of me. I was certain I was going to die. "Get it out of me, Daddy! Please, get it out of me!" I screamed and screamed.

Daddy Clay was kneeling between my spread legs. I didn't care what he saw and felt now, just so he got that baby out. "Push, Mary. Push as hard as you can!" I pushed with all I could, feeling like I was having the biggest movement of my bowels ever. Then, something gave and slid and my body jerked and the horrible, hard, squeezing sharp and ripping pain was gone. Just like that. Panting, I fell back onto the stack of pillows Kate had put behind me. It was over with. I could breathe again. I'd done it. We'd done it. I heard the faintest little gurgle and cry as Daddy tied a bit of string around the cord before cutting it with his pocket knife.

Then the room was real quiet. Other than the wind howling outside and ice-crusted snow pellets smacking hard on the glass, it was still. I turned my head and opened my eyes. Daddy had the baby in his arms, all bundled up snug in one of the towels. He was rocking on his knees a little. Back and forth, he went, like he'd smashed his thumb with a hammer and was trying not to curse. Kate stood beside him, still in her nightgown. She was so pretty like that, blue eyes looking at the little foot that was poking out from the corner of the towel.

"You had a baby, Mary," she said with a smile.

"I know," I smiled back at her.

I looked at Daddy Clay who had got real still all of a sudden, still clutching the bundle tight to his chest, so tight his knuckles were white and he was shaking. "Daddy?"

He flinched as if snapping out of a dream, eyes wide, scared. His hold on the baby loosened. "A boy, Mary," he said.

I held out my arms, "Can I…"

Daddy Clay shook his head. "No, you better not, Mary. It ain't right."

Another cramp suddenly washed over me and I moaned. What was going on? I'd had the baby. "Daddy?" I looked at my father desperate for help, for answers.

"It's the afterbirth coming, Mary."

"The what?"

"Just a few easy pushes, not like before. Kate, get another towel ready."

He was right. It wasn't like before. It was so easy Katie did most of the work. Her little face crinkled up, "Ew," she said but never turned away or hesitated. "That's yucky."

All the while, Daddy Clay stood there, holding the bundle that my baby was in. I didn't understand at first why he wouldn't let me see my son. A baby needed its mother.

"Go run your sister a hot Epson salts bath, Katie," he said.

Katie was more than ready to get out of the bedroom.

"What's wrong with him, Daddy?" I asked when we were alone.

"Born blue," my father explained. "Cord got wrapped around his neck."

My stomach soured. "But I heard him, I saw ..."

Daddy made the buck grunting sound again. His jaw was set firm. His eyes were narrowed. "Baby was a stillborn, Mary. Like that last baby sister your mama had. You understand what that means? It never took a breath of life. It's dead."

I was too tired to cry. I wanted to hold my baby. I wanted to see his face. Daddy Clay shook his head no at my silent, pleading look. He turned and left. I never did get to see anything but that tiny, delicate, blood and goo-coated foot, a foot I was sure I'd seen wiggle its toes.

Katie helped me stand and climb into the steaming hot water of the claw foot tub. While I soaked and cleaned myself up, I heard the rattle of the mop bucket and the gentle swish of the mop being pushed over the rough wood floorboards of Kate and Seth cleaning up. Katie brought me clean panties, a nightgown, and thick socks while I was trying to dry off and keep from bleeding more down my legs. Mama had showed me the box under the sink full of old cloth diapers and sock rags. She told me what they were and I figured this was pretty close to the same thing I'd been using them for since only a few months after she'd died.

"Daddy says you're to stay in bed a couple days," Katie told me as she stood there watching. "He's heating up some broth and tea for you."

I wasn't going to argue with that. Katie helped me back to our room and tucked me in.

I couldn't sleep. From the bedroom window I could see the sweeping field across the road. Everything was white. I wondered how long it would last and how deep it would get. I wondered about my baby boy's tiny foot and the way his toes had curled closed and opened and how Daddy Clay had held him so tight, so very, very tight.

I stayed abed for three days, feeling guilty all the while knowing how hard the chores was what with all that snow we got. There was a good two feet of it. Way out where we were the plow trucks didn't come until late, if at all sometimes. On the second day, I heard the driver talking with Daddy saying everything was closed up, even the mine, at least until tomorrow. By then things should be passable and Daddy wasn't missing any work time so that was good. It was real nice of him to stop. Most folks didn't pay us much attention, but he was a good man and stayed a bit longer to get our driveway cleared and Daddy's old truck dug out properly.

That night, I got up the courage to ask Baby Kate something I didn't dare ask Daddy. "What happened to my baby?"

"Daddy said it died," she said, setting a bowl of soup down on our bedside table along with a glass of cold milk.

"I know," I whispered. "But what did he do with it? Where's it at?"

She gave an indifferent shrug as if a dead baby weren't no big deal. "Buried it in the basement."

I leaned back on my stack of pillows, "Oh." He couldn't really have dug a hole outside in two foot of snow so it made sense, I suppose.

I think Daddy done the right thing. It was better I didn't see my baby, because then I would have felt more empty in my heart than I already did, and he buried it close so I could go and visit any time I wanted, in rain or shine, heat or cold.

By spring it was almost like none of the business of it happened. Nobody talked about it. Sometimes Kate and I would go down and put some flowers on the little dug up spot in the back corner. Nigel found a flat rock in the creek that summer. We painted it and I come up with a name, Allan, after Mama's daddy.

Chapter 4

Two days passed before a chance came to visit the old house. There were no further sightings of the woman Brandon had taken to calling The Sugar Lady. Sam grinned as Renee placed the last of the breakfast dishes into the machine. "You have such a cute ass," she said.

Renee gave her jean-clad backside a shimmy before straightening.

"Don't start something you can't stop, little mama." Sam leaned against the doorframe, feeling like the luckiest woman on earth.

"You started it," Renee jibed back.

"Guilty as charged." Samantha Whalen, who stood a stocky five foot ten in her well-cushioned work boots, tipped her head with a sheepish grin. "Can't help it. I'm a natural born perv."

Renee's soft, lithe body crossed the kitchen floor. "And that's why I love you," she said, wrapping her arms over Sam's shoulders and planting a peck of a kiss on her partner's lips. The moment didn't linger. Brandon was in the living room watching television and though neither had a problem expressing their affection publicly, like any parents, they kept it down to a dull roar when the kid was around.

Sam gave Renee's butt a little squeeze before they parted. "Sure you don't want to go over there with me to meet the freak?"

"Very sure." Renee backed away. "But do give Sugar Lady my best wishes." She'd filled the jar the night before. It sat waiting on the dining room table, a little yellow sticky note adhered to the side with Renee's written salutations.

"I wanna go!" Brandon chirped. Just when you thought they weren't listening, they proved you wrong.

"I'd rather you didn't, buddy," Renee crossed her arms.

Sam's brown eyes twinkled. "C'mon, Mom! Don't be a meanie."

"Yeah, Mommy!" Brandon chimed in from the other room while rolling to his back. His hair still lay smashed to one side and stood on end by his right ear. "Don't be a meanie," he giggled, got up, and wandered over to where they stood in debate.

"We don't even know if that's where she lives, little man. I'm betting she doesn't."

Judging by the look on Renee's face, she wasn't going to budge no matter how much Sam insisted they'd be careful. Sam reached out and mussed Brandon's hair up even more. "Your mom is right, Bee." Brandon slumped and groaned. "But I'll go over, have a look around and, if anyone is there, maybe we can stop in again another time."

The boy's face screwed up with disappointment. "I never get to do anything fun," he grumbled.

"What if we go to that pumpkin farm when I get back?"

There was another grumbling sigh from the six-year-old as he tried to hide the twinge of a smile. "Can I get a candy apple?" he mumbled.

"Sure," Sam agreed before Renee could protest against that, too. "Anything you want. I don't have to be to work until three o'clock so we have plenty of time. We can even do the Spook Barn. How's that sound?"

Glee ignited the boy's face exposing the missing top front teeth again. "Awesome! Can we, Mommy? Please can we do the Spook Barn?" He turned on the charm with puppy-dog eyes and that gap-toothed grin towards his mother. "Pleeeeeeease!"

With a skyward roll of her eyes, "Fine, but you need to be ready when Mama Sam gets back. Teeth brushed, hair combed, clothes and sneakers on."

"Yeah!" Brandon shot off like a rocket up the stairs.

"Brush your teeth extra, extra good if you're going to be eating junk later," Renee called after him.

Sam smirked, "Thanks, Mom."

She was rewarded with a kiss. "We need some family time. Now, go take that jar back to its owner so she can make her pies, though I doubt you're going to find anyone over there."

Sam gave her a quick kiss back, scooped up the filled canning jar of sugar, and made a beeline for the front door. "I promise not to dawdle too much."

"Don't dawdle at all," Renee called, following her only as far as the top step of the front porch.

The ear-splitting pound and scream of Slayer erupted from the Jeep as soon as Sam started it up. Cupping one ear in Renee's direction, Sam mouthed the words, "What? I can't hear you?" before shifting into reverse and backing out the driveway.

The Jeep drew to a slow, easy stop in front of the house. The amateur photographer in her was cursing the fact she'd left her camera at home. This place could make for some awesome shots and now was the best time of year to be capturing images of spooky old houses. The weeds she and Brandon had seen at the start of summer were easily twice as thick and tall and tangled now.

A waist-high wooden post that yawned backwards may have once held a mailbox and the vaguest indications of a driveway long past its prime lingered to the right of the house. Sam didn't dare pull the vehicle into it.

Along the roadside, a gray fence teetered back and forth, at times so tired it lay all the way down, lost in the overgrowth, only to rise again a few yards down and fall back again. Sam recognized it as that cheap snow fence people put up around here, narrow slats of wood wired together and rolled into a neat, portable bundle. It appeared as if once upon a time it had been someone's idea of a white, picket fence. If that was the case, this fairy tale clearly did not have a very happy ending.

Grabbing the jar, Sam climbed out and stood by the Jeep, eyeing the front of the house and what little she could see of the property beyond. Nothing but the orange and blue reflection of the yard's massive maple tree and the sky above shifted in the two upstairs windows, one of which had a corner broken out of one pane. A faded orange and black sign stapled to the front door proudly proclaimed to keep out.

Sam waded with caution into the tall grass crowded with flowering stalks of Goldenrod, mauve-toned Joe-Pye weeds and clumps of Black-eyed Susans. It could be someone's idea of a wildflower garden, she speculated. Not hers, but someone's. Someone who didn't drive a car. She looked for some sort of worn footpath, but the lawn yielded no such thing. She was forced to giant step her way to the porch stoop. The center of the bottom step sank in on itself, crumbling to splinters from years of exposure with no maintenance.

This was nuts. It was obvious no one lived here. "Hello?" Sam called out, not daring to put her weight on the steps. "Anyone home? Yo!" She held up the jar, shaking it in the air, just in case the paranoid inkling sprouting at the root of her spine was right and she was being watched. "I brought your sugar jar back. We filled it." The front of her brain told her to turn and go and take the full canning jar back home with her. The back of her brain had other ideas. It nudged her forward. It dared her to ignore that first rotten board and try the second step. It told her it would be okay to grab hold of the railing and hoist herself onto the porch itself and walk to the door.

"*Knock,*" the dark part of her subconscious urged. "*Go ahead and knock.*"

Sam's fist rapped on the door that had once been a very pretty shade of green. Now it was a dull, dusky, rotted-grass color. Flakes of the paint crumbled away, joining hundreds of other chips already at the threshold. "Hello?" She called, knocking again before leaning to one side, trying to peer into the window to the right. She couldn't see anything and quickly realized why. A yellowed and drawn pull shade blocked her view. Sam moved down the porch to the next window. It was patched over with cardboard from the inside.

She went back to the door and rapped a third time. Instead of the desolate silence of before, Sam was certain she heard movement on the other side of the door. It wasn't much, maybe the slightest shuffle of feet, the hesitant crunch of a shoe on broken glass, of someone lurking, listening, not wanting to be known.

"I brought your sugar," she repeated. All was quiet again. "Hey, Sugar Lady, open up! I wanna give you some sugar." She snorted at her own perverse humor. That sort of remark would have gotten a punch in the arm and verbal chastisement from Renee. Snarkiness was such a great way to make new friends.

Taking a step back, she studied the door with its rusted knob and weather-pitted keyhole plate. It reminded her of a face covered with spreading scabs. Someone had to be standing on the other side of that door. She felt it. She'd heard something.

The black eye of the keyhole blurred then swelled into perfect focus. "*Take a peek*," it whispered. "*Just lean your big ass self over and put your eye right up close.*"

Images of needles, screwdrivers, and ice picks jabbing through the hole flashed through her head vividly enough to make her jerk back. That was ridiculous.

Sam inched forward. Leaned in.

Whatever she'd heard on the other side was more likely a squirrel or chipmunk than this crazy Sugar Lady. Maybe there would be another eye looking back at her, a bloodshot eye. Was it any wonder Renee didn't want Brandon staying up late to watch scary movies with Sam? Here she was a grown woman pushing thirty, on a bright, sunny day in autumn, letting her imagination get the better of her thinking of her eyeball being poked out by some weirdo hag.

"Fuck it," Sam shoved the images aside, forcing herself to look through the tiny hole and into the room beyond.

Her eye peered in. Right. Up. Close.

Dark Hollow Road

Just a room. That's all it was, a small and narrow entry hall with peeling wallpaper and little chunks of fallen plaster on a floor covered with brown and yellow linoleum. It wasn't much wider than the door itself. She couldn't see much other than that. Sam straightened herself, staring at the doorknob as she took a step back.

The pattern of black rot on it shifted. First spiraling right, then left. Right. Left. Full stop. Was it really moving? Squinting her eyes didn't seem to make a difference.

"Ninety-seven, ninety-eight, ninety-nine. One hundred! Ready or not, here I come!"

Tiny hands shoved her backwards. Staggering, she clutched for the railing but missed completely and prepared to meet her maker. The jar of sugar hurtled into the air as Sam landed hard on her ass before flopping flat to her back, breathless, stunned. "Shit!" Her arms flung up protectively over her head as she rolled to her side, expecting to be stampeded by the feet of a running child. "Jesus H. Christ, watch it, kid!"

Sam held her breath. Waited in a tense semi-ball. But the feet never came. There was no kid. Instead, a blue jay screeched to her left from somewhere in the overgrown lilac bush. Sam sat up, eye level with a clump of Queen Anne's Lace.

Wind gusted through the leaves in the trees and the tops of the tall flowers and grass around her. The world seemed to sway with them, twisting like a long line of fun house mirrors. Sam's eyes darted back to the porch where the door stood tall, firm, and shut beside the window where the faded shade hung and did not stir.

Nobody's home. Gone fishing. Keep out.

Groaning, Sam hoisted herself up. Nothing seemed out of place, sprained, or broken, but she might have a

39

bruise on her ass by the end of the day. Ten feet away the canning jar remained miraculously intact in a thick clump of browning weeds. She scooped it up and gave it a quick inspection. Not a scratch.

"We're not done," she addressed the house and whatever mute, unseen occupant it harbored. "And you aren't getting your sugar until you can come to the front door like a sane, decent human being, you stupid bitch." Sam turned and worked her way to the Jeep quick time. Not running, but a far cry from a casual stroll back through the weeds and ruts and toppled fence line. Anger smothered any fear and Slayer drowned out the growl Sam used to throttle the fear that dared linger around the edges of that anger.

"Well?" Renee met her at the door.

"Nobody was home." Sam marched by, slamming the jar a bit harder than necessary onto the counter. "I need to change my pants," she added.

"Wait. What?" Renee snorted out a laugh. "What happened? Did you shit yourself? Sam?" Renee's giggles followed her up the stairs, and into their bedroom. "What did you do?"

"Fell off the porch. Bad railing."

"Oh my god, Sam. You aren't hurt, are you?" Renee tried to sound concerned, certainly she was under all the snickering at the large, brown smudge of dirt on the ass of Sam's pants that could simply not be ignored.

Brandon suddenly appeared at the bedroom door. "Can we go now?"

Renee giggled again, doing her best to block the view of Sam standing in the middle of the room without any pants on. "As soon as Mama Sam changes her pants."

Dark Hollow Road

The boy's eyes grew big. "Did she have an accident?"

"Jesus," Sam groaned. "Can I have some privacy here?"

Laugh-snorting, Renee scooted her son away. "Yeah, sort of. Let's let Big Mama change in private then we can go to the pumpkin farm."

"And the Spook Barn."

"We'll see," Renee looked over her shoulder, still grinning, then pulled the bedroom door shut.

Sitting on the edge of the bed, one leg half into the clean pair of jeans, the other still naked, Sam's vision blurred around the edges while her mind's eye came into sharper focus. Sure as she was sitting here half naked, she'd heard a kid yelling, a kid who was "It" playing Hide-and-Seek. It could have come from anywhere, from around the back of the house, from any place in the fields of corn around them, or from across the narrow creek she knew ran not too far beyond the big "Bridge Out" sign.

What bothered her wasn't the voice that counted down, it was why she'd fallen backwards. She was a big girl, not easily pushed around, and yet something had caused her to move back so quickly and with such force that she'd struck the porch upright, bounced off it, and landed ass over end in the front lawn. One minute she was standing there looking at the doorknob, a good six feet from the edge of the porch, the next she was sprawled in the grass. She'd felt someone push her, pure and simple.

Sam slid her right leg into the jeans, stood, pulled them up and walked to the window as she zipped and buttoned them into place. The view from here wasn't as good as from the guest room, but she could still see

41

part of the other house's roof a bit. No one lived there, she repeated in her head. How could anyone possibly live there? What you heard was a rodent or maybe a bird. That piece of glass broken out of the upstairs window would give easy access to either. And there were probably another hundred holes big enough for chipmunks or squirrels, hell, maybe even a raccoon or woodchuck had worked its way through some gap under the porch and down into the basement.

She may not have known what she'd heard, but she'd heard something and she wanted more than ever to go back and find out what it could have been. Despite her real age, what remained of Sam's teenage brain twitched to sneak around back, jimmy open a door or window, and wiggle her way inside. She wanted to find out what was in there and who had lived there.

Young Samantha spent a couple weeks every summer with her grandparents. On many of those long, hot summer days there was nothing better to do than go yard sailing. One memorable and exceptionally hot day, while they were out hunting down yard sales, Grandma stopped along the roadside in front of a small, abandoned house with a screened in porch. Sam couldn't remember much about the place beyond sheets of gray, water-stained Homasote and old wood planks used to board up the windows and the porch.

"There's a window around back," Grandma had said. "Go see if you can get in, then come through the house and let me in that way."

Innocent Sam had been horrified. "It's posted," she'd said. Despite the bold black ink that had faded nearly to the same color as the white cardboard it was stamped on, you could still read the sign tacked to the side of the house.

Dark Hollow Road

"Then we better be quick about it."

And so it was that Sam's addiction began. No sign was too new or too bold back then to keep her out if she wanted in. Thing were different now and she was wiser, but Sam wanted in to the house on Dark Hollow Road. She wanted in bad.

Chapter 5

I slipped up again in 1956. I didn't mean to, but I was getting older and boys were getting better to look at. Bobby was still around, but after what happened that first time, I was afraid to be near him anymore. Daddy never did find out who I'd been kissing that first time.

This time I knew right off I'd made a mistake. I knew those feelings my body had and them cravings for things. I also knew Daddy Clay wouldn't be happy I'd done it a second time, even if it weren't my fault, but I had to tell him. He'd be more angry if I tried to hide it again. Besides, he'd know soon enough since he wasn't with his lady friend no more. Daddy was sure to never, ever kiss me on the mouth. That made it alright. I'd seen enough in the movies and, speaking from personal experience, knew that no good could come of it.

Daddy was usually real nice during what he called the Loving Times. He taught me that this was something men and women did in private and that it was special and that I wasn't to tell no one about it, not nobody, not even Kate. It was something he and Mama had done except they kissed a lot and that was how me and my brothers and sister come into being.

Dark Hollow Road

There were other times when Daddy Clay'd been drinking that the Loving Times weren't so nice. He was rougher then and it was hard for me to be quiet and keep him from kissing me. He'd turn me over on my belly and have me put my rear end in the air, too. It felt funny that way because sometime Daddy didn't always put himself in the right spot, but at least I didn't have to worry about getting kissed.

Anyway, back to my mistake. I went to the pictures that night to see a film called "North By Northwest" starring Cary Grant and Eva Marie Saint. It was real good and about this guy who is mistaken for another man and he gets chased because they think he's a spy. I didn't get to go to the movies much so it was important to pick a good one. I wanted to see "Some Like It Hot" but Daddy didn't like the idea of me going to a picture with Marilyn Monroe in it.

I was coming out of the theatre just as a group of three boys from school were walking by. I recognized all of them: Richard Barrows, whose folks ran the general store, Elmer Murphey's uncle and daddy owned the two places the town was named after, and Larry Yagar, the midwife's son. The cutest was Richard. His family had money.

"Hey, Mary," Elmer greeted me first.

"How you doing, Mary?" Richard added.

Larry just stood there shuffling his feet.

"I'm fine," I said.

Richard looked up at the theater marquee and smiled, "How was it?"

"It was real good. In the end..."

He held up a hand quick. There was a lit cigarette wedged between two of his fingers. "Don't tell me, doll. I may want to go see it."

"Oh," I laughed. I had that funny feeling in my stomach when he smiled at me, like I wanted to kiss him.

"Where you going now?"

I shrugged, "Home, I suppose."

Richard looked at the other boys quick, grinning ear to ear, then came over closer and put his arm around me. "We're headed to Kelley's for a burger and malt. Want to come?"

My heart fluttered. Was Richard Barrows asking me out on a date?! I hesitated. I didn't have any extra money for even a soda, let alone a malt. "I don't…"

He squeezed me a little closer, "My treat, baby. C'mon, I got a flip top now and we can get you home loads faster than if you walk even if we hang at Kelley's for half an hour. It'll be a kick. You deserve some fun, don't you, Mary?"

"I guess," stammered out of me.

"Course you do, right fellas?"

"Of course, she does," they echoed.

"It'll be like a triple date, Mary. You ever been on a triple date?"

I'd never been on a single date but didn't tell them that. "No," was all I said.

Richard laughed, "Ain't that a bite? Mary's never had a triple date. You need to get off that farm more, doll. Let's beat it and show Mary a swell time. You know the fellas here, don't you, Mary?"

"I seen them around."

"Cool. C'mon, let's beat it." Richard draped his arm over my tight shoulders.

The others chuckled, falling into place behind Richard and me as we crossed the road to Kelley's.

There ain't much to Murphey Mills, Pennsylvania. Along with the theater, which was real old and had once been called an opera house, and the diner, we had the general store, a single-pump gas station, a couple of small shops, a post office, and a church, of course. Murphey Mills had its own fire department, but there were only two trucks and one police car. Last, but not least, there was Murphey Mills Hotel. There were rooms upstairs you could rent for cheap and a bar and dining room on the first level. The official name of the big road through town was Pennsylvania Route 9 Spur, but we all just called it Main Street.

Even though I hadn't been to school in almost four years, there were still kids at Kelley's who knew me. It's not like I was friends with any of them, but we knew each other.

They all looked when the door to the malt shop opened and I walked in on the arm of Richard Barrows. Some of them right out laughed. Others rolled their eyes and turned away. A few, like Sarah Wilson, shook their heads and looked kind of angry. I figured they were jealous. Maybe they'd never had a triple date like I was having.

Richard marched us right up to the counter. "What you want, Mary?"

It was all so overwhelming. This wasn't but the second or third time I'd been in there. I never had extra money for this sort of thing. "A soda would be nice."

"A soda? That's it? C'mon, doll. You can get more than a soda. I'm buying, remember? Get yourself a cheeseburger and fries and a chocolate malt if you want."

"Okay," I smiled at the man behind the counter. "What he said sounds good."

"That's my girl. Make it two, barkeep," Richard laughed. "Sit down, fellas. I'm feeling generous tonight."

The other two scurried onto counter stools. Elmer sat to my left. Larry Yagar sat on the other side of Richard.

We were five minutes into waiting for our orders when someone came up and nudged in between Richard and me. "What's the buzz, cuz? Who's the babe?"

"This is Mary," my date said and I felt myself blushing. No one had ever called me 'babe' and I didn't much think of myself as being pretty or cute. "Mary, meet Chester. He's a bit of a spaz, but we love him."

Chester shook my hand rather awkwardly, "Pleased to meet you, Mary."

"Thanks. Nice to meet you, too."

Richard rolled his eyes. "Spaz," he repeated in a half whisper. "Now, scram, Sam," he added. "Can't you see we're having a date here?"

Chester chuckled and strolled away. I glanced over my shoulder. "I thought you said his name was Chester."

"It is, doll."

"But you just called him Sam."

"It's slang, baby doll, slang. Don't you know what slang is?"

I shook my head, "No, I guess not."

"Oh, Mary, Mary, Mary. We are in for a good time tonight. I can tell that already."

I smiled at him.

Our burgers arrived.

On the way home, Richard had me sit in the front seat between him and Larry. Elmer sat in the back. We weren't a mile out of town before Elmer leaned up and pushed a cheap bottle of whiskey up to the front. I knew the smell right away. Daddy drank it a lot. I knew what it did to men and I guessed it did the same to boys my age. Suddenly I was kind of scared.

Richard pulled his arm away from around my shoulder, grabbed the bottle and took three long swallows of the amber liquid inside. He waved it in front of my nose and I shook my head. Larry took it instead and drank a bunch down before handing it back to Elmer. They did this a few more times, before Richard slowed the car and turned right. We were still a few miles from home.

"Where we going?" I asked. "This ain't Dark Hollow Road."

He pulled the pack of cigarettes out of his front pocket, shook one out and handed the pack to the back seat. "Can't light a smoke with all that wind blowing," Richard explained. "And, I need to take a leak." He smiled and kissed me on the cheek. "Wait here, doll. I'll be right back. We'll have you home in no time." Much to my surprise he nodded to the others. "C'mon, fellas. Let's talk, huh?"

Elmer jumped eagerly out of the back without waiting for the front door to open. Larry lit his cigarette and leaned back in his seat. "I don't have to go. I'll wait here with Mary. Don't want to leave her sitting her all alone, do we? It's kind of scary out here at night."

There was no mistaking the annoyed look Richard gave his friend. It was the same look Daddy Clay gave one of us kids when he thought we were lying to him. "We need to talk, moron."

Larry didn't back down. "I'll wait here." He drew in a lungful of air and blew it up towards the black sky of sparkling stars.

"It's okay, Larry. I'm not afraid. I walk home after dark all the time." I really didn't mind. Dark roads didn't frighten me one bit, or the sound of the night animals or any of it. I kind of liked it. It was one of the few times I could really relax and think. Sometimes I even let myself dream a little bit of a life away from Murphey Mills.

"See, she's fine," Richard was already out of the car and slammed the door a little harder than I think he needed to. "It'll take five minutes. Let's go." It wasn't a request. It was an order.

"Fine," Larry scowled at the other two boys and opened the passenger side door. As he walked around the front of the car and the parking lights shined on his face, Larry looked right at me and half smiled. The others had already wandered off to the other side of the road and over the ditch to the bushes. Reluctantly, he joined them.

Not five minutes later I heard, "I ain't doing it!" Larry suddenly growled from the dark place across the road, "It's wrong."

There was a lot of scuffling sounds and man grunts and loud whispers I couldn't quite understand before Richard and Elmer emerged. "Hey, Mary, come here a sec, will ya? Larry twisted his ankle or something. We need some help."

I hurried from the car but didn't hardly get the door shut before the two of them was suddenly beside me. Richard had come around the front of the car and Elmer the back. "What's wrong with Larry?"

"He's a chicken shit asshole, that's what's wrong with Larry," Richard announced and grabbed my arm. "Take your stockings off, Mary. We aren't done having our good time yet."

"What?"

Elmer suddenly had my right arm and was reaching up with one hand, yanking at my dress slip. "Get her on the ground."

I was half-pushed, half-slipped into the ditch along the roadside. It only had a few inches of water in it, but it was cold and slimy. "Stop it," I tried to push away from them. I tried to fight, but there were two of them and they were big and there was only one me. I really did try, though Daddy Clay didn't believe me at all when I told him.

Elmer held my shoulders tight while Richard pulled my panties, my very best panties, down to my ankles. My head filled with my own screams and the sounds of them laughing. Richard lay on top of me, kissing me hard on the mouth, his tongue pushing into my unwilling mouth as his stiff man part went up between my legs. Daddy Clay said if I'd not been asking for it, I would have bit Richard's tongue off, but I wasn't thinking too clear at the time.

When Richard was done, they turned me over, one side of my face under the muddy ditch water so I couldn't open my eyes or barely breathe, and Elmer did what Daddy does, but Elmer wasn't as gentle about it. It hurt and I screamed, sucking in water and coughing it back out, and oh, how I tried to scramble away, but Richard held me in place, barely letting me lift my head up out of the water.

"Get away from her!" Larry's voice yelled. "Get the hell away from her, you sick bastards!"

Larry came charging in, tackling Elmer right off my back. I fell to my side and just lay there trying to figure out what to do. Richard let me go. He jumped onto Larry's back and yanked him off, half tossing him to the ground. "Shut the fuck up, pecker head."

I staggered to my knees and crawled from the ditch, hoping I could get far enough away and maybe hide until they decided to leave. I didn't mind walking home from here. I wasn't afraid.

"Get back here, slut," Elmer's voice raged. He swooped down from behind me and yanked me to my feet.

Back at the car, Richard stood with his arm draped around Larry's shoulder. Larry was looking down at the road, but I could still see the blood coming from his nose and there was a big clot of it on his head that had bled down into his left eye. Elmer marched me over to them.

"Take her hand, Larry," Richard ordered. Larry didn't move, but his jaw muscles tensed up. "Take your girlfriend's hand, DAMN IT!" Richard pulled himself away from Larry and for a minute I thought he was going to punch him again.

Larry held out his hand and Elmer pushed me towards it. It was cold and shaking, but his fingers curled around mine real tight all the same.

The other two laughed. "You two lovebirds have a nice walk home," Richard called out, going around to the driver's side of his car. Elmer leaped into the passenger's side same way he'd gotten out of it. The car started up. "Fucking pussy." Richard shifted and hit the gas, kicking up dirt and pebbles into our mud- and blood-spattered faces. The car drove about a hundred feet before the taillights flashed and my purse came flying back at us. Then they were gone, becoming nothing but two pinpricks that looked like tiny red eyes before vanishing all together.

Larry still hadn't let go of my hand. "You won't tell, will you, Mary?" he asked. I couldn't see him much in all that dark, but his voice was full of shame and fear.

"You didn't do nothing wrong, Larry."

"I should have stopped them."

I sighed, shuffling my feet to get us going in the right direction. "Can't do nothing about it now," I said. I picked up my scuffed purse as we went by it. No telling where my panties ended up.

"But you won't tell, will you?"

"Daddy Clay will find out whether I tell him or not, but I promise I won't say nothing about you being there."

"Thanks, Mary." He gave my hand a squeeze. His was warmer now and stronger and together we walked hand in hand all the way to the head of Dark Hollow Road.

I didn't say a thing to Daddy Clay for another month, but when I did, he was hopping mad. He said he'd not let this one get as far as the first. I told him who it was, but he never went to the police about it. He said he didn't want everyone knowing what a dirty slut his daughter was.

One night, real late, about two months later, Daddy woke me up and told me to come down to the root cellar. The bare bulb was glaring down bright as day on Daddy's makeshift work bench and someone had put an old, ratty blanket on top of it. As we got closer, I saw someone else there. He had a mask up over his face like doctors wear for operations and alongside the workbench was one of our metal television trays. There were doctor tools on it.

"Get up on the bench, Mary," Daddy told me. My knees were weak and shaky. I knew what they was going to do. Daddy picked me up and lay me down.

"We're going to take care of this one for you, little girl." His smile was all lopsided. He smelled like whiskey.

"That's right," the doctor reassured me. "Just close your eyes." He held a piece of damp white folded cheesecloth up to my nose. "Take a deep breath and close your eyes. We'll be done in no time."

My heart was racing. Would they cut me open? Would they put knives up into my girl parts? I'd heard sometimes coat hangers was used and I started crying. I couldn't help but breathe in the acrid smell of chloroform through my sobs. The last thing I remember was half-gagging, trying to breathe, and pure terror.

When I woke up the next day, I was back in my own bed knowing the baby that had been inside me was gone. Kate and I put a stone next to Allan's grave that we wrote "Baby" on. There wasn't no body to bury. The doctor had taken it away, but we wanted to do something.

It was a long, long time after that before Daddy and me had any Loving Time between us.

Chapter 6

Saturday morning probably wasn't the wisest time to visit Yagar's Farm. Every parent, grandparent, aunt, uncle, and child in the area seemed to be there, taking their dear, sweet time walking up the middle of the rutted hayfield path that now doubled as a parking lot row. Beside Sam, Renee clung to the Oh-Shit handle for dear life. In the backseat, Brandon giggled with each sharp dip in the path and curse that was jarred from between Sam's clenched teeth. She maneuvered the Jeep through the narrow lanes, keeping an eye on the man in the day-glow yellow vest who was working to direct them into a space, while at the same time trying to avoid a variety of obstacles that included but were not limited to, traffic cones, woodchuck holes, rocks, and wooden stakes tethered together with orange string to form the parking sections.

"Jesus Christ!" It was all Sam could do to resist gunning the engine and plowing down the two old ladies walking at a snail's pace in front of them. Each tugged along a wheeled wire basket contraption more suitable for a grocery store than a hay field, while carrying an over-sized purse. The Jeep took a serious dip to the left before leveling out again so Sam could crawl it into the parking space being offered by the man in the vest. She smiled, gave him a thank you nod, and cut the engine. "This place better blow my mind," she grumbled, releasing the seat belt. Another car filled with two women and three elementary-aged kids pulled up and parked beside them.

Oblivious to Sam's mounting stress, Brandon pressed his nose to the back window, squirming and eager to get out and explore this exciting new world full of miles of pumpkins and cornstalks, candied apples, cider and donuts, and by the looks of it, a tractor-drawn hayride. As she waited for the neighboring vehicle to release its occupants, Sam looked back at Brandon in the rearview mirror. "Looks like fun, eh, Bee?"

"Yeah!" Brandon was clearly in awe.

Renee hoisted her purse to her shoulder and climbed out. "Don't forget your camera, hon," she said before slamming the door and going to the back to free her son.

Finally the others were done fumbling with backpacks, water bottles, and strollers so Sam could get out. "Camera, right. Thanks, babe." She grabbed it from the backseat and, with Brandon out and chomping at the bit to run towards the main attractions, locked up the Jeep, steeling herself to make the best of a landscape of screaming, running kids with sticky fingers and ketchup-smeared faces. It wasn't that she disliked kids, but she didn't exactly like them, either. They were fine in brief doses and Brandon was cool, but he was only one kid, not a hundred, or a thousand, by the looks of this place.

Brandon tugged on Renee's arm as they crossed the field made parking lot, drawing them closer to the wooden picket fence and eight-foot-wide archway that formed the entrance to the grounds. Beyond it, long mounded rows of pumpkins waited to be selected by dozens of children and adults. Wooden crates of apples, Indian corn, squashes, and gourds could be seen even further in, under a low-roofed barn-like structure. Through the open-air market, another closed-in greenhouse had been transformed into a massive gift shop. The place went on and on. Maybe it would be worth the trip and madness after all. Sam pulled the cap off her camera lens and started taking pictures.

"Can we get a pumpkin?" Brandon eyeballed the rows of plump, round, orange squashes. The first row they passed held pumpkins no bigger than a cantaloupe. Further on down the line they ran about beach ball size.

"We'll grab a few on our way out, Bee," Sam said. "Let's go see about that Spook Barn and maybe a hayride. You ever been on a hayride?" Despite her misgivings, Sam was feeling herself getting a bit excited about the place.

Brandon shook his head. "Nut-uh." His head swiveled back and forth. Sam wasn't the only one having a hard time deciding what to do or where to go first.

"How about a corn maze?"

"Nope."

"This way," Renee headed in the direction of what looked like a vegetable market. Holding tight onto Brandon's hand, she wove her way around the barrels and crates and people while Sam did her best to keep up. It was like following a charging bull through a china shop maze. Sam, being wider and less agile, had to take greater care side stepping kids, wagons full of pumpkins, and a large table stacked and packed full of locally made preserves, before they emerged on the other side and into the open expanse that was the inner core of the farm's offerings. Behind them was the market. To the right down a long, wide dirt path was a barn with a series of stalls that appeared as if they might contain various small farm animals.

Food aromas wafted from straight ahead where two red and white food trailers had been set up. Half a dozen gray picnic tables covered with checkered tablecloths that matched the trailers waited for patrons. A short, generously hipped woman in a blaze orange t-shirt marked staff in all capitals across the back was wiping the plastic cloths off with a wet rag. Brightly painted signs announced that this was the place to buy hot coffee, cider, fresh made donuts, burgers, hot dogs, fried dough, French fries, and the most important items of all, candied and caramel apples. It was too early for there to be anyone in the burger and hot dog line, but a few people stood around with steaming Styrofoam cups, and one table held five kids sipping cider. Powdered sugar from two large fried dough patties covered their faces, hands, and in some cases, their shirts. The coffee-sipping chaperones seemed oblivious to the mess.

Sam was glad they'd eaten a hearty breakfast, or she, too would have succumbed to donuts or fried dough and walking away would have been far more difficult than it was already proving to be. Some sort of narrow, wooden bridge formed an arch over the walkway in front of them. Beyond that more signs announced hay rides, a corn maze, games, and the Spook and Boo Barns they sought. Sam had had no idea there would be so much here. They'd driven by it countless times but hadn't really paid much attention until the place started to come to life with thousands of pumpkins made into fairytale characters.

Dark Hollow Road

Renee shifted her purse on her shoulder. "There, first gauntlet cleared," she laughed.

"Goats!" Brandon hooted with excitement. Before either of them could even locate the goats, the boy was nothing more than a brown head of hair atop a striped green and white shirt, bobbing and weaving itself into the wandering hordes.

"Brandon Michael Evenson! Get back here!" Renee shouted, following in hot pursuit.

By the time Sam arrived, Brandon was getting a firm reprimand by his mother who squatted in front of him. "... you hear me? You do that again and we're done here. We'll go right back home and we won't be coming back until next year."

The boy's puckered lips turned first in one direction then the other. With a head half hung down, his eyes remained on the lookout to the right where goats did indeed play an active role in entertaining the nearby children and adults alike. "Yes, Mommy."

"Do we need to put you on a leash like a three-year-old?"

"No, Mommy."

Renee grabbed her son's hand with a firm, protective shake and stood up. "Alright then. Now, about these goats."

The back of Brandon's hand swiped across his nose before he looked up. A white goat was climbing up a caged in ramp that led to the bridge Sam had seen before. Brandon's eyes were riveted to the creature. The trio headed over for a closer look. More goats lingered and begged through sturdy fencing at the base of the ramp inside a large grassy and hay littered yard. There were dozens of them. Sam had never liked goats. Their eyes were messed up, narrow slits turned sideways. What the hell was that all about? Oh, they were cute from a distance, but up close and personal, no thanks. Their soulless eyes freaked her out.

"Can we feed them?" Brandon's fingers played over what had once been a gumball machine but now held brown pellets of food. A quarter apparently gave you a handful of the stuff. Some clever farmer had rigged up an old soup can to a pulley system that carried the goat chow up to the bridge where it could be dumped. The goats knew this. The white goat had a following. Behind her they nudged each other and sniffed at the boards. Several looked over the railing, their disturbing eyes demanding the humans below pay them homage.

Sam fished a couple quarters out of her front pocket and gave them to Brandon.

"That's Ruby," a voice piped up from behind them. "She's the boss."

Sam turned and smiled at the woman. "Oh, yeah?"

"Yeah. The alpha." Her smile and expression were that of a child, but she was clearly much older than that, how old Sam could not determine. Short and heavy set, her slightly tipped eyes watched as Brandon pulled the rope that moved the can closer and closer to the awaiting goats. The name tag pinned to her bright orange shirt declared her name was Lisa. Sam knew immediately it was the same person she'd seen earlier wiping off picnic tables. "That one behind her with the brown spots is Jade, then is Opal with the black ears, Diamond, Amber, and Pearl. Amber is kind of mean. She bites."

A chuckle rose in Sam's chest. "I sense a theme."

Lisa's grin widened with growing pride revealing smaller than usual teeth. "I named them."

"You did a great job."

"I'm Lisa," she announced. "I work here. My brother Lee owns it, but I help." When she wasn't talking Lisa's tongue ran back and forth slowly in front of her bottom teeth and behind her lip. She held out her hand.

Sam shook it. "Nice to meet you, Lisa. I'm Sam."

"Hi, Sam. Nice to meet you, too." She went back to watching Brandon feed a second quarter into the machine, pour it into the can and haul it skyward as if she were seeing it for the first time as well. Once the can tumbled over the edge and headed down again she looked away. "I should get back to work."

Brandon and Renee turned and headed over before Lisa could go.

"Hi, I'm Lisa," she repeated. "I work here."

"Hello, Lisa."

The woman stuck her hand out towards Renee who gave it a warm shake. "I'm Renee and this is my son, Brandon."

"Hi, Renee. Hi, Brandon."

"Hi," Brandon leaned against his mother's leg, staring pie-eyed at the stranger. He tucked his hands deep into his pockets when Lisa held hers out.

"He's shy," Renee excused before quickly changing the subject. "What's the difference between the Boo Barn and the Spook Barn?"

Lisa either didn't notice or didn't care, or both. Her answer came without a flinch. "Boo Barn is for little kids. It's not scary. The Spook Barn is supposed to be scary. I don't think it is, but I've helped set it up for a long time so I know it's not real. It was Lee's idea. Lee's real smart. He thought up this whole place

"Wow," Sam added. "Well, thank you for the help, Lisa."

"You're welcome. Have a nice day."

"We will," Renee added.

Lisa marched off towards the market area with big, waddling strides, her arms pumping in determination.

"She was nice," Renee said.

Brandon didn't look convinced.

"What's wrong, Bee?"

He shrugged. "I dunno. She was kind of weird."

"We're all kind of weird, Bee. Get over it," Sam tussled Brandon's hair. "Your mom or I will explain later. Meanwhile, time's a'wasting. Which will it be? Boo or Spook? That's what we came here for, right? That and a candy apple."

Much to Renee's sour-faced chagrin, Sam bought three tickets for the Spook Barn. From behind a window covered with warped chicken wire, the man in bib overalls and a flannel shirt smiled. "You big enough for the Spook Barn, young man? It's pretty scary."

Brandon's chest puffed up. "I'm almost seven."

"Practically ready for college," he chuckled back, handing the three tickets over to Sam. "You folks been here before, I take?" His blue eyes smiled behind sagging eyelids.

"Nope, we're pumpkin farm virgins," Sam announced.

He frowned. "You sure about the Spook Barn then? It really is for kids a bit older than almost seven."

Renee stood a few yards away from the short line of people buying tickets, her arms crossed and an I-told-you-so smirk on her face, and said nothing. She'd already argued that the Boo Barn would be more appropriate.

"It's all fake," Brandon announced.

With a shake of his head and another soft laugh, the ticket man grinned. "True enough, I suppose, but just because something is fake doesn't mean it isn't scary."

"I'm not afraid of fake things," Brandon assured him. "I'm only afraid of real things that are scary, like closet monsters and snakes and big rats. Are there any of those in there?"

Renee pressed a hand over her mouth to cover the laugh.

"Well, you know, I ain't been through there this year, myself, so I don't really know for sure what all's in there. I just sell the tickets, but if them things are in there, I'm pretty sure it's just like you said, all fake. All just pretend. Although, we are on a farm and farms do tend to get a rat now and then." He looked up at Sam and winked. "You still sure you want to go in?"

At the mention that real rats might be in there, Brandon's mouth dropped a little bit open. He snapped it closed quickly enough, straightened his spine, and gave a stiff, confirming nod. "I'm sure. I don't think real rats would stick around with all these people. They'd hide."

"Alright," the ticket man said. "Have a good time in there. Don't say I didn't try to warn you."

"Thank you." Chuckling, Sam gave the tickets a little flap in the air and turned away, her free hand coming to rest on the top of Brandon's head. "Let's go get spooked, Bee."

Brandon didn't often take Sam's hand, but now it wiggled into place and gripped it tight. Renee marked their approach with an eager grin, pretending she hadn't heard a word of the formidable warning. "All ready to get spooky?"

"Yup," Brandon's reply was a little too quick and sharp. After almost seven years, Renee knew that an answer like that meant Brandon was not at all ready or sure of what was coming next. He was excited and he put on a brave face, but the curtness of the answer always gave him away. He was a lot more scared that he let on.

She scooped up his other hand, letting him walk between them as they headed in the direction the Spook Barn arrows pointed. "I think we should make Mama Sam go first," she said.

"Me, too," the boy agreed. "And you go last, Mommy."

Renee mock frowned. "Me? Why do I have to go last?" Of course she knew perfectly well why Brandon wanted her to go last, so he could be safely tucked between the two grown-ups.

"So me and Mama Sam can protect you, Mommy. We'll punch the scary things so you can get through safe."

"Sounds like a plan, little man," Renee replied.

They'd reached the short line of people waiting to get in. Brandon's grip on Renee's hand tightened. Every time a loud scream echoed through the faux-rock painted walls, Brandon's eyes flashed bigger. They took a step closer as the door was opened by the attendant to admit a teenage boy and girl.

"We're next," Sam said. "Ready, Bee?"

Brandon didn't answer. He just nodded as Renee felt his grip grow even tighter.

Their tickets were gathered and ripped in half before being tossed into a nearby orange bucket.

The old barn door was pulled open just enough to let them pass into the pitch black void beyond.

Chapter 7

"You hear that?"

"Yeah."

"What you think it is?"

Moonlight was shining in bedroom window. We'd propped the window open with an old piece of wood from the crumbling outhouse out back. It was a week after my July thirteenth birthday. I'd just turned eighteen. A little breeze was pushing into my and Kate's stuffy bedroom. I'd left the door open, hoping it would help. I was still covered in sweat.

I'd heard the sound before and knew it very well. It was the soft squeak and knock of Daddy Clay's bed as it rocked. Once in a while the headboard would hit the wall. I closed my eyes. "Go back to sleep, Katie. Ain't nothing to worry about."

"But what is it?"

"Daddy's loving on someone," I explained.

She was quiet for so long I was sure she'd fallen back to sleep, but then she startled me by saying, "I wonder who."

My heart fluttered and for a minute I couldn't breathe. I had a feeling I knew who.

I'd seen Daddy Clay eying our oldest brother the past few days the way he used to eyeball me. I found him just before bed out in the kitchen going through the cupboard. "We out of Crisco?"

Daddy didn't know nothing about where I kept things in the kitchen. "It's in the baking pantry." There was a little room off the kitchen about four feet wide and twice as deep. Along the right hand wall was all shelves. On the left, an old wooden table stood. That's where I learned how to make my first pie crust and loaf of bread. I nibbled my lip as he went and found what he was after.

"You going to bed?" he asked.

I nodded a yes.

"See you in the morning." He brushed by me and went back into the living room to read the paper.

"Night, Daddy." I paused by the doorway into the front room, at the foot of the stairs.

He didn't look up or nothing. That's how he'd been around me lately. Barely acting like I was there at all unless he really needed something. I was starting to feel like a ghost whenever it was just him and me at home. I went upstairs where I found Kate sitting at the same table I'd once used for my homework.

"It's time for bed," I told her.

"Almost done." She was doing her figures with that same look of concentration on her face that I'd seen on Daddy's when he was calculating things.

I moved to undress and put on the lightest nightgown I had, but all the while my head was buzzing a little. I figured I'd messed up too many times. Daddy had abandoned me. There would be no more Loving Times. And there was Kate, getting prettier and prettier every day while I was like a full grown woman. I was the same age Mama had been when she and Daddy Clay got married. When I looked in the mirror it wasn't Mary Alice Brown I saw anymore but my Mama and how she must have looked when her and Daddy went on their honeymoon.

Now, there I was, lying in bed listening to Daddy's bed squeak and knock and it wasn't me in there with him. I know it wasn't right for me to think that way, but I was glad it wasn't me down there. I wasn't glad it was Nigel, either.

The wall banging finally stopped and soon after I heard Daddy's door give itself away with a squeak. The floor boards in the hallway did the same. I counted the steps, a dozen, tiny and timid steps trying to be quiet, as they tip-toed closer and went into the bathroom across the hall. Someone snuffled their nose just before the latch on the door clicked. Even the sink wouldn't be quiet when the rusty spigot handle was turned and water came gushing out. And under it all I heard Nigel doing his best not to cry. He was nearly fifteen after all. Boys don't cry and certainly not fifteen year old ones.

Katie was quiet all this time. Maybe she was listening, too. Maybe she'd gone back to sleep. I never knew for sure. Her and I never talked about it after that night, but I did notice she and Seth talking real close and hushed down by the chicken coop a few days later. At the time, I didn't give it much thought, but now I know I should have. Maybe things would have ended different if I had. That's neither here nor there, because at the time I had more important matters to consider and I was brewing a fine plan of my own in my head.

I'd been thinking a lot about Mama during those days and nights and how pretty she'd been even when she was near dying. Everybody said so and none could reckon how she ended up with a fella like Clayton Brown who was all rough and cracked and stubby. Mama smelled like laundry soap, rose water, and good home-cooking. Daddy was all coal, dirt and wood smoke. Sure, I looked like Mama alright, but I didn't have any rose water. There was only two ways I could get it.

I'd seen some at the five and dime, but that meant going into town and, boy, Daddy Clay wouldn't like me wasting money on something like that. And with a town as small as Murphey Mills, there weren't no chance I could go there in secret to buy it. Someone would see me. Someone would tell Daddy they'd seen me and Daddy would start asking questions. Telling the truth wouldn't work. He'd accuse me of lying and meeting some boy in secret.

The other way was to sneak into Daddy's room and get what was left of Mama's. Daddy'd kept Mama's dressing table exactly as she'd left it the last time she'd used it. If a person didn't know better they'd expect to see Mama come walking in any second, her hair pulled up in a bun at her neck and her skin glistening with sweat from hanging the laundry or working in the garden. Even covered with dirt and sweat, Mama sure could turn heads. When she dressed up, she and Daddy would be the talk of the town for weeks, though it weren't such nice talk at all from what I heard of it.

I knew sometimes Nigel was hurting real bad. I did up the laundry and knew every stitch of clothes everyone had so I knew when a pair of Nigel's underpants was missing. He got real mad when I asked, said they was full of holes and that he'd burned them. I knew he was lying. Didn't make no sense, burning them. First off, he didn't have no underpants that was in that bad condition. Second off, they could have been used for a cleaning rag. But, weren't no point in arguing over it. There was a scared look in my oldest brother's eyes that pleaded with me to be quiet and not say anything to anyone. It was just a pair of underpants, that's all, but I needed to do something to take away my brother's pain even if it meant having to lie under Daddy Clay's grunting, sweating body again myself.

It was a chilly October morning when I stepped outside wearing one of Mama's old sweaters and heard the arguing. Frost dusted the grass, making it crunch as I walked across the back yard to the chicken coop. From there, I could hear everything.

"Keep your grubby hands off me, old man!" Nigel bellowed. "You touch me like that again and I swear to God and on Mama's grave, I'll kill you!"

"You think I can't still whoop your ass, boy?"

"I'd like to see you try! You're so damn drunk all the ..."

Next thing I hear is a lot of thumping and banging around like someone getting themselves thrown against the wall. The cows started bawling in protest.

I looked down, tried to ignore the sounds, and gathered the eggs under the bellies of the protesting hens that fluffed and clucked and pecked at my less-than-gentle hand. Normally, I was a lot nicer about it, but that morning all I could think to do was get them eggs and get back to the house as quick as I could.

I couldn't endure it too much longer. I had to do something. I was supposed to be taking care of things like Mama had and I wasn't. It weren't my fault though, was it? Daddy'd stopped visiting me. I made up my mind then and there to make sure he didn't love on Nigel no more. I should be the one to take it, not him. The Lady of the House had to put a stop to it once and for all. That's what Mama would have done.

That's what I would do, too, even if it meant going into her and Daddy's bedroom against orders.

Seth was up to his elbows scrubbing up after feeding the pigs and Kate was pouring the scrambled eggs into the pan when Daddy and Nigel come stomping in, their misty breath vanishing once they stepped into the warm and cozy kitchen full of the smells of coffee, bacon, and toast.

"Colder than a witch's tit out there," Daddy chuckled, nudging up next to Seth for a place at the sink. "Getting them pigs nice and fat, son?"

"Yes, sir," Seth said with pride. We'd be butchering them real soon. "I found a nice old hickory must have been knocked over that last storm out in the woods the other day. Figured it would be perfect for smoking time."

Nigel leaned against the counter waiting for his turn at the sink, his eyes narrowed and arms crossed as he glowered at the way Daddy was carrying on all sweet as pie with our little brother. "We should cut and haul it Saturday," he said. The cold edge in his voice covered my arms in chicken skin. He sounded a little too much like Daddy Clay. "Give it some time to dry out a bit."

Seth turned around, towel in hand, young eyes eager and bright. "Yeah, alright."

I prayed that look meant he'd not been touched by Daddy Clay's dark blight. It wasn't until Seth handed the towel off to our father that Nigel moved to the sink. To my seeing, there was no mistaking the way he was sure to walk around the other side of the table, steering clear of Daddy who took up his place at the head of the table.

Seth and Katie did most of the talking that morning. Katie was getting really good at sewing and wanted to get some fabric in town to make herself a new dress. Daddy grumbled about the money, as he always did, but I'd been saving up in that little coffee can over the stove just like Mama always had. Just dribs and drabs of change whenever it came my way.

"I'll go into town today, meet you after school, Katie. We can pick something out together," I suggested, my eyes flicking towards my father. He frowned like I knew he would, but didn't say anything. "I need a few other things, too. Soon as the dishes are done up."

Daddy took a slurp of coffee, leaned over slightly, and reached into his back pocket. Everyone's eyes, including mine, had gone round as saucers. "You need money? What you getting?"

Daddy Clay never gave out money willingly. I licked my lips, while glancing over at Nigel. His jaw was clenched as he gave me a silent and brief nod. Though there weren't no outward signs of it, I got a feeling in that moment he'd gotten the upper hand in the fight.

"Five?" I said, giving a little shift in my chair.

He pulled out some ones, counted them and tossed them on the table, "Here's three."

"I need laundry soap, Daddy. Tomorrow's washing day."

His bushy eyebrows touched over the bridge of his nose and he snuffed his nose. We held our breath. If Daddy offered you three dollars, you took that three dollars and didn't quibble about needing more. You'd be grateful and say thank you and move on, making the best of it. Doubly so after he'd gone and offered the money without anyone even asking.

71

His eyes turned towards me. Smoldering fury curdled my stomach. "Finish your breakfast," he growled.

"It's okay, Mary. I don't need to make a new dress," Kate offered with hope. "Maybe we can fix up one of Mama's old ones. I got ..."

Daddy Clay's fist slammed on the kitchen table, jarring the butter knife right off the tub and onto the floor. "You leave your mother's things alone!" He rose, so red-faced I expected one of the pulsing veins in his neck or on the side of his head to explode. "You hear me? You stay out of my bedroom and away from your mother's things!" The wooden chair behind him clattered backwards, "My lunch ready, Mary?"

I gave a curt nod. "On the counter, Daddy."

He lurched around the fallen chair, grabbed the battered metal box shaped like a miniature barn and stormed out, smacking the door against the woodpile first then letting it slam shut in a way that would have sent Mama to yelling. No one at the table moved as the old truck sputtered in protest at being brought to life, followed by a string of livid cursing and the eventual turning over of the engine. The rusted body of the vehicle rattled as Daddy left, not even trying to miss the numerous potholes.

The first to move was Nigel. He reached over and scooped the butter knife from the floor. "I got a little bit of money, Mary Alice. Was going to buy the new Spider Man comic with it, but you need it more."

"Thanks, Nigel," I picked at my eggs. I'd lost my appetite, but food was too precious to waste.

"It's time we took care of ourselves more," my brother continued.

"We're doing alright," I said.

Nigel shook his head. "We could do better and," he said with what, I think, was supposed to be a frown but somehow looked more like a smirk, "Daddy Clay ain't gonna be able to work too much longer."

That confused me something fierce, "Daddy ain't even fifty, Nige."

My brother scoffed. "I bet his liver is half pickled and with that temper, he could have a coronary any day. Don't take much for folks like him to have coronaries, I hear."

"What's a cor-o-nary?" sweet, innocent Kate asked just before taking the last swallow from her glass of milk.

Seth rolled his eyes. "It's when your heart explodes, dummy."

"I ain't a dummy," Katie shrieked back.

"Stop it!" I shouted. I wasn't one prone to shouting. We had enough of that with Daddy Clay, so when I done it, they sure took notice. "Seth, tell Katie you're sorry for calling her a dummy. Ain't nobody here a dummy." I glared at Nigel, "And Daddy Clay ain't gonna die from no coronary."

Nigel shoved the last bite of toast in his mouth as he rose from the table. "Maybe not today," he said, "and maybe not tomorrow. Either way, ain't no guessing that we need more money and we can't rely on Daddy to give it to us anymore. Tomorrow I'm going to start asking around about places for work. Maybe can do some mossing or hunt down a patch of ginseng. There's good money in ginseng."

"What about school?"

"Don't worry. I ain't quitting school for nothing. Mama wouldn't want me to quit."

It was too late for me, but Nigel could make it, then Seth and Kate. Three out of four wasn't bad and it wasn't terrible keeping house. Someone had to do it. Plus, as much as I hated to admit it out loud, Nigel had a point. Daddy Clay might not be an old man yet, but I had a really bad feeling he wasn't going to live long enough to be one, either.

Dark Hollow Road

Chapter 8

Black walls pressed in on either side, narrowing a little more with each step, forcing them to walk single file. In the dark, a low, rhythmic bass pulsed. It's all pretend, Brandon reminded himself. Black ebbed into deepest, blood-blue just enough for him to see thick wisps of mist swirling around them. A single string of purple lights faded gradually into blue, dimming and glowing in time with the throb he could feel under his feet.

Ahead, through some sort of curtain, white pinpricks of light turned like the inside of a huge dryer. Brandon liked to sit in front of the dryer and watch the clothes tumbling around, but he wasn't liking what loomed ahead. Mama Sam parted the drapes. Brandon's world tipped sideways, bashing his right shoulder against the midnight blue wall that was returning to black again and meshing with the spinning tunnel ahead. In the dimness, to the right of the tunnel, a tall, thin alien creature stood. Its eyes were as big as the hand that the young boy gripped in front of him. The spindle-thin creature's dull skin was a mottled greenish-gray. As they inched closer, its oversized head turned in minute increments on the stalk that passed as a neck. All the while, the tunnel spun with a

75

slow, grinding rumble and the pulsing tone grew ever louder.

His stomach churned. Brandon held back the urge to puke.

"Mommy, I don't like this."

"Close your eyes, honey."

He did and the sensation of tipping and spinning and walking sideways vanished. Mama Sam's hand held firm and tugged them slowly forward. "I'll go slow, Bee."

The solid floor beneath them changed a few more steps in. It felt like the open grate of a bridge they had to cross every time they went into town. Brandon turned his head down and dared to crack his eyes open. They were halfway through the swirling tunnel. The grating, grumbling sound of huge boulders being rolled against each other pressed in on him from all sides. They were going to be crushed, crushed in a giant tumble dryer on a bridge in outer space. He tipped with the spin and thudded against the railing before he could grip his eyes shut again. A few more strides and the solid floor returned. Brandon let out a breath and let his eyes open full. Still dark, still rumbling, but the dizziness was behind them.

"We made it," Sam announced. "How you doing back there, Bee?"

"I'm good," he said in the bravest voice he could muster.

Mama Sam shuffled them forward into the deeper, darker depth of the Spook Barn, passing through black rubber curtains like they had at the grocery store when you went into the beer cooler. It wasn't cold on the other side of this curtain though, it was hot and steamy. Mists rolled around them. The walls glowed red, flames shot up on all sides, things with leathery wings swooped and twirled over their heads. Brandon could see the dark line of the bridge they'd have to cross to make their way through this room. Under their feet, a molten river seemed to flow as thick, red and black cones, like they'd seen in one of the caves they'd visited, climbed towards the ceiling. Other cones, hung downward and something, thick and red and gooey, dripped from the ends, splatting onto the ones below, trickling like blood. Always there was the throbbing of an oversized and weary heart. Brandon stared at the outlines of human figures with glistening red skin, black horns, huge batwings, and snakelike tails. They rocked side to side, hypnotic. Something moaned.

A woman's scream jolted him to the right, her scabbed and slimy face rocketed from a wall he hadn't noticed before. Brandon jumped back and bashed against the railing, forcing him closer to the bat-winged things. The rattle of clinking chains drew his attention upward. Bodies, wrapped in shrouds or tattered rags, descended from above. Some were bound by their feet, their arms flopping, mouths open and eyes wide. Others drew closer with their wrists bound. Shrill shrieks echoed though the cave. Deep, guttural laughter ran beneath it and a figure, one taller than even Mama Sam, stepped into a red glow. It was real. It wasn't a dummy or a robot, it was a real live creature with glistening black eyes and glowing, pointed teeth that gleamed behind thin, black lips. The horns that topped its head twisted a foot high.

The massive devil laughed. The room's pulse quickened. Steam rose from around the thing's feet as Brandon pushed hard against Mama Sam's back, pulling Mommy along. Mama Sam picked up the pace, leading them forward and leaving the horribly real pit of fire, blood, and screaming behind them.

Brandon was having serious doubts about all the begging he'd done to get in here, but he couldn't take it back now. No. He wouldn't let them know he had almost wet his pants when the lady's head had come flying out at him. It's pretend, all pretend. Fake.

"This is horrible," Mommy said. "We are not doing this again, ever."

Brandon swallowed, "It's okay, Mommy. It's not real, remember?"

"I know," she said, but Brandon didn't think she sounded convinced of that which only made him more afraid.

The fiery-red morphed to black, passing through another short tunnel and more rubber freezer flaps, stepping into shades of deepest forest green. The walkway morphed into what looked like old-fashioned cobblestones scattered with dirt and leaves. They were surrounded by trees whose scraggly-armed branches hung down only a foot or so above Mama Sam's head. Glowing eyes shined and blinked in the distance with the cawing of a crow and the hooting of an owl. Tucked back in the trees, a rustic log cabin no bigger than the storage shed Mama Sam had put up this past summer, sat. There was a glowing fire pit out front and over it hung a big, steaming, black cauldron.

He jerked to a halt. Dangling from a long, iron bar, hung upside down by their tails, were huge rats. Their bodies would jerk every now and then as if they were still alive. Something whooshed over their heads. He couldn't see what it was but felt the breeze it trailed behind it. There was a loud thump followed by an even louder startling cackle and a witch came around from the back of the hut.

Dark Hollow Road

She leered at them, eyes so wide the whites showed all the way around her pupils, teeth stained green, lips painted black. She carried a primitive broomstick and her hair was a tangled mess that held piece of twigs, leaves, and cobwebs.

The witch approached, stopping just short of the not-very-strong-looking fence that separated her from the path on which Brandon now stood. "Oh, more lost souls have dared enter my woods. Come closer. Don't be afraid." Her voice sounded like she'd swallowed sandpaper.

Mama Sam moved them along the walkway slowly.

"Wait," the woman beckoned, reminding Brandon a little too much of The Sugar Lady and her gray-streaked hair. "I have something to show you." She shifted away, did something at the rod that held the dangling line of rodents and turned back quickly, thrusting both hands forward, each holding a live, beady-eyed rat.

Brandon screamed, swung around, making quick work of putting Mama Sam between the rats and him. "I don't like this!" he heard himself crying as a warm, wet spot bloomed in the crotch of his pants. "I don't want to do this anymore! I want to go! I want to go, now!"

The witch only laughed, pulled the animals close and let one climb to her shoulder while the other she petted tenderly in the palm of her hand. "That will teach you to trespass, little boy! From now on stay out of my woods!" She walked backwards towards the cabin until she pushed the door open with her butt and vanished inside.

"I want to go," Brandon whimpered.

"We're going," Mama Sam sounded annoyed and hurried them along.

After that, Brandon didn't want to see any of it. He kept his eyes closed as much as he could. He blocked out the weird sounds, the screeches, and the warped carnival music that could only mean they had entered a circus and if there was a circus, there would be clowns and clowns were nearly as bad as rats. Brandon was ashamed and scared and couldn't seem to stop whining and shaking. People ahead and behind them screamed and laughed. Cobwebby things brushed against his bare skin. Animals of some kind growled and gurgled. Toads croaked and snakes hissed.

And repeating in his head that it was all fake didn't do any good at all.

Cool, fresh air and brilliant sunshine jolted him back into reality. They had emerged back outside into the crowds of people and the smells of fresh-made popcorn. The steady chug-chug-chug of a farm tractor waiting to pull its next load of passengers on the hay wagon behind replaced the pounding throb of the terrifying darkness.

Mommy had never let go of his hand. She crouched down on her knees and pulled him in close. "It's over with, little man. We made it through." She reached up, wiping away the last of the tears that still trickled down his cheeks.

"I wasn't very brave," he snuffled.

Mama Sam's big hand patted his shoulder. "You did fine, Bee."

Brandon's head hung low. What had once been warm in the center of his pants was cooling quickly, reviving the flood of tears all over again. "I want to go home," he said. He didn't really want to go, they'd hardly done a thing, but he didn't want his friends from school to see the big wet patch, either.

Mommy leaned forward and kissed his cheek. "I have a secret," she whispered, pulling back to brush the hair off his forehead.

Brandon didn't say anything. He just didn't want anyone to see him like this, like a baby standing here bawling who'd wet his pants.

Mommy looked up at Sam, "There's a blue plastic bag in the back of the Jeep, under Brandon's seat. Go get it. We'll meet you over at the port-a-johns."

Mama Sam mussed Brandon's hair again. "Go with your mom. I'll be right back."

"I don't have to use the potty," Brandon protested. Couldn't they see it was too late for that? Besides, the potties were the other way from the way they'd come in. He might see someone he knew. They'd see. They'd know he was a baby. No one would be his friend anymore, not if they saw what he'd done.

Mommy stood up and took his hand, anyway. "I know you don't, but I do. C'mon," she said.

He didn't have a choice and making an even bigger scene about wanting to leave would only make matters worse. The port-a-johns were closer than the exit and so Brandon allowed himself to be tugged along, never looking up at anything or anyone.

The toilets were hidden behind a tall, blockade-style fence. Five ran down once side, five the other and two bigger ones at the end with pictures of wheelchairs on them. No one was there that he could see. Mommy went to the nearest one and opened in. "Scoot in," she said then added with a whisper, "Mama Sam is bringing you some dry pants and undies. I hope Sponge Bob is alright."

Brandon's leaden heart lifted along with his gaze and the corners of his mouth. "You brought extras?"

She nodded. "I always bring extra, little man. Accidents happen. Sometimes we slip and fall in the mud like Mama Sam did this morning, remember? Sometimes we drop ice cream or spill juice. Sometimes, well, sometimes other things happen." Her smile was so tender and loving and she wasn't mad at all.

He wrapped his arms around her waist, "Thanks, Mommy," he chirped, then slipped into the port-a-john to wait.

Mama Sam hoisted a third pumpkin, a good twenty-pounder that Brandon and she had determined would be the centerpiece for an epic display in the front yard, into one of the little orange wagons that Yagar's Farm provided. Mommy had wandered off to the piles of baby pumpkins and was still lingering there when they rolled up.

"Holy pumpkin head," she laughed. "That's huge."

"It will be our masterpiece," Sam announced. Mama Sam knew her way around a pumpkin. Brandon could still remember last year's carving. It had looked just like the face of the witch from the Wizard of Oz. After his experience in the barn, Brandon had quickly voted down doing that one again and Mama Sam had assured him she never carved the same one twice, and certainly not two years in a row. Mommy just did triangle eyes and nose with the grinning mouth. Brandon would do better, with a little help from Mama Sam, of course.

Mommy grinned and rolled her eyes, selected two small pumpkins and added them to the cart. "And these will be mine, two made-from-scratch pumpkin pies. One for Thanksgiving and one for Christmas. Now, let's go get a bag of apples and I'll make us a pie for tomorrow."

"What about my candied apple?" Brandon worried. He still hadn't gotten it.

"They have them right over there by the register. We'll get it then," Mommy assured him.

Mama Sam tugged the wagon's handle and grunted. "Oof, Bee. Help me get this puppy rolling. This dog is heavy."

Brandon pushed, moving the cart easily, but still pleased he was helping.

At the register, Mommy let him pick out a candied apple.

"Hey, folks. Have a good time today?" The cashier lady had dark-blue hair, an arm full of colorful tattoos, and rings on every finger which made Brandon smile.

"Just great," Mama Sam answered, reaching for the monster pumpkin first.

"Oh, no, no. Leave them there." She came around and drew black X's on each with a magic marker. "That'll wash right off," she added as she went back and started to ring up their items. "First time here, huh? Where you from?"

Mommy was already reaching into her purse for her wallet, "Just up the road, heading into Murphey Mills. We moved here from Jersey back in May. We got a house about half a mile from the end of Dark Hollow Road."

"I'm in kindergarten," Brandon blurted,

"You bought the old Brown house?" She looked completely shocked at first before quickly returning to her previous pleasantries and addressing Brandon instead. "Wow, kindergarten. That's pretty exciting. I

see you got a candied apple. Those are my favorite."
She glanced at Mommy with a weak smile.

He grinned, "I can't eat it until I get home 'cuz it's
too sticky for the car."

"Good idea," she replied. "Let's see. Fifteen for
the pumpkins, twenty, twenty-two fifty and a tiny bit
for the government," she said. "Twenty-two sixty two
will take you all the way."

Mommy handed the lady a plastic card. "No, we
bought the little house on Route 9, just this side of
Dark Hollow Road, white with blue shutters."

"Oh, gotcha. Cute place. I was going to say, that
Brown house has been empty for years. I didn't think it
was even for sale."

Mama Sam tapped an index finger against her lips.
"The Browns were the last family to live there then?"

The cashier folded the receipt and handed it across
to Mommy. "Yeah, but it's been ages. I've been
around these parts all my life and don't remember
anyone ever living there."

"Who owns it now?"

She shrugged, "No idea. Mr. Yagar might know.
His family's been here for generations."

"That would be Lee Yager?" Mama Sam asked.

"He's the one."

Mommy was giving Mama Sam that look she gave
when she was feeling annoyed and impatient. "Another
time, hon. We need to get home and you need to get to
work."

"And I got a candy apple to eat," Brandon
proclaimed.

The woman laughed, "Well, we don't want to
postpone that any more than needed, do we?"

"Nope."

"Have a nice day, folks. Come again soon."

Chapter 9

For a while things got better with Nigel working a few hours after school plus, he and Seth found a ginseng patch. He was right. There was good money in ginseng. Just between me and Nigel, he would give me half of whatever he brought home, I'd tuck it away and not in the coffee can Daddy Clay knew about. We agreed right off that if he knew how much Nigel was really making, he'd try and drink it all away. The only one who changed his spending habits was Nigel. We always made a big show of it at the dinner table when he got paid for one of his odd jobs. He'd dig into his pocket, pull out some money, and count me off five or ten dollars to go towards whatever we might need it for. I'd smile all proud and get right up and tuck it into the coffee can.

It was all a lie. If Nigel made ten dollars, he'd give me five in private then another two dollars and fifty cents at the dinner table in front of Daddy Clay. Next morning, after Daddy Clay was gone to work, I'd give Nigel the extra back from what was hidden in my room under a loose floorboard. Daddy Clay was never the wiser.

There was a price for Nigel's and Daddy's fight, though. He left Nigel well enough alone, but every

Friday night when Daddy'd come home late from work after spending most of his paycheck at the bar, he'd want some Loving Time with me. When it got to be regular, I started taking to sleeping on the sofa with the radio on, so he'd not sneak up into Kate's and my bedroom. I was so afraid he was going to wake her up if he come stumbling in stinking of beer and cigarettes. It was better we done his business downstairs.

I'd given up on my notion of dressing up pretty in one of Mama's old dresses and using some of her perfume to protect the others from Daddy's ways. I was afraid I'd see my father fall apart even more if he saw and smelled me like that one night only to realize the next morning Mama was still dead and buried out back. I didn't want him to lose the job he was barely clinging to keeping, and I was afraid what he'd do to me, too. Truth of the matter, the only time I wasn't afraid was when Daddy was gone from the house, but we needed him. We needed every dollar he managed not to drink or smoke away.

One Friday night just before Christmas, I woke up to the sound of the kitchen door clicking shut and being locked. I kept my eyes closed, laying real still and breathing like I was sleeping, slow and steady. It's funny how hard it is to breathe normal when you start thinking about it. Daddy's lunchbox clunked down on the kitchen table before one of the chairs was dragged out and creaked under his weight. He was taking off his boots, I figured, all the while hoping he'd just leave me be, let me sleep, and go on upstairs to his own bed.

A few minutes later, the door on the stove opened and the heavy wooden thud of logs being added reached me. I knew he'd be heading my way soon. My heart pounded hard in my chest. The heavy quilt I'd pulled up over me should prevent him from seeing that. The weary scuffing of slipper-covered feet approached the open doorway between the formal dining room that was never used and the front room where I prayed so fervently.

I could tell when he reached the carpeted part of the room. There was a long pause. I fought the urge to yank the blanket over my head. Wound tight as a spring, I somehow managed to keep my expression passive and relaxed. I'm sleeping, I repeated to myself. Just sleeping, now go away, Daddy Clay. Go away and go to bed. Please, God, make him go away and leave me alone. His feet shuffled closer. His labored beer-breath tried to make me gag, but I didn't move. Logs shifted in the fireplace as he poked at them. He added three more pieces. Silence whooshed and pounded in my ears. Don't scrunch your eyes, Mary Alice. Don't let him see you so much as flinch.

The next sound I heard was Daddy walking away. I dared to sliver my eyes open. His back was to me and, sure enough, he was leaving. One soft clunk and moan after another on the stairs marked his retreat. I let out my held breath and took in a deep one. My chest hurt. I listened.

The bathroom door closed, toilet flushed, water ran, door opened. And still I listened, realizing now that my eyes had sprung wide open and that my mouth was agape. He wasn't coming back down the hall to his room. I'd have heard the floor squeak at the top of the stairs. Where was he? What was he doing?

The baritone rumbling of his voice barely touched my straining ears.

"Daddy?" a little girl's voice, one startled from her sleep filled me with dread. "What you doing, Daddy?" Kate asked.

Tears trickled from my eyes as the additional logs he'd lain into place ignited. I wanted to scream. I wanted to leap up from the sofa, run up those stairs and down the short hallway to my bedroom and just scream and scream at him. I wanted to take the fire poker and bash him in the skull with it. That's what I wanted to do.

Instead, I lay there in terror and shame, shaking all over, unable to think. I buried my head under the throw pillow, covered my ears with both hands, and tried not to hear anything. I don't know if I did hear it or if I was just remembering the sound of it when it had been me with Daddy's big, coal-stained hand clamped over my mouth. The memories consumed me into total paralysis and I couldn't help but wonder if Mama had known what he was doing to me like I knew what he was doing to Kate.

If she had, she'd not have let it happen. She'd have stopped it, right?

I wasn't a bit surprised the next morning when Katie didn't come bounding down the stairs ready to start the day. If she felt anything like how I'd felt back then, she was curled into a ball with a deep ache and burn in her girl parts.

"Where's Katie?" Daddy Clay asked at the breakfast table as if he didn't know. He was in the best mood I'd seen him in for weeks. "I think we should go get ourselves a Christmas tree today." He actually smiled.

I hadn't actually checked on her yet, but I knew well enough what to say. "She has a bellyache," I said. "I'll take her up some ginger tea once we're done eating."

He scowled and for a minute I considered maybe he didn't know. Maybe in his drunken state he couldn't remember what he'd done. It could be that way. It really could. I'd seen situations like that in the movies and on the daytime stories I liked to watch. Drunk people forgot a lot of things. "That's too bad. You think she'll be feeling better by lunchtime?"

"I don't know, Daddy." I said. "You boys can go and get the tree without us if she ain't."

"It's man work, anyway," Seth chimed in.

I got up from the table just as Daddy Clay reached over and mussed up Seth's already tousled head of hair. "That's my boy."

"We going after lunch then?" Nigel drained his glass of milk.

"Seems so, with or without your sisters."

"Besides, we don't do anything but tag along and get in the way," I said. "I'll have hot cocoa waiting when you come back and I can make up some donuts, too. How's that sound?"

"Sounds great," Nigel pushed himself away from the table. "I told Widow Avery I'd get her upstairs coal barrel filled today, Daddy. Won't take me but a couple hours. I'll be back in time for lunch and to go with you and Seth to get a tree. That alright?"

"Got your morning chores done?"

"Yes, sir. Got up extra early." Nigel was already shoving his feet into a second pair of socks as he spoke.

"Best get to it then," Daddy encouraged. "You're growing up to be quite the hard worker, son. I'm proud of you." Compliments from Daddy Clay were few and far between. Why was he being so nice this morning? It was almost like how things had been before Mama died.

My oldest brother stumbled over his words, "Th-thank you, Daddy." He tugged on his boots and pulled on his coat and hat saying "I won't be long," as he let a gust of chilly air into the warm and cozy kitchen, puffs of white breath trailing out behind him like cigarette smoke.

"I should check on Katie." Something in the air felt tainted and greasy, like when you walk into a place fouled with pet shit and piss and you didn't dare touch nothing. It didn't matter that I knew my kitchen was clean. It wasn't that sort of filth. I turned my back to the table and washed my hands. It didn't help much.

Daddy squawked his chair away from the table, "And I need to go sharpen up the ax. Want to come help, champ?" He rubbed his hand on top of Seth's head again. "You can get toboggan dusted off and waxed up."

"It needs a new string, too," Seth chirped and was off, scampering to get his outdoor clothes on.

"You feeling alright, Mary Alice?"

Was then I realized I'd been standing there drying my hands over and over again on the kitchen towel staring off into space, listening to all this and wondering how long it would last. Daddy's mood was just too good this close to Christmas. It cost him too much. It was a waste of time all this foolish decorating. He had better things to do than stomp around in the woods looking for a god-damned tree. Now, here he was all eager and chipper and smiling.

"Yeah, I'm fine, Daddy. I'm just worried about Katie."

"Well, you go tend to her," he said and reached for his coat. "Meet me out in the barn, boy!" He yelled towards the staircase.

"Be right there!" Seth hollered back.

Dark Hollow Road

Daddy grinned, looked at me, winked, and headed outside leaving me feeling dirtier than ever.

Kate was buried under the blankets just like she was when I'd snuck in a couple hours earlier to get dressed. With as much cheer as I could muster, I opened the bedroom curtains. It was cold, but the sky was as blue as blue could be and the sun was shining bright. It would have been a good day to go for a walk in the woods with the boys, but that all depended on Katie. "Katie Sue," I nudged the lump under the blankets playfully. "Time to get up. Daddy and the boys are gonna chop us a Christmas tree this afternoon."

A faint grunt rose from the pile.

I nudged it a second time, "C'mon, Katie. I need your help making a spot in the window and getting the decorations from the attic and washing them off." I figured the best cure for what was ailing her was not to wallow in bed nibbling on toast and sipping tea, but getting up and dressed and thinking about something happy like Christmas and scheming about presents.

The lump shifted and groaned, elongating just a tiny bit as Katie stretched out her legs.

Should I say I knew what had happened? I figured she understood better now about that night we'd heard Nigel. I'd wised up a lot since my first time. I also knew them babies I'd had weren't anyone else's but Daddy's. And I was pretty sure I knew why he'd left me alone for so long and gone looking at Nigel and now Katie. I didn't know if he'd messed with Seth or not.

The springs on my baby sister's bed whined as I eased down to sit beside her. "Kate?" I gave her shoulder a little shake.

She didn't respond.

I took a deep breath and let it out, "I know what Daddy Clay did last night," and waited.

Her pillow-and-blanket-muffled reply finally came, "Hurts," she said.

My hand slid from its perch, helpless. "I know." A piece of my heart cracked. "He done it to me, too," I offered, wanting her to come out of hiding on her own. That feeling of grime covered my fingers again. "You been to the bathroom since?"

"No."

"You should do that," I said. "I told Daddy you had a bellyache. I'm gonna go make you some tea and toast while you do that, okay?"

"Okay." Kate's nose snuffed.

I leaned over and wrapped my arms around the warm pile under which my little sister hid, hugging her as best I could. "It'll be alright, Katie. I promise. Daddy don't mean no harm in it. I don't think he knows how much it hurts those first dozen times." I stopped short quick of saying how much more it must have hurt Nigel than it did us girls.

"I don't like it."

"Me, neither," I confessed. "But sometimes we have to do things we don't like to and it don't matter how much it hurts."

"Do I have to help with the tree, Mary?"

Knowing that she wasn't really sick but just hurting from Daddy's ways, I figured it was best to compromise. "You can stay up here all morning if you want, but maybe you can start feeling better while the boys are off in the woods. I'm going to make hot cocoa and donuts. 'Sides, you can't hide from Daddy forever. You may as well get it done with more sooner than later."

Dark Hollow Road

Kate rolled over and pulled the blanket away from her face. Her eyes were puffy and red from crying. "I love you, Mary Alice."

I embraced her again. This time it was a real hug, tight and warm and protective. "I love you, too, Katie Sue." I knew she would never be the same again. My innocent little sister was gone. Daddy Clay had killed her and for that I hated him.

Chapter 10

"Hey! There she is!" Brandon shouted from the back seat.

"There who is?" Renee's eyes flicked towards the rearview mirror, watching the boy twist around to look behind them.

"The Sugar Lady," he proclaimed.

Halloween was only days away. The pumpkins they'd bought at Yagar's a week ago were carved and the front lawn was decorated, not that they figured they'd get too many trick-or-treaters out this way, but it was Sam's favorite holiday and to do nothing merely because they didn't think any kids would stop in was pure sacrilege.

"Really? You sure?"

"Yeah. She was walking down the road. Go back, Mommy. We need to go back and talk to her. She might still need her sugar."

Renee shook her head. "We have groceries to get put away before things start to melt." Her gaze darted back to him again. He looked disappointed, but it couldn't be helped. "Maybe we can go over after we eat. You want those SpaghettiOs for lunch?" He perked up and smiled at her in the mirror.

"Yeah!"

Dark Hollow Road

SpaghettiOs to the rescue. It worked every time.

Moments later she turned the minivan into the driveway. The modern, small, two-story house with an offset, single-car garage, sat back some fifty feet from the main road. The white picket fence that had won Renee's heart, protected the yard along the road edge only. It served no other purpose than to look pretty, unlike the less attractive, gated, chain-link fence out back. Renee loved it along with the closest town of Murphey Mills, both were a far cry from the cramped living they'd left behind in Passaic.

Once upon a time, Murphey Mills had boasted two large industries, each owned by one of the Murphey brothers, Hector and Harry. One mill took advantage of the bounty above ground, lumber. The other, technically a mine, had been used to haul out ton after ton of coal for nearly half a century.

The closing of the lumber mill in 1984 had been the town's near fatal death knell. Dozens of jobs were lost and most of the families who'd relied on that money soon moved away, heading towards Scranton, Wilkes-Barre, or Towanda. Without the steady supply of quality hardwoods, the small furniture factory was the second business to pass away. Six years later, the last of the dump trucks hauled the final loads of coal to the railroad station and there went a hundred more jobs and families.

The theater was still open, but barely. It ran three shows a week. Friday and Saturday nights and a Sunday matinee. Nothing new had played there in years. The pharmacy and its once-gleaming chrome fountains and sparkling shake glasses now sported a double padlock on the front door and layers of faded newspapers taped over the windows from the inside. The five and dime hadn't faired any better, but a small grocery store remained open. The gas station's two pumps saw a fair amount of business, too. Kelley's Diner was the hub of life and gossip in Murphey Mills. The food was good, the portions generous and with the prices set so low, it was a wonder the place had survived at all.

Rundown and deserted as it was, Murphey Mills still had an air of charm. It was that feeling of old-fashioned simplicity that had drawn Renee and Sam to the place. It was Mayberry and Walton's Mountain combined: picturesque, peaceful, and relatively crime free. Real estate was cheap and bountiful and other than Sam's ten minute walk turning into a twenty minute drive to her new job, it was all worth it.

With any luck at all, Renee would hear back soon on the offer she'd put in on a village storefront. She loved antiques and in their numerous jaunts searching for a new home, Renee had realized how popular little collectible and antique shops were in the area. Folks who stopped for gas and a bite to eat as they passed through would, she hoped, decide to spend some time and money at her place, too.

Renee placed one of the lighter bags of groceries into Brandon's eager arms and grinned. "Thanks, little man," she said, snatching up two heavy ones of her own and following him up the front steps.

Six years old, she thought with a shake of her head. How was it possible that her son was in kindergarten? That was another reason they'd chosen this year to move. The school near their old place in New Jersey was overcrowded and understaffed. Murphey Mills Central School was very small and very old fashioned. All the grades were housed in the two-story original brick school built in the mid-1950s and class sizes almost never topped ten kids. It was almost like having a private school education without the expense. They had a very high graduation rate, too. Every now and then someone would suggest they consolidate with a nearby district. The vote never came close to passing.

Three more trips between the house and van eventually loaded the countertop with goods. Brandon immediately began digging through them in search of lunch. "How many minutes?" he asked holding up the promised SpagettiOs can.

"Two, but all the groceries need to be put away first."

His narrow shoulders suddenly slumped and arms dangled to his sides as he looked up at the ceiling, rolled his eyes, and whined, "I'm hungry now, Mommy."

"Then you better work a little harder to help get these things put away faster. Work first, food and playtime later." She pushed the bag of lighter items his way. "You know where these all go. Hop to it."

"Moooommy ..."

"Braaaanndon ..."

Brandon pouted and set the can in front of the microwave with a heavy hand. He stomped to the bags on the floor and commenced grunting and moaning as if the boxes of crackers and oatmeal weighed a ton, hauling each one to its spot. Renee filled the refrigerator and freezer. Sam hated the idea that Brandon ate SpaghettiOs at all. Renee argued they were a once-a-week treat or used for bribery, and sometimes making everything from scratch like Sam would do, was just too exhausting. Besides, Sam was the cook in the family. Not that Renee's skills were terrible, far from it, but her menus were a whole lot simpler than her partner's. When it was time for a dinner party, Sam ruled the kitchen which suited Renee just fine.

"I'll get it!" Brandon suddenly shouted, practically throwing the new container of seasoning to the floor. Renee hadn't even heard the phone. She transferred the eggs into the refrigerated container and tossed the cardboard carton into the recycle bin just as Brandon returned with the phone. "It's for Mama Sam." He held the receiver out at arm's length towards his mother.

Renee took it. "Hello?"

"Hello, this is Doug Martin. I'm looking for Sam Whalen?"

"She's still at work. This is her partner, Renee. Can I take a message?"

There was an awkward pause on the caller's end that, to Renee, meant they were either digesting the fact that Sam was really a woman or that Sam's partner was one. "Um, yeah," Doug's hesitant reply finally came. "I had a message from her about getting into the old Brown place to get some pictures."

"Oh?" Sam had mentioned wanting to get a closer look at the rundown house, but she'd not said she'd contacted the owner about it. Renee was not pleased with any of it.

"Yeah. Talked it over with my brother and we guessed it would be alright if your ... if Sam would be willing to sign a waiver about not suing us if she gets hurt over there. Neither one of us has been inside in a few years. No telling what condition the place is in."

Renee watched Brandon fighting to get the pull tab lid open on the SpaghettiOs can. She tucked the phone against her shoulder and held out her hand to him. "I'll let her know you called, Mr ... Here you go, kiddo." She returned the can to her son.

"Martin, Doug Martin."

"Yeah, alright, Mr. Martin. I'll pass the message on to Sam when she gets home, usually around five-thirty or so."

"Great. Thank you."

"No problem." Brandon retrieved his favorite bowl. He'd done this a hundred times before and Renee had no problem turning her back on her son and walking to the next room for just a few minutes. "Mr. Martin, you're saying no one has lived in that house for a few years?"

"Close to thirty. Why? You seen folks down there?"

Renee absent-mindedly chewed a nail. She turned to watch Brandon again but kept her voice low, "No, no, I haven't seen anyone down there."

"Has Sam?"

"I don't think so, no. I was just curious, that's all. Sam probably told you where we live, huh? We can see the roof through the trees, but that's about it. She went down there just over a week ago." Renee had no intentions at this point to tell Mr. Martin why. "I guess that's where she got your name and number from, a no trespassing sign or something?"

"Don't really know. Anyway, have her give me a call when she can and we'll figure out a good time to get together."

"Yeah, alright. I'll pass on the message."

"Sounds good. Thank you." Mr. Martin hung up before Renee could press the button to end the call on her own.

Brandon practically inhaled his lunch, while Renee took her dear, sweet time over a bowl of chicken noodle soup and a tomato sandwich.

"I'm done!" he announced triumphantly. "Let's go."

"Go? Oh," she sighed. "I really don't think it's a good idea."

The boy retrieved the jar from the counter. "You said we would, Mommy."

"I said maybe," Renee corrected.

His eyes narrowed a touch as his lips pursed. "You're not being very neighborly."

A laugh snorted out of Renee before she could stop it. It was such a mature and serious thing for a six-year-old to say with such a somber face. "You're right. I'm not. We'll go over, but we're not staying and you are not getting out of the car."

He slumped and rolled his eyes with a loud exhale. "That's no fun."

"Mr. Martin just told me no one lives there, little man."

"But I saw her, Mommy! I really and truly did."

"We'll go look, quick, just so you'll be convinced there's no one there."

The smile returned to his face. "I'll get my jacket."

Not five minutes later, Mommy's mini-van occupied almost the exact same spot Mama Sam's Jeep had when she and Brandon had been here the first time. "See, it's empty."

He craned his neck. "Maybe she lives in the barn."

"No one lives in the barn."

"Someone could live in the barn," he said with conviction.

"Where would someone who lives in a barn bake apple pies?"

He hated to admit it, but it sure didn't look like a place anyone would live, let alone make pies in. "I saw her," was the best answer he could come up with.

Dark Hollow Road

"Maybe there are old apple trees somewhere out back and she's just down here picking apples. It's that time of year, after all, and lots of old farms used to have their own apple trees. That would explain why she was around before, too."

"I guess," he moped. "Can we go look?"

"No," Mommy said. "Are you convinced now that no one lives here?"

He knew someone was there. Someone was watching them, he could feel it. He studied the windows, one by one, all dark, all vacant. No one was there and yet, something was. His gaze was drawn down to the darkness under the porch. That's where it was, hiding behind one of those narrow, black windows at ground level. "I guess," Brandon finally said. He really wasn't convinced, not in the least, but he didn't know how to explain that to Mommy. "We can go home now, Mommy."

Mommy turned the van around. "We'll keep the sugar jar handy just in case she comes knocking again. If she's around picking apples, maybe she'll come back to our house to get it."

"Okay," he said. Brandon turned in his seat, watching the thick cloud of dust the tires were kicking up behind him. He didn't see The Sugar Lady, but he knew she was there.

"Why didn't you tell me you found out who owned that place and called about it?" Renee had delivered the message as off-handed as she could at the dinner table. Knowing Sam had kept a secret like this had nagged at her all day. Anger mixed with annoyance which would yield to Renee convincing herself it was really no big deal. It shouldn't be a big deal, anyway, so why had Sam not mentioned it? It was best to wait until Brandon was down and out for the night than to bring it up during quality family time.

Sam took a long swig from her bottle of Yuengling. "Why would I? I didn't know if we'd be able to get in or not. Why mention something that may not even happen, at least not legally." She gave Renee a wink.

"We?" Renee found no humor in the situation. "Really, Sam? We? I told you from day one I wanted nothing to do with that place and I didn't want you traipsing around over there. There may not even be a floor left, and if there is one, maybe it's all full of dry rot. You could get halfway across, fall through the floor, and break your neck for God's sake."

Sam's head dropped back onto the propped up sofa pillow. "That's not going to happen. There's a floor. I was up on the porch. If the porch is sound, the inside can't be any worse, can it?"

"You don't know that."

She closed her eyes and drained the beer bottle. "You worry too much. I'll be careful. Mr. Martin and I will do a walk through together. We'll make sure it's safe before I take up even one pixel on my camera."

Renee crossed her arms with a sigh of reluctant resignation. "I'm not happy about this, I'll have you know. Not one bit happy."

Sam reached over and patted her on the knee with a soft chuckle and smirk on her lip. "No shit, Sherlock."

Renee cracked a smile and gave up trying to be mad. "So, how'd you find out?"

"I stopped back at Yager's on my way in the other day, like that girl suggested. I was able to talk to Mr. Yager." Sam studied the empty bottle of beer resting on her thigh. "Weird old guy."

"And he told you what you needed to know?"

Sam shook her head, "Not at all. Just the opposite. He was nice and friendly until I asked him about the place. Said it was best to let those sleeping dogs keep right on sleeping, that place has been empty for years and the family was long gone. I assured him all I wanted to do was get some pictures, but that didn't seem to ease his mind at all."

"You didn't tell him about The Sugar Lady then either, did you?"

"Hell, no," Sam scowled.

Chapter 11

We soldiered on as we had always done. Most of the time Kate appeared to be her usual happy and playful self, but I knew by that haunted, hunted look in her eyes, that wasn't entirely true. I busied her with the approaching holiday preparations. We sewed together every chance we got. She wanted to make new shirts for the boys. I sat nearby knitting them sweaters ready to help when she hit a snag. Nigel and Seth spent more time than usual out in the barn. We all had our secrets to keep and Daddy Clay's mood remained surprisingly upbeat. He even gave me extra money to buy what we'd need for the best Christmas dinner we'd had since Mama's passing.

Everyone loved their presents. The four of us kids were speechless when Daddy gave us ours. Four new bicycles! Not ones he'd hauled from the junkyard and hammered back into shape, but really and truly brand new ones. He said it was so we could get into town faster, especially now that Nigel was a working man. Apparently he'd gotten a nice bonus that year and, in untypical fashion, had managed to spend the money on others instead of himself. It would be the last time I ever felt proud of my father for any reason.

Dark Hollow Road

All the while I did my best to protect Kate whenever I could. I stopped sleeping on the sofa for starters. Kate was having bad dreams. I asked Daddy if I could put one of those latch-hook locks on the door from the inside because Kate had taken to sleepwalking, too. I was afraid she'd walk right out into the snow in nothing but her nightgown one night. He said no. He didn't like the idea of us being locked in our room. What if there was a fire? It made sense, but I sure would have felt better with one.

Katie's nightmares were unpredictable and violent. The last thing we wanted was for Daddy Clay to wake up to the sounds of her screaming or thrashing around. If he did that, he'd come rushing into the bedroom. He'd gather her into his arms and hold her close, rock her gentle and stroke her hair. The next thing you knew, he'd be carrying her to his bedroom where he said it was safe. No monsters dared go into Daddy Clay's room, no sir. Daddy would scare them away. No one was allowed to hurt his children, least of all his pretty, precious, sweet, Kate.

I told Nigel about it, but despite our best efforts, things still happened between Katie and Daddy Clay. I'd even offer to take her place, pleading that it should be me, but he wouldn't listen. Once he had a notion, it stuck. He'd make it clear he was the man of the house and things would be done his way. He was still bigger and stronger than us. We depended on him for almost everything we had, and he made sure we understood he could beat us black and blue if he were so inclined.

In January I missed my period. To say I was petrified don't even come close to explaining what I felt. I knew I'd be showing by spring. Daddy Clay would surely find out long before that. When he did, I knew exactly what he'd do. He'd bring that same abortion doctor to the house and force me into the basement under that terrible blinding bulb. They'd tie me down, drug me up, and pull me open to get rid of the whole unpleasant business of Mary Alice not being able to tell a boy no. It would be turned into my ugly sin.

It wasn't right for a girl to carry her daddy's own baby in her belly, but it wasn't right to kill the poor thing, either. I wanted that baby nearly as much as I wanted my mother to be alive again. None of this would be happening if she were here. Daddy would have her to love on and that would be that. Everyone would be happy again.

"Why you crying, Mary?" Kate whispered from across the nearly pitch black bedroom.

I blurted out the truth of it, "I got a baby in my belly again."

She must have been giving that a good, hard think because it was quiet for some time followed by, "How'd you get another baby in there? You ain't kissed nobody on the mouth, have you?"

The truth gushed out of me again. "That ain't how it gets done," I told her. "Daddy Clay put it in me with his man thing."

More quiet, an even longer pause than the first. "I won't get one in me, will I?"

"No," I assured her. "You're too little. You have to get your time of the month before you can have babies."

"I hope I never get that. I don't want to have any babies, ever," she replied. She shifted on her bed. "Daddy don't like it when you have a baby in you, does he?"

"No."

"He'll kill it like he done before."

My heart sank. Cold prickled my skin despite my warm night clothes and heavy blankets. Katie had been so young the first time I'd hoped she didn't remember. "I won't let him."

"How you gonna do that?"

I shrugged. "I don't know. I'll think of something."

"I'll try to think of something, too."

"Alright," I said. "Don't say nothing to the boys, okay?"

"Our secret like before?"

"Yeah," I whispered back. "Just like before. Now, go to sleep."

"G'night, Mary Alice. I love you."

"Good night, Katie Sue. I love you, too."

It was a long while before I fell asleep.

By Easter, I was starting to see the changes in my body.

In May, Daddy Clay's fate started to come into focus.

I was cutting up some potatoes to boil when Nigel slammed into the kitchen with such rage the knife I was using clattered to the floor. Katie Sue nearly dropped the stack of plates she was carrying to the table. There our brothers stood. Nigel's fists were clenched and his face was beet red with anger. Seth's was blotched from crying and there was mud and bits of hay scattered all over the front of him. He didn't say nothing, just stared at the floor, sniffing back snot.

"I'm going to kill him, Mary Alice! I swear on Mama's grave I'm going to kill him!" Nigel seethed.

I didn't really have to ask, but I did anyway. "What happened?"

Nigel cast a glance at Katie, but we knew how Daddy was, and I reckon he figured it was alright to talk in front of her. "He was doing his disgusting business to Seth out in the barn. Had him bent over the pigsty wall. He hurt him bad, I think, Mary Alice. I saw blood."

My attention turned to Seth again. He seemed to be shrinking, crowding himself into the corner as far as he could. "Go up to the bathroom, Seth," I spoke to him gently, trying to sound as much like Mama as I could. "Someone will be up in a little while."

Seth didn't move at first. "Go on," Nigel encouraged. "I'll help you after me and Mary have a good talk. Katie, you can tend to dinner for a few minutes, can't you, while me and Mary talk in private?" For someone of fifteen, Seth was sounding and acting very grown up.

Kate gave a somber, little nod, put the plates on the table, and retrieved the knife I'd been using from the floor. Seth hurried as quick as he could, retreating up the stairs to the bathroom and slamming the door hard.

"Where's Daddy?" A hardness had formed in my throat and chest.

"Out in the barn," Nigel said. He took hold of my arm and gave it a gentle tug, "Let's talk in the front room for now."

I didn't like the idea of leaving Kate alone out in the kitchen without knowing what sort of situation this really was. What if Daddy Clay come crashing in all crazy and did something?

"Lock the door, Katie, and pull down the blind," I instructed. "And don't you let Daddy in until me or Nigel says to."

She wasted no time following orders, and as soon as it was done, I went with Nigel to the front room.

"We can't kill him, Nigel. As much as I wish we could, we can't. Social Services will come and split us apart soon as they find out. We'll never see each other again," I said in earnest.

He paced back and forth, "You're eighteen now, Mary Alice, almost nineteen. You can take care of us. They'd let you take care of us!"

"What we gonna do for money, Nigel? We barely got enough as it be. What we gonna do when we ain't got Daddy's money coming in? And what we gonna say killed him? They find out it was our doing, we'll be worse off than we is now!"

He knew I was right and that infuriated him even more. I'd been thinking about this a lot more and a lot longer than Nigel realized I had. Since January. Maybe a little bit before that.

"What about Uncle Eli? He'd help us. He'd let us go live with him, don't you think?"

I'd thought of him, too, "Uncle Eli ain't come to see us in years," I reminded my brother. "I think he's forgot about us since Mama died."

"He ain't forgot, Mary. How could he forget? We're his kin. You can't just forget your kin like that and he's got plenty of money to take us all in. I bet he does. I bet he's got a fancy, big place where we could all live together." His voice was so full of hope, desperate, aching hope.

My lips pressed together tight as I thought about our uncle in Scranton. Sure, he'd brought us real nice presents, but he never stayed but the one day. Mama would get letters from him once in a while, but other than that, I didn't know much about him. I'd never seen another letter from him or heard Daddy say he'd gotten one. I didn't think it was a good idea to put all our eggs into Uncle Eli's single basket. We needed to be smarter than that.

Frantic pounding erupted from the kitchen door accompanied by Kate shrieking. Nigel and I raced into the kitchen to the sounds of Daddy's cussing. "Let me into this house, you little fuckers! You hear me?! God damn it, let me the hell in!"

"Katie, go upstairs," I kept my voice low for some reason, still in the hushed tone I'd been talking to Nigel with.

Her sweet little face was filled with terror.

"Go!" Nigel insisted.

The moment she raced from the room, Nigel and I exchanged glances. What were we going to do? Daddy sounded like he was in a blind rage.

"Open this door, you little shits, or I'll take the axe to it!"

No doubt in either of our minds he would, too.

Out of the corner of my eye, I noticed Nigel standing a little straighter. "You going to leave Kate and Seth alone?" I bit my lip while covering my mouth with both hands at the same time.

The glass in the door's window rattled with each pound of Daddy's big fist. "OPEN. THE. GOD. DAMNED. FUCKING. DOOR. NOW!!"

"Better open it, Nigel."

"We'll open it, but you have to promise you'll never touch any of us again. Not any of us!" Nigel squared his shoulders as we waited for an answer.

"Let me in. I'm bleeding bad," Daddy replied.

"So is Seth. Promise you'll stop," I was so proud of my brother for standing up to Daddy like he was but at the same time terrified of the consequences his bravery might bring.

Heavy footfalls shuffled on the porch. "Fine. I'll stop."

"Promise!"

"I promise, God damn it, now open the door before I bleed to death."

Nigel extended one long, thin arm to unlock the dead bolt. He snapped back into place beside me, placing one hand on my shoulder. His hand was trembling, but his jaw and stance were both firm as the door opened and Daddy trudged in.

A dark patch of blood clung just above his right eye where his hairline started. Most of it had already clotted into place, but not before a good wide stream had run down into his eye, along the side of his face and drew a few trickling lines half down his neck. He glared at the two of us, mostly Nigel whose hand squeezed my shoulder.

I was revolted at the sight of him, but he was my father. For that reason alone, because I knew I was supposed to love him and take care of him as Mama had asked, I stepped away from my protector and pulled out one of the kitchen chairs. "Sit down, Daddy. I'll clean you up."

He sat, barely giving a look my way, eyes riveted with darkness on the one who had dared step up and strike him down. I learned later Nigel had used a shovel. "You should check on Kate and Seth," I told my brother.

"Ain't leaving you alone with him." Nigel's eyes narrowed.

Retreating to the sink, I got out a clean dish rag and wet it down. "I'll be fine. Daddy Clay won't hurt me. Go and check the others."

"You sure?"

I gave him a tight nod. "The fighting's over."

I figured it was done for the rest of the night, anyway.

Reluctant, Nigel went upstairs while I went to nursing Daddy. He had a good gash on his head but nothing so bad to need stitches. He'd have a well-deserved lump and bruise come morning, not to mention a pounding headache to go with it. At least, I hoped he would.

He didn't so much as thank me when I was done and handed him a glass of water and two aspirins. He swallowed them down, stood, and went upstairs. A few minutes, later I heard his bedroom door slam shut.

After cleaning up, I joined the others upstairs. They'd all crowded into my and Katie's bedroom. Seth didn't look a whole lot better, but he wouldn't let nobody look at what Daddy had done. I could only hope and pray it wasn't anything too serious even though Nigel said he'd seen blood. No good could be had from blood coming from where I figured it was coming from. Seth persisted though, saying he was okay and it only hurt a little bit.

For about a week after, we all slept in the same room. We'd butted the dresser up against the door. Kate and me slept in one bed and the boys the other. I think those were the best nights any of us had had in years. We felt safe. We felt like a family.

Despite Daddy saying no to it before, Nigel went to the hardware store and bought two of those chain locks for our bedroom doors. Daddy never said a word as he passed by while Nigel was putting one into place. He kept his distance and his word, at least for a while. Meals were strained and mostly taken in silence.

In the meantime, my belly was growing. By June there was no hiding it. I didn't even bother to try. Course, I heard the whispering behind my back when I went into town. Sometimes I heard them guess right who got me that way. Richard Barrows and Elmer Price called me a slut. I bit my tongue and walked away.

I saw Larry that summer, too. He was nice enough and, unlike the others, I felt like his smile at me was real even if it was a little sad, too. I think he knew the truth. I think he wanted to help but was afraid what folks would say if he was seen with me too much. They'd think he was the daddy. I didn't want folks thinking that any more than he did.

Daddy Clay's drinking took a turn for the worse that year. It weren't no surprise when he was sent home from work and told not to come back until he'd sobered up. Lucky for us, the foreman was willing to let Nigel work at Daddy's wage after school for three hours and even more hours over the summer, filling in whenever he could for our sad excuse of a father.

Chapter 12

Up close and personal the place looked even more terrifying to Renee's motherly sensibilities. Carrying Brandon piggyback, Sam lingered around the property edges while they waited for Mr. Martin to arrive. Renee had not wanted to come, but when Brandon had overheard Mama Sam making the arrangements a few nights ago, it was all her little boy talked about. When could they go see? Could they take her a can of SpaghettiOs? Did Renee have a dress she could give to the old lady, because her blue one sure looked like it needed to be replaced? Better yet, a nice warm sweater and mittens.

"Brandon, enough about The Sugar Lady. She's not there," Sam snapped three days ago. She'd brought her bad day at work home with her.

Brandon's eye stared in horror. "But I saw her when Mommy and me came home from grocery shopping."

"Alright, enough," Renee tried to intervene.

Sam lowered her fork and gave Renee a glare. "You're right. It is enough. You know as well as I do no one lives there. Mr. Martin said the place has been empty for a good thirty years." The butch looked at her

114

son. "She isn't there, Brandon. Stop pretending she is. I don't want to hear another word about her from you."

"Samantha Whalen! How dare you say that to him!"

"She is too there, Mama Sam. I seen her!"

"You didn't see her. You imagined her."

"Stop it, the both of you."

"I did so see her! She was wearing a blue flower dress and an ugly sweater both times. Mommy said maybe she went down there to pick apples."

Sam growled, "Oh for fuck's sake."

"Enough!"

Big tears were rolling down Brandon's cheeks. "Yes, I did!"

"No, you didn't."

"For God's sake, Sam, stop it! You are arguing with a six-year-old. Knock it off."

She couldn't stand to see her son crying and what did it matter if Brandon saw this Sugar Lady or not. She was beginning to wonder if he really hadn't made it up, though that didn't explain the old canning jar. Maybe he'd found it somewhere. Either way, to him she was real, just as real as the imaginary friend he'd had before they moved.

"I'll take you with me when we go meet Mr. Martin and prove it." Sam just wouldn't let it go.

"He most certainly will not go with you over there."

"I want to go, Mommy!"

"It's not safe."

Sam let out a deep sigh, "I'm not going to let him run wild over there, Ren. Jesus, trust me once in a while to keep the kid safe, will you?"

Brandon's emotional resilience snapped into place. The tears were barely dry and already he'd switched sides. "I'll be safe, Mommy. I want to go."

"We can all go," Sam studied her partner without smiling. "Mommy can keep a better eye on you than I can."

It was clearly a jab at Renee who scowled in reply. She knew she was overprotective and not as trusting of others to watch her son, even Sam. She'd spent five years in an abusive relationship with Brandon's father. And, near as she could figure, he'd been cheating on her the entire time, even when she was pregnant with their son. He led two lives. When they were together as a family in public, he was the vision of tenderness and love. At home, not so much.

Trust became a thing of the past, not just towards him but everyone who approached her. Everyone until Sam. Sam had turned Renee's world on its head. It wasn't that she was surprised to be attracted to a woman. She'd always felt some of that, but in her family you got married and had babies and lived happily ever after. In the world she grew up in, lesbians were a joke. Renee didn't want to be anyone's joke and so she'd done more than just tuck that part of herself away, she'd buried it deep.

Things changed quickly after meeting Sam at a carnival three years ago. Sam had been confident about who and what she was. She didn't hide anything. She was strong, honest, and so butch it had made Renee's head spin. On top of that, Sam's family and friends had totally accepted it. Renee wanted that kind of life and love for herself and her son. After a year of dating, Renee had built up enough confidence to be honest with her parents. The response was mediocre at best. They didn't yell or disown her, but they hadn't embraced the whole idea, either. They said they were alright with it, but Renee knew they were lying, just like her ex-husband had lied to her time after time.

No, trust did not come easy to Renee though she wanted it to on a desperate level. It was happening with Sam, but the going was still slow and her confidence still flailed more than it flew.

"I'll be busy talking with Mr. Martin and it's probably a good idea you not go in with us. Mommy is right. It could be dangerous. Maybe you can go play down by the creek while we're inside."

Renee's brain screamed in panic. Don't tell him there's a creek, she thought. He'll be wanting to play down there all the time. Christ, one more thing for her to have to worry about. But it was too late.

"Can we, Mommy? I want to play in the creek."

Renee's gaze fell to her plate which held nothing now but a chicken breast picked clean. She gave her head a shake and sighed, "Fine, but if you wander off once, just once, we leave immediately."

Brandon grinned ear to ear and bit into his chicken leg. How had an argument about Mary being imaginary turned into Renee agreeing they'd make visiting that death trap a family outing?

And yet, here they all were, turning with expectant smiles as a beat-up, green Ford pickup began rattling its way towards them, swerving to miss a plethora of ancient potholes, and kicking up a long plume of late autumn dust regardless of how slow it was going.

The driver pulled up behind Sam's Jeep. "Hey, ladies," he said as he climbed out of the cab then gave a nod and grin to Brandon who was in the process of sliding off Sam's back. "And you, too, young man."

"Mr. Martin," Sam stepped forward offering her hand. "Samantha Whalen."

The hesitation was brief before he gave Sam's hand a firm shake. Mr. Martin was a lot younger than Renee had expected him to be, late forties, maybe fifty. He was clean shaven and sported a full head of blond hair, parted neatly to one side. His attire was simple. Brown work boots, jeans, and a heavy flannel, green-and-black-checkered jacket that covered an upright frame. This was clearly a man who wasn't afraid of hard work. In fact, Renee got the feeling he enjoyed it. She liked him. "Nice to meet you, Sam." His smile was genuine.

"This is my partner, Renee, and our son, Brandon."

Mr. Martin shook Renee's hand and then Brandon's with a warm chuckle. "Ready for some exploring, kid?"

Brandon's face bloomed.

"No!" Renee snapped, rushed forward, and grabbed her son's hand. "I mean," she said with an uneasy laugh, "we, we're not going in, just Sam. It's not really a safe place for a child."

"Smart woman," Mr. Martin added. "Not likely a safe place for anyone to be. We really should tear it down. It's beyond the point of being a handyman special."

"What happened to the Browns?" Sam asked.

Mr. Martin's mouth turned down into an exaggerated frown as he shook his head. "Not sure. Mary was the last one who lived there. Back about twenty years ago, word got 'round a relative of theirs from Scranton wanted the place auctioned off. It was either a brother or an uncle, I think. Only a handful of folks showed up. Ed and I won the bidding. Got the place dirt cheap. We planned on fixing her up and reselling. They call it house flipping now. It was in

118

pretty good shape back then." He shrugged, "Well, life got in the way before we could do much. Ed's wife got sick with that Lou Gehrig's disease. Took her five years to succumb. By then Ed's finances were pretty well shot. We replaced some of roofing and a few panes of glass. It was enough to keep the weather out."

The owner looked up at the looming house. "Roof and walls still look pretty straight. That's a good sign." His attention turned to Sam. "You bring a flashlight?"

Sam shook her head, "No, didn't even think of that."

"I got a spare." He headed back to his truck still talking, "Course, then there was the matter of the septic tank and plumbing and wiring." He chuckled, handing Sam a smudged, but sturdy looking, yellow and black flashlight. "Seems the Browns had treated it like a maintenance free home since the early seventies or so. Nothing's up to code. Nothing."

"What a shame," Renee looked up at the place. "What became of Mary? You said she was the last one to live there?"

Mr. Martin shrugged and frowned again. "No one seems to know. We're guessing she went to live with the relative who put the place up for auction. They were a pretty isolated family. Real poor. Didn't associate much with the rest of the people in town. I hear Mary was real pretty in her day, though, real pretty. There's still folks around here who remember her and her brothers. Had a little sister, too, I think. Mary can't be more than seventy or so. Could still be alive and well and living in Scranton with her family."

"Makes sense," Sam said. "Ready to head in?"

"Let's get this done." He patted his front pocket as if checking for the keys and gave Renee and Brendon a mischievous grin. "Get ready to call 9-1-1 if you hear us screaming for help."

Renee grimaced. "Not funny."

With Mr. Martin leading the way, they waded through waist high grass all the way up to the front porch. "Steps look a little sketchy." He tentatively approached the first step, giant stepping over the first broken one, before allowing his full weight to settle on the second. It creaked, but held firm. "Just don't be doing any jumping jacks and I think we'll be good." The next three steps, as well as the entire length of the front porch, were crossed with equal care.

He pulled the keys from his pocket and slid one into the hole Sam had so nervously peered into before. It took three hard nudges and a sharp kick of his steel-toed boot at the bottom before the door finally gave up and swung inward, releasing a plume of dust, a tumble of crumbling plaster, dry paint chips, and snapping thousands of cobweb threads that had formed on the inside.

"Maybe I should have brought some dust masks," he joked.

"Maybe," Sam replied, trying to see beyond Mr. Martin's right shoulder and into the dusty realm beyond. Wafts of stagnant air tainted with the aroma of must, dust, and decay tickled the inside of her nose. Sam gave it a defiant rub.

The first room bordered on claustrophobic, being little more than a narrow ten-foot-long hallway with a single window on the left hand side, just as Sam had spied through the keyhole. Despite the sunlight, the space felt anything but bright. Sam couldn't put her finger on it, but she didn't want to linger in here for too long. Other than the thick layers of dust, dead flies on the floor, and lacy cobwebs everywhere, the space was relatively clean.

"So far, so good," Mr. Martin noted. "Maybe it's not as bad as I thought it would be after all this time."

There were some serious cracks in the walls, but from what little Sam knew about old house construction, it could just be that the old plaster had separated from the lath beneath. All that held it in place now was the wallpaper. In a place like that, that could actually save you a lot of time in demolition. Any contractor with an ounce of sense would have that all ripped out and replaced with sheetrock.

They moved forward, Mr. Martin waving one arm back and forth slowly to fan away drifting cobwebs, and stepped into another small room that didn't seem to have much of a purpose to Sam's eyes. It was half the size of the entry way and turned them to the right. The bottom three steps of the staircase leading up jutted out. Sam could almost hear Renee in her head calling it a tripping hazard. Danger lurked at every corner. Sam smirked at the thought.

"What do you think so far? See anything worth taking a picture of?" Mr. Martin had passed under the doorway to the left.

Sam followed suit. "Not just yet," she said.

With one window blind drawn and the other window covered with cardboard, the kitchen proved difficult to see in. Shadowy black and white linoleum squares were starting to peel up from the floor in places. Some were just cracked. Others were missing entirely, revealing the tattered remains of dull, black paper and below that, hardwood planks. The center of the room was barren, but there were indents in the floor when four table legs had once rested. The marks were surrounded on all sides by scratches, scrapes, and barren worn spots where boots, shoes, bare feet, and chair legs had long ago all left their impressions.

Against the wall to Sam's left, a massive cast-iron cook stove squatted. "Now I do," she grinned. "That's some monster stove there."

"That's why it's still sitting there," Mr. Martin replied. "Can you imagine how much that bastard must weigh?

Sam studied the relic from various angles, catching the glimpse of the creative process as she moved. "It's a start." She dared to open the oven door. Soot and cobwebs mingled with flakes of rusted iron. "No one's been baking any pies in there, lately," she laughed. "And it says a thing or two about the sturdiness of this floor."

"Yeah, I think we're pretty safe in here. Oh, this might interest your artistic eye." Mr. Martin moved to an odd little door in the opposite corner of the room and pulled it open. "Walk in pantry." He clicked on his flashlight and shined it into the windowless darkness.

Sam added her beam and the hair on her arms prickled to cold attention. "Wow."

Row upon row of dust-covered Ball canning jars lined the shelves. Jars exactly like the one sitting on the countertop back home filled with sugar. These jars, however, held murky gray substances, a combination of dust on the outside and seals that had broken, allowing the food to rot on the inside. Some, however, still looked intact and in perfect condition. Cold sweat dappled Sam's forehead as the borrowed flashlight scanned the tight space. A cane-seated wooden chair sat against the back wall. A wider shelf than the rest jutted out at about waist level, clear of jars but scattered with rusted lid rings, a cutting board and some utensils. It was probably used as a prep counter, Sam figured. Mr. Martin's beam moved to the left, landing on what appeared to be a blanket tacked up over the exterior wall.

"Do you know what's behind that?" Sam asked.

"Cardboard and a window," Mr. Martin replied. "You can take it down if you want some natural light in there, just be careful. Try and get it down on one piece if you can."

"Why'd they do something like that?" she mused further.

He gave a shrug, "Maybe it was bad for some of the food to be exposed to too much sunlight? You can see the cardboard from the outside."

"Yeah, could be. Cool and dark is the best way to keep some things preserved." Apart from watching her grandmother, mother, and aunts going to town on a bushel of tomatoes, canning was beyond Sam's realm of experiences. She stepped back from the doorway, making a mental note of what she'd need to safely remove the window covering. "Awesome, what else we got?"

"Dining room, front room, and the upstairs. I think you'll like it up there better."

"Lead on," Sam urged, eager to see more.

Chapter 13

Things were almost normal for a while. Seemed Daddy had learned his lesson about messing with us. We watched out for each other. Everyone knew what to listen for. Weren't no more secrets like that.

I was harvesting the first wave of late summer squash when the baby decided it was time to come. Daddy and the boys were out cutting hay. I come trudging up the little hill, holding the underside of my belly, watching the row of freshly laundered shirts and dresses flapping in the wind just as Kate secured another one from the back. All I could see was her bare knees and feet.

When she saw me, her eyes got just as big that time as they did the first. "It time?"

I nodded. "Uh-huh. Pretty sure."

"Ain't it early? I thought it weren't supposed to come 'til next month." Her eyes went towards the field across the road where we could just make out how far along they were coming with the bales.

"A baby comes when a baby comes. And it ain't too early, I don't think. Maybe just a month." I turned my head to follow her gaze and I shook my head. "Just us, Katie."

She looked across the way again before giving a curt nod of agreement. There weren't no further need for words about the why. "One more shirt to hang up. That okay?"

I smiled, "Yeah, I'll get the old towels and blankets like we planned and meet you upstairs."

By the time Katie joined me, I had my bed stripped down and was putting a plastic shower curtain on top of the mattress in hopes of keeping things as clean as possible. On top of that we spread a moth-holed wool blanket Daddy said came from the Second World War. Water sloshed onto the floor as Katie set the basin down beside the bed.

"Lock the door," I whispered, pulling my dress up over my head. Another pain doubled me over with a groan. They was coming fast. Faster than either time before.

"Mary…"

Panting, I lifted my head and let out a slow breath. She was real pale. "We got to do it ourselves, Katie Sue. You hear me? Daddy Clay ain't gonna take this one away."

She was staring at the window, lips trembling. "But what if something happens? What if something bad happens like with Mama?"

"Ain't nothing bad gonna happen this time. You lock the door?" I was able to stand up straight again and shuffled towards the window to pull down the blind. The hay wagon was way out. They'd never hear me scream. I pushed the window down all the same, followed by the blind. With the door shut and the window closed, it was going to get real hot in here real fast.

By the time it was over, both me and Kate looked like we been swimming in the river. The itchy wool blanket was ruined, but the shower curtain done the trick and in my arms was a little baby girl. She was maybe a little smaller than other babies I'd seen, but her color was good and she let out a healthy loud wail at first. I knew that was a good thing. Even better that there weren't no one around but me and Kate to witness it. The baby had sleepy, almond-shaped eyes, a flat, pushed-in button nose and the cutest little ears I'd ever seen. A blessedly cool breeze filled the room when Kate opened the window again. She tossed the soiled towels into a pile while I gathered my senses and rested. "How long's it been?"

Kate looked out the window. "Not too long. Four hours is all." She walked over and smiled at the baby wrapped in the cleanest towel we had. "What you gonna name her?"

The baby's short fingers wrapped around one of mine as her tongue poked out of her mouth a little. "Alice," I said, looking at her, "Alice Katherine, after you and Mama."

"We can call her Ali," Kate sighed with a grin on her face. I hadn't seen Kate smile like that in a long time. Things were going to be better. "We did it, Mary. We really did it."

"I knew we could."

"I'll get you a bath going."

Closing my eyes, I heard the water running in the tub across the hall. I must have dozed off. Next thing I know, Kate is coming back in saying it was ready and that she'd heard Daddy and our brothers come back. They was down at the barn unloading now. We probably had another hour before someone came into the house. "They're gonna be wanting lunch," I said.

Dark Hollow Road

"I can fix it. Let's get you and Ali washed up. I can finish cleaning the bedroom while you do that. I'll be back in about half an hour to help you back to bed."

It took some doing, but I hauled myself and the baby out of bed slow and easy. We was both a mess. The scent of the fresh chamomile and lavender Kate had added to the water reached my nose before I saw the bits of it floating in the tub. While I climbed in, Kate held Ali then handed her to me once I got settled. "It's going to be okay, Katie. Don't worry."

"I ain't worried."

"Don't be lying. We're both worried, but nothing bad's gonna happen. I promise."

Her brief smile had fallen back into the look that had become far too common for her the past few months, sullen and blank. She took two steps toward the door and stopped. "What should I tell them?"

"That I'm resting."

"That's all?"

"Sun got too much for me and started feeling sick. I come inside to get a drink and cool bath and rest. That's all they need to know for now."

"Alright. Be back in half an hour," she repeated and left, closing the door behind her.

The little hook patted at the doorframe, reminding me there wasn't any protection between me and the hallway but an unlocked door. Daddy could come storming in easy as you please. I closed my eyes against the thought of his red face and clenched fists. Alice fussed in my arms. I couldn't let her cry. It was too soon. I prayed Daddy would stay away long enough for me to get back into my room and lock the door.

Resting against my left arm, Alice settled down into the warm, scented water. The rinse cup trickled water over her chest and head. Soon all the blood and goo was gone from the both of us. She smacked her lips. That little pink tongue of hers poked out every now and then as if she was tasting the air. Leaning over, I kissed my baby girl on the forehead. She was beautiful. I knew she weren't perfect on account of how her face was kind of squashed in and her head seemed a touch small, but she was mine and I still thought she was the prettiest baby I ever had seen in the world. I knew right then and there that if anyone ever tried to hurt her, I'd do my best to kill him. I'd die for her. I hoped my brothers and sister would feel the same way.

My tub water was getting cool before Kate came back and Ali was starting to fuss. "Don't let her cry just yet, Mary," I kept telling myself. "Give me twenty-four hours, Lord," I prayed as I heaved the two of us from the water. I needed to be strong enough to defend us. I needed to rest and Ali needed to get stronger.

One handed, I dug around under the sink for the cotton pads and belt. I was still bleeding from my lady parts and sure as shooting if Daddy Clay saw a drop of it, he'd suspect something. I'd no sooner taken a final look around the bathroom, when there was a timid knock at the door.

"It's me. You okay? Can I come in?" It was Kate.

"Yeah."

The door inched open just enough to let Kate slip inside. "Everything alright?"

Ali snuggled against me in the towel, "Yeah. They back yet?"

She shook her head. "No, but soon. Everything's ready."

128

We scooted across the hall on tiptoes, guilty as burglars in the dead of night even though we were alone in the house. I was going to climb right into bed but realized that would leave the bedroom door wide open. "Go on down. I'll get settled. I want to lock the door behind you."

Before she left, I wrapped my free arm around Kate's shoulders, pressing baby Alice between us. "I love you, Katie Sue. Thank you."

When we pulled apart, there were tears in my sister's eyes. "Love you, too, Mary." She looked to her newborn niece. "And you, too, Ali." I let her plant a kiss on the baby's forehead.

Kate hurried away. Soon as I heard the stairs creaking under her feet, I locked the door. It wasn't much of a lock, that's true, but it was something. It would at least give fair warning if someone tried to get in while I was sleeping. We all knew that if he really and truly wanted to, Daddy Clay could have smashed in the door.

As Ali took turns between sleeping and nursing, I dozed in bed and listened to the voices that rose up from the floor grate. Kate and my bedroom was right over the kitchen, allowing us to be the first to smell anything cooking down there and to hear just about any sound that rose up from below. It also meant that ours was the warmest room when the wood stove was hard at work. In the winter, that was a blessing. Not so much on that day.

Wooden, chair legs scraped across the floor. Daddy honked his nose and hacked. One of my brothers sneezed.

"Where's Mary?" Daddy asked.

"Not feeling good," Kate replied. She did a fine job of sounding casual about everything that had really happened in the past few hours. "Sun got to her so she come in for a cool bath and said she was gonna lay down for a spell."

Daddy grunted.

"You think me and Mary should go visit the midwife soon, Daddy?"

"Don't care what you do," his words were spoken around a mouthful of food.

"I think we should. Tomorrow maybe if Mary is feeling better and it ain't so hot." Kate was trying to sound cheerful. "Right after the morning washing is done."

"You done the washing already," Daddy Clay retorted. Of course he'd seen it all on the clothesline when they come up from the barn.

"Shirts and dresses, yeah, but it been so hot, Mary and me was saying it would be a good idea to wash up the linens. I always sleep better on a bed sheet that smells like fresh mowed hay and sunshine."

He grunted again. I smelled cigarette smoke. Daddy didn't care too much about being clean so long as he was fed a good meal. If he hadn't been for me and Kate, he'd likely of ate right out of a soup can or bit off hunks of bread from the loaf instead of cutting off a slice. He didn't even bother to shave his whiskers or get his hair trimmed but maybe once every couple of months. "You boys about done? We need to get them dead trees I seen last week drug out before sunset. I want you splitting and stacking wood tomorrow while I'm to work. God knows I won't get shit for work out of you once school starts up. Best I get as much out of you as I can before then."

Spoons clanked against bowls. Chairs legs whimpered as they drew new lines into the floor.

"Gimme your thermoses and I'll fill them back up for you," Kate offered.

Boots clunked and not soon enough the final pair retreated down the back steps as the screen door squeaked and slammed. Apart from Ali's suckling sounds, the house fell silent. I closed my eyes and relaxed, imagining Kate standing in the door frame watching them go.

Exhaustion sank deep into my strained muscles and bones. My body demanded sleep and I was in no condition to fight it.

Tap-tap-tap. Pause. Tap. Pause. Tap-tap.

I opened my eyes to a room in twilight. How long had I slept?

"Mary?" someone whispered.

Tap-tap-tap. Pause. Tap. Pause. Tap-tap.

"Mary, unlock the door. It's Seth."

"Seth?" My brain was still fuzzy around the edges. What time was it? Everything still hurt. "Just a minute."

Alice's eyes cracked halfway open for a second. She was being such a good baby. It was like she knew to be quiet.

"You okay?"

"Yeah, just a minute," I retorted. He had no idea how raw and burning my lady bits were right then. I shuffled to the door. "Wait 'til I get back to bed before you open it. I ain't got no clothes on."

"Alright."

Slow but sure, I unlocked the door and made it back to bed, Ali held protectively against me all the while. My arm was wet from her soaked through diaper. How I wished it had been Kate at the door instead of my youngest brother. "Alright. You can come in now." I double checked to make sure I was covered up on top.

He slipped in, re-hooked the latch and approached the bed, his hands wringing together just a bit. "Is it like Katie said? You had the baby already?"

"It is," I said. "Come see. Her name's Alice Katherine."

Seth approached, biting his bottom lip a little bit. I drew the thin blanket away from the little face that was once again calm with sleep. "She's tiny," he said. His head tipped a bit as he studied her in the darkening twilight. "She's like one of them Munchkins from *The Wizard of Oz.*" He joked. "Kate told Daddy she thought you and her should go to the midwife tomorrow."

"I heard." I nodded towards the floor grate.

"I think you should, if you can. Nigel and me can help get you there if you ain't up to walking that far."

"Alright. Where is everyone? What time is it?"

"In the front room listening to *Gunsmoke*," he said. "It's going on eight."

"Daddy ain't asked no more questions about where I'm at or how I'm feeling?"

Nigel shook his head, "Nope. He ain't said a word."

I wasn't sure if that was good or bad. "Okay."

"I should get back. Had to use the toilet, figured I'd stop and see how you were before I went back downstairs."

"Thanks, Nige. See you in the morning."

"Yeah, see ya."

The door shut with a soft click. I didn't bother to get up and lock it again. I figured Katie would be up in about an hour to get ready for bed.

Chapter 14

With each step, the air cooled yet somehow felt heavier and increasingly humid. Apart from the dead starling lying sprawled and skeletal on the fireplace hearth amongst a tangle of pink insulation, the dining room and front room had held nothing but more stale, hot air. Sam wasn't interested in photographing empty rooms. She'd been hoping to tell a story with the images she captured, but so far all she had was an old woodstove, a pantry full of canned food, and a dead bird.

"Damn, it's a little chilly up here." Mr. Martin tugged the collar of his jacket closer to his neck.

Sam wished she could do the same. "Gotta love these old houses. Maybe we should open a window to let the warmth in."

Mr. Martin chuckled. "Unfortunately, most of the windows are nailed shut."

Sam scowled. "Why would you do that?"

"Didn't. Was like that when we bought the place. Closed up tight as a drum top to bottom. I suppose to keep nosy teenagers out when the last of the Browns left."

Sam was no stranger to the teenage penchant for breaking and entering into old, empty houses.

Sometimes she and her friends would find nothing. Sometimes the house they ventured into looked like the owners had sat down to dinner then suddenly changed their minds only to up and leave. Closets full of clothes, food in the pantries, and lives that had just been left behind for reasons unknown still lingered. Those were the creepy ones. That's the kind of place Sam wanted to find. The Brown residence was proving to be a bit of a disappointment.

She rubbed the palms of her hands together to warm them, scanning the dark hallway. All the doors were closed and she felt like she was breathing cobwebs. The back of her throat itched. "So, what's so interesting up here?"

Mr. Martin pointed to the door behind Sam, the one on the left. "Let's start there."

Curious, Sam turned to the door. Her hand was on the knob before she saw the three inch long metal hook that dangled from the doorframe. An eye bolt was screwed into the door next to it. Sam looked over her shoulder at Mr. Martin wondering why there'd be a lock on the outside of what appeared to be a bedroom door. "You do that?"

He shook his head. "Nope." He gave her a smile. "Makes you wonder, doesn't it."

"Just a little bit."

"Go on in."

Turning back, Sam opened the door and stepped into an empty room streaming with sunlight. Her eyes went to the source of that light, the dirty window with a broken pane. Streaky white bird droppings ran down the glass on both sides. More had found a home on the floor with bits of feathers. It was nothing of any great interest.

"What do you think?"

Dark Hollow Road

Sam studied the dull, blue wallpaper, the cracked ceiling, and the dirty hardwood floor. "Not much to look at, unless the image of the Virgin Mary is hiding in that bird shit."

Mr. Martin chuckled. "That'd be pretty funny, wouldn't it, but no, that's not what I mean. Look again. At the floor, specifically."

There was a faded outline of where an area rug had probably once lain, slightly off center as if it had been beside a bed. She shook her head still not seeing anything of interest.

Mr. Martin brushed past her and went to the center of the room. He pointed at the floor, along the faded line of the missing rug. "What do you make of that?"

Sam put her hands on her knees and peered at the spot. "There's a line of some sort." The stain spread out like fingers before hitting a crack in the wood floor that channeled whatever had left it towards the window. "Looks like someone spilled something," she noted as she straightened.

"It does, doesn't it?" Mr. Martin rubbed the sweat at the back of his neck again. "Brother Ed thought it looked like blood. I told him it was probably furniture stain."

"Why would he think it was blood?"

Mr. Martin smiled. "He was the town butcher until a couple years ago when Parkinson's made it too hard to hold the knives steady. He said he knew spilled blood when he saw it."

Sam looked at the stain again. "That's would have to have been a lot of blood, wouldn't it?"

"That's what I said. I still think it's wood stain. Cherry, by the looks of it." Mr. Martin was grinning ear to ear.

"You're messing with me, aren't you?"

He chuckled, "Not at all. I've no idea what it is. It's interesting though, isn't it?"

Sam wasn't sure what to believe now. Clearly her host had a sense of humor, and a rather dark one to boot. "I'll give you that. It's interesting all right."

"Let's have a look at the other rooms."

As they left and Sam closed the door behind them, she felt the strangest urge to slide the hook into the eye and lock the room up tight.

Mr. Martin nudged open the door directly across the hall. Inside, two twin bed frames, minus any mattresses, framed a solitary window that offered a view of the road below and the cornfield. Once the corn was gone and all the tree branches made barren by winter, there was no question one would be able to see their house from up there. To the left, Sam found herself staring at the long, dark opening of a closet door. It hung half open with missing chunks of plaster on the wall on either side, as if someone had been throwing a ball at it. Stepping closer, she spied two wire hangers dangled from the wooden bar. Another lay on the floor. Other than that, there wasn't much to look at.

"Let me show you the bathroom and other bedroom."

Sam followed Mr. Martin down the hallway, brushing her hands across her arms at invisible cobwebs. There was nothing there when she looked, just the feeling. She didn't care for the sensation at all. Places like this had never bothered her in the past, even the ones that people for miles around boasted were haunted. Sam didn't think for a minute they were being watched by ghosts, but she sure wasn't as comfortable as she normally was. Maybe it was the sight of the locks that bothered her. She had a bad feeling about this place that had nothing to do with spirits.

"Anyone ever call this place haunted," she asked with a laugh as Doug opened the bathroom door and walked in.

Mr. Martin laughed. "Oh, sure. The normal urban legends. No facts behind any of it. One of them hitchhiking stories passes through now and then, someone or another will claim they seen Mary hitchhiking a few miles down towards town. They pick her up, she'll tell them where she lives and when they get here, course, she ain't in the back seat. Stuff like that, but those stories are a dime a dozen."

Sam felt herself grinning at what remained of the bathroom. "So, no one ever died here then?" A pale, rose-colored toilet, sink, and claw-foot tub filled the room. It was usually the one room Sam could always get pictures in. People didn't tend to take their bathroom furnishing along when they moved out of a place.

"Didn't say that," Mr. Martin stepped out of the way while Sam opened the medicine cabinet. "Mrs. Brown passed away here. Mary's mother, that is. Complications from childbirth, I think."

A rusty razor leaned against the inside walls of a murky drinking glass within the mirrored cabinet. Beside it an equally aged can of shaving cream sporting red and white stripes stood. There was a black comb and a white toothbrush with yellowed bristles on the bottom shelf. No sign of any toothpaste though. Sam's fingers twitched to touch the items, but her photographer's eye and sensibilities forced her hand to stay by her side. "Oh, that's sad."

"Yeah, shame, but it happened back then more than we know, I reckon."

There were dead flies in the dried out toilet bowl. Sam gave the room one last sweeping look. "I could get a few good shots in here, I think."

"Great," Mr. Martin returned to the hallway. "And last but not least, the girls bedroom." He swung the door wide open and stepped aside for Sam to lead the way in.

She crossed the threshold and stopped, eyes fixing on the empty mirror frame mounted to the back of an antique dressing table, sweeping her hands over her bare arms again in an attempt to brush away the tiny bumps that suddenly covered them. The room was far from cold. It was just as stuffy as all the others, but there was that weirdness again. It was the same creepy, crawly feeling she'd had as they'd left the first bedroom. "This where the mother died?" she asked aloud almost before the question had time to form in her brain.

"Don't know, but the wallpaper seems kind of flowery to have belonged to the boys. We figured it belonged to Mary and her sister."

Sam shook off the unease and moved deeper into the space. The placement of the beds created a mirror image to what they'd found in the boys room, minus any sort of closet. Instead, the old dressing table stood against the wall. A bed had been put on either side of the single window. The other difference was these metal frames supported mattresses. While one lay barren and stained, the other was all made up neat as can be. Sam scowled. "That's a little odd."

"You think? Just a little?"

"Bad shit went on here, man." Sam heaved a breath to look out the window, to try and clear a head that had suddenly gone milky. Where the boys' view had been of the front, this view was of the overgrown backyard. Half of the barn roof had collapsed, but there was still an chicken coop that didn't look too bad. Beyond it gnarled apple trees clung to several old trees.

"I wouldn't doubt it," Mr. Martin agreed. "No one really talks about the place, and me and Ed, well, we didn't want to start making any suggestions or rumors. The less folks around town that know what we found in here, the better. We made a pact not to say anything, so I'd appreciate you and yours doing the same. Whatever went on here is in the past. Ain't nothing any of us can do to change it."

"Let sleeping dogs lie. That's what Lee Yager told me."

"You spoke to Lee?" Mr. Martin was stunned.

"Well, I tried to," she shrugged.

"Lee's a good enough guy, though he's about as polished as a lump of coal. Real hard working, but never heard him talk much about his folks or family. Him and his little sister are tight. He's real protective of her, and given the chance, she follows him around like a puppy."

"Lisa? We met her at the pumpkin farm."

Mr. Martin gave a curt nod. "She's a sweetheart. Not a mean bone in her body and always the first one to raise her hand and volunteer. Lee had to put a damper on that. She'd offered to help so many people with so many thing at churchs, he couldn't keep up. She don't drive, of course. Once pumpkin season is done, you'll start seeing her at Kelley's. You been to Kelley's in town, the diner right on Main Street?"

"We've been a couple times."

"Lisa's a waitress there. She's good, too. Don't know how she does it, but she never uses a notepad to write anything down. I'm not sure she knows how to read or write. Never known her to do either." He tapped his left temple with his index finger, "It's all up here, though, despite the obvious disability she's got. Anyway," Mr. Martin had stuffed his hands deep into his pockets. "I think we've seen all there is to see up here. Ready for the basement? We'll go around back through the storm doors. That'll let in a lot more light. The old wooden stairs from the front room should be fine, but better to approach it from below, just in case."

"Ready when you are."

"Have that flashlight ready. If you thought the kitchen was dark, you're going to love the basement."

The moment the front door opened, Brandon jumped to standing. "Did you find her?" he yelped. He wanted to run, to leap onto the porch, push past them and race into the house yelling her name.

The man who was showing Mama Sam the house look puzzled and said something Brandon couldn't hear. Mama Sam replied back to him before raising her voice. "Nobody's home, Bee. All quiet."

"Oh," he grumbled with disappointment.

"We're heading down to the basement," Mama Sam announced next.

"Really?" Mommy whined. She didn't like waiting, Brandon knew that. She didn't like waiting for anything, and especially not for something she thought was dumb and a waste of time. Brandon had heard her complaining more than a few times about things like Mama Sam taking too long to gel and spike her short hair when they went out. And this place was definitely a waste of Mommy's time. She'd said so. It was ridiculous, she said. "How much longer are you going to be?"

Mr. Martin shrugged, "Fifteen minutes, tops."

140

"Fine," Mommy pulled out her phone and went back to leaning on the front bumper of the car and staring at the screen.

"Can I go with them, Mommy?" he dared to ask. It might be the last chance he had to get inside.

"No," came the unsurprising negative retort.

"Oh, come on, Renee, let the kid have a little adventure," Sam started walking towards the road. "I promise not to let him get killed, or have a rusty nail spike jab up through his foot. It's fifteen minutes in an empty basement with two grown and quite capable adults."

Brandon's wide eyes stared at his mother, hope and doubt mingling in the blue-green orbs. He bit his bottom lip but didn't say anything.

Mommy lowered her phone, looked at Mama Sam, looked at Brandon, then looked at Mr. Martin. "Go on," she said, resigned.

"Really?!" It was like a blast of cold air slapped him in the face. "Really, Mommy?"

"Really. Go before I change my mind, little man. I hope this turns out better than the last time you two talked me into going against my better judgement."

Brandon laughed and made quick work of closing the gap between himself and Mama Sam. Mama Sam hoisted him up and tucked him under one arm like a giant football. Brandon giggled. "I won't drop him on his head or nothing, ma'am," Sam called out and turned back around, lugging Brandon and following Mr. Martin to the back of the house.

Just before they rounded the corner, Brandon squirmed down. It was getting uncomfortable being a football even if Mama Sam was pretty round and soft. He walked carefully behind Mr. Martin, trying to step in his steps through the thick, clumpy grass.

"What have we here?" Mr. Martin paused.

Brandon had to get on tiptoes to see what Mr. Martin was seeing, but when he did it was like one of those hard landings where you couldn't breathe for a few seconds.

"That's your coloring book, isn't it, Bee?"

Mr. Martin stooped with a grunt and picked up the book, now swollen and soggy from all the time it had spent outside. "Laying right there on top of the padlock." He turned and held it out to Brandon. "This yours?"

The boy recoiled, much like when the witch had thrust those two rats at him. "I don't want it, anymore," he whimpered.

Chapter 15

In a half-sleep, Ali and I passed the night together in my bed. I kept waking up afraid I'd rolled over onto her, but she was always safely tucked into the crook of my elbow or once, on my shoulder where I must have put her to be burped after feeding. What few whimpers she made could not have been heard beyond the room's four walls. In fact, Kate told me she'd never heard a thing all night.

Heavy footsteps receding down the stairs woke me fully, followed by someone shaking down the ashes and tossing a couple logs into the woodstove. Daddy's familiar hack, cough, and spit followed. Mama would have yelled at him for spitting in the sink. Me and Kate didn't dare ask him to not do it.

As I sat up, the toilet flushed and I saw that Kate's bed was empty.

"I'll be right down to get your breakfast made and lunch packed, Daddy," I directed my voice toward the floor grate some five feet away.

"Don't bother. Going to Kelley's," he said.

She must have heard him, because Kate walked in just then looking as confused as I felt. Kelley's wasn't nothing special, but Daddy Clay hadn't gone there, far as we knew, since before Mama had died. Kate, who

143

stood closer to the grate than I, looked down at it, "Alright," she answered. "See you for supper, Daddy."

"Won't be back until after dark," came the reply. "Coffee's on," he added moments before the kitchen door squeaked and slammed with our father's quick departure. Even as the truck rumbled to life and drove away, Kate and I remained motionless and silent. What had just happened?

Kate exhaled with a giddy grin. "You and Ali can join us for breakfast now.

I smiled back. "I'll be down as soon as I can." I didn't want to waste a precious moment of Daddy being out of the house. We had a lot to do and hopefully enough time to do it.

Half an hour later, I joined my siblings in the kitchen. Seth and Nigel had scurried down the stairs while I was in the bathroom washing up Ali and me. Seth stood right up when I entered the kitchen, eager to see his niece and help me to my chair.

I'd barely gotten situated when Nigel began talking in earnest. "We got it all figured out last night, Mary Alice. Remember that old dog cart Mama always wanted Daddy to fancy up for her?" I did. "It ain't fancy just yet, but it's in good shape. We figure instead of a dog, we can hitch it to a bike. If Kate can't pull it, I can for sure. You don't care if I take you to the midwife instead, do you?"

I didn't. "Might be a better idea even, having my oldest brother with me. You okay with that, Kate?"

"Uh-huh." She spooned a heap of scrambled eggs onto my plate and added some buttered toast. "I have a lot of washing to do."

"Great. We got it all pretty near figured out in our heads last night how we're going to hook it up."

I felt terrible guilty knowing how much work I was leaving for my siblings to do. Hopefully, it wouldn't be long before I was back in full working order.

We ate as quick as we could. The boys hurried out to ready the wagon and see if their hitch idea would work. I helped by clearing the table and doing the dishes. It was the least strenuous job that needed doing. Kate ran the hose out to the back porch where we kept the washing machine and began loading it with all the soiled linens and towels, from the day before, along with Ali's diapers. A generous cup of Borax was added just to make sure it all come clean. Mama'd been so happy the day Daddy Clay had brought that thing home. There'd be no more scrubbing board for her, and that wringer on top sure would make it easier on her hands. For a time, it almost made laundry days fun.

The machine was chugging along good as you please when Seth's shout came from the front porch. "Mary! Come look!"

In the driveway, my brothers waited proud as peacocks with Nigel's big blue bike hooked to that dog cart just like they'd planned. "It's real sturdy, Mary," my brother assured me. "All we need are some pillows and blankets and you'll be just like a princess heading off to the ball."

"It's genius!" I gushed. Why hadn't we thought of this before? It would have saved us so much time and effort going into town for groceries and supplies. "Two of the sofa cushions should fit perfect in there."

And so it was that just over an hour later, Nigel pulled me, baby Alice, and two jars of raspberry preserves into the driveway of Mrs. Yagar, who come right, ain't she?"

out her front door wiping her hands off with a dish towel. "What in the world?" she laughed.

Mrs. Yagar was a short, stout woman with a generous bosom and belly. Tight, snow-white curls covered her head and her hands were gnarled with arthritis. She had the kindest blue eyes I'd ever seen on anyone and an easy smile that made you feel welcome and loved. Her bright expression changed to concern as she got closer and realized just why we were there. "Mary Alice, you had that baby. Why didn't you have someone come fetch me?!"

"Wasn't time, Mrs. Yagar," I said. It wasn't really a lie under the circumstances. "Had her yesterday afternoon. Kate helped me."

Her practiced hands reached out and took the bundle into her arms. Gentle fingers drew back the blanket. Her smile slipped even further away. "Oh, Mary Alice."

My heart skipped a beat. "What's wrong? She's alright, ain't she?"

Mr. Yagar studied the baby a bit more, drawing out one of the pudgy little hands from beneath the covering for a closer examination. "She's fine, Mary Alice, but we need to get inside and out of this sun so I can have a good look at the both of you."

After setting the preserves on the kitchen table, Nigel made a quick retreat to the front porch to sit and wait.

Mrs. Yagar had a room off the kitchen she used for her midwife appointments. It wasn't anything fancy, just a desk, two chairs, an exam table, a basinet, some cabinets for her supplies, and a long table by the window where she kept the baby scales.

"Now, let me have a good look at you, little one. What did you name her?"

146

Dark Hollow Road

I told her. She seemed pleased with the choice and unwrapped Alice from the blanket. Mrs. Yagar took hold of the baby's arms and moved them back and forth, then she done the same with her legs. She opened Alice's hand and looked at her palms, followed by looking in her ears and listening to her heart.

"She's real good. She don't hardly ever cry," I said.

The midwife gave me a little smile before carrying the baby over to the scales. "Just over six pounds," she said, jotting it down on a nearby pad of paper. Next, she measured the baby and wrote that down, too. "What time did you say yesterday?"

I shrugged. "In the afternoon sometime. Daddy and the boys was out baling across the road."

"Before or after lunch?"

"Before."

Mrs. Yagar wrote something else down, tucked Alice back into the blanket, and set her into the basinet. "I'll get a birth certificate done up for you."

"She's alright? Is six pounds good?"

She patted my shoulder, "She's a little small, but she was early. I think she'll be just fine. There's something I need to talk to you about, though."

I bit my lip.

"Don't worry too much, but I'm pretty sure Alice has something called Down Syndrome."

"Is that real bad? Is she going to die?" I guess I knew my baby wasn't as perfect as others, but that didn't mean I didn't love her any less.

Mrs. Yagar's smile was tentative. "No, it's not something that's going to kill her. If all goes well, no reason she can't live a long while. It just means she's going to be slow to learn things and she's going to be smaller than most others, too. She's going to look more like herself than you or your, or the father. She might have some other troubles, but we'll worry about them if they happen. She's retarded, Mary Alice. You know what retarded means?"

My jaw clenched as I fought back the urge to cry. People'd been calling me that all my life and saying I was stupid. It wasn't true. I was smart. I could do anything I wanted if I had a mind to. "Yes, ma'am," was all I could manage to say, though I had a million questions in my head.

"But she's healthy by the looks of her. Now," the midwife laid her hand on my knee, "what about you? How are you feeling?"

"Sore and tired."

She laughed. "Well, of course you are, but no fever? Eating and drinking alright? Have you had a bowel movement yet?"

I nodded. "I'm doing alright."

"Good. Think you can climb up on the table so I can have a look, just to make sure?"

"A look?"

"It won't hurt," she tried to reassure me. "I just want to make sure you haven't torn anything. Last thing we need is an infection."

Honestly, I didn't want anybody doing nothing down there, but Mrs. Yagar was the midwife and I figured she'd seen more lady parts than anyone else I knew. Mama had trusted her and I figured I could, too.

"Alright," I agreed.

She'd held my hand before we left and I was all situated into the wagon again. Her eyes and voice was serious as I ever seen or heard. "Mary Alice, if you need anything you get someone to come fetch me, you hear? Anything at all. I brought every one of you kids into this world and your Mama was one of the nicest people in these parts. Don't think twice about coming for help, or if you have a question."

"Thank you, ma'am," I said.

"I mean it, Mary." She looked steady at Nigel who stood beside his bike waiting to haul us all back home. "You, too, Nigel. All of you. I made it no secret from your mother how I felt about your Daddy and her being with him. I won't keep it secret from you. He's gotten worse since your Mama's passing, but I'm sure you know more about that than I do." Her eyes flicked to the baby. Without a word, that look told me she knew where and how Ali'd come into being. "My husband and the boys feel the same way. If you need anything, just ask."

Tears come streaming down my face before I could even think to try and stop them. "Thank you, Mrs. Yagar."

"Oh, Mary, don't cry. Just know folks is watching out for you. We really are. It may not seem so, but we are." She bent down low and gave me a hug which only made me want to cry all the more. "Now, get on back home."

"I will," I whispered.

"We will, Mrs. Yagar. Thank you," Nigel climbed onto his bike and began the long trek back to Dark Hollow Road.

Mrs. Yagar had given me half a dozen new diapers, a couple of knitted, pink baby blankets for Alice, and some vitamins for me. It was what she gave to all her new mothers, she said. They were all stuffed into a brown paper sack beside me in the cart.

I kept looking back over my shoulder as the distance between us grew. She didn't move the whole time, watching us. It was the first time I felt like we weren't alone and totally at Daddy Clay's mercy.

Daddy hadn't been kidding when he said he'd be late getting home. Everyone was to bed when I heard the rumble of his truck getting closer. I rolled to my side and squinted at the wind up alarm clock. It was almost two in the morning. He'd be drunk. He always was when he come home at that hour. I felt my body tense under the covers, drawing Ali closer to me. She was over a day old now and there was a witness just two miles away that she existed. If anything happened, I knew in my heart that Mrs. Yagar would testify to that. Hearing the kitchen door open made my chest grow tight. Had Kate locked the bedroom door? I was pretty sure I remembered her doing it, but not so sure I wasn't afraid. Nigel and Seth would have locked theirs, too.

Ali whimpered beside me. Maybe I was holding her a little too tight. "Not now, baby girl," I tried to be calm.

Daddy's boots trudged across the kitchen floor then echoed a heavy thud up each step. I held my breath and closed my eyes. Suddenly I had this vision of Daddy standing at the top of those steep stairs, teetering a little in his drunkenness, losing his balance, and falling backwards. I imagined it was me standing there in the dark, reaching out and pushing him with both hands as hard as I could. And he went back and back, tumbling ass over end, and there would be this loud snapping sound when his neck broke. I'd walk to the edge of the steps and look down. Daddy Clay would be lying there, arms and legs all akimbo, his head twisted at an unnatural angle, and his eyes staring blank.

I know it's wrong to pray for things like that and it wasn't like I was really praying. It was only a random thought, a wish that he wasn't there anymore and we could have more days and nights like we had that day without him being around. That's all it was.

His footfall drew closer. I stared at the bedroom door, wondering if Kate was awake and listening, too. If she was, she was probably just as scared as me to make a sound. There was a click and a squeak so faint that normally you'd not have heard it, but it was the middle of the night, stone quiet, and I was wide awake. Cold fear made me suck in a breath. Kate had forgotten to lock the door. Daddy was going to come in. He was.

Metal tapped on metal. The door held firm. The hook and eye lock was in place.

He'd smash it. If he was drunk enough and wanted in bad enough, he'd step back and throw himself forward and smash it open. A scream started to work its way up my constricted throat. Alice squirmed, whimpering a little louder, demanding I pick her up and hold her. She was hungry, but my heart was pounding so hard it made my hands shake. I couldn't get the buttons on my nightdress undone and I was afraid to take my eyes off the door.

Another squeak moved my terror further up my throat. The latch wiggled. The knob shifted. The floor groaned, once, twice, three times before the bathroom door shut and the sound of Daddy Clay taking a piss covered the sound of my trembling exhale. While I could, I opened my gown and brought Ali to my breast.

Beyond the bedroom door, the toilet flushed and my prayers were answered. Daddy's leaden steps retreated away to his own bedroom, his door closing with a satisfying click.

I waited in the dark for the sound of his snores. Only then was I able to get back to sleep myself.

Chapter 16

After that, Sam didn't feel she had any other choice than to tell Mr. Martin about The Sugar Lady. As Sam relayed the tale, Brandon's initial panic settled down to the point where he picked up the spongy remains of his coloring book and began peeling the pages apart one by one. The outer edges had been hit pretty hard, but given some time in front of a fan or on top of a heated air vent might make the book usable again.

"Doesn't sound like anyone familiar to me, but there could be most anyone living around here up in the woods. Even then, why would she leave without taking the sugar?"

"That's what doesn't make sense," Sam agreed. "You saw her again a little while ago, too, right, Bee?"

He nodded, not looking up from the tender task of separating pages. "Uh-huh. She was walking down the road, heading here."

"I'll ask around town, see if anyone recognizes the description," Doug said. "Obviously she's not been in the house. It's all been locked up tight, including the basement," he jingled the keys he'd been just about to use on the padlock. "Still want to go down?"

"Of course. You, Bee?"

The boy gave a little shrug.

The metal, ground-level Bilco doors showed very little wear and tear. Apart from a few scratches here and there, they were in good shape. Nothing seemed to have disturbed them, no jimmy marks, no dents, and the padlock was just as pristine. It took a bit of work to get the key to turn before the lock finally popped up, and together Sam and the owner lifted both the doors wide open like a pair of square, dull brown butterfly wings. Brandon's silence was disturbing. He was normally such a chatterbox, but now he just stood there watching, the battered coloring book dangling limp in one hand.

Cold air rose up from the concrete steps that led into the darkness. Sam rubbed her nose to get the aroma of rot and decay out, but it did little good. The smell was too pungent and clung where it landed. Brandon coughed.

"I don't wanna go down there," Brandon's apologetic eyes begged forgiveness.

"You don't have to, buddy. Maybe just sit on the top step there, while Mr. Martin and I look around for a few minutes. Would that be okay?"

He nodded, followed them to the edge, and sat with the book on his lap. "You'll be quick, right?"

"Quick like a bunny," Sam assured him and meant it. The kid wasn't looking good. He was almost as pale now as he'd been when they'd come out of the Spook Barn. "You sure you're okay? I can take you back to your mom if you want."

Brandon's face tightened, but he shook his head, "I'm fine. Just hurry."

"We will." Sam gave him a reassuring pat on the knee before she turned on the flashlight and joined Mr. Martin in the cellar.

Sam bowed her head to avoid the draping cobwebs that hung from the cellar's open beam ceiling. Between two massive uprights, a set of wooden stairs stood. Doug walked over and gave one of the posts a good, hard shake. "Still solid as a rock, it seems. Maybe there's hope for the old place for someone with a good wad of cash burning a hole in their pockets."

On the opposite side, an old workbench had been slapped together with bits and pieces of unmatched wood. None of it was new, but some parts looked newer than others. To Sam the work surface looked like nothing more than a discarded door, salvaged from some shed or barn. Red stain was still visible around the edges, but the central work surface was rubbed pretty clean. Overhead, a cord swagged down from the cobwebs, ending in a single socket still holding a light bulb coated with dirt and dust. A single shelf, as large as the top, had been installed halfway down the bench. Sam's flashlight played over it.

"Old hacksaw here," she said, moving on, light illuminating a jumble of rocks in one corner. "What's that all about?"

Mr. Martin's beam joined hers. "Just leftovers from when the basement walls were put together, we figured." His light quickly darted away.

Sam moved on as well, studying the years of neglect and dust that coated everything in the musty darkness like gray cheesecloth stretched beyond its limits, ripped and fragile.

Mr. Martin's backlit and hunched shadow shuffled in the dark. The beam of his light flashed and cast stretching shadows along heavy stone walls and makeshift wooden shelves that sagged with age. "This place is full of strange things." Wood scraped on layers of dirt and stone. "Check this out. It's a box of old light fixtures."

Sam headed in his direction just as he was lifting out a small lamp base. "I got a friend who'd love that stuff."

"Hell, take it!" Mr. Martin urged, pulling the container out even further, dragging an old ragged piece of fabric along with it in the process. He tugged it off the tack it clung to and tossed it into the box of lighting supplies.

"He'll be thrilled." She gave the basement one last sweep with the flashlight. "I think I've seen enough," she said. "Might need some floodlights for pictures, but I see a lot of potential down here."

"Great. Let's get topside. This dust is starting to stuff me up."

They headed for the wide span of daylight and fresh air offered by the open Bilco doors.

Brandon's warped coloring book rested on the top step, but the boy was nowhere to be seen. "Where you at, Bee?" Sam retrieved the book and tossed it on top of the wooden crate Mr. Martin was carrying, before taking hold of it herself so he could close and lock the doors behind them.

"Probably got bored and went back to his mother." He glanced up. "Looks like we got some rain coming."

"Bee?" Sam scanned the yard gone to field, the apple trees, and the barn beyond. "You still back here?" There was no reply.

Doors secured, Doug and Sam retraced their steps to the front of the house. "I really appreciate you coming out here like this, Mr. Martin. I'd love to get in and get pictures soon."

"No problem. It was past time I came out here to check things out. Really should do something with it, put it on the market or tear it down, one or the other." He lifted his hand in greeting to Renee who had moved from leaning on the Jeep's bumper to being inside it with the radio on. "Tell you what, why don't I just leave the keys with you? Come over when you can, as often as you like."

"Sounds great. Thank you."

Renee was looking grouchier than ever by the time they reached the vehicle. "Sorry it took us so long, babe. Some interesting stuff down…"

"Where's Brandon?"

Sam's heart paused in her chest. "He's not out here with you?"

"No," her partner replied, the grumpy expression morphing into terror. "You took him with you. You were supposed to be watching him."

"Shit, I was."

Renee shoved the Jeep door open so hard and fast it practically knocked Sam off her feet. "You weren't! Where is he, then?" A red flush of anger spread over her face. "BRANDON!" she screamed. "Brandon, you better answer me!" She headed towards the house, repeating her son's name over and over again, each time a deeper level of dread touching the edges of her voice.

Sam and Mr. Martin followed close on her heels, echoing Renee's cries.

"You don't think he snuck into the cellar while we were down there, do you? He'd have said something," Mr. Martin suggested.

Sam didn't know what to think. "He'd have yelled when he saw us leaving," but even as Sam said it, Mr. Martin was working the lock to open the Bilco doors a second time. Since the Spook Barn the boy had been even antsier in the dark than he was before. There was no way he'd have remained quiet knowing he was going to be left behind.

"I told you to watch him. You promised you'd not let anything happen," Renee was frantic. "Brandon, where are you?" her voice raised again.

They scrambled into the basement. The two flashlights were a far cry from the light they really needed to have. "Brandon, answer your mother, you hear? If you're down here, you come out right now."

"Brandon, please. You're scaring Mommy. Stop this."

Mr. Martin's lights illuminated the shelves and workbench. "No one's here," he finally said. "I don't think he's down here."

"Jesus Christ," Renee swirled around, retreating back to the surface. "Brandon!!!"

The thin gray clouds had thickened considerably, releasing a scattering of cold raindrops down on their unprotected heads. "He can't have gone far," Sam offered, moving to wrap her arm around Renee's shoulders.

The effort was thwarted by an angry shove and backhand that just missed Sam's arm. "Damn it, Sam! I trusted you!"

"Let's check the old coop and barn," Mr. Martin, the voice of age and reason, suggested. "Never yet have met a boy who could resist sneaking into an old barn."

Halfway to the chicken coop, the sky rumbled and opened with a vengeance. Renee continued to scream her son's name. Behind her, Sam trudged, yelling as well, but the clamor of a cold, hard rain on the trio of tin rooves that surrounded them made it nearly impossible to hear much of anything else.

Mr. Martin stopped dead in his tracks, "Lookie who I see." He pointed towards the small, ramshackle building that leaned just slightly off center and had once housed the property's numerous generations of chickens.

Through the wire-covered window, a tiny face was peeking out. Locks of hair hung soaked with rain over the child's wide eyes.

"Brandon!" Renee shot forward, miraculously missing any number of tripping hazards hidden under the bowing and dripping weeds and clumps. "Why didn't you answer?"

He smiled. "I was hiding and didn't want to be 'It' next."

For a moment Sam feared the ferocity Renee used to open the shabby door was going to pull the whole structure down on top of the boy, but the cold that trickled down the back of her bare neck refused to let her speak momentarily. "Get out of there," she said, finally finding her tongue. "You scared us to death, Bee. Don't ever do that again."

Renee yanked her son out and pulled him into the circle of her rain-drenched arms. "Little Man, don't ever, ever run off like that." Tears and rain poured down her face.

"I was only playing." The gravity of the situation was completely lost on the pouting child.

"Let's get home and out of the rain. We'll discuss this then," Renee started marching the boy back in the direction of the car. Renee glanced over her shoulder once as Sam and Mr. Martin, both soaked to the bone, slogged along behind. Sam didn't have to be told that the discussion would not just be between mother and child.

Brandon peered at his mother from under the towel she was rubbing much too hard on his wet head. Her lips were nothing more than a faint pink gash under her nose. She'd barely said a word since they'd gotten back home.

"I'm sorry, Mommy," he said. And he really was. He was only trying to have some fun and pulling the ruined pages of the coloring book apart had gotten boring real fast. It really wasn't his fault. "I only wanted to play."

Finally, she stopped rubbing his head and pulled the towel away. "I know, just don't ever run off like that by yourself. You should have told Mama Sam you wanted to go. She would have brought you back to me. We could have played a game."

Mama Sam appeared in the doorway. She'd changed into a pair of sweats and her favorite sweatshirt. Mommy hadn't said much to her since they got in the Jeep. He knew it was his fault. He'd done bad, but he wasn't thinking and he didn't like sitting there on the steps. He didn't know why. Maybe it was the cold, smelly air that kept blowing past his nose. Maybe it was because it was so dark. Even though he could hear Mama Sam and Mr. Martin talking, it had still been scary.

Mommy pulled a clean, dry t-shirt forcefully over his head followed by a sweater. "Go brush your hair then get downstairs and sit in the Time Out chair until I say you can move. I need to talk to Sam."

Dread swelled up in Brandon's stomach. They were going to fight. He could tell. It was the same voice Mommy had used with Daddy. Brandon had been little, but he still remembered. They'd fought a lot. Mommy told him it wasn't his fault and maybe then it wasn't, but it sure was now. He looked up at her but couldn't find any new words so repeated the only ones that seemed to fit. "I'm sorry, Mommy."

"Go downstairs, little man. Mama Sam and I will be down soon."

Brandon headed towards the bathroom to get the hairbrush, head down, eyes cast to the carpeted hallway floor. The air grew even heavier, filled with pained sadness. Brush in hand, he thudded down the steps to the Time Out chair in the corner of the dining room.

Chapter 17

The next day I introduced Daddy to his granddaughter. Somehow he managed to get up and go to work despite only five or so hours of sleep, was ornery as a bear at the supper table, and probably would have preferred to be left alone after, but I didn't want to keep her hidden any longer.

He was sitting on the front porch in the rocking chairs when I carried Alice out. Across the valley, dark gray clouds were gathering and the wind was picking up. We all hoped the storm would bring cooler, less humid weather.

Daddy looked up at the sound of the door closing. His bushy eyebrows jumped briefly before returning to their usual somber scowl. "I hope you don't expect me to give you any extra money for that," he said. He didn't even act like he wanted to see her.

"No," I said.

"Good," he leaned back and relit his cigar. "Maybe that will teach you to stop slutting yourself all over town."

My teeth ground together. "You know that ain't how it happened."

Daddy's eyes narrowed and he smirked. "Don't lie to me, girl. I heard all about it in town. You're no better than a two-bit Jap whore. Your Mama would be ashamed."

My fingers pressed into Ali's flesh, my rage at his lies. With my heart racing, I couldn't hold back no more. "Mama ain't got nothing to do with this. You done it and you know you done it. You're the liar, not me, Daddy."

The sound of the rocker smashing backwards reached me in the same instant Daddy grabbed my arm, pushed me back against the wall, and wrapped that big hand of his around my throat. "You better be watching your mouth, girl, or you're going to find that brat of yours in a sack with a rock, tossed into the river."

I couldn't scream. I'd kill him if he set one finger on Ali. I tried to jerk away, but his other hand was on my shoulder, pressing me hard to the siding. His eyes were like the old bull one of our neighbors had years ago, red, deadly, and without feeling or remorse.

With a grunt he let go and shoved me sideways. Ali started crying. There just ain't words for the amount of hate I was feeling. I went back inside drenched in that blind rage and shaking head to toe.

Mid-August heat gave way to cooler, late September nights. Halfway through the second week of Nigel's senior year of high school, he come crashing through the house, gasping and yelling nearly two hours earlier than I'd expected. "Mary Alice! Damn, Mary Alice, where are you? Come quick. Lord, sweet Baby Jesus, come quick."

I'd barely got my hands out of the dish water when he stumbled into the kitchen, "What's going on?"

His gaze darted towards the basinet I usually kept Alice in while I was working downstairs. "Where's Ali?" He took two frantic steps towards the wicker basket.

"Upstairs," I said.

The color of his skin flip-flopped from pale to red and back again. "They ain't been here, yet?"

"Who? Nobody been ..."

"The police."

"What would the police be doing here?"

He grabbed my arm a little too hard. There was a feverish glint to his eyes. "I was in math class. The window faces the parking lot. I seen two policemen and a lady dressed up come walking up the sidewalk, all business, no smiles. Didn't figure nothing about it. Ten minutes later, there's a knock on the door and Miss Kelsey from the office is there saying I need to come with her. I knew I hadn't done nothing wrong, but then I thought about the lady and the police. Miss Kelsey wouldn't tell me nothing. Sure enough, they were waiting for me in the principal's office. Seth and Kate was brought in, too."

I could barely breathe. My first thought was Daddy was dead.

"Been an accident," Nigel went on, "at the mine. Daddy showed up drunk after lunch and got into a brawl with the foreman. Both gone to the hospital. One of the officers said Daddy was going to be in jail for a while once the doctor's patched him up and released him."

Part of me was disappointed. Part of me was relieved. "Where are the kids?"

"They went back to their classrooms. I rode here as fast as I could. Police said they'd come and tell you, but I said it was best I do it. Plus," he shook his head with a frown, "the lady that come with them …"

He swallowed and pushed the wide flap of hair away from his eyes. "What?" I urged. "Who was she?"

The look of terror in Nigel's eyes made me hold my breath, "She was with D.S.S., Mary. They're coming here to look at the place."

"So?" My housekeeping was every bit as good as Mama's. Weren't like we were living in a leaky barn with no comforts.

"I think they want to take Seth and Kate away. They asked me a lot of questions about Daddy and you and how we live and if we got relatives around."

"And what'd they say?"

"They said they wanted to talk to you, too. If they think you and me can't take care of Seth and Kate, they're going to take them. They didn't say it like that, but that lady was looking them up and down like. She even put her hand on Kate's head like she was just comforting her about the news about Daddy, but I saw her checking closer, like looking for lice or dirt or something. She held Seth's hand and looked at his palms. Sorry to say, they was as filthy as ever."

"Damn." It started to sink in. This was real serious. If they decided we wasn't good enough to take care of them, what about Baby Alice? Cold, damp fear coated my bare arms. They couldn't take her, could they? I was over eighteen. I was an adult.

The sound of cars was coming closer. No one ever came down Dark Hollow Road unless it was to see us. We were the only ones down here. By the time Nigel and me walked out the front door, a police cruiser and a black Chrysler were parking in the driveway. The lady who had been driving the New Yorker wore a dark-blue pencil skirt with a white blouse. A pair of glasses dangled from a beaded chain around her neck. She smiled and waved, maybe to try and put us at our ease. It didn't work, not with the set of police officers trailing so closely behind her.

Nigel took up a guarded stance beside me. His feet were planted. He'd put his hands on his hips. I half expected him to hold one hand out and shout, "Halt!" He didn't.

"Are you Miss Brown?" the lady stopped about ten feet away.

"Yes," I replied.

"I'm Mrs. Hayes from Social Services," she smiled again and held out her hand, inching her way closer, so I could take it and make her feel welcome.

I took it even though she wasn't welcome in the least. "Hello."

"Can we go inside and talk?"

The policemen had become cross-armed posts standing some five feet behind her. "Why the armed guard?"

She turned, looked, and twittered out a laugh, "Oh, don't pay them any attention. The department gets a little over the top in cases like this. Believe you me, I wish they weren't here just as much as you do."

Nigel's eyebrows arched. "Cases like what? Since when is there a case?"

Her attempt to be lighthearted faded. "Since the moment your father was brought into the ER and said he had underage children at home and no mother here to take care of them."

"I take care of everyone just fine," I said. "I been doing it since I was eleven."

"And I'm sure you are doing a wonderful job, Miss Brown, but there are laws."

"I'll be twenty come spring. Nigel will be eighteen in October, less than a month."

She nodded, "I understand that, too, but we are still obligated to inspect the residence. Neither of you is a legal guardian to your siblings. I'd just like to ask a few questions and look around, that's all."

"Daddy Clay ain't going to be in jail forever, Mrs. Hayes. What's it matter we're here on our own for a few days until he's back home?" Nigel asked.

"May we go inside and talk?"

I looked over at my brother who peered with untrusting eyes at the three intruders. "You can come in," he said, sounding like Daddy through and through, "but they need to wait outside."

My insides was flopping back and forth as we headed inside. Part of me was saying this was a good thing. Here was our chance to get out of this place and away from Daddy forever. We could go and live with Uncle Eli. We could be free of Dark Hollow Road. The deeper, more stubborn part of me didn't want to leave. This was our home. It was the house we'd all been born and raised in. Daddy may be a miserable old man with his flaws, but he was still our father. Mama had taught me to respect that even if I didn't like the man much.

Mrs. Hayes silently observed her surroundings as I led her back to the kitchen. I'd never been more self-conscious about the way we lived or my housekeeping. Clean as it was, it was run down and careworn. Everything struck me as being in a dull, yellowed haze that I'd never seen before. Not much about the place sparkled and shined.

"Would you like a drink?" I asked. "I can make up a pot of tea or coffee or even some iced tea if you want."

Nigel leaned against the sink and crossed his arms.

"Tea," our guest said. "Iced tea."

"Have a seat." I went about the business of fetching three glasses of iced tea and was just setting the last one out when little Alice decided to make herself known.

Mrs. Hayes looked up, more than able to hear the baby's crying from the ceiling grate. She offered a wan smile. "I'd heard you had a baby. Go on then. Don't let her cry."

By the time I come back down, Nigel had moved to sit at the table and Mrs. Hayes had put on her cat-eye glasses and had gotten out a notebook and pen. I could already see she'd written down half a page of notes. I sat down opposite her at the table.

"How old?" she asked.

"Just a month," I picked up my iced tea and took a sip.

Mrs. Hayes looked surprised, picked up her pen and wrote something down. "What's her name?"

"Alice Katherine, after my Mama and little sister."

She wrote that down, too.

"You going to write down every little thing we say, Mrs. Hayes?" Nigel leaned forward and put both elbows on the table, giving her a long, hard look.

Her eyes flicked to my brother. I understood now why there were two policemen waiting outside. "A lot of it, yes. I need to know the conditions here to file a report."

Nigel didn't move. "Conditions here are fine, ma'am. We take care of ourselves, always have. We got food. We got clean water. We got enough wood stacked to keep the place warm just like our Daddy and Mama done before us. We even got electric and indoor plumbing way out here."

Her red-painted lips drew in on themselves. "Then you have at least one bill to pay," she said, not quite meeting Nigel's stare. "How do you intend to pay the electric bill if your father loses his job?" Her eyes flicked up, but didn't rest on his face for long. She shifted in the chair.

"I work," Nigel said. "I make twenty dollars a week at the mine, plus me and Seth got us a good ginseng patch. There's good money in that."

She wrote that down. "What about food?"

"I do a garden, Mrs. Hayes. I can and freeze most everything we need. I can show you the pantry if you want. We got cows for milk. We got chickens for meat and eggs. We got pigs and two Herefords that are going to be butchered right soon. We don't get much from the stores in town, ma'am. We don't need to."

The woman frowned, scribbling in that notebook all the while I was talking. "What about a doctor? What if one of you gets sick?"

"Mrs. Yagar's our baby doctor," I said. I figured her knowing the little ones was taken care of first was real important. "Me and Nigel, we don't get sick much."

"But what if you do? What about the bill that's going to come from your father's visit to the hospital today and the jail fine?"

Nigel's chair creaked as he leaned back. "We got money put away. We'll pay it." He sure did look a whole lot older than his seventeen years. I sure was glad he was there.

"How much?"

I felt my eyes narrow. "Enough," I said. "Plus, we need help, we can always write to Uncle Eli. He'll send what we need."

Dark Hollow Road

Nigel scowled and looked at me a little puzzled, but played along. "Yeah, and so far, we ain't never had to get hold of him, but if we did, he'd do right by us."

Curiosity bloomed on Mrs. Hayes's face. "Uncle Eli?" Even upside down, I could read it as she wrote down his first name.

"Mama's brother, Elijah Gunderman. He lives in Scranton," Nigel explained. "He comes to visit twice a year." That was an out and out lie. We'd not seen or heard from Uncle Eli in over five years. Nigel shouldn't be lying like that. This lady was just the type who'd check it out.

"He didn't come this year though. Busy, I suspect. Maybe for Christmas," I added. "He usually comes around Thanksgiving or Christmas time."

"But even if he don't, we don't need his money. We have enough, more than enough."

"Gunderman, is that with an E or an A?"

"A," I swallowed hard. She was going to check. Sure as I was sitting there, she was going to check.

"Any other relatives nearby?"

"None closer, no. The rest of Mama's family's up in New York. We ain't seen them but a handful of times."

Mrs. Hayes took another drink from her glass of iced tea. "I'd like to see that pantry of yours, Mary, and the rest of the house, if I may? The more I know now, the less I'll have to bother you in the future. I can see you're the sort who likes their privacy." The smile was meant to make me feel better. It didn't.

"Sure," I said. Weren't any point to saying no. If we didn't let her look around, she'd somehow force her way. She'd bring more people, more folks stomping through the house invading our lives.

169

I showed Mrs. Hayes every inch and cranny of the house, attic to basement, pantry to bathroom. She never stopped writing in that little book of hers. By the end of it, baby Alice was crying and squirming to be fed.

Nigel took Mrs. Hayes and the two henchmen out to the barn so I could feed the baby in private.

By the time they all come back to the house, it was pushing three o'clock. Seth and Kate would home by three-thirty. I wanted these people long gone by then.

Finally, Mrs. Hayes let her glasses dangle from their chain again, closed her book up, and put the pen away. "Someone will be in touch with you," she said, slipping behind the wheel of her car.

"What about our father?" I asked.

"If bail isn't posted, he'll be in jail for three days. After that, he'll have a court date and will likely be given a fine. If the fine isn't paid, he'll spend a little more time in jail and that will be the end of it."

"Thank you," I shifted Alice to my shoulder and patted her back. That's where I stood as the Chrysler came to life and rolled away, tossing up a cloud of brown dust in the wake of the police car before it.

Nigel stood beside me looking grim and annoyed. "We got three days," he finally spoke when the majority of the dust storm was gone and the two cars were little more than specks at the end of the road.

Three days. It didn't seem like much, but we were grateful for it.

Chapter 18

"Better?"

From his bed, with the covers pulled all the way to his chin, Brandon nodded.

Sam bent down to plant a kiss on his forehead. "We had quite the adventure this weekend, didn't we?" Something had been nagging at the back of her brain since finding the boy peeking out of the chicken coop window.

He frowned. "I guess," he said. "You aren't still mad, are you? We can still go trick-or-treating tomorrow, can't we?"

Sam chuckled. "Yes, we can still go trick-or-treating and, no, I was never mad, Bee. I was worried, just like your mom was worried and scared that something bad had happened. There could be a lot of things out behind that house we can't see because of the grass."

"I know," his eyes darted towards the closet door where Sam had set up a small night light inside. It was round and stuck on the inside of the door. It should last all night.

"I know you know," Sam grinned and sat down on the side of the bed. "There is something I've been

171

wondering, though. Maybe you can help me out?"

The blanket under the boy's chin lowered just a touch, eyes a little more alert. "What?"

"You said you were hiding because you didn't want to be 'It' next."

"Yeah."

"What did you mean by that?" Sam asked.

"It, like in Hide-and-Seek. 'It' is the one that counts and if you get caught by 'It', you have to be the next counter. I'm not a good counter, yet."

Despite the sweatshirt, Sam's arms felt a little bit colder. "So you were afraid if you had to be 'It' next, you'd mess up the counting part?"

Brandon nodded. His smile was vague and a little embarrassed. "But I still wanted to play," he added.

"Of course, you did. Who doesn't like to play Hide-and-Seek?"

"Mommy," the smile melted from the boy's face. "It makes her real mad when I do it."

Sam felt sorry for the kid. As much as she loved Renee, there were times that she seriously questioned the woman's sense of fun. There had to be more to it than being hurt by her ex-husband. The man was a cheater and a liar, but what did that have to do with playing a simple game of Hide-and-Seek or Tag with your own kid? It was as if Renee thought Brandon was made of sugar glass and would shatter if he tripped and fell. "I know," Sam said. "We'll have to play when she's not around, that and maybe some football." Sam winked already hearing Renee's rant if she ever caught Sam teaching Brandon how to tackle.

The smile was back, "Really? You'll teach me?"

"Sure, our secret, though. Deal?" Sam held out her fist, knuckles towards the six-year-old.

Brandon pulled his fist out and bumped it against Sam's. "Deal."

"Cool," she said. "I have another question for you."

"Okay."

"When you were hiding, who was 'It'?"

"Allan."

"Who's Allan?"

He gave a little shrug. "He came over and asked if I wanted to play Hide-and-Seek with them. It was him and two other kids, two girls. I think they were his sisters."

Sam leaned back to think. There had to be a house nearby with kids. She'd heard them playing herself. Now Brandon was saying he'd joined them in a game of Hide-and-Seek. Maybe that's where The Sugar Lady came from and the children Brandon had seen were hers. "Did they say where they lived?" she ventured.

"No," Brandon was starting to look concerned. "I don't think they go to my school," he added.

"Why?"

"I never saw them there and the one girl, she was too little."

"Maybe they're home-schooled."

"Maybe," he yawned.

"Okay, Bee. Time to get some sleep. I'll stop by the hardware store and get you a real nightlight tomorrow, okay?"

"Thanks, Mama Sam." He sat up and gave her a big hug around the neck and a kiss on the cheek.

"You're welcome, buddy. Sleep tight and sweet dreams." She returned the kiss. He really was an awesome little guy. "Night."

"All tucked in?" Renee leaned into the corner of the sofa, magazine in one hand, cup of tea resting at her elbow on the side table, and a Steelers throw draped over her folded knees.

"Yeah," Sam headed into the kitchen to grab a beer before settling in beside her. She cracked the bottle open, took a swig, and patted her partner's warm thigh. "I think we all learned a valuable lesson today," she said with a grin.

Renee was mostly out of her grump now that everyone was settled in. "Sorry I flipped out on you, hon." She lowered the magazine to her lap.

"You had every right to flip out," Sam took another long drink from the dark brown bottle. "I should have kept a better eye on him. When he didn't want to go down into the cellar with us, I should have brought him back to you." Sam's hand slipped over top of Renee's and gave it a squeeze.

"I love him so much." The quaver in her partner's voice was totally unexpected. "I can't lose him." There was real terror there, in her eyes and in her voice.

Why was she so afraid? Of course it was normal to want your child to be safe and happy, but Renee's fear had weird, obsessive quality lately. "I promise I'll do a better job seeing that you don't."

"Thanks, Sam," Renee smiled and Sam fell in love all over again. "I love you."

"Love you, too, baby." She leaned in, giving Renee a soft kiss. Pulling back, Sam's eyes lingered over the curve of Renee's cheek, the way her nose turned up just a tiny bit, and the full outline of her lips. The cheeks suddenly bloomed with color and the lips smirked.

"You're staring."

"You're worth staring at," Sam laughed and leaned back fully on the sofa. "Told Bee we'd pick him up a real nightlight tomorrow. Kind of strange he suddenly wants one after all this time."

"I told you not to take him into that Spook Barn," she lifted her magazine and went back to scanning the page.

"He's not said two words about the barn. I don't think that's what bothering him."

She didn't even look up. "Trust me, it's what Brandon doesn't talk about that's bothering him the most."

"Did you hear any kids over there today?"

Renee glanced up and shook her head. "No. Why?"

"Brandon said there were three other kids over there playing. That's who he was playing with, not us, them. He said some kid named Allan asked if he wanted to play Hide-and-Seek and that there were two girls, too."

The magazine lowered to Renee's lap a second time. "Three kids?" she shook her head. "I think we would have heard that many kids playing Hide-and-Seek, don't you?"

"That's why I'm asking. Maybe being in the cellar muffled it, but you were outside. I thought maybe you'd heard something."

"Not a peep," she said.

"Weird." Sam fell silent, staring at the blank TV screen. "I heard kids when I took the sugar jar over, too." she finally admitted, but was not yet ready to confess the very real sensation of being shoved backwards by invisible hands. "I figured it came from the other side of the creek."

"Maybe they have a boat, or it's shallow enough to wade across."

She reached for the remote. "I'll check it out next time I'm over there."

It was a lot quieter here than it had been in their apartment. There you could hear other people talking, televisions babbling through thin walls, music thumping in cars as they rolled by, and sometimes the train at night. You could hear that coming from a long way off. It started as a low, vibrating hum. As it got closer, the whistle would blow, and the steady chunka-chunka-chunka sounds could be heard. There was always something to listen to. Now, Brandon didn't hear anything but his own heart stampeding in his chest. Not even the wind blew to rattle leaves in the trees or rustle the stalks of corn on the other side of the chain-link fence along the back yard.

He'd tried very hard to go to sleep, but he just couldn't. Ian, a boy in his class, called it Hamster Brain. Ian said it was like when your pet hamster was running and running and running in his wheel all night and making it squeak and the squeak kept you awake. Brandon had never had a pet hamster, but if this was anything like it, he didn't want one. Besides, hamsters were like mice and mice were like rats.

Most of the time he liked living in Murphey Mills. He liked his new friends in school and his teacher. He liked having a big yard to play in and the swing set Mommy and Mama Sam had put together for him. They said next year he'd get a sandbox. But right now, and for the past couple of weeks, Brandon did not like being here at all.

Before the corn had just been corn. Now, he looked at it and expected The Sugar Lady to come walking out. Other than the blue dress with white flowers on it and her tattered sweater that dangled bits of shaggy yarn from the sleeves and bottom edges, he'd forgotten what she really looked like. In his head, she had the face of the Spook Barn witch.

The hamster racing in its wheel became one of those rats. Tiny black nails chattered against metal. Two beady eyes the size of pin heads glistened at him. A dark gray nose twitched over yellowed teeth, snarling, snapping, biting at the wires, working them apart bit by bit. It would get out soon and once it did, it would hide in his room, under his bed, behind the trash can, inside his basket of dirty clothes, under a pair of socks, beneath a pile of stuffed animals, disguised as one of them.

Brandon's open, dry mouth trembled. He looked towards the warm, comforting glow of the light inside his closet as he pulled the blankets up closer to his wide, watering eyes. Maybe it would be safer in there. If he got inside and closed the door the rats and The Sugar Lady with her jars couldn't get him. He could hide under the shoes and clothes and toys and blanket. But to do that, he'd have to get out of bed, have his bare feet touch the floor, and risk one of those horrible creatures attacking, lunging at his ankles with its sharp claws and tainted teeth.

Maybe safer to stay where he was, with blankets pulled all the way up now, teddy bear held tight, head under the pillow, and body curled into a ball listening to the silence of his room, of the house, of the world outside his window that faced the cornfield where The Sugar Lady waited and watched. Lying very still and very quiet, quiet as a mouse, not at all like Ian's hamster. Brandon scrunched his eyes shut and bit into the back of the teddy bear's head. *Go away, hamster. Go away. Go away. Go away*, his little boy brain screamed.

Tap-a-tap. Tap-a-tap.

Brandon's eyes flashed open. His lungs tightened, holding in the sound he wanted to make.

Tap-a-tap. Something tiny, something like toenails, little rat toenails, rat-a-tatted on the window glass.

Rat-a-tat-tap-a-tap-tap.

"Hey," a whispering voice tickled the cusp of Brandon's ear. "Hey, kid, you up there?"

Tap-ta-ratta-tap-tap-tap.

Pebbles. That's what it was. Not toenails, but pebbles. Little pebbles like you found alongside the road or in the driveway, like the ones Mommy always told him not to throw. That's all it was and someone outside was tossing them up at his window.

Warm air that smelled like pee gushed into his lungs. Brandon pushed his pillow out of the way and pulled the blanket down, but only a little bit, just enough to turn his head and get some fresh air and hear a little better. Arty Bear was still held tight even, as Brandon uncurled from the fetal position ever so slightly.

The wind still didn't blow, but now the gentle tick-tick-tick of the heat run in his room came on. Mama Sam snored down the hall. Brandon swallowed, inching his way out of the safety of the mummy wrappings of sheets and blankets until he was sitting up, knees drawn to his chest and the dampness just below his bellybutton grew suddenly cold and uncomfortable. He looked towards the window with its curtains drawn shut and slowly climbed out of bed.

Another spray of pebbles clattered against the glass. "Hey, kid! Wake up."

Dark Hollow Road

There weren't any streetlights here to help guide him across the room. Were it not for the nightlight in the closet, Brandon's slow steps across the floor would have been even more groping and tentative. The pale blue curtain barely quivered from the warmth being released by the radiator beneath it, but the room still felt cold.

Don't do it, Bee, his brain said in Mama Sam's voice. *There's nothing outside that window but trouble. Scoot right on back to bed.*

"But the sheets are wet," the boy replied. "Besides, if I don't go look, they're going to keep throwing rocks at the window and wake you and Mommy up."

Me and your mommy can't hear a thing. Go back to bed, Mama Sam's voice insisted.

Brandon swallowed back the lump in his throat and took another step, his bare toes curling into the soft, plush carpet. In three more steps he was at the window, his fingers holding the edge of the curtain, eyes focused on the narrow gap where the two curtains met. For some reason, the waft of heat on his hand made him shiver. Brandon pulled back the curtain.

At first all he could see was the rectangular reflection of the light coming from the partially open closet door behind him. Brandon leaned in until his nose touched the cold glass of the window then cupped both hands on either side of his eyes, squinting down. He didn't see anything different.

There was the swing set and the ball he'd left out there. There was the chain link fence. There was the cornfield with barely shifting stalks, yellowing leaves, and dark brown silk hair tufts. He could even make out the elongated clumps where the cobs hid, waiting for the farmer to come through and harvest them all down. He wished the farmer would hurry up and do that already. "I hate corn," Brandon's warm breath rose a fog over the window, obscuring his view. He wiped it away with the curtain edge.

Allan was suddenly standing there, between the first and second row of stalks, looking up. His hands were stuffed deep in his pockets. He grinned. One of Allan's hands slid from his pocket, lifted like he was standing under water, and waved. He made a motion, one that said, "C'mon out. Come out and play."

Brandon didn't actually hear the words, but he shook his head all the same, "No," he whispered back. "I'll get in trouble."

Something deeper in the corn shifted, raising tiny goose bumps on Brandon's bare arms, and the two girls, holding hands, came into view. The littlest one of the girls wasn't any bigger than his cousin, Jason, and he was only three. The other girl looked like she might be in sixth or seventh grade. She was a little bit taller than Allan. The girls moved up closer, so thin they didn't even disturb the corn as they passed between the rigid stalks.

Allan motioned again. "Come on. Let's play Hide-and-Seek," he urged. This time Brandon did hear it, even saw Allan's lips moving. "No one will ever know. I promise. I'll even show you my best hiding place."

Oddly, Brandon was not in the least bit tempted. Maybe if he hadn't just been in trouble and maybe if there wasn't the possibility of not being able to go trick or treating tomorrow night as punishment if he were caught, he would have felt more inclined to venture out. But right now? Not no how, not no way. His head shook in a stubborn, firm no. "Go home," he said. "I don't want to play."

Allan looked back at who Brandon assumed were his sisters. Their big eyes gazed at the boy as he appeared to be talking to them, then turned back to stare up at Brandon's window again. He didn't like the look. He couldn't tell if they were sad or mad. None of them smiled.

Like a somber and curious puppy, the taller girl tipped her head to one side. "We'll come back." Brandon didn't see her mouth move at all. It kept the same slightly downturned corners; and suddenly Brandon was very afraid.

The curtain fell from his fingertips as he took a quick and uneasy step backwards before running from the room.

Chapter 19

Daddy's truck pulled in Friday afternoon. He cradled a brown paper bag like a baby in one arm. Seth and Kate sat at the kitchen table doing homework. I was doing some ironing. Nigel hadn't got home from his three hours of work at the mine.

Daddy halted in the doorway as if surprised to see us. His bushy eyebrows knitted together with a grumbled, "I'm back."

"Welcome home, Daddy." I tried to sound cheerful. Dumbstruck, Seth and Kate just stared, their pencils poised over math worksheets.

"Welcome home, my ass," he snapped. "Couldn't bail your old man out?"

I choked back the venom I wanted to spew. "Didn't have the extra, Daddy."

"Bullshit," he snorted. "And not one visit to your old man either?"

I shrugged. "Wasn't time, Daddy. Been busy, what with Social Services paying us a visit and all." He let out another of his buck snorts. "I'm making meatloaf for supper," I added.

He turned on his heel and stomped up the stairs. The glass babies wrapped in their brown paper blanket clanked together with each heavy step. I thanked God baby Alice was in her basinet in the kitchen with us. The slamming of Daddy's bedroom door rattled the windows and our nerves.

Seth scowled, "I hate him, Mary Alice."

"Don't say that, Seth."

"Me, too. I wish he was dead," Kate added.

"Stop it." I kept my voice low, but stern. "If anything happens to Daddy Clay they may not let us live together no more. Me and Nigel done told you what that Social Services lady said. We gotta stick together."

My little brother's face was turning redder by the minute. "We'd be better if he was dead," he stewed.

Kate sniffed, silent tears running down her face.

"Seth, you can't be talking like that."

But he was on a roll and in a mood, and truth be told, can't say as I entirely disagreed with him. "What if Uncle Eli don't come? What if he don't care about us no more? What if the Social Services lady is right? What if we can't …"

"We can! We will! We're a family and I won't let nobody take you and Katie away." I hoisted Alice from the basinet, quieting her down with gentle kisses.

Daddy's boss, Mr. Murphey, not the foreman he'd punched, but the owner of the mine, come to the house the following Monday. They talked a good long while out by Daddy's truck. After he left, I saw Daddy taking big, firm strides across the back yard with his fists clenched at his sides and I knew the news wasn't good. I carried a bucket of hot water out to the washing machine on the back porch and poured it into the tub, paused and listened, and pretended to be fiddle with something on the wringer.

With a basket full of underclothes, Kate followed me out. "What you suppose he said?"

"Don't know," I confessed. "Don't think it was good, though."

She bit her lip and pouted. "I don't want to live with Uncle Eli, Mary Alice."

I turned to her sharply, "Nobody's gonna live with Uncle Eli if they don't want to." My little sister had been paying attention far more than I gave her credit.

The tears were already spilling over in her eyes. "If Daddy don't got a job, we're gonna have to, or worse."

I softened my expression. "We'll do what we have to do to stay together, Kate."

Mrs. Hayes showed up again two weeks later with a plain manila envelope firmly in hand and no bodyguards. She didn't waste no time in getting right down to business. "Miss Brown, we have much to discuss."

"Sure," I said. "C'mon in."

We settled into the same chairs we'd used before. "I hear your father was not permitted to return to work."

"No, ma'am," my stomach twisted.

She gave a curt nod. "Perhaps he'll find something else soon." She took in a deep breath before speaking again. "I have also been in touch with your Uncle Eli."

I swallowed, hoping the grimace I felt myself make didn't show too much. "Yes, ma'am."

"He confirmed what you and your brother said and apologized for not being able to contact you about his usual visit this past summer," she half smiled. "Apparently, he's been quite busy with work."

My heart sang. Uncle Eli had lied for us. We weren't forgotten. "Yes, ma'am."

"You really should see about getting a telephone installed out here, Mary Alice. It would make things so much easier."

"We talked about it," I told her. We had and she was right. There was a dozen times over the past year I'd wished we had a telephone. "We ain't decided, yet."

"Do give it serious consideration. I believe it would increase the likelihood of things going your way should we find ourselves in a similar situation as what we had last week. The monthly rental fee is quite reasonable."

"Yes, ma'am. I'll talk to Daddy and Nigel about it when they get home."

"It would be a very wise investment," she paused only long enough to take a sip from her cup of tea. "Now, in regards to the baby and her condition. I spoke to Mrs. Yagar about it and ..."

"Wait. Her condition? Ain't nothing wrong with Alice other than she's a little small and Mrs. Yagar said she'd be slower to learn than other kids."

"Precisely. Alice has Down Syndrome, Miss Brown. I don't think you understand exactly what that means. She will have more medical difficulties than most children and she may require special housing and education facilities."

The knot tightened in my stomach even more.

"For the time being, we will play it by ear, but the department will be keeping a close eye on her progress. We'd like you to take her to a real doctor, Miss Brown, and have her evaluated properly." Mrs. Hayes pulled a sheet of paper from out of the folder and slid it across the table to me. "This is a list of doctors who specialize in the condition. You are free to pick any one of them." She added another paper on top of it. "Have him fill this out and return it to us. We'll proceed from there based on his evaluation. You have ninety days."

I didn't even look at the papers. "Proceed with what?" My stomach turned sour.

"To see whether or not Alice can remain in your care, Miss Brown, based on the severity of her condition and the type of care you can provide under the circumstances."

"You want to take my baby away?"

Mrs. Hayes sighed and shook her head, "I want no such thing, Miss Brown. I want what is best for your daughter, for you, and for the rest of your family. Take her to a doctor, have her checked out, and we will see where we are then."

"And what if I don't take her to a regular doctor?"

The social worker's expression darkened. "That wouldn't be a good idea. Trust me on this. I am not the enemy here. I want to help. No one was happier than I when your uncle confirmed he'd take care of things if he was needed. No one was sadder than I to hear your father had lost his job. My job is to keep families together, not tear them apart."

"You want to take Alice away, though."

"No, I don't. I want what is best for her just as much as you do."

"What's best is she be here with her Mama and family. You ain't taking her away."

"That won't be up to me, Miss Brown. I only submit what I see and give as honest an evaluation as I can for each case. The judge decides."

"Based on what you tell him." I stood up, clenching my teeth so I'd not scream at her. "Please leave, Mrs. Hayes."

She didn't argue. Upon standing she tapped the papers on the table. "Ninety days, Miss Brown."

Dark Hollow Road

"Good bye, Mrs. Hayes." I walked her to the door and watched from behind the screen as she got into her car and drove away. "No one is taking my baby girl away," I simmered. "No one."

After supper, I took Nigel aside and told him the news. As good as it was about Uncle Eli, he was as angry as me about baby Alice. "They can't really do it, can they, Nige?" I whispered just barely over the clank of the dishes I was trying to wash.

He looked grim. "I think they can. Could take Kate and Seth, too, I reckon, if they was of a mind to do that."

"Just because we're poor?" My hands sank into the soapy water, useless and trembling.

He put an arm around my shoulder. "I know it ain't right. We'll get that telephone, too. I'll see to it."

"What about the doctor?"

Nigel give my shoulders a squeeze, "We'll do what we have to do, big sister. Go and talk to Mrs. Yagar first thing Monday morning. Take that list with you. I'm sure she'd be happy to help you make an appointment."

"And Daddy?"

Nigel's encouraging hold slid away as he stepped back. "Don't worry about him."

It wasn't so much the words, but the tone that sent the spiders walking up my arms. "What you meaning to do?"

"Ain't meaning to do nothing." He smiled and gave me a brotherly kiss on the cheek. "Don't worry about him is all." Nigel walked away and suddenly even the dish water felt very, very cold.

I went to see Mrs. Yagar. Nigel was right. Our reliable family friend helped me with everything, even calling the telephone company to see about running a line down to our place. Finding a doctor on the list proved to be a bit harder, but by the fifth call we'd gotten a place in line for the third of January, just barely within the ninety day limit.

When he wasn't in town, supposedly looking for a job, Daddy skulked around the property smelling like booze and cigarettes. He missed his court date and went back to jail for another week right after Thanksgiving. We paid the doctor bill, but not a cent went towards getting our father out of the mess he'd made of his life. No one missed him. Everyone dreaded his return.

Daddy Clay, out of jail again at least for the time being over Christmas, wasn't happy about the phone company coming. Lucky for them, he was away when they come knocking with a shiny new black phone. I had them put it in the hallway just outside the kitchen. The first person I called was Mrs. Yagar. She called me back to make sure it worked. The next I called was Mrs. Hayes. She wasn't in, so I just left a message to let her know we was doing what she said to do about the phone and the doctor visit. I was feeling really hopeful.

We made the best of Christmas that we could. No one was surprised when Daddy hadn't gotten any of us gifts. I put hard candy sweets in Seth and Kate's stockings. Kate had knitted everyone scarves and mittens, reusing the yarn from some sweaters that no longer fit her. Nigel, Seth and Kate had picked out a bottle of perfume for me and Kate got bubble bath. I ain't sure why we bothered to get Daddy anything, but we did, a new shaving brush, cup, and soap cake along with a packet of razors.

"So you can look nice for your job interviews, Daddy," Kate said. She hadn't quite given up on Daddy being a decent man.

"Don't be nervous," Mrs. Yagar held the door open for me and Ali as we walked into the clinic. "I think the baby is going to pass with flying colors all things considered."

Despite her encouragement, I was terrified. I hadn't slept nearly a wink the past few days worrying and wondering. She was just a baby. How could they know how smart she was going to be? Ali's sleep had been just as bad as mine. She woke up a lot and fussed for hours. She'd gotten a bit of a cold, but I didn't figure that was anything too serious. At least, I hoped not. I'd heard the horror stories. One little thing out of place and them Social Services folks would swoop in and take what they wanted while saying it was for everyone's good.

"Mrs. Brown?" The sound of the nurse calling my name startled me out of my skin.

I got up, holding Ali close. "Miss Brown," I corrected the woman.

She frowned slightly. "Miss Brown. Follow me, please."

Ali was measured and weighed. The nurse even measured around the baby's head and listened to her heart, never saying much of anything to me, like I wasn't even there until she was all done. She took the folder with her when she left, "The doctor will be right in," she said barely before the door clicked softly shut.

I didn't like this place one bit. I didn't like that nurse even more.

Two sharp raps on the door announced the doctor's arrival and the door opened before I could say a word.

"Miss Brown?" He seemed nice enough. He was a bit on the heavy side, salt and pepper colored hair and a pair of gold, wire-rimmed glasses that rested just on the tip of his broad nose.

"Yes," I said, smiling.

"I'm Dr. Ashcroft. Nice to meet you." He shook my hand. "And this must be Alice." I had her perched on my leg, one arm wrapped around her tummy to keep her from toppling over. She was still a bit wobbly. "How old is she?"

"Almost six months," I let him scoop her up and take her to the exam table.

"Six months?" He seemed surprised as he pushed his glasses into place and looked at the form the nurse had written on earlier. Laying her on her back first, he listened to her heart as the nurse had already done then took hold of her hand, and pulled, trying to bring her up to a seated position. Her head was still a bit too heavy on her neck for that.

He worked her legs like she was riding a bicycle. She waved her arms up at him. He looked up her nose and into her mouth, tickling her little pink tongue that seemed unable to stay still or in her mouth for more than a few seconds.

Dr. Ashcroft looked into her eyes with a tiny flashlight and smiled when she followed the movement of the light. He peeked inside her ears. "Could you come over and hold her up to sitting? I want to check her hearing."

I sat her up. From behind her back the doctor snapped his finger first by one ear then the other. He got a little squeak toy and repeated the exercise, gauged her reaction, and added his observations to the chart.

"She making any sounds, other than crying, I mean? You know, baby sounds, reacting to your voice and that sort of thing."

"Not too much. She's real quiet most of the time, unless she wants something or something scares her."

"Scares her how?"

"Like a door slamming or Daddy's truck backfiring."

"Regular bowel movements?"

I nodded.

"Any jaundice?"

I had to think for a second what that was. "No, sir."

"Sleeping through the night?"

"No, sir, but close. She been fussy lately. I figured it was because of the cold, but normally she been going about four hours, sometimes six on a really good night."

Like Mrs. Hayes, the way he scribbled all these things down was making me nervous.

"By what I'm seeing, she does have Down Syndrome, but we'll have to run some bloodwork and I'd like to do a series of x-rays to have as a baseline. It's very hard to say at this point how severe it's going to be. For now, I'm going to rank her as mild. That could change as she gets older. We'll just have to see how quickly or slowly she develops over the next year."

I felt a sense of relief. He didn't act too concerned. "Alright."

"She does seem to have a bit of a hearing problem, which is normal for these children and her muscles aren't as developed as I'd like. Again, normal in a baby with her condition. I'll give you some exercises to help her with that. You're going to have to work with her, Miss Brown, if you want to keep her progressing.

There are a lot of things she's going to need help learning to do that most babies would go about doing themselves. Otherwise, I think she's doing rather well." He rubbed her head before pulling some pamphlets out of a nearby drawer. "Read these over. If you have any questions, you can always call. I'll send in a nurse to get the blood sample and she'll take you back for a few x-rays, then you're all done. I'd like to see her again in three months."

He talked real fast. I guess it was then that I began to realize that something really was wrong with Ali, but I loved her just the same, if not more, knowing she'd be needing my help. I wanted to be a good mother and I'd do what I had to. "Thank you," I said, lifting her back up into my arms.

Maybe it would be alright. Maybe I was wrong about Mrs. Hayes and Social Services wanting to take Alice away from me and her family.

Chapter 20

From the backseat, Brandon gazed out the window far too seriously for a six-year-old with a yellow hard hat on his head and a Bob the Builder costume folded beside him in a plastic bag. Around two in the morning, Brandon had tumbled into bed between Renee and Sam. He'd been cold, shivering, and the front of his pajama bottoms was wet. Renee hadn't been able to get much information out of him while cleaning up her son in those early hours of the day. That he'd had a bad dream was all she could discern. Nor had he been any more talkative over breakfast. That's what bothered her the most. Chatterbox Brandon, who had been so excited about his costume and Halloween and trick-or-treating the day before, barely spoke at all.

It must have been one hell of a bad dream for him to come running in as he had, clambering over the top of her and wedging himself between the two grown-ups. Renee's questions only made the boy more tight-lipped. Even Sam wasn't able to break the boy's silence.

She smiled and looked at Brandon in the rearview mirror. "It's going to be a fun day, huh?"

"Yup," he said, not looking at her, but a little smile did play on his lips.

"Looking forward to trick-or-treating with Mama Sam tonight?"

"Uh-huh," Brandon said, lacking the enthusiasm Renee felt he should have.

She slowed and turned down the side street towards the school. The ten or so cars that stopped and started like synchronized car ballet in front of the school, was about as jammed as traffic got in Murphey Mills. She took her place in the slowly moving line, inching her way towards where Brandon's teacher stood to greet her arriving students. Renee still couldn't get over the fact that the entire school district occupied only one building, with Brandon as one of only five kindergarten students.

She pulled the car to a stop as Mrs. Fitzsimmons stepped up to open Brandon's door. "Good morning," the middle-aged blonde chirped.

"Morning," Brandon took off his seatbelt and gathered his things, handing them off to his teacher so he could climb out.

"Good morning," Renee replied. "Happy Friday!" she added.

"Oh, yes. Happy Friday!" the teacher said, laughing a bit, making sure Brandon had everything easily in hand. "Go on inside, Brandon. I'm still waiting for Nicole to get here."

Brandon turned and smiled. "Bye, Mommy," he said and trudged towards the school.

"See ya, buddy," she called after him. "Mrs. Fitzsimmons?" she added before the teacher could close the back door. "Brandon had some sort of nightmare last night. He won't talk about it, but he wet the bed and came charging into our bed at about two this morning. I just wanted you to know, in case he acts a little off."

Mrs. Fitzsimmons gave her a reassuring smile, "Alright. I'll keep an eye on him. See you this afternoon." The car door slammed and the teacher took a step back onto the sidewalk. Dismissed.

"Thank you," Renee muttered with a sigh, knowing it went unheard. She needed coffee and she needed it bad.

Ian, Micha, and Torey all sat on top of their desks as Brandon entered the room. Their heads turned as one, three faces touched with that look of fear of having been caught doing something bad like sitting on their desks. Seeing that it was only Brandon, the looks snapped back into smiles. "Hey, Brandon!" Ian shouted, his feet hitting the floor with the soft thud of rubber to concrete. "Nice hat."

Brandon finally found the joy to smile. Those other kids had been creeping him out all morning and Mommy just kept reminding him over and over about it, but these kids were his friends and he liked all of them. "Thanks," he said, lugging his backpack and the plastic bag containing his costume over to his cubby.

"We were talking about our favorite candy. What's yours?"

Brandon left the hard hat on. "Cow Tales," he said without hesitation.

"Oh, those are good!" Ian scurried back to his desk. With a little jump he sat on top of the work surface again, legs swinging back and forth. "Mini Snickers is mine."

Torey raised her hand in a half wave, "Red Twizzlers." Torey, with her short cropped hair and jeans, didn't look much like the girl she was.

195

She liked frogs and snakes and playing with cars and trucks outside on the dirt pile just as much as hanging out with Nicole at the doll's house or in the play grocery store. And she could climb the jungle gym better than any of the boys.

Micha worked at tying his shoe, his tongue sticking half out of his mouth as he mumbled something about loop-de-loops and rabbit ears before completing the task with a satisfied nod of his head. "Sour Patch Kids," he added to the conversation.

"Want to be candy names with us?"

"Huh?" Brandon scooted his bottom on to the top of his desk and adjusted his hat.

Ian laughed. "I'm going to be Snicker, Torey is going to be The Twiz, and Micha wants to be called Patch."

"Oh!" Brandon grinned, "Yeah, call me Cow Tale."

Mrs. Fitzsimmons cleared her throat, her arms crossed as she stood in the doorway. Nicole hugged a brown paper back to her chest, giggled, and walked to the cubbies. With a clattering of scraping metal and thuds, Brandon and his friends half jumped, half tumbled off their desk tops.

The teacher shook her head, smirking, as she went to her desk, "Hat off, Mr. Cow Tale."

Laughter erupted in the classroom.

"Bless you," Renee clutched the sides of the coffee mug like a sacred communion cup, brought it to her lips, sipped, and sighed.

Janet, the waitress, laughed, "Bad morning?"

Renee shook her head, lowering the cup, "No, not really, just didn't have time for a cup at home, that and my kid dive bombed me in bed at two in the morning with a bad dream." She slid the menu towards Janet, "I'll have the Western omelet, rye toast, and sausage."

"You got it," Janet jotted down the order and headed towards the kitchen.

A row of six tables, four chairs each, ran down the center of Kelley's dining room, with two sets of booths on either side of the front door and a counter with another dozen seats along the back. A large, chrome-framed window offered a look inside the bustling kitchen which was accessed by a swinging door behind the counter. One woman minded the customers at the counter, while Janet moved with practiced ease amongst the table and chairs with plates full of steaming breakfast dishes and a coffee pot. A man in his early twenties, with a mop of black hair that he kept flipping out of his face, bused tables.

Renee looked out at the parking lot from her booth seat. Her new landlord should be showing up across the road with the lease papers in about forty-five minutes. With the rent so reasonable, there was no way Renee could have said no to the place. From here she could see her future business venture's front windows, grimy and newspaper-covered on the inside, but that would soon be remedied. She hoped to spend all weekend over there cleaning up the place and putting up some sort of simple displays and a sign in the window. She grinned to herself. Brandon would be tickled when she told him the name she'd decided on, Aunt Eeks Antiques.

"Here you go, hon." A plate settled down in front of Renee's perched elbows.

"Looks great. Thank you." Renee swapped out her coffee cup for a fork. "We're going to be neighbors," she grinned up at the waitress.

"Oh?" Janet stood poised to turn away.

With a nod Renee indicated the general direction of the future shop. "Going to sign a lease on the store across the way."

"Oh, yeah?" The waitress looked genuinely pleased. "What sort of business?"

"Aunt Eeks," Renee joked, wondering if the woman would catch the mispronunciation.

She didn't. "Nice. Was a tailor and dress shop back when I was a kid. Lots of antique places up and down Route 9 in these parts. You'll fit right in. Welcome to the neighborhood. Maybe you can help bring some life back into this old town."

"I hope so. Thank you."

Janet lingered only long enough to be polite before heading back to work.

Hunched at the counter and slopping up eggs with a piece of toast, an older man with a full head of snow-white hair and dressed in denim coveralls and grease-stained work boots, twisted ever so slightly on the stool to turn a baleful eye towards Renee. His lower lip jutted out ever so slightly under a bulbous, pockmarked nose. The bushy white eyebrows lowered as he grumbled, "Good luck with that. Folks don't take too kindly to strangers in these parts." He gave a mild snort and turned back to his plate.

Renee's jaw dropped.

"Lee, really?" Janet blocked the space between the two halves of the counter. One hand rested on her jutted left hip, the other held the nearly empty pot of coffee. Her eyes flicked to Renee. "Don't pay him no mind, hon. He's just being a pain in the ass like always."

Beside Lee, a younger, but similarly dressed, man shook his head as he pressed a napkin over his mouth. "Say you're sorry, you old bastard." He nudged Lee in the arm with his elbow, jostling the older man's loaded fork.

"Hey, I'm eating here," he retorted.

From the opposite end of the counter, a heavy-set woman laughed. "Tell the lady you're sorry, Yagar. Jesus, why you gotta be so grumpy all the damn time?"

"I ain't grumpy. I'm hungry and my asshole nephew here's smacking my fork around."

"I'll smack more than your fork if you don't apologize," the younger man retorted with a snicker.

Renee's mouth closed again. Yagar? Lee Yagar. This was the man who owned the pumpkin farm.

"You're Lee Yagar!" Renee blurted out.

Lee didn't turn around. Instead he cut the sausage link on his plate in half with the side of his fork. "Yeup," he said and shoved the meat into his mouth.

"My partner and I took my son to your pumpkin farm last weekend. It was amazing."

"Thank ya." Lee slurped from his coffee cup.

Renee really wanted to get on the good side of the people of Murphey Mills. "That spook barn of yours gave Brandon nightmares," she laughed. It wasn't anything to laugh about, but in the moment she needed to make light of it. "Well, that combined with that stupid house we can see down on Dark Hollow Road. Sam insists on going over to …" The diner had suddenly become very quiet. Those who weren't staring at her were paying an undue amount of attention to their plates or bottoms of their coffee cups.

Lee's stooped posture lifted, his head turned, and he looked at her even more sourly than he had the first time. "That house needs to be burned to the ground and the land sown with salt," he said. "My father should have seen to that when he had the chance."

"What's wrong with it?" Renee ventured. It wasn't that she disagreed with the old man, but his reaction had her curiosity up. She wanted to know more.

"Everything," he said. "If ya got a single lick of sense in that head of yours, keep yourselves away from it. Don't go near it. Don't take nothing from it. Leave it to its slow, miserable death."

"What happened there?"

The way he rose from his seat reminded Renee of a biker who'd just been told some asshole had knocked his Harley over in the parking lot. His fists were clenched, his eyes were squinted. The tall, husky man, old but by no means past his prime, was out for blood. She couldn't help but shrink back in her seat a little. "You and yours don't need to know that, just don't be stupid. Do as I tell ya and stay away from Dark Hollow Road." He looked Renee square on. His tone was deep and harsh, but what Renee saw in the depths of his eyes was not anger. It was cold fear. Lee suddenly turned away and headed for the door. "Pay the tab, Fred. I'll meet ya in the truck."

The bell over the door jangled cheerfully despite the dark emotional cloud Lee left in his wake.

Lee's nephew shook his head and stood as well. His apologetic look said it all. "Sorry about him. That place is a real touchy subject for Uncle Lee." He took the few steps over to where Renee no longer cowered in the corner and extended his hand, "I'm Fred Yagar, by the way."

"Renee Evenson," she said, shaking the offered hand. Around them people began to talk again, spoons clanked inside coffee cups, and the sound of sizzling bacon and eggs rose once more, as if even they had been afraid to make a sound during Lee's speech.

"Nice to meet you, Fred." Renee adjusted herself in the booth seat. "Why does it upset him?"

Fred offered a vague shrug. "Uncle Lee's ma was a midwife back when the Browns lived there. She and Grandpa knew them as well as anyone could. They were a real private family. Grandma Ruth delivered all them kids herself, I'm told. I reckon nearly anyone around here older than sixty was brought into this world by Ruth Yagar."

Renee didn't understand. "Why would that make the place so bad?"

"Weren't the kids that was the problem, was their father, Clayton Brown. Rotten to the bitter core. He went missing back in the 60s, I think it was. It was a huge deal for a couple of months. Made the Scranton newspaper. He was never found. Rumor has it the kids did something, but no proof was ever found. From what little Uncle Lee will say, the whole town figured if the Brown kids were to blame, it wasn't none of their concern." A horn blasted two harsh honks from the direction of the parking lot. Fred looked up and gave a single, open-palmed wave to the figure of his uncle visible behind the windshield. "I better get before he has a stroke out there."

"What happened to the kids?" Renee pushed forward.

Fred pulled out his wallet. "Don't know. Uncle Lee won't say. I don't know as anyone else around here knows. If they do, they're as tight-lipped about it as he is."

The horn blatted again, long and loud this time.

"I won't keep you." She didn't want to dig an even deeper thorn into the side of Lee Yagar.

"And don't pay no attention to him saying we don't take kindly to strangers around here. He's full of bullshit. We're happy to have you in town. Like Janet said, maybe you can bring some new life into the place. God knows we need it. Have a good day."

"Thank you. It was nice meeting you."

As the pick-up truck backed out of its parking space, Janet strolled over to Renee's booth, ever present coffee pot in hand, only now it was full again. "Fred's good people. Lee, not so much. More coffee?"

"Yes, please." She watched at Janet refilled the off white mug. "Do you know anything about the Browns?"

"Not anything much more than what Fred's just told you really. That's about all anyone knows or is willing to say."

Renee managed a smile, "Small towns and their secrets, huh?"

"They all got 'em. Some's just bigger than others."

Dark Hollow Road

Chapter 21

By mid-January, Mrs. Hayes had gotten in touch to let us know everything looked good with Alice's paperwork. I prayed that was the last we'd hear or see from that woman in a long time. Twice a day, I spent half an hour working with the baby to make her muscles stronger.

"You want me to switch out those tires for you today, Daddy?" Nigel shoveled thick, hot oatmeal into his mouth at the breakfast table. He'd bartered better truck tires for a load of wood with a neighbor across the creek.

"If you want." Daddy drained the last drop of whiskey from the bottle into his coffee cup. He didn't even bother to try and hide his drinking now.

Seth piped up, his eyes wide. "Can I help?"

"Sure," Nigel agreed.

"Radio was saying there's going to be a storm later this week," I tried to sound cheerful though my insides wanted to take that bottle of cheap booze and smash it against Daddy Clay's thick skull. I spooned a tiny bit of watered down oatmeal into Ali's mouth. Most of it stayed in.

"Almanac says we're in for an early spring." Daddy drained his second cup of coffee and belched.

"We'll make it through no matter what comes. We still got plenty in stock," Nigel shoved himself away from the table. "Good breakfast, Mary. Meet you out at the barn when you're done, Seth."

"Alright," my youngest brother mumbled through a mouthful of scrambled eggs. "Gimme a minute."

"I'll give you ten," Nigel laughed and reached for his coat. As he stood behind Daddy's chair and tugged on his hat, something in his eyes belied the laughter. Nigel looked up at me, just a flick, half a second, then turned away and was out the door.

I trembled against the cold blast of Nigel's departure into the great outdoors and the look he'd cast my way. "What you going to do today, Daddy?" Standing, I pulled Alice from her highchair.

He gnawed on the last piece of bacon. "Same thing I do every fucking day, Mary Alice."

Kate's chair scraped across the floor. She gingerly began clearing the dishes away. Her hand reached out towards Daddy's.

He slapped it away. "Ain't done!" he bellowed. "Can't you see I ain't done eating?"

She jerked back, staring at his livid, red face. "Sorry, Daddy."

My heart was about pounding out of my chest. "Katie Sue, I think Ali needs her diaper changed," I said as calmly as I could.

Seth was frozen in place, a spoonful of oatmeal poised and dripping over his nearly empty bowl, jaw lax.

Katie shuffled back as Daddy's chair teetered and crashed to its back when he stood up. His barrel chest expanded and his fists clenched. He picked up his empty plate and grinned. "She ain't done clearing the table, Mary Alice."

"Yes, she is. Katie, take the baby upstairs."

My little sister took another reverse step, edging her way closer to where I stood.

"I said she ain't done!" Daddy bellowed, slamming his fist on the table with one hand, while the other catapulted the dirty plate towards my head. It smashed against the stove pipe.

The moment the plate struck, Seth sprang from his chair and darted towards the back door. Daddy's bear paw of a hand snatched at Seth, caught him by the arm and wrenched him backwards. The arm attached to that paw curled around Seth's body and pulled him in tight to Daddy's chest. "Not so fast, you little son of a bitch."

Seth squirmed and twisted, and started to yell. "Let me go!" His feet kicked back. One managed to land a blow.

Daddy Clay roared.

Seth turned his head, opened his mouth, and chomped down hard on Daddy's forearm with a crunching and snapping sound. I shoved Alice into Katie's arm, "Upstairs! Now!"

Kate didn't hesitate. Within seconds, she and the baby were gone.

By the time I turned back, Seth was free and stumbling for the door, screaming our brother's name at the top of his lungs. "Nigel! NIGEL!'

Daddy Clay's rage was blind. Kate and I were forgotten. The source of his pain was Seth and he rushed forward, slamming into the casing hard before getting the door open again. "Get back in here, you bastard! Get back here, little fucker!"

But Seth was fast and Daddy Clay was drunk. Daddy half fell down the back steps, staggering across a lawn heavy with half a winter's worth of snow as he followed Seth's straight line of running footprints with weaving ones of his own. I slammed the door, locked it, and waited. I watched and listened while two fingers clasped the pale-yellow curtain off to one side. My shivering breath fogged the tiny pane of glass. My mouth hung dry, while my heart jack-hammered in my chest.

I stood and waited as the kitchen clock counted off the seconds. Tick Tick. Tick. Ticking the moments, the minutes away, watching the open barn door where Daddy Clay had last been seen in his red-and-black plaid flannel shirt and baggy, denim dungarees.

A shadow shifted in that dark, square space. Small, hesitant, skin and bones, Seth.

Nigel appeared behind him, put his hand on his little brother's shoulder, said something to which Seth nodded and hurried towards the house. Nigel remained barely in sight, until Seth reached the distant edge of the clothesline and I opened the door. When I looked again, Nigel had vanished.

"Seth!" I opened my arms to the tattered, trembling body of my sixteen-year-old baby brother. It seemed more like he was six. He shivered against me. "It's okay," I pulled him against me, rubbing his back, feeling him shake with something more than just the cold. He didn't speak as I closed the door and walked him to the warm woodstove to sit in the chair I slid into place.

I waited. The clock ticked. Seth finally spoke. "I think Daddy's dead."

"He can't be dead." Didn't they know that Daddy couldn't be dead? If he was dead, life changed. Everything changed.

Heavy footsteps echoed from the back porch and the door opened. "Mary Alice," a stream of blood ran down the front of Nigel's forehead and into his eye. The other eye was starting to swell shut.

"Nigel, Daddy, is he ... Seth said he was ..."

"Where's Katie and the baby? He didn't hurt any of you, did he?"

"No. We're all fine. I sent them upstairs where it was safe."

Nigel wiped the blood out of his eye. "Good. Seth, I need you to help me get Daddy upstairs."

Seth shook his head, shaking so hard I thought he was going to fall out of the chair.

"Seth!' Nigel barked."We can't leave him out in the barn." Too much like Daddy, just too much. "Stop being a sissy and go get that wool blanket off his bed."

Reluctant, Seth rose, squared his shoulders, and went upstairs.

They dragged him inside then up the stairs, using the blanket like a hammock. And when he was in his own bed, they stripped off his boots and flannel shirt before tying him to the metal frame. I cleaned up the bloody gash on his head. It needed stitches, but the best I could do was cover it with some clean gauze and wrap it with a long piece of old sheet. His lip was split and one eye was swollen shut. All the while he never made a sound, never moved, never even flinched, but he was breathing. At least he was alive. When I was done, I covered him with warm blankets and checked to make sure the small kerosene heater in his room was full of fuel.

Nigel, Seth, and Katie were sitting around the kitchen table when I came downstairs. Baby Alice snuggled in Kate's arms. I lifted my baby away. "What we going to do now, Nigel? What we going to do? What if he dies? He needs a doctor."

"If he dies, we'll bury him out back somewhere, but he ain't gonna die. He's too mean-hearted and stubborn to die."

"We need him alive, Nigel. Don't you understand that?"

"We don't need him for anything. All he does is drink our money away. That's all he's ever been good for since Mama died."

"What we going to do then? Leave him tied up in his bed all the time? Folks are going to notice. Folks are going to figure out they ain't seen him in town, at the bar, at the diner, at the liquor store. They'll come asking questions. Then what?" I was screaming. I hadn't meant to scream, but I couldn't help myself. "Mrs. Hayes will come. The police will come! We won't be a family no more!" I slumped into a vacant chair, sobbing now, the screaming all out of me. "We won't be a family no more."

Nigel got up, came over, and squatted down beside me. The warmth of his palm covered my hand. "Mary Alice, we'll be fine. We don't need Daddy Clay."

"We do," I sniffled.

"Clayton Brown ain't nothing. No one's going to miss him for a good long while. We got time. Folks know we stay to ourselves. This storm coming on is all the more reason to keep to home. After me and Seth get them snow tires on, we'll go into town. We'll stock up more. Folks will see us doing that. Toilet paper and bread and all them things the townies get when there's a storm coming." He leaned in closer, putting a hand on each of my knees, looking me straight in the eye. "We got this, Mary Alice. You got to trust me. Ain't we always stuck together before? Ain't we always made it through?"

He was right. We had. I didn't know what he had planned, if anything, and I didn't believe we could get away with it for long without Daddy Clay, but I wanted to trust my brother.

"All you got to do is carry on like usual, like nothing is different. Maybe when Daddy wakes up, he'll realize we ain't taking none of his crap no more. He'll cooperate, but we got to stick together and show him we mean it. Can you do that, Mary Alice?"

Didn't seem I had much choice in the matter. "Alright," I said.

"Outside this house, it's business as usual." Nigel patted my knee and rose up, turning to look at the others. "Everyone in?"

Seth and Katie nodded in silence, their somber expressions as full of fear, dread, and doubt as my heart felt.

List in hand, Nigel took Katie with him into town. It seemed safer to have at least one of the boys home. Lord only knew what sort of state Daddy would be in when he come to.

"What happened out there?" I asked after checking on our father a second time. He still hadn't moved. Seth and me sat at the kitchen table while Ali napped happily nearby in the bassinet.

"Nigel winged him with the tire iron," Seth explained. "Threw it like he was pitching a baseball. Would of killed Daddy outright if Nige had really hit him with it. Almost hit me when it went flying past. That only made Daddy madder. Started cussing a blue streak like he does. Daddy said he was going to kill Nigel for that and when he was done killing Nigel, he was going to kill the rest of us." The color of Seth's blue eyes stood out all the brighter in contrast to the bloodshot whites. He wasn't crying no more. He was

209

just plain mad. "Nigel's right. It ain't right we have to live like this and be scared all the time."

I knew nothing good would happen as long as things stayed like they was. "Maybe I should call Uncle Eli," I said with an aching heart.

"You think he'll help?"

I shrugged with a heavy, grim ache in my soul. "He won't if he don't know what's going on. And if he don't help, we won't be in any worse waters than we are now, right?"

"What about Mrs. Yagar? She's always been good to us. Maybe she could come look at Daddy just to make sure."

I'd thought of Mrs. Yagar, too, but something in my mothering instincts didn't want to go there. "No," I said. "She'll only start asking questions about how this or that happened. She'll talk, maybe not meaning no harm, but I think it's best we not say nothing to anyone unless we have to. Nigel is right about that. Outside this house ain't nobody needing to know anything."

"Except Uncle Eli."

Frankly, I didn't like talking to Uncle Eli about it, either. He was our last resort now but we were desperate. "I'll ask Nigel soon as he gets back, but I don't see any other way to get around things."

Ice pellets struck the plastic stretched over the kitchen window like a million miniature drum sticks. Tink-tink-tink, each strike increasing my worry as Nigel and Kate still hadn't come back over two hours later. It was bad enough that this year I had the added worry of taking care of Alice, but now there was Daddy Clay to deal with.

"What the hell is this?" he peered at me through bloodshot eyes from his bed. I was not about to untie him despite the way he twisted his wrists back and forth. "Who did this?"

"You said you were going to kill Nigel." I stood at the foot of his bed.

A loud gust of a laugh erupted from him. "I did no such thing. Let me up, Mary Alice. I got things to do."

"Can't do that, Daddy. Not until Nigel gets back from the store."

His head sank heavy into the pillow beneath it as he looked up at the ceiling. His eyes were funny looking, kinda drunk like. "Where's your Mama? Get her up here. She'll see sense."

Sleet beat on the rattling plastic. "Mama's gone, Daddy," I said.

He blinked in slow motion. "Went with your brother, I suppose?"

"No, I mean she's gone. Been gone a long time."

His eyes closed. Tap-tap, tick went the sleet. "I remember now," he said with a hesitant slur and sigh.

The familiar rumble of Daddy's truck coming down the road broke the spell enough so I could close my mouth to swallow. "I'll bring you some soup, Daddy," I backed from the room.

He didn't answer.

Chapter 22

All day long he'd kept an eye out for one of them, but with no luck. "Mrs. Fitzsimmons?" Brandon had worked his way through the small groups of other children, all munching on cupcakes with orange icing and candy corn faces. They'd already bobbed for apples and played Pitch Witch. The ordinary brown paper lunch bags stuffed with newspapers and painted to look like jack-o-lanterns sat on the window sill to dry in a nice neat row.

"Hey, Bob, I mean, Cow Tale. You need something?"

Brandon swallowed and looked casually around just to make sure no one would hear. "Is there a kid here named Allan?"

The teacher tipped her head in question and scanned the room. The kindergarten through fourth grades only made up about thirty kids, so she didn't have to look too hard or long. "I don't think so, Brandon. Why?"

Near as he could figure, Allan was the closest one to his own age and he didn't know the older girl's name so he couldn't ask about her. "Just wondering."

Dark Hollow Road

Mrs. Fitzsimmon's expression fell with concern. "Is something wrong? Is one of the older kids picking on you?"

Yeah, he thought. Yeah, they're picking on me all right. Throwing rocks at my window in the middle of the night and telling me to come play Hide-and-Seek and their mom stole my coloring book, too. He shook his head. "No. I was just wondering, that's all."

She wasn't buying it. "If someone is bothering you, Brandon, you need to tell me so we can make them stop. It's important everyone feels safe and happy here. Are you sure you don't want to tell me what's really wrong?"

"I'm sure," he said. "I don't think they go to this school anyway."

Her brow darkened even more, "So, there is someone then?"

Brandon dared the vaguest nod. "His name is Allan. Him and his sisters came out of the cornfield last night and threw rocks at my bedroom window."

The teacher's eyes widened considerably. She took one of his lax hands into hers and gave it a reassuring squeeze, "That's awful. Did you tell your mother?"

He shook his head.

"Why not?"

He shrugged.

"Tell you what, I'll ask the other teachers about a boy named Allan. How old do you think he is? What grade?"

"I don't know," Brandon admitted. "Not a lot older than me. Maybe nine. His sister is a little older, probably twelve or something like that. I don't know her name."

"Alright. You don't worry about it anymore. I'll ask for you and we'll find out who they are." Her

213

hands shifted to rest gently on his shoulders. "You did the right thing coming to me, Brandon. We can't allow bullies to be hurtful. Did you finish your snacks?"

"Yes."

"Then go and play. We still have another fifteen minutes before we need to clean up and get back to our schoolwork."

Brandon returned to his table where Fairy Princess Nicole picked at what remained inside her cupcake wrapper. He plopped down in his chair with a weighted sigh.

"All party pooped out?" Nicole asked, licking off her fingers one at a time.

Brandon didn't want to make everyone else feel like he did. He shook his head. "No, just saving my energy for trick or treats. My Mama Sam is taking me."

Nicole leaned on the table with both elbows while she shifted to sit up on her knees in the little plastic chair. "We're going to the fire station party, are you?"

"Maybe," he said.

She twisted around on the chair some more. "You should come. Last year they did a pumpkin pie eating contest, and we carved real jack-o-lanterns, and there was a hayride, and there was a big scarecrow walking around." She leaned in closer, half-sprawling onto the top of the table and whispered, "It was really my Uncle Jim in a costume so I wasn't afraid, but some of the other kids were. I thought he was funny."

"I'll have to ask again," It sounded fun, as long as they got to go trick-or-treating, too.

"Wanna go play something?"

"Okay."

Nicole tossed her mangled cupcake wrapper onto the pumpkin face of her paper plate. "Let's go play."

She grabbed his hand and pulled him towards the beanbag toss board set up in the corner.

Tom Murphey, like all the men in his family, was tall and stocky and carried the frame with confidence. Blessed with a full head of hair even at sixty-five and a thick beard, all of which had been a chestnut brown in his youth but now heavily streaked with white, he watched as Renee made her way across the road. Once she was close enough, he stuck out his hand and, taking hers, gave it a firm shake. "How was breakfast?" he asked.

Renee laughed, "Delicious and somewhat disturbing at the same time."

His wild-haired eyebrows shot up, "Disturbing? Didn't get a gangly hair in your eggs, did you?"

The woman made a gagging face and shuddered, "No, just had an encounter with Lee Yagar."

Mr. Murphey shook his head with a chuckle, "Good old, Lee. He's always good for a bit of sunshine and gaiety on a cloudy day." He pulled a plain ring of keys out of his front pocket and turned to the front door of the shop Mrs. Evenson would officially be renting in less than an hour. "That man's got some sort of bug up his ass. Good, strong enema is what he needs," he joked and swung around. Renee looked horrified. "Sorry, pardon me for being vulgar like that. I forget my manners around the pretty ladies."

She smirked. "It's okay. I just wasn't ready for that sort of image to come at me so early in the morning."

"Is it possible to prepare for that kind of thing?" He was relieved when her smile grew and she actually laughed. "Anyhow, my apologies."

"Accepted," she said as they stepped into the chilly main room of the future store.

215

The slightly warped floorboards creaked and moaned as they entered. They were in desperate need of sanding and varnishing, but his new tenant had assured him they were fine just as they were. They added atmosphere, she'd said. As long as people weren't walking around barefoot, they'd be safe. The front portion ran thirty feet back from the double bay windows on either side of the front door, and was some fifteen feet wide. Along the right hand side, a closed in staircase ascended to the upper level.

A nice sized office space at the back was accessed via an old Dutch door. It was towards this room the two of them now headed.

"The wainscoting in here is so wonderful," Mrs. Evenson noted for about the tenth time since her first visit.

"Get it cleaned and oiled up and it'll shine like new," he said. It wasn't particularly fancy wainscoting, just tongue and groove and topped with a nicely curved chair rail, but Mrs. Evenson seemed enthralled with it all the same. If it was something that helped him rent the old place out, he was glad for it.

"Nothing some Murphy's Oil Soap, Old English polish, and elbow grease can't fix." She grinned as they entered the office space, "Oh, it's perfect!" her hands clapped together with glee.

"Told you." Inside was a wooden desk that had previously been upstairs. Like the wainscoting, the desk had a simple beauty to it and was in need of some TLC. The thick sides held four drawers each that were joined by a desktop made of a single piece of hefty, solid oak. Chips and scratches decorated its years of use, but it was still very functional, beautiful, and fit the room like it was meant to be there. "You'll have to get your own chair," he said, pulling the contents out of the manila envelope he'd carried in and set them on the desktop. "Right," Tom rubbed his hands together. "All we need do is put our signatures on a few things and you'll be free to clean and polish, paint and wallpaper to your heart's delight. Your check cleared the other day so we're good to go."

She let out a trembling breath just as Tom turned to look at her. Her eyes were glistening with tears as she gushed, "You've no idea what this means to me, Mr. Murphey."

He'd seen his wife in a similar state, all gushing and weeping when something as simple as some nice scenery tugged at her tender heartstrings. Women, Tom thought, as he pulled the pen out of his shirt pocket. "I'm just glad to be part of making someone's dream come true. It means you'll take good care of the place. I appreciate that."

Renee brushed aside the tears and blushed. "Silly, I know, to cry like this. It's just so exciting." She drew in a deep breath and let it out slowly. "Where do I sign?"

He showed her and together they made it official.

"Any questions, comments, concerns, bad jokes?" he asked.

Her lips pursed in hesitation. "Um," she started out. "Not so much about all this, but, you said when we first met that your ancestors were actually the town founders? They were the Murphey's of Murphey Mills?"

"Yes, that's right."

"Would you know anything about the abandoned house on Dark Hollow Road?"

A cold spot formed in the center of his chest. "I know it."

"You know who lived there then?"

"The Browns, yes. They've been gone a long time, since the early 1980's, I think."

"Do you know what happened to them that would make Mr. Yagar warn me so vehemently to stay away from the place?"

Tom gave his head a slow shake. "Lee tends to exaggerate more than most, but the place always has had a bad reputation of sorts."

"How do you mean?"

"Just a bad place where bad things happened, I guess. I remember when Mary and her brother, what was his name, Nigel, that's it, both lived there. Anyway, the place never did look all that good that I recall. The bridge washed out back in '72 when Agnes came and was never replaced. We had no reason to go down past the house after that. The grounds have always been run over with weeds, though."

Her brow crinkled, "But what happened? What bad things happened there?"

"Abuse, mainly. Clayton Brown, Mary and Nigel's father, was a mean drunk and he drank a lot. He drowned or something back when they were all pretty young. That's what my folks told me. I only vaguely remember hearing about it as a kid."

"Then you didn't know any of the Browns?

"No, nobody really knew them. They kept to themselves and only came into town when they had to. Lee, though, Lee seems to know more than most about them."

"Fred Yagar said Lee's mother was a midwife and delivered all the babies around these parts for a long time."

"She was a good woman, Lee's mother. Don't know where Lee got his horrible disposition from, but it certainly wasn't from her. Maybe it was on account of his brother passing away. Lisa, on the other hand, is sweet as a button. Have you met her?"

"Yeah, at the pumpkin farm."

"She came along when Lee's mother was getting up there in years. Probably why she come out the way she did. Couldn't ask for a nicer girl, well, she isn't really a child, is she? She's a grown woman."

"How old do you think she is?"

"Can't be more than fifty or so. I remember seeing her during the flood, back in '72. She must have been about twelve. Lee's quite a stretch older, ten or fifteen years, I reckon, and very protective. Half the town was down there at that old bridge once we heard it had been washed out. We don't get much excitement around here. Mary and her brother were there, of course. They got flooded pretty bad. Me and a bunch of other kids were down there on our bikes checking out the creek and remains of the bridge. Mary made a scene, screaming about folks stomping around on her property. The Yagars were there in their station wagon and there was some sort of fight. We got our asses out of there quick after that."

Scowling, Renee shook her head, ""So she was one of those crazy, you-kids-get-off-my-lawn people, huh?" Renee emitted a soft, thoughtful hum, followed by a broadening grin. "Well, Lee can't be all bad if he has a soft spot in his heart for his baby sister."

"Why else do you think we tolerate the old codger the way we do?" Tom chuckled.

"And the other two siblings? Were they there, too?"

Tom looked thoughtfully at the floor, digging deep into the recesses of those long ago times. "Nope," he eventually said after searching through as many visual files as he could muster. "Don't remember them at all. I couldn't even tell you their names. I was just a little guy back then.

"Did anyone else live on that road? On the other side, I mean."

"There were a couple farmhouses, but it was mostly just hay and corn fields. Them that were on it were a good four or five miles up from the bridge. Eventually, most forgot that shortcut ever even existed. Dark Hollow Road's been a dead end a long time now."

Concern cast a shadow over Renee's face and she appeared about to ask another question, but held it firmly behind her closed lips. "Anyway, I should let you go. I have a trunk full of cleaning supplies to haul in. I plan on practically living here this weekend," she laughed.

He checked his watch and picked up the completed paperwork. "I'll get these copied over at the post office and send them to you as soon as I can, or drop them off if I see you over here this weekend. In the meantime," here he held out the keychain from which dangled three keys, two for the front door and one for the back. "These are yours. I hope you'll stay as happy with the place as you are today. If you need anything, just give me a call."

Her fingers wrapped around the keys, her face beaming with delight. "I will and thank you again, Mr. Murphey. I'm so happy to be here and part of the community."

Chapter 23

The days and nights of late January into March of that year ain't ones I care to recall, but I'll do my best so folks might one day understand.

It was clear right away, the whack Nigel give Daddy's head had done some serious damage. Thinking back, we should have taken him to the hospital. It may have turned out better for everyone. But we didn't do that.

Some days Daddy was alright, almost civil, almost like he was before Mama died. Most of the time he was more difficult to tend to than baby Alice.

What also come clear in short time was we couldn't keep him tied to the bed. Doing that meant I had to go in and change the bed linens too much and someone had to sit there and feed him. Nigel come up with another plan. He went into town and come back with two more hook-and-eye locks, except instead of putting them on the inside of the bedroom door like he done on ours, he put them on the outside.

We tried to make it as comfortable as we could in there for him. The boys lugged up his favorite chair, Seth gave up his portable radio. Every chance we had,

Kate and I would pick up some used Western books for a few pennies a piece. Nigel and Seth tended to toilet duties before and after school, then again just before bedtime. They were getting bigger and stronger while Daddy was losing weight and strength because he wasn't working or eating like he used to. Even in his weakened state, I was afraid of him, especially when we was to home alone and everyone else was at school.

But that fear was nothing compared to the day a phone call come for him.

"He's out doing chores," I said to the voice on the other end of the line that fateful day in late February. Kate stood in the doorway, a clean plate in one hand, a drying rag in another.

"Everything alright out to your place? Ain't seen Clay in months, it seems."

"We're all fine," I hoped my voice wasn't shaking nearly as hard as the phone was in my hand. "Daddy got a job over in South Wakefield." Wakefield was a solid fifty miles to the south of us. South Wakefield went out another five miles. We hoped it was far enough away to keep folks from going there and asking questions.

"That's quite a haul. What's he doing? He can't be driving that every day."

"No, sir, Mr. Barber. He leaves Sunday after supper and don't come back 'til late Friday night, sometime not even 'til Saturday afternoon, or at all. He's got a cousin down there he stays with, one that got him the job."

"You kids are there alone, then?"

I steadied my breathing, working to get my heart to slow itself down to normal. "More or less. We're fine, though. I'll be turning twenty in a couple weeks. Nigel, well, he's eighteen last fall. Ain't like we're little kids or nothing, Mr. Barber."

Mr. Barber chuckled. He'd worked with Daddy Clay a long time at the mine. "Damn, you really that old already? Doesn't seem possible. What sort of work did you say it was?"

"Lumber mill," I answered. "He likes it a whole lot better than the mining, fresher air, he says. Pays good. Thinks maybe that's what drove him to drinking too much, the coal mine, all that dark and soot. He's cut back a lot, he has. Ain't barely touched a drop since after the holidays." Well, at least that wasn't a lie.

"Glad to hear it. Well, I'll let you go. Tell Clay to give me a call when he can."

"I'll do that soon as he comes in from helping Nigel and Seth with chores."

"Take care now."

"You, too, Mr. Barber. Bye." Heart pounding, I hung up and leaned against the door frame. For a minute my hand wouldn't let go of the receiver. I closed my eyes, breathed in slow and deep, swallowing the nerves back into place.

"He believe you?" Kate asked.

I nodded and righted myself, finally able to uncurl my clenched fist from the molded piece of black plastic and hang it up. "I think so."

Her hands went back to drying the plate. "How long you think it'll be until someone catches on?"

"Don't know." Eventually someone would ask more questions than we could answer.

March was long, gray, and rainy in 1960 and it was cold enough near the end of the month to spit snow. I'd just finished making an appointment for Alice like the doctor told me, when a loud crash shook the house and rattled the windows from above. Kate and Seth jolted in their chairs at the table, their school papers and books so scattered you could barely see the tablecloth.

"It come from Daddy's room," Seth whispered.

Nigel wasn't due home for another two hours. My stomach filled with a hunk of lead the size of my fist. Knowing what you should do and actually doing it are two different things sometimes. As much as I knew I should go and see what had caused the noise, I stood there, too terrified to move.

Three sets of eyes looked up towards the ceiling when a long, slow dragging noise followed soon after. Wasn't like walking. Was more like something big being pulled real slow across the floor, something heavy and stubborn. My brain was racing trying to think what all was up there in Daddy's room that he could be making so much noise moving it around. Bed. Dresser. Chair. Mama's dressing table. Army trunk.

"You gonna ..."

"Sshh," I hissed back, still trying to listen, to determine, to decide if I should go up there.

I swallowed hard. The noise stopped with another weighted thud. "You two stay down here," I finally said. I handed Alice over to Kate and picked up the baseball bat that rested in the corner by the cook stove.

"Mary ..."

The horror in my brother's eyes made me wince. "Seth, you're in charge of protecting Kate and Ali, you hear? If something bad sounds like it's happening, get Daddy's rifle and do what you got to do."

Seth's jaw clenched with a nod.

Hoisting the ball bat for a better grip, I headed up. Each step sang out its own off-key moan like an old funeral dirge playing one dark, hollow note at a time.

Dark Hollow Road

At the landing I stopped to listen again. It was dead still.

My chest ached while the grip I had on the bat grew slippery. By one slow step at a time I came to stand in front of Daddy Clay's bedroom door. My free hand balled up, lifted, almost knocked. Instead I pressed my ear to the door. There was a steady, fuzzy sound coming from the other side. It took me a bit to realize it was the radio, only it weren't playing music. It was stuck between the stations, static.

I knocked twice, "Daddy?"

Listened.

Knocked again, "Daddy? You alright in there?"

My fingers stretched to the first of the three hook-and-eye locks. What if Daddy was standing on the other side waiting? Soon as I had these locks undone, the door would come flying open. I stopped, tried to breathe, tried to think.

"Daddy, I got the rifle with me. You try anything, I'll blow your head off," I lied, but truth be told a baseball bat wouldn't do much against the likes of my father if he was ready for it. He'd rip that thing from my hands and turn it on me so fast I'd never know what hit me. And it would hit me.

There was still no reply.

Another trembling breath followed my fingers to the latch, as they pulled it up and set it free. Stop. Listen. Wait. The second one was unlocked. Downstairs little Alice gave a tiny cry. Kate's gentle tones followed. A chair scraped below. The baby was quiet again.

I stared at the door. If Daddy meant to get out, I reckoned maybe he could do it now. "I mean it, Daddy. No funny business. You hear me?"

The radio hissed its static song.

I released the final lock, turned the knob, and pushed.

The door struck something solid. I put my shoulder to it and pushed harder. It budged as wood scraped on wood. "Daddy?" I pushed again, barely able to shift whatever it was enough now to see into the room through a two inch gap. The dresser blocked my way. Pressing my face up to the opening, I peered in. All I could see was the window and the area of the wall to the right of it. Last year's calendar, its top edged curling downward, hung there. "Daddy? You alright? Move the dresser so's I can get in."

"What's going on, Mary?"

I nearly jumped out of my skin at the sound of Seth's voice. He stood at the top landing, rifle in hand, looking at me from the shadows. "He's blocked the door," I was too relieved not to be alone anymore to be mad at him for disobeying. I could hear Kate downstairs talking to the baby. Even if something happened up here, the two of them still had a chance of escape. "Radio's on, but just static."

Seth drew closer. "Daddy?"

"He won't answer," I said.

Seth's voice lowered to a whisper, "You reckon it's a trap?"

I shrugged.

"Only one way to find out," he said. He handed me the rifle and started to push on the door like I had been. Seth wasn't just taller than me by now but a lot stronger. He angled himself low and started pushing. At first the dresser refused to move. Seth kept shoving and bumping the door. Increments of the room became more and more visible through the widening crack. I could see the corner opposite the window now, then the nightstand, then the front left bedpost.

Seth stopped. The gap was wide enough so he stuck his head in to look. He drew in a sharp intake of breath. Seth retracted himself from the opening and turned towards me looking pale and numb.

"What is it?" I shoved him aside to look myself.

There Daddy Clay hung, a big wet spot in the center of his pants, eyes bulging, tongue half out of his mouth, twisting ever so slowly from a length of braided bed sheet he'd tied to the overhead light fixture. He was still twitching. Choking sounds rattled in his throat. As he started to turn away from me, his eyes shifted and met mine. I bashed my head on the door frame as I pulled away to escape the sight of him.

A cold hand that I barely recognized as my own, covered my mouth as I stood there looking at my brother. I wasn't really seeing him, though. I was still seeing Daddy's body turning slowly away from me, his neck twisted at an awkward angle, his protruding tongue, his eyes, his yellowed and dying eyes flicking.

"We gotta do something," Seth whispered.

I couldn't get my brain to think.

The stairs creaked. Kate, with Alice propped up on her hip, appeared around the corner. "What's going on?" Alice had the middle fingers of her left hand stuffed in her mouth and was sucking on them happily until she saw me, then her pudgy little arms reached out, her fingers opening and closing as she made a little grunting sound.

Kate's brow darkened and furrowed as she came over closer and I took Ali from her. "You may as well look."

My little sister didn't say anything as she pulled back away from the door.

"We need to cut him down," Seth offered. His voice was flat. "Need to make it look like we at least tried to help him." It was more like he was talking about fixing up an old truck than trying to save our father's life. Weren't no life to save in there. "Help me get this door open more, Kate," Seth went on. At least he was thinking and doing.

Alice rubbed her nose with the back of her hand before resting her head on my shoulder. Her fingers had gone back to her mouth and her eyelids were drooping. I watched, holding my baby against me, swaying back and forth as she fell asleep blessedly unaware.

My two siblings got the door open enough so they could squeeze into Daddy's bedroom.

"Take my pocket knife," Seth said. "We'll have to cut him down. I'll try and hold him."

Why couldn't I move? I stood in the hallway, my eyes drifting in and out of focus as the heaviness of the day began sinking deep into my body. I wanted to be like Alice. I wanted to not know anything about any of this. I wanted to sleep. This was bad. This was real bad.

"I'm going to put Ali down for a nap." The words rose from my lips as if echoing from the bottom of a very deep, very dark well. Whether or not my siblings heard me or not, I don't know. I remember turning away from the door, looking down the brown-shadowed hallway towards my bedroom, and then walking into the room. Ali was sound asleep as I put her in the crib and covered her with one of Mrs. Yagar's knitted blankets.

Kate's hand shook my shoulder. "Mary Alice?"

My eyes either opened or focused. Somewhere along the way I'd come to be sitting on the side of my bed. The shadows had grown longer in the little bedroom us three girls shared. "We need to make supper," I remember saying.

My sister's frown deepened. "Soon," she said. Her tender, cool palm covered my forehead. "You're warm."

"I'm fine," I replied, wondering what to make for supper. "Nigel home, yet?"

She shook her head. "On his way, I reckon." She swallowed. "We got Daddy back to bed," she added.

My mind was locked inside a useless body. Only my eyes obeyed as they scanned the darkening room. "What fell?"

"Mama's dressing table. Mirror's busted."

Seth appeared in the open doorway. "I closed his eyes. Put some quarters on 'em to keep 'em shut. She okay, Kate?"

"Tired," I replied for her. Ali rolled over in the crib. "We need to make supper," I repeated. "Things are always better on a full stomach." I found my legs. They didn't want to work, but I forced them to push me to standing.

"What we going to do with Daddy?" Kate asked. She picked Alice up out of the crib, dragging the blanket with her.

"After supper," I said. "After Nigel's home and after we've had supper, we'll figure something out then."

The back and forth creak of footsteps on the kitchen porch pulled me from a restless night's sleep. As I lay listening, eyes wide open, light would occasionally flash outside the window followed by the low, long distance rumble of thunder echoing up through the river valley. At first I thought it was Daddy down there. With the next flash of lightning, I remembered it couldn't be.

Dinner had been tasteless and tepid. Baby Alice did most of the talking. The rest of us sat in nervous, mute silence. It wasn't until I stood at the sink scraping the leftovers into a coffee can that Nigel said anything more interesting than, "Pass the butter." He'd put his arm around my shoulders. "We'll figure something out," his voice was low and hushed. He watched me a few more minutes, kissed me on the cheek, then turned away, dark and brooding. We didn't speak for the rest of the night.

I slipped out of bed, put on my robe, and crept down the stairs.

"Oh," I said, stepping into the chilly, spring air. "It's you." I could smell the earth again, the soil and dampness, and things wanting to grow after a long, cold sleep.

Nigel didn't turn around, but he had stopped pacing for the time being. He studied the back yard with what little light the moon, stars, and flashes of the encroaching storm offered. We watched and listened in silence, the worry of our situation unspoken until Nigel finally replied, "I have an idea."

My voice was a whisper full of fear and dread. "What is it?"

"It ain't going to be pretty, but I think it will work."

"Tell me," I urged.

He did. He was right. It wasn't pretty at all.

Dark Hollow Road

Chapter 24

Brandon poked at the lump of cold, stagnant spinach on his plate. He hated spinach. Even with butter and salt on it, it still tasted like farts smelled. "Do I have to eat this?" he whined again. Sometimes if he complained enough, he didn't have to eat the yucky stuff on his plate.

"Three more bites," Mommy said.

Tonight was not going to be one of those nights. "But, it's gross."

"It will make you strong like Popeye," Mama Sam said. "You can do it."

He didn't know who Popeye was, nor did he care. He just wanted to be done with this horrible stuff so they could go trick-or-treating. Brandon scooped up a few strands of the dark green mush.

"More than that," Mommy was watching. She was always watching.

Brandon put a little more on the fork and looked at her with the vague hope it would be enough. "I'm going to puke if I eat it."

"Bee, just eat it," Mama Sam was watching, too. "You're not going to puke. Plug your nose, shovel it in, chew, and swallow. It will be done before you know it."

231

Pamela Morris

"But ..."

"Eat. There will be no trick-or-treating and no fire station party if you don't eat three more real bites of spinach. This is not open for discussion. Do it, or go to your room for the rest of the night. Your choice." Mommy got up with her plate in one hand and her utensils in the other. "You done, hon?"

Sam put her knife and fork on the plate, "Yeah, thanks, babe. That was great."

Mommy set the plates together and carried everything over to the sink.

Brandon let out a sigh. It was so disgusting. His eyes pleaded with Mama Sam.

"Eat up, Bee. You have an hour before the party. Let me know when you're ready." Mama Sam wasn't being very helpful tonight. Lots of times she'd gobble down whatever it was Brandon was supposed to eat while Mommy's back was turned, but not tonight. Tonight, she just got up and carried the serving bowls over to the counter before heading towards the bathroom.

Fighting back the urge to gag, Brandon pinched his nose shut, filled the fork, and shoved the spinach in. He kept his nose plugged while his jaw worked frantically to break down the green lump. It felt like a giant, soggy spitball in his mouth, but Brandon swallowed, coughed, swallowed again and filled the fork for the second mouthful of torture. The second bite wasn't as bad, but it was still pretty bad. The third forkful was almost to his wide open mouth when Brandon looked up and straight into the eyes of The Sugar Lady standing on the other side of the sliding glass door.

With a scream, his fork flew across the room, spinach detaching itself as it swirled in midair, leaving a scattered trail of greens and butter on the pale brown carpet.

"Brandon! That is just about enough of that!"

He pointed at the door, still screaming, hardly able to breathe, "Sugar Lady! She's there. She's right there!"

"Stop it. You're just saying that so you don't have to eat the spinach," Mommy's face was livid red.

Brandon burst out crying. "But she is! I saw her, Mommy! I saw her. She was looking right at me."

Mommy marched over to the table and looked towards the door with growing disgust. "There's no one there, Brandon. I've had enough of this nonsense, young man. Do you want to go out tonight or not, because right now you're much closer to not."

"I saw her. I did," he protested through sobs and gulps for air. "She's gone now, but I did see her. Please, Mommy, I did and them kids was outside my window last night, too." Why wouldn't she believe him? He wasn't lying. He wanted to go trick-or-treating. He didn't want to eat this spinach and he didn't want to see that lady or them kids ever again.

Mama Sam came out of the bathroom, still zipping up her pants, "What the hell's going on?"

"Brandon says she saw The Sugar Lady."

"I did see her. I did, Mama Sam. Please believe me. I did." Snot was stuffing up his nose while at the same time dribbling from it.

Mama Sam growled, "Probably just some asshole in a Halloween costume." She stormed to the sliding glass door, yanked it open, and lunged onto the back deck. "Nice job, asshole!" she screamed. "You just scared a six-year-old. Ain't you a fucking tough son-of-a-bitch!" She stuck her head back in. "I'll walk around the house just to make sure," she said, ducked back into the darkness, and slid the door shut.

The yelling made Brandon tremble and cry all the more. Mommy picked up his napkin and wiped his nose as she rubbed his back. "It's alright, little man. Mama Sam will scare them away. It was just someone in a costume. It's Halloween night after all, right?" She gave him a little smile and kissed the top of his head. "Go wash up and get ready to go."

He sniffed his nose and nodded. He knew what he'd seen and it wasn't someone in a costume. It was her. He knew it even if no one else believed him. "Okay, Mommy." Brandon slid from the chair with a thud. There wasn't much to do to get ready but brush his teeth and comb his hair. He was still wearing the costume and his hard hat was … was where? Upstairs maybe.

Halloween was when the ghosts and monsters came out. That thought was not comforting. Before, he would have hurried through brushing his teeth and combing his hair. He would have raced up the stairs to grab his hard hat. Tonight, he went about the tasks with a feeling that was growing all too familiar, dread. What if they were waiting out there at the edge of the cornfield again tonight? What if The Sugar Lady came knocking? What if she didn't knock at all, but opened the door and slithered in? She would walk around the house, looking in their cupboards, stealing his toys, maybe dipping one of her creepy hands into his treat bag and helping herself to some of the candy he was going to bring back.

The candy. If it weren't for the mounds of free candy and sweets, Brandon thought maybe this whole Halloween thing wasn't such a great idea. But the candy was calling and lots of it! Tons of it! And games and carving pumpkins and that scarecrow guy, also known as Nicole's Uncle Jim, to see.

Brandon flipped on the switch to fill his bedroom with light. No hard hat on the bed or in the chair. Not on the dresser, not on the floor. It wasn't under the bed or in the closet. He stood there thinking, trying to remember where he'd last seen it when a sharp popping sound jolted him to the bone and the room was cast into darkness. He screamed and ran. They were coming!

Mama Sam appeared at the bottom of the stairs as Brandon scrambled down them. "What now?"

"My light! It went out!" he blurted, cold sweat and a rapidly beating heart making their second appearance of the night. He squeezed by Sam. No one could get past Mama Sam if she didn't want them to. It was a lot safer to have her as a barrier.

"Bulb probably blew. I'll let your mom know."

She didn't even bother to check. She should check. One of them could have gotten in by now, squeaking around under the cracks of the closed window, getting ready for when he came back. They'd be tucked under the bed and in the closet, waiting, waiting, waiting. That's what monsters did. And the witches! Don't forget the witches with rats in their hands, hands that were just like The Sugar Lady's. But Mama Sam didn't seem to understand that. "Where's your hard hat? You can't be Bob The Builder without the hard hat."

"I think I left it in Mommy's car."

"Well, go get it, Bee. Time's a wasting. There's candy to be had!"

Right. The candy. He hurried towards the kitchen where Mommy was filling up a big bowl with miniature chocolate bars just in case someone came way out here.

"What's all the screaming about?" she asked.

Mama Sam was following close behind. "The light bulb in his room just blew out," she said like it was nothing. "Go get your hat, Bee. I'll get the Jeep started."

Mommy actually laughed, "Well, we're just full of spooky surprises tonight, aren't we? 'Tis the season. Where's your hat, little man?"

He stood there gap-mouthed for a second. "In your car, I think."

"It's unlocked. Hurry up. You don't want to miss the start of the party."

No, he didn't want to do that. After tonight, everything would be better. That's what it was. It was this Halloween thing. Once they got through tonight, everything would go back to normal. Brandon headed towards the garage door, making sure to flip on the switch before he even touched the knob.

Naturally-chilled air whispered up his shirt sleeves as he walked around to the passenger side of the car, opened the door, and found his hat lying upside down on the floor in the back. Brandon scooped it up and was heading back to the door when something fluttered in the corner of his eye, something blue, something with little white and yellow flowers on it and so thin and fragile and old it made his blood run cold.

Sitting on top of the small workbench that ran along the left hand side of the garage was a battered wooden crate. A narrow ribbon of fabric, no longer than a foot, shifted in the faint drafts and dim shadows, dangled over the crate's edge. Brandon couldn't breathe as his feet sank into the concrete floor, eyes wide, riveted.

Flip, flap. Flip, flap it went in the trickle of air that touched it. Just a little piece of fabric that couldn't hurt anyone if it tried. That's all it was. Harmless. Perfectly, harmless. One little work-boot-clad foot scuffed forward. Two steps, three, four.

Flap, flip. Flap, flip.

Five steps closer and within arm's reach, the boy's hand extended, fingers stretched, tips touched the blue fibers. He could barely feel them they were so light, but he could see them. He knew what they were and where they'd come from, but how had it gotten here? Maybe he was right that The Sugar Lady snuck in the house. Maybe she was here while they were sleeping or when no one was home. Maybe she was here right now. His fingers wrapped around it and pulled, drawing it from the box of jumbled and rusted pieces of metal and wire. Like a snake slithering from the water, it came and fell limp, dead, in his hand.

"You coming, Bee?"

Brandon yelped, clutching the ribbon of fabric tighter as he spun in place. Mama Sam was standing in the doorway. "Yeah," he croaked.

Her head tipped as she frowned, "What you got there?"

He held it out, realizing for the first time how cold the fingers that wrapped around it were. "It was in the box." The words came out just above a whisper.

Mama Sam came closer, looked at it and shrugged, "So. It's a piece of old fabric."

"It's hers," he said.

"Hers?"

"The Sugar Lady's. It's from her dress."

Mama Sam's interest rose along with her eyebrows. "Oh?"

"I think she comes into our house when we're sleeping or away."

The raised brows sank down into a scowl. The fabric slid from Brandon's finger to Mama Sam's. "The wooden crate with the lamp parts in it?" Brandon nodded. "It was in there when I brought it home."

Brandon hadn't been paying a whole lot of attention to anything but getting yelled at by Mommy. She'd steered him by the nape of his neck pinched between her thumb and fingers, as they marched back to the car.

Mama Sam crumpled it up and stuffed it into her jacket pocket. "Let's not worry about it. Time for some fun. Got your hat?"

He held it up.

"Let's head out then."

Brandon didn't like the idea of just leaving without first inspecting the garage to make sure The Sugar Lady wasn't still lurking around, but he wanted to get out of there as fast as possible, too. "Tell Mommy to make sure no one's in there," he said, climbing into the backseat of the Jeep and pulling on his seatbelt.

Mama Sam put it in reverse, "I will, soon as we get settled at the party. You want to trick-or-treat along the way out or on the way home?"

"On the way home," he said. He didn't want to miss any of the party. Something fun might happen.

"Home it is."

As they drove past the end of Dark Hollow Road, Brandon couldn't help but look down the long, wide dirt path it had become. He expected to see one of them there, waiting and watching. The road was blessedly empty.

With the volume of the television turned way down low, Renee headed into the kitchen. In minutes, the room rang with the familiar rapid popping sound of popcorn in the microwave quickly followed by that oh-so-delicious aroma of melted butter. Barring the arrival of any trick-or-treaters way out here in the boonies, she had the house to herself for the next few hours and meant to take advantage of every second. Renee nabbed her book off the counter, grabbed the now swollen and steaming bag of popcorn, and headed for the comforts of her favorite spot on the sofa. Two, maybe three, hours of undisturbed reading stretched out before her. She pulled the throw blanket up over her tucked legs and opened the book with a satisfied sigh.

The conclusion of Chapter Nine came half an hour later. Renee wondered how she'd gone this long through life without having read Christie's *By The Pricking Of My Thumbs.* Good old Tuppence and Tommy, Renee thought to herself.

A fist rattled the front metal storm door in five rapid-fire knocks.

How about that. She was going to have to give away some of that candy after all. It was probably for the best. If they didn't take and eat it, she would. Grinning, Renee uncurled from the sofa and grabbed the bowl just as five more knocks struck the other side of the door.

She pulled it open, bracing herself for the onslaught of the shouted chant of children all across the country this night, "Trick or Treat!?"

The front porch was empty.

Bowl in hand, Renee opened the storm door and stepped out. "Hello?"

Not so much as a cricket made a sound.

Annoyed, she went back inside, giving the front door a slam to make sure whoever it was heard it.

"Stupid kids." It had to be teenagers. Who else would come way out here?

Renee went to the kitchen to get a bottle of ginger ale. No sooner had the soft hiss of the pressure inside the bottle been released when the knocks came a second time. Five again. Fast. Urgent. She walked to the door, stood on the other side with it still closed and waited, listening for the sound of childish giggles or the rapid retreat of footsteps as they went to hide again.

Renee moved close enough to wrap her hand around the knob. As soon as the knocking started, she'd yank it open. She'd catch the little bastards in the act.

Knock! Knock! Knock! Knock! Knock!

The door flew open so hard it shook the one beyond. The porch was still empty.

Renee rushed out, fuming mad and slopping soda onto her hand from the open bottle. "Knock it off, you stupid kids!" She stepped off the porch a few paces, ears straining to hear anything at all, eyes squinting into the pitch darkness created by living in the country where street lights didn't exist.

Nothing moved, not even the wind to rustle the rows of surrounding field corn. Other than the barely audible drone of her television, all was still. Renee hugged herself against the chills that sprouted goose bumps on her arms. Turning, she scanned the front yard, knowing she should probably look around back. She wasn't one to spook easily, but there was something wrong about this moment. Renee moved to the front corner of the house and peeked around. Nothing but the dark and an army of cornstalks.

And a pinprick of light barely visible near the end of Dark Hollow Road.

Chapter 25

The sun wasn't even up when Nigel came tapping on the bedroom door. Kate rolled over, mumbled something, then sank back into sleep. Saturdays were meant for sleeping in. Nigel and me felt it was up to us to take care of the business at hand without involving our younger siblings. The less they saw and knew the better.

I got out of bed as quiet as I could and dressed like I was going to do barn chores, in jeans, a long sleeved shirt, and a pair of sturdy work shoes. Nigel was leaning against the wall when I opened the bedroom door and joined him in the hallway.

"You ready for this?" he whispered.

"Ready as I'm going to be," I replied, falling into soft steps behind him.

It was cold in Daddy's room and his body was tucked neatly under its blankets. He wasn't even twenty-four hours dead, but things were already starting to look funky about him. His skin had a weird shine to it, like a lump of used up caning wax, all white and yellow and blue at the same time. His hands didn't look real at all. The colorless flesh was mottled with blotches of pale pink and stretched over bones, tipped with pale blue fingernails. The mouth that had spewed so many foul words and committed such disgusting deeds against us over the years, hung open and slightly off to one side. The hatred in me hardened into marble. He was dead and I was glad. I wanted to spit on him, but my mouth had gone dry. I wanted to scream, but my throat had filled with such a big lump of ice I could barely swallow or breathe, let alone make a sound.

"C'mon." Nigel's warm touch made me flinch and I was back in the moment, back to knowing what needed to be done.

The springs on the old bed creaked and moaned, doing their best to cry out and wake the dead along with whole damn house. Nigel took hold up under Daddy's armpits while I held up his feet. It seemed he'd gained a heap of weight overnight. Dead weight's what they call it.

Grunting and sweating despite the cold, Nigel and me hauled him out the back door and flung him like a big old sack of rotten wheat into the awaiting wheelbarrow. "Go get the scrap can," Nigel's breath came out in puffs of white mist. "I'll meet you at the barn." Without waiting, he headed out, the wheelbarrow bouncing and swerving along its intended route.

I hurried back inside, grabbed the coffee can full of scraps from the day before then headed into the pantry. I hated to waste even one jar of food, but it was the price we were going to have to pay. I scanned the shelves, judged what we had the most amount of, and yanked off a quart of tomatoes. After breaking the seal, I dumped it into the coffee can with the rest of the slop, sloshed it all around, and headed back out.

My brother was waiting. The slumped mass of flesh that was our father waited in the wheelbarrow beside the wooden outer wall of the pen. Inside, grunts and thuds jostled for position. Squeals rang out louder than I would have liked. Nigel swallowed hard when he saw me. Without a word, I set the can down and moved into place. Daddy weren't wearing nothing but old stained underpants and a grimy tank top. "Should we take those off him?" I asked.

Nigel gulped, looking almost as ghastly pale as our dead old man. "Yeah, I suppose we should."

The shirt came first, then the underwear. It wasn't like we'd never seen those parts of our father before, and in doing so now, at least we knew we'd never have to look at them again.

The pigs thrashed and oinked, grunted and squealed with growing unrest, eager for breakfast. Somehow they knew. "Ready?" Nigel asked, eyes staring into mine, pleading that we get this over and done with, begging me not to chicken out.

"Ready," I said and we lifted as one, as we'd done countless times before when we were much, much younger, lifting bales of hay together, lifting bags of cracked corn, or oats, swinging the load just a little for the needed momentum and then tossing it, end over end into the pig sty, watching it hit the edge of the trough and roll until it lay face down into the sloppy mud and shit.

I grabbed the scrap can and leaned over, dumping its contents onto Daddy's back. Nigel took the can and filled it with cracked corn, tossing it over the body as best he could as the pigs chowed down, not caring what or who they were eating. In fascinated horror, I watched as one bit into Daddy's shoulder, snapping the skin, stretching the withered muscles, and tugging at the chewier sinews beneath. Other parts snapped as teeth hit bones. I turned away, my stomach souring as I stumbled away from the scene and towards the fresher, quieter air.

Nigel was not long behind me.

"How long you think it'll take?"

"Don't know," he said. "Six pigs, two or three days maybe. We'll have to pick the bigger bones out. I don't think they'll eat his skull. Wait until I get back before you come down here again." Nigel touched my shoulder. He pulled me around to face him and held me close. It felt like one of Mama's hugs, warm and safe and comforting. His hands stroked my hair and together we rocked a little, trying to hold on to what was left of our sanity. "We done it, Mary Alice. We're done with him. We're done with him and we can get on with our lives. He ain't never going to touch any of us ever again."

My body shivered despite the warmth of his arms around me as I let myself cry.

We stood there a few minutes longer, still able to hear the grunts and occasional squeal of the pigs. "C'mon, I need to get going soon," Nigel said. "It's going to take a long time and the sooner I head out, the sooner I can get back."

I wiped my nose with the sleeve of the flannel shirt. "You can't even stay for breakfast?"

He shook his head. "Make me up some sandwiches and a thermos of coffee. That'll do just fine." He cupped my head between his hands and lifted up my face until I looked into his eyes, so much like my own. "It's going to be alright, big sister," he smiled, leaned in, and kissed my forehead. "You trust me, don'cha?"

"I trust you," I said, some of the fear loosening its frozen grip around my heart and lungs.

"Then get inside, make me up a nice big lunch, and fill that thermos. I'll get the truck ready."

Half an hour later, Nigel pulled out of our short driveway. Beside him on the seat was Daddy's lunch box and a full thermos of fresh coffee. On the floor was Daddy's suitcase, neatly packed for a week's worth of work down in South Wakefield. In the bed of the truck was Nigel's bicycle, a fishing pole, a folding lawn chair, and Daddy's tackle box all hidden under a heavy, oil cloth tarp.

I watched until there wasn't anything to watch no more. Maybe I should have felt some sense of relief, but that wasn't the case. Despite Nigel's words, mortal fear crept so deep and dark into my soul it bordered on hysteria. My arms wrapped around my shoulders, fingers pressing deep into my cooling flesh, trying to hold together the pieces that still remained of a normal life. I don't know which feeling was worse, listening for Daddy's footsteps coming down the hallway to claim his Loving Time, or waiting for the outside world to find out everything we so desperately wanted to hide.

The house was still quiet when I stepped back inside. I headed to the kitchen, feeling dull-headed and numb. In the kitchen, cozy warm now from the fire I'd started in the woodstove to make Nigel's coffee, I sat chewing my nails while the last pieces of clothing Daddy Clay would ever soil burned and crumbled to nothing amongst the wood ashes.

Seth and Kate were forbidden to visit the pig sty that day, but I can't say for sure they obeyed my orders. I'd be surprised if they did. Nor did I tell them where Nigel had gone or what he was doing. Were anyone to ask, he was to home with us going about the business of chores. We agreed on our alibis, because when you really got to thinking about it, what we'd done was murder. It didn't matter that Daddy was already dead when we heave-ho'd him into the sty. It didn't matter he'd hung himself. It mattered that we'd not called for a doctor or taken him to the hospital right off.

Noon came and went. Nigel should have gotten to South Wakefield no later than nine o'clock. We guessed it would take him at least five hours to get back on the bike.

Three o'clock come. Then five. When he still wasn't back by seven, I was well on my way to a nervous breakdown. The minutes ticked by in agony and every time a vehicle went by I found myself at the window. I half expected a police car to show up, or at the very least someone to arrive telling me that Nigel had been found dead in a ditch somewhere along the route. It got full dark early that time of year in Pennsylvania. Nigel's bike didn't have a headlight on it and unless he'd thought to grab a flashlight out of Daddy's truck, he'd be pedaling along on pitch black back roads with sharp curves and blind spots a plenty.

With Seth and Kate out in the living room watching the little black and white television Nigel'd picked up at the thrift store, I started Alice's bath in the kitchen sink. She was sitting up real good by then, and with the woodstove going the room was nice and warm for her. Alice loved her bath and within only a few minutes I was feeling more relaxed by her smiles and giggles. Things were going to be fine. I truly believed that as I soaped up her chubby feet, tickling while I did it. Everything was alright, I kept telling myself. I was twenty years old. Nigel was eighteen. In June he'd be graduating high school and he could work full time in the mine then. He'd make just as much as Daddy had, maybe more.

I'd already scooped my slippery baby up from the sink and wrapped her into a towel, when the heavy thud of footsteps come to the kitchen porch. A cold, wet wind gushed into the room as the door crashed open and Nigel tumbled in, a soggy, dirty mess. Blood darkened his upper lip, ran down the outer edge of his mouth and looked like it had dripped from his chin at one point. Now it was dry and caked with mud.

"Nigel!" I clutched Ali close against me, quick to shut the door before she caught anything in the gust of chilly air. Seth and Kate rushed in from the other direction. "Get some towels and a blanket, Kate," I ordered. Seth was already helping his brother over to kitchen chair nearest the stove. "What happened? What took you so long?" I didn't mean to crowd and fuss, but I couldn't help it.

Kate handed Nigel a towel then draped a wool blanket over his shoulders. "You want something hot to drink, Nige? There's still coffee left over, I think."

He nodded, starting to shiver under the coverings as he rubbed his head and coughed. "Sounds good, Kate." His voice was hoarse and scratchy.

"What happened to your nose?" I drew closer, putting my fingers under his chin like I seen Mama do a hundred times to us kids when we was hurt. Was then I saw more blood on his forehead from a big gash. "And your head!"

Nigel tugged his head away, "Ain't nothing, Mary Alice. Quit fussin'. I'm fine."

I was Mama all over the place that night. I handed Alice over to Kate, "Go and get her pajamas on for me, Katie, and a bath going for your brother. I'll tend to the coffee and something to eat. You hungry, Nige? Still some stew left from supper."

"That sounds good, Mary Alice," he knew it was senseless to balk too much. By the looks of him he was tired and sore and if he was as much like Daddy as I was like Mama, he'd be getting cranky with me if I pushed too much.

He drank the coffee while I heated up the beef stew. "Made it down fine. No problem," he said between sips. "All set up just like we talked about." Eating the stew quieted him down a bit, but he still managed to tell the story as he ate.

Nigel said he'd headed out right on time, around twelve-thirty or so. The going had been fast and easy at first. He was making good time until it started raining. Even then, he lowered his head against it and kept pedaling. Worse than riding in the rain, is doing it at night without so much as a match to light the way. Worse more than that, was doing the two on the twisting roads this part of Pennsylvania is known for.

He'd just crested one of the more miserable hills and was taking advantage of the equally as steep decline on the other side. Here, the road was a relatively straight shot through a narrow gully valley and up the other side. With any luck at all, Nigel had hoped to get up enough speed to make the next hill not so taxing. He almost made it, too.

Moments before reaching the bottom of the valley's U-shape, the bike was knocked out from under him and he and it both went flying all the way across to the other side of the road, crashing through a maze of trees and snapping, whipping branches and saplings. Leaves were tossed in the air and rocks tumbled down into the twenty foot ravine. With what little light there was, all Nigel saw from his sprawled position in a ditch was the flash of a white tail bobbing and bounding away.

Dark Hollow Road

My brother didn't know how long he lay where he landed, cold rain pelting his upturned face, soaking him through to the bone. He tasted blood and his head throbbed as he sat up. It took another long while of time to realize he didn't know where the bike had gone to.

He'd gotten to his hands and knees and was just about to stand when twin points of light appeared at the top of the hill he'd just careened down. If he was seen, the driver might stop and help. But, Nigel didn't want to be seen. If he were seen by someone he knew, our plan would be ruined.

The vehicle was coming full speed, bringing with it the blessed light he needed to find the bike, but also a cursed light that could ruin the entire thing. He ducked back down into the ditch, peering up as much as he dared, eyes not on the vehicle, but on the road and ditches nearby. A flash of familiar metal is all he wanted, something to point him in the right direction. He'd worry about the state of the bike if and when he was able to find it.

The car shot by with not so much as a flash of brake lights.

The bike was not in the road, but he'd not seen it anywhere else either.

Chapter 26

Something in Renee's throat squeaked, but she couldn't move until the light suddenly winked out. Halloween night, she reminded herself, taking a step backwards, afraid to turn her back on the house nearly half a mile away. This was all just Halloween night pranks and teenagers breaking into an old, empty house at the end of a forgotten road that no one went down anymore. She turned away and hurried back inside, making sure both the storm and main door were locked. Renee didn't care how many times someone knocked, she was not going to answer it.

Mind racing, Renee plopped back down on the sofa, took a swig from the soda bottle, and stared at the television screen. What about all those locks Mr. Martin has on the place? The Brown house was locked up tight. She'd seen that for herself. Someone was over there now, though; she knew that, too. Upstairs. They were upstairs. She'd not have been able to see the light otherwise, not through the stalks of corn.

"Alright," she reassured herself with a calming exhale. "Get a grip, Renee. You aren't six years old like Brandon. You are a grown woman. Just calm yourself down. Maybe a shot of rum in that ginger ale is in order." She got back up to return to the kitchen to fetch a bit of the Captain from the cupboard over the fridge. "One, no, two shots will do," she said and grinned, pouring the soda from the bottle into a tall glass and adding the alcohol. Renee added a bit of orange juice to the concoction and took a sip. "Perfect."

Rattled nerves steadied themselves as she moved back towards her perch in the living room. After another deep swallow of her adult beverage everything was as it should be, calm. Renee gathered up the throw blanket ...

Knock! Knock! Knock! Knock! Knock!

... and the cool glass in her hand seemed to leap of its own accord from her hand to the edge of the coffee table ...

Knock! Knock! Knock! Knock! Knock!

... catching it, cracking into three large chunks, liquid flying ...

Knock! Knock! Knock! Knock! Knock!

Not on metal this time. Not rattling the storm door off its hinges.

Knock! Knock! Knock! Knock! Knock!

On glass, thick glass, sliding glass.

Knock! Knock! Knock! Knock! Knock!

"STOP IT!" she shrieked, leaping away from the glistening shards that pointed upwards from the soaked carpet, her body bending away from the sliding glass door.

Knock! Knock! Knock! Knock! Knock!

"I said stop it!" Renee yanked open the drapes, livid and screaming.

Movement fluttered at the corner of the lawn. She snapped the lock free and heaved the heavy door wide open, flew out onto the back deck and down the steps before she could even think about what she was doing.

"God damn it! What the fuck is wrong with you people?!"

Shadows darted and weaved through the rows of corn. The stalks quivered. They were out there. She could almost see them, but they were too fast, way too fast and in a darkness deeper than deep that Renee could not get a good look.

"Ready or not, here I come." The sing-song voice of a child sifted up from that bleak blackness, almost seemed to touch her face and lift her hair like a soft kiss of icy wind.

Renee batted it away, turning in a circle, trying to see and hear what clearly wasn't there.

"You better stay away, you little brats! Do you hear me?" Her stiff arms and clenched fists shook at her sides. "Stay the fuck away! I'm calling the police in the morning. You're trespassing and I saw your light over at the Brown house, too! It's all going to be reported! All of it!"

Renee spun on her heels and marched back into the house, drawing the door shut with a resoundingly firm thud. One more time, she seethed to herself, one more time and I won't wait until morning to call 9-1-1.

While lifting out chunks and slivers of glass from the carpet and soaking up all that she could of the drink, Renee gave up on the idea of reading. She filled a second glass and turned up the television. And that's exactly where Sam found her when she arrived home with a very tired, but happy, six-year-old draped over her shoulder.

"I'll call Doug after breakfast." Sam nabbed a piece of cooling bacon as she glanced at the clock. Renee had wasted no time telling her about the events of the previous night. It only seemed right to let Mr.

Martin know and now that Sam had a key, the last thing she wanted the owner to think was she'd messed with anything over there. "Boy, Brandon must have been wiped out."

"I'm glad the two of you had fun." Renee cracked a final egg into the bowl and began to whisk it all together. "You should go wake him up. Breakfast will be ready in about ten minutes."

"Yeah, alright." Sam planted a kiss on Renee's cheek and headed upstairs to the boy's room. She gave the closed door two quick raps and opened it, letting a cool breeze escape in the process. "Damn, Bee, what's the window open for?"

The rounded lump on the bed didn't move. Sam gave what felt more like a stuffed animal than a small boy, a pat. "C'mon, buddy. Your mom's got breakfast on." She crossed the room and closed the window that was only open a few inches, enough to put a chill in the air. On the floor next to the bed, Brandon's trick-or-treat bag lay on its side, part of its contents strewn about with a suspicious scattering of wrappers tossed under the bed. Clearly someone had been snacking after lights out.

Sam shook her head and chuckled. "Wakey, wakey. Eggs and bakey!" She reached for what appeared to be foot poking out from under the blanket but ended up being the arm of a sock monkey. Brandon liked to make a nest of his stuffed animals and curl up in the center of them, surrounded and safe. Sam pulled back the blankets.

The nest was there, but Brandon wasn't.

Sam looked towards the closet. Bee sometimes ended up there and with all the excitement with Halloween, maybe something had spooked him into hiding. She opened the door, parted the clothing, and found nothing but a floor covered with clothes and toys.

She gave a thoughtful, "Hm," while scanning the room. Maybe he'd slipped off to the bathroom and she hadn't noticed.

He wasn't there, either. Sam trotted down the stairs and stepped into the kitchen just as Renee was finishing up the eggs and pushing the toast down. "Morning, sleepy head," she chirped and turned. Her smile replaced with a questioning tip of her head. "He coming?"

"He's not up there. Did he come down here?"

Renee shook her head. The steaming pan of eggs lowered back to the stove top with a gentle thud. "I didn't hear him if he did."

"Brandon?" Sam turned back, heading towards the downstairs bathroom and the room they'd set aside for the computers. "Come on, Bee. Breakfast is getting cold."

"Did you look in his closet?" Renee had left the sanctuary of the kitchen and stood at the bottom of the stairs as Sam emerged from the other rooms.

"Yeah."

"Under the bed?"

"No," Sam snickered, remembering the candy wrappers. "Little devil is probably laughing it up."

"I'll get him. Go ahead and get the toast buttered."

Renee ascended the stairs. "Little man, your eggs are getting cold."

Sam withdrew the warm toast and was halfway through buttering the second slice when her partner's hurried steps came thudding down them. "He's not up there, Sam." She'd gone at least one shade paler than usual. "And his slippers and robe are gone."

"You don't think he went outside, do you?"

"Where else could he be?"

"Why would he go outside?" Toast forgotten, Sam went to the door that led into the garage. A quick flip of the locking mechanism admitted her into the cold, semi-dark area beyond. "Bee? You out here?" Sam looked in the minivan, fear that she could not let Renee see starting to seep into her head. The van was empty. Movement by the door turned her around. It was only Renee. Sam shook her head.

"Nope." Renee looked like she was about to cry.

"We'll find him, hon. Don't panic."

It was too late. Renee darted back into the house. Moments later Sam heard the front door open and slam shut then the sound of her partner out front yelling for her son. "BRANDON!" She screamed at the top of her lungs and ran around back before Sam could get inside, grab her jacket, and go out through the sliding glass door of the living room.

Renee stood on the edge of the cornfield, one hand on her forehead as she cried out. "Brandon! Answer me. This isn't funny!"

"Answer your mom, Bee!" Sam called as she moved up beside Renee and put an arm around her shoulder. "He ever do any sleepwalking?" she asked, looking between the rows of tall corn.

Renee gave a slight nod. "When we moved the first time after his dad and I split up, but he was real little. He didn't get far. Couldn't get the door open." She swallowed. "You think he wandered off into the cornfield or something? Jesus, Sam. What if he walked down to the creek and fell in. He can't swim, yet." The edge of panic in her voice was sharp and tears ran down her face as her whole body trembled. "We need to call 9-1-1."

"Let's look a little bit more. He could be asleep out there." She scanned the field, eyes settling on the rooftop of the house across the way. "Or maybe he went over there."

Renee startled at the thought. "God! What if he's fallen into an old well?!" She pulled away and headed back towards the house. "We need to call for help, Sam." Sam hurried after her. Renee's Mama Bear Mode was in high gear.

"I have keys for the house. Let's go look over there first. If he's not there, we'll call the police and Mr. Martin."

Renee's eyes said she wanted to call the police now and Sam couldn't blame her, but Sam was more of the mind to look everywhere they could think of first before calling in the authorities. Renee let out an impatient sigh, swallowing again and putting her hand over her mouth. "Alright. Hurry up and get your keys."

Renee was opening the Jeep's passenger side door before Sam could even come to a full stop in front of the abandoned house.

"Brandon!" Renee called immediately, running onto the front lawn and up to the porch. She gripped the knob with both hands and twisted and tugged, but the door held firm. "Brandon, are you over here? Answer me, baby!" Her eyes were wide as she turned towards Sam who was only then reaching edge of the lawn. "I'll check out back."

Sam let her go and went to the door as well. It was just as she and Doug Martin had left it, locked tight. Sam walked around to the back of house. She examined the rest of the decaying structure for any evidence of breaking and entering. There were no signs of jimmied doors or newly broken windows and the few windows she could reach, she checked to make sure they were just as firmly in place as ever. Hadn't Doug said they were nailed shut? Renee's frantic calls echoed through the valley as she headed towards the chicken coop where her son had hidden before.

The bulkhead doors of the cellar were still padlocked. Sam turned back and headed up the steps of the kitchen porch, cupped her hands around her eyes, and squinted through one of the dirt and cobweb-coated panes in the door. Everything looked the same. Except.

Except the air pulsed with a low humming, a buzz, as if a hive of bees had taken up residence in the nearby walls. Stuffing her cold hands into her pockets, Sam stepped back and listened, looking at the walls on either side, unable to determine the direction the sound was coming from. It seemed to surround her on all sides. Movement flickered in the kitchen, a shaft of light faltered. Sam moved in close again and studied the interior. Maybe it was just a bird trapped inside like the dead one that had been upstairs. All the same, some odd compulsion lifted her hand to rap on the door. "Hello? Is there someone in there?" She had the keys. She should just go inside. "Brandon?"

The light shifted inside those four walls and for a scant few seconds Sam stopped breathing. A woman of slight build walked across the floor holding what looked like a pot of coffee. At a table Sam knew very well wasn't there, child-sized figures sat. One was kicking its feet. None of it was solid. It blended perfectly with the reflection of the buildings and fields behind Sam. She opened her mouth to call Renee over and the illusion evaporated. The kitchen was void of everything but the big old cast-iron stove. No table. No chairs. No children. No woman with a coffee pot. No buzzing bees in the walls. Only Renee's reflection as she marched through knee high weeds from the chicken coop to the barn.

"Hold up, Babe," she called and hurried back down the stairs. "Watch out for woodchuck holes!"

Minutes later, they emerged. Renee's face was red with tears and Sam was dialing 9-1-1.

Chapter 27

"I figure it was a good twenty minutes from the time that deer come crashing through to the time I give up looking for the bike," Nigel said. "I'm hoping it's gone way down to the bottom of that drop where nobody is likely to find it for a good long time."

We didn't entirely change the truth about Nigel's missing bike. Everyone knew how crazy the deer were around these parts. Deer been jumping out in front of cars a good many years, probably were jumping in front of the old horse and buggies before that. Why not a bike? Deer are kind of dumb that way and Nigel was always riding his bike into town on errands. All he had to do was show up on Seth's bike and say a deer come barreling out of the woods and knocked him clear off his own bike, ruining it. Folks would believe it.

The story of Nigel's bike passed all well and good, but we all knew the days and nights of Daddy's truck remaining wherever it was Nigel'd left it and Daddy's whereabouts going unquestioned, were numbered.

On April eleventh, just short of three weeks since we fed Daddy Clay's remains to the pigs and in the first weeks of trout season, a sheriff's car pulled up into the driveway. It was one of the first warm and sunny days of spring free of rain, one of those days that makes you glad to be alive when you can smell the earth again and everything seems right with the world.

My last load of washing was being wrung through the wringer while Kate hung what was already done on the line.

"Afternoon, Mary Alice," Officer Webster startled me as he rounded the back corner of the house. "Your father around?"

My heart skipped a beat, but we'd rehearsed this very situation many times over. "No, sir. He went fishing," I replied, barely missing a beat as I guided Nigel's dungarees through the rotating pair of wringers that helped squeeze the water from the heavy fabric.

"First thing this morning, I'm guessing?"

I paused and forced myself to look as calm as could be, "Yes, sir, before it was even sunup. I packed him up a lunch and thermos of coffee and off he went. Something you need me to tell him?"

"Did he say where he was headed?"

I shrugged, "Not specifically, no, sir. Said he found a new spot, down towards Wakefield."

Officer Webster's face crumpled a little. "Nigel around then?"

"Out in the barn." I dropped the pants into the awaiting basket, "Is there something wrong?"

He rubbed at the back of his neck, shaking his head back and forth ever so slowly, "Not sure, Mary Alice, but if you say Clay went fishing, there may be. You sure he didn't come back with someone else? Could he be out in the barn with Nigel?"

I nodded and supposed he could. After all, me and Kate had been busy with laundry the past hour and not paying much attention to who came and went from the barn. Kate and I exchanged glances as Officer Webster turned away and made his way over to the barn. It wasn't a stretch to guess that Daddy's truck had probably been found. We waited, going about the chore of hanging the final load of washing until Nigel and the policeman returned, Seth trailing along behind the two. Everyone looked suitably grim.

I stuffed a clothespin over a shirt tail, pausing as they all drew near. "What's going on?" I asked, looking from one to the other.

"They found Daddy's truck," Nigel said.

I gave a shrug, "So?"

"There's no sign of your father, Mary Alice," the officer answered.

"Well, he went fishing. Why would he be with his truck if he was fishing?"

Officer Webster cleared his throat. "His chair was all set up along the edge of the stream a little ways down, or had been. Fella found it toppled, facedown half into the water. Only thing that kept it from getting washed away was a little sapling the leg got snagged up on."

My hand went to my open mouth. "You think he fell in and drowned?"

The officer gave an uncertain shrug. "River's pretty high. The fella said there are some pretty deep trenches and tricky currents around there. Someone not familiar with the lay of the creek could slip."

I looked to Nigel, my voice trembling. It was no act, at least not all of it. Nigel had been real smart to tell me nothing about what he'd done in any detail. "Daddy's a real strong swimmer. He's always real careful. Maybe he just got washed down a ways and is sitting somewhere on a bank wringing himself out even now. "

"The sheriff's office down there has been notified, just in case, but now that I know for sure he hasn't come home, we'll get an official search team organized. Don't fret too much, Mary Alice. Maybe you're right. Maybe he just took a little spill and has made his way back to his truck already, covered head to toe in creek mud." He chuckled. "I've done that a few times myself, I'm not ashamed to say."

"Oh, I hope you're right. I really do," I said.

"Someone will call when we find something one way or another. Say, you got a picture of Clay we could show around, just in case."

Nigel frowned, "We ain't got too many, but I can find you something. C'mon inside and we'll look."

He followed Nigel in through the back door. Five or ten minutes later, they both come back out, Nigel holding one of the few images we had of Daddy Clay in one hand and a stuffed paper grocery bag rolled down at the top in the other, "I'm going to go down to Wakefield, Mary Alice. Got a clean change of clothes for Daddy and going to help them look."

I nodded. "Yeah, sure, of course. We'll be fine here, but you call, yeah? Soon as you hear anything. Soon as you find Daddy."

"Someone will get in touch with you, Mary. You sure you're alright here by yourself?"

I couldn't help but laugh a little, "Sure, I'm sure. Been chief cook and bottle washer here ever since Mama passed. We'll be fine. Now, you two get going and give me a call with any bit of news."

I scooped Alice up off the porch floor where she'd been playing during all this time. Me, Seth, and Kate followed the men around to the front. Nigel give me a hug, "It'll be alright, Mary. I'm sure we'll find him just fine."

A wan smile twitched at the corners of my mouth. "I'm sure, too," I said. Kate come up beside me and held my hand, giving it a squeeze. I'm sure in the eyes of the law, we looked a pitiful sad and worried bunch. And that's the way we remained as Officer Webster's cruiser started up and backed from the driveway before heading towards the bridge and Wakefield.

Of course, they didn't find nothing. Daddy's body done been eaten up and shit out by the pigs good by then. The bigger bones they didn't eat we'd picked out of the pen, smashed up with a hammer and tossed into the woodstove where they got nice and charred and black. We spread them out with the wood cinders onto the front steps and driveway so folks wouldn't slip on the snow and ice.

The police came and went from the house every day for a solid week. Mrs. Yagar and her youngest son, Lee, come by a few times. Usually bringing things they thought we might need for food. Sometimes just to see how we was holding up.

Mrs. Hayes showed up, too.

"And Kate is what, twelve?" She studied me over the metal line of her glasses as she sipped coffee with cream and sugar.

"Yes, ma'am," I said, bouncing Ali on my knee while she sucked on the arm of her rag doll.

Mrs. Hayes set the cup down on the saucer. "You've been in touch with your uncle, I hope?"

"Yes, ma'am."

"And he's going to help with things?" Her lips were a little too puckered for my liking.

I nodded. "Yes, ma'am, but we can do just fine without. Nigel will be graduating high school come June and will be working full time then. Don't worry, ma'am, we got plenty of money to see us through."

She took a deep breath and sighed it out slowly, "The money isn't what concerns me, Mary Alice. Seth and Kate are underage and have no legal guardian according to the law."

"I can take care of them just fine, ma'am. Been doing it since I was Kate's age, since Mama passed."

Her smile was as fake as the day was long. "Of course you can, Mary Alice. I have no doubt, but it's the court and judge that will need to be convinced of that, not me. And with your baby's difficulties on top of that ..."

My temper flared, "I'm twenty years old, Mrs. Hayes. I can take care of my little one just fine. I can take care of my brothers and sister, too. You ain't got no right to take them from me, none at all."

"And I don't want to," her words said, but her eyes, oh those holier-than-thou eyes of hers told me something completely different.

It was like they was wolves in the bushes and she was the alpha female, waiting all this while to circle us together and pounce. There wasn't no reasoning with them, no explaining that things then was the best they'd ever been for us on Dark Hollow Road. They didn't want to hear. They wanted to do what Mrs. Hayes kept calling in the best interests of the children. Problem was, Child Protective Services didn't know anything about us or our ways. Daddy being gone was a blessing.

Our final hope rested on the shoulders of Uncle Eli. Mrs. Hayes had called him and set up a family meeting the first Saturday of May. He was all we had left. The day he pulled into our driveway in a big, old, white Mercury, just like a knight riding in on his white horse, we was certain was the day of our salvation.

"Mr. Gunderman," Mrs. Hayes rushed forward, hand at arm's length before any of us could so much as flinch. "I'm Mrs. Hayes, the social worker. So pleased to finally meet you."

He shook her hand, but the smile on his face was anything but warm and eager. "Nice to meet you, too, Mrs. Hayes." Uncle Eli looked almost exactly the way I remembered him, tall and thin, what Mama called willowy and Daddy called queer, with big brown eyes and hair trimmed short. It was oiled and combed neat as a pin. His pale-brown suit didn't have a fleck of dirt on it, and the narrow, brown tie he wore was smooth and straight as a freshly ironed pillowcase. He wore a pair of them Oxford shoes like you saw lawyers and gangsters wearing in the movies. They were brown and white and shiny new. A gold wedding band shined on his left hand.

Mrs. Hayes scanned him up and down with an approving eye. "How was the drive up?"

"Fine," he said, turning slightly away from her and towards me and my siblings. "Nigel, you've shot up a good foot since I last saw you and Mary Alice, oh, you do look the spitting image of little sister." He reached out and took little Alice's hand, "And this must be the one I've heard about, Baby Alice. What a doll."

Nigel shook his hand while I gave him a one-armed hug. "It's been a long time, Uncle Eli," I said.

"Too long, but life gets away from us sometimes, doesn't it?" He gave me an odd sort of wink.

"Sure does," I hefted Alice up onto my hip a bit more.

Uncle Eli turned towards the two others, "Seth and Katie Sue, I just can't believe it. You're practically all grown up. Time has raced away from me and I apologize for staying away so long." He gave them both big hugs before turning back to Mrs. Hayes who didn't look happy about having been kept waiting during our little family reunion.

"You're here now, Uncle Eli," Nigel stepped up. "That's what counts."

"Indeed, I am. Now," he rubbed his hands together and gazed at the social worker with an intensity that would have sent me crouching in the corner, "Let's get down to business, shall we?"

"I made some iced tea and sandwiches, Uncle Eli. I thought you might be hungry after the long drive."

"That I am, Mary Alice. What's on the menu?"

I blushed as he wrapped an arm around my shoulder just like he used to do when we were all so much younger. "Just sandwiches. Ain't nothing fancy as I suppose you're used to."

He laughed, "There's a lot to be said about good old home cooking, Mary, even humble sandwiches."

It all looked normal enough, us all sitting down to the table with paper plates and napkins with a pile of tuna fish sandwiches sitting in the middle and glasses of iced tea all around. A breeze came in from the open kitchen door, rustling our napkins.

Uncle Eli put his on his lap. "You brought all the paperwork?" he asked Mrs. Hayes, casual as you please and with no more feeling than if he'd asked her to pass the mustard.

She gave him a curt nod that I didn't like one bit. "In my briefcase, but I thought it best we talk before going any further with that."

"Of course." Smiling, as he reached for a sandwich. "Things are going to be a lot easier for you after today, kids. I promise."

Finally, after all these years, maybe we could all rest easy again.

Chapter 28

He didn't want to play with them, but if he didn't they'd keep bugging him. He'd tried a long time to ignore the calls from below followed by the tink-tink of little pebbles being thrown at his closed bedroom window.

Brandon stomped over to the window and yanked the curtains open. All three stood along the edge of the cornfield with Allan a few steps in front of the two girls. He waved and motioned for Brandon to come down. Brandon shook his head. He mouthed the words, "GO A-WAY." Yelling them would wake people up.

The older boy didn't move. He stood there, looking up, waiting, and smiling. "One game!" he shouted up.

The window didn't open very easily, but Brandon managed to get it about halfway. It was enough. "Go away," he insisted. "I don't want to play. I'll get in trouble."

Allan held up a finger. "One game," he repeated. "Just one game. C'mon. It's Halloween night. Everyone plays outside on Halloween night."

The boy looked out across the tops of the shifting stalks of corn and sighed, "You'll leave me alone if I play just one game?"

Allan nodded. The older girl, holding onto the hand of the youngest, smiled but didn't say anything. "We'll wait here," Allan said.

Brandon shoved the window down, but it stuck and wouldn't go any further. Leave it, he thought. He'd close it when he came back. Brandon stuffed his feet into his slippers, tugged on his robe, and grabbed his Bob The Builder flashlight, tucking it into his pocket next to the little green Army Guy he'd forgotten was in there and tiptoed down the stairs.

As promised, Allan was waiting. Brandon squeezed out the back door. "I better not get into trouble," he told the other boy.

"You won't," Allan said. "C'mon," he took Brandon's hand, tugging him towards the rows of uncut corn. The two girls were already heading into the field. Within a few paces Brandon had lost complete sight of them. "Ginny's gonna be it. I'll show you the best place to hide. No one will ever find you there."

Brandon turned on his flashlight. His heart pounded like a frantic rabbit's as he followed Allan into the tall, rustling stalks of corn. Allan moved with sure and steady strides, changing rows as they went deeper. Bob The Builder's light struggled to keep up, bouncing from the center of Allan's back to the thin, cutting, snapping blades of pale-brown corn leaves that seemed to want nothing more than to reach out and draw little red lines against Brandon's face and the back of his hands. The slits stung, but Brandon didn't dare stop to check. Allan was getting further ahead with each step

"Hey, slow down," Brandon panted after him. Allan changed rows again. Brandon couldn't even tell where they were now. All he could see was corn on all sides, a big, star-filled sky above, and the figure of

Allan moving faster and growing small until Bob the Builder's light no longer illuminated the other boy's back at all. "Allan! Wait up!" Brandon started to run, not sure where to go, when to change rows, when to stay on the straight and narrow.

The ground suddenly rose up and sent Brandon sprawling flat on his face. The flashlight flew, landed, and spun with a flicker but didn't go out. Pain throbbed through Brandon's big toe. He'd tripped. He crawled to the flashlight, grabbed it with both hands, and shown it back the way he'd come. A rock about the size of one of Mama Sam's boots stuck up out of the hard-packed ground.

Brandon turned in place. "Allan! Where you are?"

A soft fluttering of dry corn leaves and fall crickets replied.

"ALLAN!"

Something moved to Brandon's right. "Allan?" he asked more softly, fear creeping up the back of his throat and making his voice squeak. Bob's light wasn't helping at all. In fact, it was making it worse by fading off into the pitch black of what felt like an endless field of tall, thin aliens with razors for arms just waiting to bite him.

"Here," came a distant voice.

Brandon turned and ran towards the sound.

The field snapped away behind him. The ground dipped suddenly. Brandon flew through the air for a second time, sprawling like a broken scarecrow to his side as Allen watched from the middle of a familiar dirt road, his hands resting on his hips, and his lips turned up into an impish grin. "Gotcha," he said and snickered.

Anger fired through the six-year-old's brain as he hauled himself back to his feet. "That wasn't funny! I don't want to play, anymore. Take me home!"

Allan stopped laughing and sighed, "Look, I'm sorry. It was a joke. It's Hide-and-Seek, right? It was a test. That's all." He held out his hand. "C'mon."

Brandon dusted himself off and looked to get his bearings. "But this is ..."

Allan ignored him. He was turning around and heading to the other side of the road where the older girl smiled and still said nothing before turning away. "What you gawking at?" Allan paused by what had once been a driveway. "It's just an old house. We play here all the time. Ginny's going to start counting soon and she only counts to fifty so we gotta hurry."

The dark windows glared down at him under heavy wooden brows as Brandon followed. Blank walls of warped cardboard covered the front windows. It didn't take much for him to imagine someone standing behind those things, watching through the cracks. He tried hard not to listen or see anything as Allan led him around to the back porch.

It wasn't so dark back here. Dim light streamed from the kitchen windows, illuminated by a single bulb that dangled from the center of the room. A woman stood with her back to the door slicing a loaf of bread. Brandon had no doubt who that pale blue dress and ratty sweater belonged to. "It's her," he said, unable to speak any louder than a breathless whisper.

Ginny, eyes covered, leaned with her face towards a post. "Fifteen, sixteen, seventeen, eighteen ..."

"Who?"

"The Sugar Lady," he answered, not sure if he should be scared or not. The other three kids didn't act like they were afraid at all.

Twirling a long strand of hair around her index finger, the smallest child sat on the stoop. She was far too young to be running off to hide by herself.

"Nineteen, twenty, twenty-one …" Ginny counted.

Allan shook his head as if he didn't understand. Maybe, like Mommy and Mama Sam, they didn't see the lady at all. "We need to go hide," Allan urged. "C'mon." Brandon's hand was grabbed again and he was towed across the yard. If Brandon didn't know better, he'd have sworn he heard chickens clucking and rustling in the coop as they passed it by. But he knew it was empty. Or it had been. But so had the kitchen.

Allan was making a beeline towards the yawning black mouth of the open barn door.

Ginny's voice drifted on the cold breeze, "Twenty-nine, thirty, thirty-one," as Brandon was swallowed up by the barn's brutal darkness. His hand clamped, bone white, around the flashlight. Its meager beam offered little comfort as Allan pulled him deeper.

"In here," the older boy's voice whispered from the depth. In front of them stood a large, wooden box with a sloped lid. Its old hinges gave out a squeaky protest as Allan opened the top. "You're gonna have to climb in. It's the best place. Ginny never looks here."

He didn't want to go. It smelled like animal poop and corn and oatmeal and it all seemed to stick to the back of his throat. "Allan, I don't …"

"Sshhh… she's almost done counting. Just get in there. I still need to go hide."

"Thirty-seven, thirty-eight, thirty-nine, Forty!"

Allan half-lifted, half-shoved Brandon over the waist-high wall then pushed him on top of the head.

"Keep your head down and turn sideways," Allan instructed in a whisper.

"What is this?"

"Just an old feed box. It's kinda small, but if I fit, you should, too. I'm gonna close the lid. Just keep your head down so I don't bonk you."

Brandon was too scared to do anything but follow directions. He shifted to sit on his bottom, crossed-legged and shivering. Bob the Builder's light shuddered on a dark and stained wooden wall not three feet in front of him. He could no longer hear Ginny counting. He couldn't hear anything but his own ragged breathing and heart pounding in his head.

He'd make noise, he decided. He'd make noise on purpose so Ginny would find him quick and he could be done and he could be back home in his own bed and this would be over with. He'd drop the flashlight, no. No, better not do that. It might go out and that would only make things worse. He'd thump his elbow or knee against the side of this little box. That was a good plan. All he had to do was wait and listen for her footsteps.

Brandon shivered and tucked one hand into the pocket of his bathrobe. His fingers brushed over a tiny, plastic figurine. He had Army Guy, too. That was good. Army Guy wouldn't let anything hurt him. His fingers curled around the toy and squeezed it tight, scrunching his eyes closed at the same time. Any minute now and he'd hear Ginny.

Any minute now and he'd be free.

Three patrol cars, one K-9 unit, an ambulance, and Doug Martin's pickup had joined Sam's Jeep in front of the empty house. As she sat on the top step of the kitchen porch stoop, Renee's mind reeled. This couldn't be happening. This happened to other people, to strangers, to people on television, in movies, not to her. Where was her baby? She clutched the yellow flashlight between her clenched fingers. Bob the Builder smiled and waved up at her. Her tears wouldn't stop.

"Where is he, Bob?" she asked the cartoon figure.

The dogs had found and followed Brandon's scent through the cornfield and into the barn but then they'd stopped. The officer couldn't explain it. It was as if the trail had suddenly vanished at an old feed box that still smelled faintly of the corn and grains it had once housed. The yellow flashlight had lain on the floor beside this box, its battery dead. And that's where the dogs lost the scent.

The only other explanation they could conceive was that someone had picked Brandon up and carried him from that point. If that was the case, they were looking at a kidnapping and not just a lost child. Renee had told them about the previous night and the knockings that had terrified her and seeing a light over here. Someone had been here. She was certain of it now, even though the police had found no evidence that anyone had broken into the old house, Renee had seen a light. Someone had taken her son.

Fresh tears slid down her face. Her throbbing head felt stuffed with soggy moss. Her eyes burned. She rubbed a thumb over Bob's chest, staring at his happy, little face. "Yes, we can," was printed in black under his feet.

Someone sat down and put an arm around her.

"We'll find him." Sam's hold tightened as Renee felt a tender kiss on the side of her head.

Bob's face blurred. Renee's mouth would not connect with her brain. She stroked Bob's round cheek with her thumb.

"I told them about The Sugar Lady and the kids Brandon said he'd been playing with. They're already calling in more help to go door to door. We'll find him."

"Yes, we can," Renee thought. Somehow those three little words gave her just enough hope to stop crying. Renee leaned into her partner's arms and sighed. "It was her," she said.

"The Sugar Lady? You really think so?"

Renee nodded. "I don't know how I know, but I know. Mother's intuition, maybe."

Sam sat up a little straighter. A thoughtful hum vibrated against Renee's inclined head. "I don't think Bee would have gone with her. He was afraid of her," she said. "He walked over here alone," she continued. "They found his tracks in the cornfield and only his tracks. The ground was pretty soft in spots. If someone had been with him, they'd have left tracks, too."

She wiped her eyes with the cuff of her sweatshirt as she straightened. "Sleepwalking?"

Sam gave her hand a reassuring squeeze. "Yeah. I think so. And she, The Sugar Lady, was here. Maybe she sleeps here or something."

"There wasn't any evidence of anyone staying in the barn or anything."

"No, but let's say she was and Brandon wandered in, sleeping, not knowing or seeing anything really. She saw him and picked him up and carried him to wherever it is she really lives. That's why the scent trail suddenly stops. And that's where he is now."

Renee pulled her gaze away from Bob's yellow hardhat and stared at the gnarled, apple-laden trees beyond the chicken coop instead. "But why wouldn't she bring him back home? She knows where we live. She must know we'd freak out when we found him

274

missing." The urge to cry threatened to rise up and take control of her again. Renee bit into her tongue just enough to shove the sensation away.

"She's not right in the head," Sam said. It wasn't what Renee wanted to hear, but it probably wasn't far from the truth and it wasn't like the idea hadn't occurred to her. "Even if you and I have never seen her, I'm pretty sure she's real, I mean, she did bring that jar over. It makes the most sense."

"We just need to find out who and where she is."

"We've got half the county police and the state troopers out looking for both of them, Babe, and those kids. They must belong to her. They can't be too far away if they're within walking distance. We'll find her and when we do, we'll find Brandon."

Renee gave a nod. Sam was right. They couldn't be very far away.

Not far away at all.

Chapter 29

We ate, talked about school and work, baby Alice, and the garden I was planning for that year. It was all real nice, even though Mrs. Hayes seemed like she had ants in her pants. She kept looking at Uncle Eli until finally he put down his empty glass of iced tea and took a deep breath.

"I'm sure you both know this is pretty serious?" he looked at me and Nigel.

"Yes, sir," Nigel said acting every bit like the man of the house.

"Mrs. Hayes and I have talked this over a great deal, and we think we've come up with a solution that will satisfy everyone. It's not going to be easy, but it's what we think will please the court. I'd like Seth and Kate to come live with me until they are of age."

My mouth dropped open and I must have made a sound, because Uncle Eli held up his hand. Nigel started to protest, too.

"Hear me out," Uncle Eli went on. "We're hoping nothing will have to change until the school year is out. The court will want an appointed guardian that has all the resources and qualification to be a guardian. My wife and I have that. We have no children of our own, we have plenty of money, space, and time to take two children in, especially my own nephew and niece. It will pose no hardship on us whatsoever. I know Mary and Nigel are more than capable. However, if we let this go before a judge he may not see it that way. You risk having them sent off to foster care. If that happens, they may get separated. You'll lose contact with them until they are of age. I know you don't want that to happen."

I could hardly breathe as he talked. I tried to listen and understand and hoped Nigel was taking it in better than I was. His eyes were narrowed and his face was getting red, but he didn't say anything.

"If you let them come with me, I'd have no problem bringing them up here one weekend a month and over the school breaks. Certainly, I'd have no problem letting them spend the summer months here. You could write, call and visit any time you want. Foster care won't let you do that. Lastly," he said, studying us a second before he went on. "I'm willing to provide the three of you with a steady monthly income. Nigel would still have to work as it won't be a lot, but it will be enough for you to get along on and be sure and keep your bills paid."

"It's a very generous offer your uncle is making, Nigel and Mary," Mrs. Hayes added. "I'd strongly suggest you take him up on it. If we have your cooperation, this could all work out very well for everyone. If we don't, then we more or less leave it all in the hands of a judge and total stranger."

"What do you think?" Uncle Eli looked around the table.

I looked around the table, too. It was then I realized that this wasn't just my decision. I'd always had the loudest voice on the matter without really thinking what my brothers and sister would want. I saw an uncomfortable eagerness in Kate's eyes that I didn't care for. "Can we talk about it between us first?" I asked, shifting my gaze to Seth who sat there with his arms crossed and a furious scowl on his face.

Mrs. Hayes and our uncle both nodded. "Of course," they said as if they'd rehearsed this whole thing.

It was Mrs. Hayes who added, "I can give you until Friday morning. You're planning on staying around awhile, aren't you, Mr. Gunderman?"

Uncle Eli's lips shrank to a narrow line as he nodded, "Yes. I've rented a motel room in Tunkhannock for the rest of the week, though I'd like to spend as much time here as I'm allowed." It was his way of asking if he was still welcome. I wasn't so sure about that now.

I wanted to leave the table and drag my siblings with me, but it was best I held myself together until these two people, who thought they knew better than me, were out of here.

"We'll have to talk about it," Nigel spoke up. His face wasn't quite so red now. That was good. Nobody was going to get punched in the face, for a while, anyway.

Uncle Eli shoved his chair back and stood. "Good. It's best you do." He smiled. "Mrs. Hayes, I think we're done here for now."

"I think you're right." She wasn't looking any happier than the rest of us as she gathered up her purse and unopened briefcase. "You can call me any time you want, Mary or Nigel, with any questions at all."

"And here's the number for the motel I'm at. I'm in room twelve." He handed Nigel a white business card with a number written on the back.

My brother took it without a word.

"You gonna come to supper, Uncle Eli?" Kate piped up. "Me and Mary make supper together every night. What do you like best?"

Our uncle smiled as he turned towards Kate, gathering both her hands into his. "I'd love to come to supper, but that's up to Mary Alice."

She looked up at me with pleading eyes. "Can he, please, Mary? Can he?"

Despite wanting to spit in my uncle's face, I couldn't turn down Kate. "Chicken and biscuits on Wednesday?"

"That sounds great. Thank you."

"We eat at six-thirty," I added, heading towards the door to hurry them on their way.

"I'll be here."

I hadn't seen my little sister smile so big in a very long time. Without her having said a word, I had a feeling I already knew what she wanted to do about this whole situation. All the way out to his car, Kate practically skipped while swinging their hands between them. She pouted, looking more like she was two than twelve, as she waved. "Bye! See you Wednesday!" she shouted after the white Mercury.

"See you Wednesday," Uncle Eli shouted back and tapped his horn twice before rolling up the window.

Nigel came up beside me and put an arm around my tense shoulders. "We got a lot to think and talk about," he said as we both stood there watching the two vehicles grow smaller and smaller.

"It ain't right what they're doing to us," I said. "It just ain't fair."

Nigel sighed. "I know it ain't, but we got to make a decision.

I studied my brother's profile. He'd grown up so much the past couple years and he was a good four inches taller than me. He was real handsome and I could see how Mama must have seen Daddy back in the day. I put my free arm around his waist. "I know," I said with a sickening dread in my stomach.

Dressed in a long white nightgown and sitting in the middle of her bed, hugging her knees that were drawn up to her chest, Kate watched me brush out my hair. Her own hairbrush rested forgotten beside her on the bed. "Why can't we all go live with Uncle Eli?"

I stopped in mid-stroke, looking at her face reflected in the small, free-standing mirror I'd put on Mama's old dressing table. Seth and Nigel had moved it into the room Kate and I still shared shortly after Daddy had met up with the pigs. "I reckon he ain't got room for us all."

"I wish he did."

I went back to brushing my hair. I didn't want to talk about it. I didn't want any of us to go anywhere. Why did Mrs. Hayes and Uncle Eli think the only choices were to make Kate and Seth live somewhere else? If Uncle Eli wanted to really help and if money was the only issue, why not just give us a more generous monthly allowance? If we had the money to pay the bills and fix the place up, then Social Services wouldn't have no reason to split us up, right? Both me and Nigel was of age. Why couldn't we be made the legal guardians of our own siblings? "Ain't nobody going nowhere until we get more questions answered."

She scowled. "What if I want to go, Mary Alice?"

The hand that held the brush lowered to my lap as I turned around to face her. "Do you?"

Dark Hollow Road

Guilt settled on her face, but she nodded all the same. She knew better than to lie to me. "I don't like it here, Mary. I don't like not having pretty things. I don't like the way everyone stares at me when I go into town, whispering behind their hands, or how kids at school pick on me. I don't like being poor." The corners of her mouth had drawn down and her chin was starting to tremble. "Everything here reminds me of Daddy." A sob caught in her throat. "I hate him with all my heart and I'm glad he's dead." The tears came out in a flood.

Before I could even think about it, I was sitting there on the bed beside her, holding her and rocking her and telling her that I did understand. I knew what he'd done to her, to all of us, and I hated him, too. "He can't hurt us no more, Katie Sue. The hogs took care of that."

She clung to me and cried. It was a sobbing that come from deep down inside her where Mama lay dying and Daddy stood by your bedside in the middle of the night looking at you then making you do things with him you knew was wrong. It was a cry that made your soul dark and bitter and miserable. It had been all building up inside her all those years and I cried with her. Not just about those things but being twelve-years-old and not having anything pretty to wear and hating to go to school because people would laugh at you and being afraid to come home even more because that's where even worse things happened.

At twelve I'd longed for just one person to tell me I was pretty even if I didn't believe it then or now. I dreamed of going into a store, a big store, and buying a dress and matching shoes. The fantasies of being popular and well-liked and to never hear the snicker behind my back when I passed were sometimes the only things that made life on Dark Hollow Road bearable. I'd hoped against hope that Richard and Elmer were really and truly being nice to me because they liked me. In the end, only Larry had shown me a kindness I never forgot.

And now, after all of Katie's life living the exact same way, going to live with Uncle Eli was a promise of starting all over again, where nothing reminded you of your nightmares or the monster in the bed that had your father's face. I understood and didn't like what Katie's tears made me know I wouldn't force her to stay when there was a way out.

Eventually the gut-wrenching sobs eased. The shaking stopped. Her shoulders eased down and her head grew heavier against my shoulder as exhaustion took the place of the black demons of the past that had just been, at least in part, exorcised.

I stroked her hair that was still wet from the bath she'd taken earlier. "You want some hot tea?" I whispered.

The slumped head that rested against my nightdress nodded. She sat up, eyes red and puffy and bloodshot. "I'm sorry."

"Ain't nothing to be sorry for. If you want to go live with Uncle Eli, I ain't gonna stop you."

She swallowed and I thought maybe she was going to start crying again. Instead she leaned over and reached for the box of tissues.

"I'll go get the kettle on. We'll have our tea up here like we used to when we were little. Remember? And, unless one of the boys has found and eaten them, I got a box of shortbread cookies hidden in the cupboard. It'll be like a little tea party. You get your hair brushed out."

She smiled and I kissed her again.

By the time we had our tea and cookies, Katie was feeling much better. The same could not be said of me. As much as I understood, my heart was still breaking.

"Y'ain't mad at me, are you?" My little sister whispered in the dark after lights out.

"No. I ain't mad."

She was quiet then, "Do you think Nigel will be mad?"

"No, I don't think so." I turned my head to look out the window at the sky full of stars beyond. Tears trickled to my pillow. "We want you to be happy. If that means you going to live with Uncle Eli for a few years, well, that's what will happen."

"Ain't like you won't never see me again." I could hear the hope and relief in her sleepy voice. If this had all happened back when I was her age, I'd have jumped at the chance to escape, too. Things would have been a whole lot different. I'd not have been raped ever again by anyone. A soft yawn came from Kate's side of the room. I shut my eyes and tried to sleep.

.

Chapter 30

Helicopters crisscrossed the sky. Dogs howled and barked in the deep woods and across acres of farmland. Boats putted downstream as well as up. Dozens of men, some in uniform, most in jeans, boots, and everyday jackets, scoured miles of roads and creek sides. Even horses clomped through the dying brown patches of the Endless Mountains that men on foot could not have passed through with as much ease. Over the course of the weekend, every house, farm, hunter's cabin, and campground was searched.

Brandon's picture was posted on the afternoon and evening news. Sam and Renee were interviewed and shown pleading their misery to the public, begging to whomever had taken the boy to please, please return him, to not hurt him, to somehow let his parents know he was safe. Amber Alerts went out.

The sun set and soon it was too dark to safely search. For the second time, Renee and Sam were told the search would start at first light the next day. For a second night, two officers in a police cruiser remained in front of the house down on Dark Hollow Road. Another sat parked at the end of Sam and Renee's driveway.

Dark Hollow Road

"Turn it off, Sam," If Renee had to see and hear herself sobbing on television one more time, she was going to go mad.

The television blinked out and went silent letting the soft rustling sound of hedges flapping against siding into the living room instead. The wind was picking up. Rain was in the forecast for the overnight. Renee's stomach felt hard and sour, as if, at any moment, she was about the throw up what little she'd put into it. Brandon was out there somewhere. Possibly alone. Certainly afraid. Was he warm and dry? Was he safe? Her head felt tight and swollen in her skull as it pounded through her bloodshot and burning eyes.

"We should try and get some sleep," Sam suggested gently beside her.

"I don't want to sleep," Renee murmured through the heavy fog. She knew she should. Her body and her mind were begging to escape. "I'm already sleeping. I'm going to wake up soon. It's going to be Saturday morning again, only this time it's going to be real. You're going to go upstairs and get Brandon for breakfast. He's going to come down with you. We're going to have scrambled eggs and bacon and French toast together and …"

"Renee, don't." Sam pulled her closer.

On any other night, Renee would have nudged her partner away. Tonight, she lacked the strength. She sank against Sam's shoulder, allowing herself to be held and rocked. It felt good to close her eyes even if those eyes were once more weeping. The hole in her heart ached to be filled, to hold Brandon as she was being held now. That's all she wanted to do, hold her little boy and bury her nose in his hair. She wanted to feel his little arms around her and hear his voice say, "I love you, Mommy." She'd not even care if he got peanut butter and jelly on her best sweater or tracked dirt and fresh cut grass across the kitchen floor she'd just mopped. "Oh, Brandon," the sob could not be contained. "Where are you, baby?"

The deepest darkness of her despair swallowed Renee whole and she didn't care if she ever saw the light of day again. Without her son, she didn't want to live.

Sam leaned over to kiss Renee on the forehead. Hot tea with a little help from two crushed up sleeping pills had finally let Renee do what was needed most. Sam wasn't proud of what she'd done, but she knew how important sleep was in times like these. Renee never would have taken them on her own, but she would drink some chamomile tea. They were helpless and repeatedly saying, "We'll find him," wasn't doing any good, now. Sam wondered who she was trying to convince more, herself or her partner.

Very much against her will, Sam forced Renee to leave the house Monday morning. The authorities had their cell phone numbers and Sam called the station to let them know where they'd be. "You need to get out of the house, Babe. Working on the shop will relax you."

"I don't want to relax," she protested. "I need to be home for Brandon. What if he comes back and we're not here and the doors are all locked?"

Sam sighed. She was tired, too. Renee kept forgetting that Sam cared just as much about Brandon as she did. Brandon may not be Sam's flesh and blood son, but the two were very close. "I told the officer at the station we'd be gone a few hours. They told me the next shift of officers was already on their way. They want to catch whoever took Bee, too, hon. You need to step away before you have a nervous breakdown. We'll get breakfast out."

Renee could barely stand the thought of leaving but agreed.

And instantly regretted it the moment they walked into Kelley's Diner for breakfast.

The place had been humming with chitchat and laughter, but as soon as they walked in, the conversations fell off and people squirmed restlessly in their seats. The whole town knew what was going on. A lot of them were part of the search teams. Renee's body stiffened, ready to flee. Sam's hand grazed her elbow. "Relax. You can do this," her partner whispered at her side.

"Morning, folks. Take a seat anywhere. I'll be right with you," Janet chirped from across the room as she refilled a patron's depleted cup of coffee.

They found an empty corner booth and slid in on opposite sides of the table. Normally Renee would have wanted the seat facing the room. Today, she wanted nothing to do with looking at anyone.

Janet slid two breakfast menus in front of them with cutlery neatly rolled up into a white paper napkin. "What can I get you to drink?"

"Coffee," Sam answered.

"What about you, hon?" Janet's voice had lowered, taking on a caring, tender softness that nearly brought more tears to Renee's eyes.

"Coffee, please."

The waitress let her hand rest a moment on Renee's shoulder and gave it a reassuring pat. "Two coffees, coming up."

Diner chat began to fill the void again and with it Renee's ability to breathe. She wasn't hungry, but if she didn't order something Sam would read her the riot act. You can't be strong for Brandon by starving yourself to death, she'd say. Sam didn't understand. She didn't know what it felt like to have part of your body, your very heart and soul, yanked out of your chest and up through your throat.

Janet appeared with their coffee. "Have you decided?"

Sam ordered her usual lumberjack breakfast as if all was right with the world.

"I'll have an English muffin and a scrambled egg." Renee doubted she'd even be able to eat all of that.

"I'll put that right in for you."

A well-dressed couple at a nearby table rose and put on their coats. They were probably commuters heading into Scranton for work. Sam should be going to work again, too, Renee realized, but the idea filled her with even more dread. She'd be home alone, dwelling on the fact that Brandon was not safely in school with his friends.

"I can't do this, Sam," Renee's whole body felt on pins and needles. "I have to get out of here. I need to go back home. I need to be home if Brandon comes."

Sam's hands reached out and held hers. "They will call if they find him. Take a deep breath and relax."

"I can't. I just can't."

"Yes, you can. It will only be for a couple hours, but you can do this."

"Told ya not to take anything from that place," Lee Yagar glared over the steam that rose from his cup of coffee. "Mary don't like when ya take things from her house."

"Lee, don't be a fool," the waitress snapped. "Mary Brown's dead."

He turned a baleful eye towards Janet. "Is she? Just because a person ain't been seen in a long time, don't mean they's dead."

The waitress huffed, "Well, even if she isn't dead, she's not around here, anymore."

Renee turned, her anger mixing with raging curiosity, as she studied Lee's face. He was a sour, old man. Deep and permanent scowls marked his brow between wild, white eyebrows that stood out over watery blue eyes. "Mr. Yagar, what makes you say Mary isn't dead?" For a moment, the eyes that everyone saw as angry appeared sad to Renee. No, she thought, not sad, haunted. It was something worse than cancer. Cancer ate away at your body. Whatever Lee had inside him, it was eating into his soul.

He shook his head and the weird sense of sorrow seemed to be shaken away with it. "Nothing. Don't listen to me," he grunted. "Get my tab ready will ya, Janet?" He rose from the stool, fished out his battered wallet, and tossed a couple dollars on the counter before shuffling towards the register on the opposite end.

"We didn't take anything from that house," Sam said.

Renee didn't think Lee was going to answer. He acted as if he hadn't even heard as he paid for his meal and stuffed the wallet away once more. "Then your boy did," he said.

Silence clung heavy and sour over the room as Lee made his way out. The little bell jangled as the door closed behind him.

Renee turned her back to the room again.

"What is it?" Sam was looking at her.

She shrugged a little, realizing she must have a very peculiar look on her face. "I'm not sure. I think he's hiding something."

Sam looked towards Lee's truck as it backed out of its spot. "Like what?"

"I don't know."

Sam scowled. "You think he knows who took Brandon and where he is?"

Renee simply could not put her finger on it and sighed. "I don't know," she repeated. "I don't think that's it, but there's ... maybe I'm just overtired."

Janet carried over a tray and set Renee's small order down in front of her. "Don't let Lee upset you, folks. He's one of them people that seems to think he needs to make everyone as miserable as he is."

"Why is he so miserable?" Renee asked.

Janet shrugged. "He's been that way since his brother was killed. They were real close. Larry had a bad car wreck just before Christmas back in '65. He was at Larry's bedside when he passed. Just the two of them." She shook her head again. "Shame."

"What's the connection between Lee and the Brown family?" Sam added a single packet of sugar to her coffee.

"That, I don't know, other than they were the Brown's nearest neighbors. We didn't move here until 1970, so anything before that I don't know much about."

Renee thought about the other houses that were nearby. There weren't many. "Neighbors? You're saying that the Yagar farm was the closest house? That's a good five miles away."

"That's what I'm saying. All the other boys married and got their own places. Lee's the youngest, other than Lisa. When their mom passed, he took over the place.'

That flash of haunted sadness on Lee's face rose up in Renee's mind again. She'd seen that same look on her own face over the past two days. For her it was the terrible fear and grief that she'd never see her son alive again. Maybe there had been something between Lee and Mary. He's quick to defend her and warn people away from the house. Maybe Sam was right; maybe Lee knew where Brandon was. It would also explain why he seemed to be saying that Mary was still alive.

"You said Lee is the youngest. Are any of his brothers still around?"

Janet thought about that for a minute. "I don't think so." A sharp bell rang out from the direction of the kitchen, "Order up!"

"Got to get that," Janet said. "I'm so sorry to hear about your little boy, but you've got to trust the authorities are doing all they can to find him and that he'll be back in your arms real soon."

Renee's heart suddenly sank as reality crashed down on her head again. Sam's hand reached out and covered that of her partner. "We're doing the best we can," Sam answered for the both of them.

"Thank you," Renee held back the sob lodged in her throat. She stared hard at the plate, narrowing her focus on what they'd just learned and the hope it contained instead of the nightmare scenarios that hadn't left her head since Saturday morning.

Sam's hand squeezed hers. "They are going to find him, Babe."

Renee dabbed her eyes with the napkin and blew her nose on the same before she could speak again. "We need to talk to Lee Yagar," she said so only Sam could hear. "Either him or his brother. There's something going on here that people aren't saying." She chanced a look up at Sam.

"Or don't know about." Relief settled on Renee's shoulders as Sam nodded in agreement.

"Lee knows," Renee picked up a packet of butter.

Chapter 31

I went through the motions helping make dinner for Uncle Eli. Kate did most of the work. She was excited. She knew she was going to leave in less than two months. Though Seth said he was less than thrilled, there was something in the way he protested that told me he wanted to go, too. I can't even tell you how horrible and lonely I was already starting to feel. They weren't just my brother and sister, but my own flesh and blood kids and I loved them the same way I loved Ali.

Feeling betrayed and angry, I watched Kate setting the table with the greatest care. She'd put on a fresh tablecloth and got down our best plates and sorted through trying to make as much of the silverware match as possible. I was half-tempted to add something nasty to the chicken gravy, but it was our meal, too. Instead, I rolled out the biscuit dough to have them ready to pop in the oven the moment our uncle arrived.

His car pulled in at exactly six o'clock.

The way Kate fawned over him twisted my stomach. At the end of the meal when she and I were clearing plates and getting ready to serve up the coffee, I realized why. It was the same way Mama had treated Daddy. It reminded me of everything we'd lost. Kate had been so young; there was no way she could have remembered much of anything from those day. Yet, there she was acting just the way Mama had.

"That was delicious," Uncle Eli said as I poured coffee into the special China cups Kate insisted we use.

"Kate did most of it," I confessed.

He grinned. "Well, you'll have to teach my wife the secret of your gravy, Katie Sue. Hers is always full of lumps." He took a sip from his coffee.

"Ain't nothing to it," Katie said. "Mary taught me."

"And Mama taught me," I added.

"And someone needs to teach Lily." He laughed as he leaned back looking full and satisfied. There wasn't a care in the world to him. He got what he come for. He got his belly stuffed and he got two of the people I loved most in the world to agree to come live with him. "She's a great lady, my Lily, but cooking's something she's never quite mastered."

After setting the stack of dessert plates down, Katie returned to her seat beside our uncle, all doe-eyed and swooning. I brought over the pie, still warm from the oven. I wasn't about to even pretend I was happy about any of this. "Uncle Eli, where you been all these years? Why'd you stop writing and coming for Christmas?" I poured Nigel's cup of coffee first, despite knowing perfectly well I should have given that honor to my uncle.

"I did write," he said. Kate set a piece of pie in front of him.

"We ain't seen a letter or card from you since after Mama's died," I pressed.

"But I did write. I sent you all birthday and a Christmas cards every year." Uncle Eli scowled deep and long. I believed him though I damned sure didn't want to, him being the bad guy and all.

"We never got anything," I replied and finally sat back down again to my own slice of pie and cup of coffee.

Nigel's lips were tight and pursed. "Daddy Clay," he grumbled. "I bet that son of a bitch got to them first." Nigel spoke that last part before I think he realized what was coming out of his mouth. His gaze darted towards Uncle Eli.

Our uncle looked back, licked his lips, and set down his coffee cup. "Let's talk about your father." It sent a chill down my spine as if we was sitting in a courthouse under oath to tell the truth and nothing but the truth, so help us God. "What happened?" We sat there in terror as he looked at each of us in turn before finally settling the question on Nigel's shoulders. "What really happened?"

"He went fishing," Nigel fiddled with his fork, working it in and out of the pie crust. "And ..."

"I don't want to hear what you told the police," Uncle Eli interrupted. "I want to hear what really happened. The truth."

Nigel looked across the table to me. "It's like Nigel said, Daddy went fishing and just never come back," I said.

Our uncle chuckled under his breath, leaned back in the chair, and rested his right ankle onto his left knee. "You and I both know that isn't true, Mary Alice."

How could he know anything about any of it? He wasn't here! But, his eyes and that smile and the way he looked at me straight on and with that serious lift of his eyebrows, was like a lawyer waiting for the witness to confess. "We done told you, he went fish ..."

"He hung himself," Katie blurted out. Her face was bright red.

"Kate!" I snapped. "Hush it!"

"It's true and I aint' gonna be lying about it to Uncle Eli when he's trying to help us," she went on. "That's what he done. He hung himself up in his bedroom."

Uncle Eli uncrossed his legs and leaned forward again, staring straight at me. "And why would he do such a thing? Clayton Brown never struck me as the suicidal type. Murdering, sure, but to take his own life? I don't see it."

"It's what happened," Nigel spoke up.

"Tell me what's been going on. Tell me all of it."

And so we did. We all told the story in pieces and parts up to finding Daddy's body swinging from the twisted bed sheet and Nigel taking the truck down to where it was found by the creek. There was one part we all hesitated to talk about, though.

"Where's his body?"

Even Kate fell mute and still now, her eyes lowering as her hands pulled back, twisting nervously on her lap. For the first time I felt shame for what we'd done, shame, yes, but regrets? Not a one. Daddy deserved what he got.

"No one will ever find it," Nigel said. "We took care of it. Probably best you don't know those details."

"How long ago did this all happen?"

"March," I said. "He died in March."

Uncle Eli reached for his fork. "If word of this ever got out, you could all go to jail, you know?"

All four of us nodded, but it was Nigel who spoke up. "You won't tell, will you?"

There was a moment of silence. "No," he said. "No, I think the four of you have suffered enough. I never pretended to like Clay and you'd not know how many times I tried to get my sister to leave him. I won't say a word. I just wanted the truth, so we can start things off on the right foot."

"Then why you taking Seth and Kate away?" I couldn't help it. "You say we've suffered enough, yet you want to break us apart."

"No, I don't. I'm trying to keep the family together. I'm family, aren't I? Mrs. Hayes and I are telling you the way it is. It's not pretty. It's not what any of us want to hear, but it's what could happen if we let the court alone decide what happens. Are you willing to let some stranger come along and decide where Kate and Seth go? They sure won't be together if they don't come with me. You won't hear from them until they're of age. That's how Child Protective Services works. No contact. Period. Our best bet is to have them come live with me and Lily. It's only for a few years. You won't lose touch. And," he added looking more and more serious, "you won't have anyone coming here asking about your father."

"We gotta trust him, Mary," Nigel said. "Last thing we need is folks coming around poking into our business."

I rubbed at my temples that were starting to ache and throb. "Alright," I whispered, though it went against the grain of everything I held near and dear to my heart. "Alright, you all win. Take them." I looked up, the pulsing pains in my head turning to anger, "But don't you ever try and taken nothing from my house again, you hear? I already got little enough as it is."

On Friday, June eighteenth, nineteen-sixty, my brother Nigel Clayton Brown became the first person in our family to graduate high school. I'd made a cake.

Pamela Morris

Uncle Eli came up from Scranton and we got to meet our Aunt Lily for the first time. She was about what I expected, real pretty and dressed up fine. Her black hair was cut short and her eyes were big and brown. Aunt Lily was also very uncomfortable. Oh, she smiled a lot and said the best and nicest words, but you could tell she maybe thought being poor was contagious or something. She kept her elbows and hands tucked in and only touched things that needed touching.

To her credit, Aunt Lily was really interested in the things that Seth and Katie liked. She wanted to know their favorite colors and subjects in school. She wanted to know what books and movies they liked, things like that. During Nigel's party, it all grew very heavy and hard in my chest and stomach. We had until the first of July before Seth and Kate left, just two weeks.

"Now, you won't need to pack a lot of clothes," Lily told them towards the end of our gathering. "Bring enough for the weekend is all. I plan on taking the two of you shopping. We'll get you both whole new wardrobes, right down to your socks and underwear." She giggled. "So only bring your favorites."

A smile had spread wide and full across Kate's face. I wanted to be happy for her and kept reminding myself how thrilled I would have been were me in her place. Seth smiled, too, but he kept it mostly in check. He claimed he only agreed to go along with it to keep an eye on Kate so she'd not be alone with strangers. He'd protect her from whatever they were going to face in Scranton.

As the final days and nights ticked by, my heart grew heavy and dark. I spent more time with Ali than usual and didn't let Kate watch her as much as she used to. I told her it was so the baby wouldn't miss her when she went away. Telling the truth, it was because I

298

was afraid Kate might try to take my little girl with her. I don't know how I thought she'd do it. It didn't make any sense. Ali wasn't some baby doll Kate could stuff into the big suitcase she was packing.

A hot bright sun shined down out of a cloudless sky the afternoon of July first. I went through the motions of just another day, making breakfast and doing chores, losing count at how many times I had to stop and wipe the tears from my eyes that poured out the agony of my soul.

The sight of the dust that billowed up behind Uncle Eli's car wrapped around my throat, choking me long before the actual cloud of it reached the front yard. It felt like dying. How was I going to live without them?

Kate and Seth came out of the front door, each carrying a single suitcase. Nigel went down to the car to shake our uncle's hand. All I could do was stand on the porch with Ali propped up against my hip. My eyes were puffy and red from all the crying. I made no effort to hide it now. Uncle Eli put the two cases in the trunk. The slam of it rang like a closing coffin lid.

My two youngest siblings walked over to me and looked up. "We're going now, Mary Alice," Seth said. For a change, Kate looked sad. The tears on her face matching mine. She was looking at Ali instead of me, afraid to make eye contact with the one whose heart she was ripping right out its chest. "We'll call when we get there," my brother added.

My head nodded, pounded, and grew fuzzy gray around the edges. "Alright," I said looking at him. He mounted the steps and took Ali's hand. "You be good now," he told her and kissed her cheek. "Uncle Seth will be back soon as he can to spoil you."

A strangled sound shuddered from Kate. When my eyes flicked back, her hands had risen to cover her face. All I could do was stand there as Seth put an arm around my shoulders and kissed my cheek. "Don't worry, Mary. We ain't gonna be that far away. It'll work out fine." I didn't hug him back. I didn't say anything. Everything was stuck in my chest, squeezing my heart and feelings down to a tiny, black speck.

"Just go," I was numb with cold.

"You gonna say good-bye, Katie Sue?" Nigel was beside her. I'd not seen him move from where he'd been standing by Uncle Eli's car only seconds ago. He touched her elbow as if to try and coax her forward, but her feet remained firmly planted.

"She don't have to," I said. "The sooner she'd rid of us and this place, the better. It's a shameful, terrible place to be. Once she's gone out of here and got her nice new clothes, no one will ever have to know what sort of horrible dirt she come from." As I spoke, a level of hatred began to rise in me like I'd never dreamed I could feel for my sister. It was as dark and miserable as what I'd felt for Daddy that first time he came into my room and pulled the blankets back. I was betrayed. I was violated. I was raped of every good thought I'd ever held towards her.

"That ain't true," Nigel started to say.

"Is true," I snapped back. "Ain't it, Katie? Ain't it true?"

She made no reply but another gut-wrenching sob as she spun around and ran for the waiting car. She scrambled in and even after the door slammed, I could still hear her anguished cries.

Seth stepped away with a sigh, descended the few steps, and went to Nigel. They boys embraced, shook hands, trying to look and act like the strong, stoic men they wanted to be. "I'll call when we get there, Nige," I heard him say.

"See that you do," my brother said. "Have a safe trip."

Uncle Eli shook his hand, too, and I saw him pass Nigel a plain white envelope. "Be kind to her, Nige."

Nigel nodded and took the envelope. "I will. We'll be fine."

"Call if you need anything," our uncle added. "Anything at all."

Seth and Uncle Eli joined Kate in the car. The dust cloud plumed once more, chasing them down the entire length of Dark Hollow Road back to the main highway. I stood and watched and didn't let myself feel anything. As far as I was concerned, they were as good as dead now. They'd get to Scranton and their new house and new clothes and they'd forget all about us and the place they left behind.

Nigel appeared beside me, touching my shoulder. "Mary …"

I pulled away. "I got things to do," I said, still watching the spot where I'd last seen Uncle Eli's car.

"Mary, it's going to be alright. You'll see."

My gaze shifted. I looked up at him for by now he was a good bit taller than me. "Ain't nothing going to be alright, Nige," I replied, turned away and went back into the house.

Chapter 32

How long had it been? Five minutes? Ten? He'd
not heard a thing and his head was starting to get
stuffed up from all the smells. He wanted out. He could
get out if he wanted to. All he had to do was push the
lid up, climb out, and go. Then what? Walk home all
alone? He wasn't going to cut through that cornfield,
no way. He'd have to take the road. It would take
longer, but he knew the way.

The glow of the flashlight shined into one of the
powder-filled corners of the box. The powder was a
brownish yellow with darker flecks of other things
mixed with it. He didn't know what and he didn't care.
Nor did he care if he won this stupid game of Hide-
and-Seek. Would they come back if he quit? He'd
promised he'd play one game. If he didn't play by the
rules, Brandon was afraid they'd come back some
other night and want him to play again.

He started to draw in a breath, but it stuck halfway
in his throat. Brandon let it out, tried again. Stuck.
Why couldn't he fill his lungs with air? God, it smelled
in here. It smelled so bad and not just of animal feed
and poop. There was something else that reminded
Brandon of the time Mama Sam had found a dead
squirrel stuck under the hood of her Jeep. It wasn't as

bad as that, but it was there, all tangy and gagging and putrid. Half breaths weren't enough and he hated that smell, but he had to breathe. He had to get out of here, or he was going to puke and that would make it smell even worse. It was all closed in and stuffy and hot in here.

Brandon pushed on the lid. It didn't open. Maybe it was a lot heavier than Allan made it look. He pushed harder. Nothing. Not so much as a budge. "Hey!" he yelled. "Get me out of here! Allan? Ginny! The top is stuck." A third hard shove did no good.

Panting, he began pounding on the walls, screaming their names with what little air he could manage to take in. The lid could not be that heavy. Maybe it got locked! The panic that washed over him was sharp and biting, sending him into panting screams and yowls. He kicked at the wall of his wooden prison that was starting to feel more and more like a coffin.

"GET ME OUT OF HERE!" he screamed. "Get me out right now!!!"

Sweat dappled his face. His arms were growing cold despite how hot it felt inside the box. Pushing and pushing on the lid first with one hand, then with two, then with his shoulder. Tears poured down his face. Desperate sobs made it even harder to draw in a breath. Brandon clawed at the walls, kicking, screaming, and gagging on that dead smell that was growing stronger. His head was spinning or maybe it was the box. Both hands flew out to the walls, pressing on them hard to try and stay sitting up. Bob the Builder turned round and round and round on the floor until he rolled into the corner. Pain shot into Brandon's shoulder as he thudded hard against one of the walls. The back of his throat stung. I'm going to puke, he thought. I'm going to puke! He fell over, curled into a ball on his side, and screamed like he'd never screamed before.

"MOMMY!" he cried out. "Mama Sam! Help me!"

Full stop.

Listen. Soft voices murmured.

Breathe in. Bacon? Was that bacon?

No more dead squirrel. No more animal poop. No more corn, hay, or oatmeal smell.

He still lay curled into a tight ball on his side, but what he felt beneath him wasn't wood. It was soft. Brandon closed his fingers. It was a bed sheet. He was in bed and the blanket was pulled up over his head. He pulled in a deep breath. It smelled of blankets and a sort of musty, old something, but that aside, there was definitely bacon being fried.

It had been a dream. That's all, just a bad, bad, dream. His body relaxed as he stretched slowly, turning slightly to his side and reaching out for one of his stuffed animals. His white bear, Ted, should be on the left, but he wasn't. Well, sometimes he fell on the floor. With his right arm, Brandon reached for Big Bear. Big Bear wasn't there either. He frowned and thought a minute. Monty. Monty the Monkey always sat at the head of Brandon's bed right above the pillow. Monty's spot was cold and empty.

Brandon opened his eyes. Morning light shown through the dark green blanket still pulled up over his head. The tight weave shimmered only a nose length from his eyes. Green. But his blanket was blue. Sliding his hand up, he ran it over the surface. It was picky like that sweater Grandma Evenson had given him for his birthday last year. Wool. Brandon didn't like wool. It made him itch. He pushed the blanket away and sat up.

Not only was he not in his own bedroom, he wasn't really even in a bed. He was too low to the floor. It was just a mattress in the corner of a room. There was another mattress beside him made up all neat and two beds, two real beds with metal frames, stood on either side of a single window. Pushed against the wall to his right was a weird-looking wooden dresser.

Brandon pulled the rest of the blankets away and rose cautiously to his feet. His slippers rested at the foot of the mattress and his robe was draped over the footboard of the nearest bed. He put these on, happy to feel the little lump in the right hand pocket that he knew to be Army Guy, and made his way over towards the room's only window.

Outside the sun shined full and bright under a blue sky scattered with puffy, white clouds. Stretching out almost as far as the eye could see beyond the not-quite-so-tall-as-he-remembered-it, weedy yard, were the gnarly apple trees, past them was a field of pale brown corn. He was pretty sure he knew exactly where he was, but something wasn't right.

Brandon stared at the chicken coop he'd hidden in the first time and then followed a clothesline, dotted with pins but no clothes, towards its slightly leaning post, then to the barn where he'd just been. The big doors gaped like a giant, sideways-opening mouth. A tractor was parked there now. Brandon was positive that hadn't been there before, nor did he remember the clothesline. Tiny, white specks of movement snapped his gaze back to the coop. Chickens had appeared, strutting, pecking, scratching, fluttering chickens.

Below him was the rusted metal roof of the kitchen porch. When he leaned forward he could just see the big, double doors that led down into the basement. Only now they were made of wood, not metal.

"You're up!"

Brandon jerked and spun around with a start.

Allan was standing in the open doorway. "Breakfast is about ready. You like scrambled eggs?"

"Where – what, how did I get here?" His heart was pounding hard and sharp in his chest.

"You're in our bedroom, that's all. C'mon down for breakfast."

That didn't answer his questions at all. "I want to go home."

Allan's shoulders sagged and he sighed. "Can't yet. Not until after breakfast, anyway. C'mon. Ma's waiting." Without any further explanation, Allan turned and walked away.

Brandon stared at the vacant doorway. He may be only six years old, but he knew a lot of things. One of those things was that when you walked across an old wooden floor in an old house, your footsteps made noise. When Mama Sam and Mr. Martin had been in the house, Brandon had been able to hear them walking around even from way outside. Allan hadn't made any noise.

Brandon looked down at his slipper-shod feet and took a step forward, paused, then took another. Nothing. It was as quiet as walking across a concrete floor. A few more steps and he was standing by the door. His footsteps had never made even the faintest creak. Brandon moved to the hallway. The scent of bacon was strong out here and now he could hear the sizzle of it, too. His stomach rumbled. Across the hall was a bathroom. He could see the end of an old bathtub with big feet shaped like dragon claws half hidden behind the partially closed door. Normally he'd have to go pee first thing when he got up, but he didn't feel that now. Maybe he'd wet the bed and that had been the musty smell, but his pajamas were dry.

Dark Hollow Road

Turning down the hallway, he headed for the top of the stairs and descended slowly and carefully, noting each step was just like the one before it, unnaturally silent. He stopped halfway down.

"He coming?" asked a lady's voice.

"Yeah. He wants to go home." That was Allan.

"Only when they give me what I want in return," the lady replied.

"That could take a long time, Mary." It was Ginny.

"I'll wait as long as it takes then," the woman, Mary, again.

Brandon moved to the bottom of the stairs and walked into the warm kitchen.

The Sugar Lady was standing by the stove pouring already scrambled eggs into a thick, black frying pan.

Yagar's Pumpkin Farm wasn't quite as crowded as it had been the first time they'd been there. Renee felt her heart shatter a little more at the sight of it, remembering Brandon picking out his pumpkin and walking through the corn maze and feeding the goats. She had no real hope of getting Lee to talk to them. He wasn't just a grumpy old man, he was a very busy one, and not one to take being interrupted well.

Sam gave her hand a squeeze as she took it and they headed into the market place. There were still tons of pumpkins to be had. There was a high school-aged boy at the checkout table now. Sam stepped up behind the person being rung out and waited.

The boy's nametag told them hello and that his name was Kevin. "Can I help you?"

"We're looking for Mr. Yagar, Lee. Is he around?" Sam asked.

Concern flashed in the kid's eyes, "Something wrong?"

"No, no," Sam assured him. "We just wanted to ask him something. Nothing to do with the farm, personal stuff."

"Oh, okay. Hold on." From under the counter the boy pulled a bright yellow walkie-talkie. "Carla, you there?"

The walkie squawked after a few minutes, "Yeah, what you need?"

"You know where Mr. Yagar's at?"

"I think he's over in the big barn. Anything the matter?"

"No, just some folks here to talk to him about something."

"Alright, yeah. Ellie tells me she saw him heading for the barn about ten minutes ago."

"Thanks."

Kevin flipped his black hair out of his eyes with a flick of his head. He pointed with the radio's rubbery black antennae. "That a'ways," he said. "Good luck. He's an old guy, but he doesn't let that slow him down none."

And they were off, exiting out the back as they'd done before. Sam was on a mission, a mission that felt urgent and angry, tugging Renee along as if she were a child until Renee dug in her heels a bit to slow them down. "Hold up," she said.

Sam stopped. "What?"

"What are we going to say, exactly? We can't just storm up to the man and accuse him of anything and certainly not here in the middle of all these people."

The reality of the situation finally registered on Sam's face. She gave a curt nod. "Yeah, you're probably right. This isn't the best place to confront him."

Renee kept her gaze towards the barn just in case she saw Lee coming or going from it. "Maybe ask if we can meet later, after hours."

"He'll refuse."

"Hi!" a loud, cheerful voice burst out from behind them.

Renee spun around. "Lisa! Hello."

The girl's smile was infectious and for the first time in her life, Renee found herself wishing that what the young woman had was contagious. She sure could use some of the happy-go-lucky attitude about now. "Hello. Having fun? Have you fed the goats?" Clearly she didn't remember them from before and why would she? Hundreds of people came through this place every day.

Renee forced herself to smile and speak as if she didn't have a care in the world, "Oh, yes. Last time we were here we did that. Do you know where your brother is by any chance?"

"He's filling the pellet machines back up, you know, the ones you put the quarter in so you can get food for the animals. He's in the barn now, I think. Want me to show you?"

"No, we know ..." Sam began.

"Yes, please," Renee interrupted. What better way to get an audience with the man than to have the one person he seemed to have a soft spot for take them. Without her, he might just turn on his heel and refuse to talk to them at all. With her, he'd at least be polite for a while.

Lisa headed out without any further ado, her stride was long and fast-paced, as she leaned forward slightly, arms swinging in a near march towards the bar. Sam and Renee double-timed to catch up and keep the pace. "Zippy little thing, isn't she?" Sam remarked with a smile.

Lee was just topping off one of the machines as they entered the darker, richer-smelling barn. The entire back wall was open to give visitors what felt like a behind-the-scenes feel of farm life. In the paddock on the far left, seemingly every goat in the place had gathered at the wooden fence, crowding each other for attention, and bleating in earnest as if they hadn't been fed in days. The middle paddock held several miniature ponies that happily munched on a mound of fresh hay in the center of their enclosure. On the far right, a group of pigs had found a shady spot under the eaves to nap.

Lisa marched up to her brother, "Lee! People here to see you," she announced, scooping out a handful of the brownish-green pellets from the open bucket in the wagon. Renee had a flash of the girl tossing them into her mouth like so many jelly beans. Instead she went over to the goat fence as her brother turned to face the visitors.

What may have been a pleasant expression on the old man's face fell immediately when he saw who waited. "What?" he growled.

"We need to talk," Renee spoke up, afraid that Sam would be too aggressive. This called for a mother's touch. "Please."

"I'm busy." He pulled the wagon down to the pellet machine on the end. "Ain't got nothing to say. There's nothing I can do about any of it."

Renee took a deep breath, forcing herself to remain even-tempered. "Mr. Yagar, please. Is there anything you can tell us about that place and the Browns? My son is missing. I'm afraid something terrible has happened to him. You must understand that."

Dark Hollow Road

"Like I said, I'm busy here and what's done is done."

Sam spoke up and wasn't so gentle and sweet about it, "What's been done? What do you know?"

"Do you know where Brandon is, Mr. Yagar?" Renee pleaded. "Please, if you know where he is, tell us. I want my son back. What if it were Lisa who was missing?"

The grumpy face softened, but Lee turned away. "Lisa's safe from that house. We stay away and we never took nothing from the place. That's what gets ya into trouble." His spine straightened as he turned back to face them full on. His jaw and eyes held the resolve of a very determined man, lips tight, brow furrowed. "Ya homos need to stay away from that place. Better yet, keep right off Dark Hollow Road all together. I can't help ya."

Renee heard Sam's sharp intake of air and saw her partner's hand curl into a fist. "Listen, old man, this isn't about us. It's about a six-year-old-boy who's lost somewhere, alone, and probably scared out of his mind. What the fuck is wrong with you that you don't have any sympathy for a little kid?"

Lee Yagar swung around, his fist clenched just as tight and ready to punch as Sam's. "Get off my property," he snapped. "Get your fag selves off my property right now. If I ever see ya here again, I'll have ya both arrested for trespassing."

Lisa's eyes were wide and her mouth open in shock. "Don't yell at the customers. That's what you said to Fred the other day."

"This isn't your concern, Lisa. Get to wherever you're supposed to be working today."

"You're being awful mean to these people, Lee. You should help them."

"Lisa, what did I just tell ya to do?"

Her mouth snapped shut as she gave him an indignant glare. "Not until you're being nice."

Renee held her smile in check. The girl had spunk and reminded Renee of a stubborn, old mule, a trait she probably got from her brother. "Please, Mr. Yagar. What can you tell us about the place that might help? There is something, isn't there?"

"Told ya to leave," he said. "I'm done talking to ya. All three of ya leave me alone."

Lisa walked over to her brother, eyes angry and lips bunched up in an odd, puckered pout. "You're mean," she said. "I'm done talking to you." The girl marched from the barn, muttering to herself. All Renee caught was something about a grumpy bully.

The old man's sour gaze turned towards Renee and Sam. "Looks like my sister's smarter than the two of ya put together. Won't take but a few minutes for security staff to get here and escort ya out."

Renee reached out and took Sam's hand. "Come on, hon. This isn't doing any good. This man doesn't care about anyone but himself."

Sam was rooted to the spot, fury still in her eyes. "If we find out you had anything to do with this, you son of a bitch, you're going to find yourself up to your neck in a shitload of trouble. This is a little boy. A little boy!"

Sam's hand was starting to crush Renee's. "Let's go," she tugged on her partner. "He'd rather hate us than help an innocent child."

Lee was already turning back around to the pellet dispenser. They'd been dismissed.

Disheartened, they headed back to the open barn doors. Tears were already starting to well up and spill over onto Renee's hot cheeks.

"Oh, hell. God damn it all. Wait." Lee said, not quite yelling, but loud enough for them to hear over the bleating goats and clucking chickens. "Not here," he mumbled. "We ain't talking about it here."

Renee's heart skipped with hope as they turned back.

"Tonight. After hours. Come to the house at seven o'clock."

"Thank you." Renee wanted to hug him, but was held back by Sam's grip.

"This is urgent, Mr. Yagar. We really can't wait that ..."

Anger flared in the wrinkled and weather-worn face. "Tonight at seven or not at all, not that it will do any good. If Mary has him it's probably too late."

"Too late? Too late for what?" Renee snapped.

"Seven o'clock," the old man said.

Renee thought her anxious heart was going to pound right out of her chest. "We'll be here."

Chapter 33

The world became hollow. I existed in a vacuum, scooped out like a Halloween pumpkin, doing what needed doing but feeling nothing. Nigel started working fulltime at the mine. The garden was tended, clothes were washed, and the animals were fed. I pretended to be getting over the loneliness. I laughed at Nigel's jokes and stories. He even started to give me a little kiss on the cheek like Daddy always did Mama when he left for work and again when he came home. Those kisses and baby Ali's constant smile got me through the days.

The nights were harder. I had no one to talk to after lights went out and the darkness settled deep into place. For weeks on end I cried myself to sleep. Every morning I'd wake with a dull headache that never quite went away.

Near mid-August, after talking to Katie on the phone, my mood sank to the lowest it had ever been.

While listening to my sister go on and on about how she and Aunt Lily had picked out new curtains and matching bed linens, I understood why I was so miserable. It wasn't just because they were gone. I was jealous to the core. I hated them for their good fortune. I hated that they were happy. How dare they be rewarded for all of my hard work, drudgery, and suffering? Realizing all this, I hated myself and wept the bitter tears of that hatred.

One night after my bath, as I sat on the side of my bed in my nightgown lost in self-loathing, I never heard the bedroom door open. I never knew Nigel was there at all until his fingers touch my cheek and draw aside the wet tangle of hair plastered there. All the fight in me was gone as he sat beside me and pulled me close. In the dim light of my bedside lamp, Nigel rocked us until my sobbing eased to sniffles.

His lips touched the crown of my head, as Mama might have done, stroking my hair, my cheek, my shoulder. "Let me love you, Mary?" The question came in a pleading, sad whisper.

I didn't answer in words. My head rested against his shoulder. My arms lay wrapped around his narrow, bare waist. I didn't pull away.

Love? What did that even mean? Little to nothing as far as I was concerned. We knew about survival and we knew it was easier to survive if you didn't have to do it alone. But, love?

Nigel's index finger traced down my jaw to my chin then nudged it upwards as he drew back ever so slightly. My tear-swollen eyes lifted to look into his. I wanted to be loved. I wanted to be needed and appreciated. I didn't want to be alone. I thought about Larry Yagar and how he'd walked me home that night. He'd been kind to me. He'd even held my hand.

My brother's lips drew closer, hesitant, barely touching mine before they pulled away.

"We shouldn't," I said, knowing I wanted to. I wanted to know what it felt like to be truly loved. I was tired of being afraid and walking through life on this dark, hollow road of hurt.

"We won't if you don't want to." I knew he'd honor that, but the desperation in his eyes looked as deep and painful as what I was feeling in my heart.

I leaned up and kissed him back.

A little past two that morning, I woke up alone in my bed. Nigel had gone back to his room down the hall. A nearly full moon was shining outside my window, making it almost as bright as day. We shouldn't have done what we did. As I lay there looking out the window at the drifting clouds against a dark-blue sky, tears came again. I pushed them aside. Wasn't nothing to be done about it, now. We shouldn't have done what we did to Daddy's body, either, but I sure didn't feel guilty about it. I wouldn't feel guilty about being with Nigel. Nigel wasn't nothing like being with Daddy. He was gentle and nice. He made me forget at least for a short while how sad I was. He loved me.

On August fifth, another envelope arrived in the mail. Like the first one that Uncle Eli had given to Nigel the month before, it contained a check for two-hundred dollars. I hated it. It felt like we was being paid off. Nigel'd opened an account at the bank and put it there for when we might need it. Being as it was my regular shopping day, we decided to go into town together.

Nigel dropped me and Ali off at the grocery store while he went down the street to the bank then to the Agway for a few things. The Red and White wasn't a very big store, but it served Murphey Mills well enough. By now Ali was sitting up just fine so I tucked her into the seat of the cart next to my purse. We didn't need much in the way of fresh vegetables, but my eyes was drawn to the oranges, bananas, and peaches. Other than apples, we didn't get much fruit, and we did have a little extra now, much as I despised where it come from.

"It's for Ali," I told myself. "So she can be healthy." I figured as long as folks seen me taking care of her and feeding her good, they'd have no reason to turn us in. That was my constant fear. I felt like everyone who looked our way was plotting against us on how to take my baby from me. They was all working for CPS. Maybe they wasn't on the payroll, but they was working for them in one way or another. I had to do everything right, so I got the fruit.

I made it as far as the cereal aisle where I was picking up a box of Cheerios before someone stopped to talk to me. Thankfully it was someone I didn't mind talking to at all, Mrs. Yagar.

"Mary Alice," she called out, smiling and waving. "Oh, and look how big little Ali is getting."

"Hi, Mrs. Yagar," I said, cringing a little as she scooped my baby out of the cart without even asking. She cuddled her close, kissing her round cheeks all over. I told myself to settle down. It was only Mrs. Yagar and hadn't she been nothing but a help in all the years we'd known her?

"Oh, Mary Alice, she's a doll."

Ali reached for the older lady's bulbous nose. She had no fear of strangers. I smiled and put the box of cereal into the cart, adding up what I had in my head already and hoping I'd be able to keep it under ten dollars this time. "She's doing real good, ma'am. Doctor said so."

She propped Ali on her hip, bouncing her a bit. "Good, good. And what about you, dear?" She frowned. Everyone knew about Kate and Seth being sent away. "You've been through so much. I worry and pray for you every night, hoping God will ease your load."

"I'm fine," I lied. "Seth and Katie are doing real good in Scranton, too. They call every week. And now that Nigel can work fulltime at the mine, we're doing real good. I even got some fresh fruit today." I didn't want to tell her about the money our uncle was sending.

She peered into my cart. I'm sure I saw some disapproval despite my best efforts. "Oh, that's good. Growing babies need their fruits and veggies, don't they, Ali?" The baby grinned, tugging on the chain that dangled from the woman's glasses. "No, no, sweetheart." She gently pulled Ali's hand away. "And you always keep such a good garden, too."

"Thank you," I said. "I should get going. Nigel's picking me up after he's done down at Agway."

"Of course." She planted another kiss on Ali's cheek before putting her back into the cart seat. "You take care now, Mary Alice, and if there's anything you need, you don't hesitate to give me a call, alright?"

"I will. Thank you."

Ali squirmed in the seat trying to keep an eye on the lady who had just been holding her. Her little arms stretched out, fingers opening and closing. She looked at me, bottom lip trembling as tears started to pool up in her eyes. "It's okay," I leaned over, kissing her forehead. "We'll see her again," I said, handing her back her rag doll and continuing on with my shopping.

Katie, Seth, Uncle Eli, and Aunt Lily come up in September for Ali's first birthday. Katie and Seth had both put on weight. Guess I'd never noticed how thin they was before. They both liked their new school and both had already made friends. It was better for them, I supposed, this new start, but I still felt the anger and unfairness, not to mention the jealousy.

Seth had gotten a new camera and set about documenting the day as we sang happy birthday to Ali. I helped her blow out the single candle. While Nigel scooped up ice cream, I sliced up the cake into small pieces and put them on plates. Kate handed them around.

"You always make such delicious cake, Mary Alice," Kate licked a few crumbs off her fork. "You should give Aunt Lily your recipe."

"Was Mama's recipe," I said. "I'll give it to you sometime." I'd be damned if I was going to give it to one of the people who'd taken part in stealing my siblings from me. No matter how nice she appeared to be, she and Uncle Eli was kidnappers. I played along as best as I could, smiling with them when Seth insisted he get a picture of me with the baby, after I'd wiped her snotty nose for the hundredth time that day. She was getting another of her colds. Uncle Eli even got all five of us to sit together out on the front porch for a family picture. It was a nice picture. One of my favorites, even if now it makes me real sad.

"You alright for money?" I heard Uncle Eli ask Nigel.

"Just fine," Nigel told him. I don't know how much we actually had. He gave me what I needed when I needed it and that was all I cared about.

Kate wrapped her arms around me and Ali and hugged us both close and tight. "I love you, Mary Alice," she said then gave Ali a kiss on the forehead. "And you too, cutie-pie."

Katie suddenly looked so much older to me. She'd grown up a lot over our summer apart. She and Seth never did come to visit like they'd talked about back in

July. No doubt, my aunt and uncle had played a heavy hand in that, filling up all their time at the parks and a trip to New York City. I'd have bet my last dollar that their time wasn't the only thing being filled with nonsense. I reckoned they was being brainwashed to stay away from Dark Hollow Road and the family they'd left behind.

"Love you, too, Katie Sue," I replied.

All too soon they were loaded back into the big, fancy car and kicking up a stream of dust as they drove away. Nigel draped his arm around my shoulder as we watched them go. Ali sneezed.

"You okay?" he asked.

I guess by now he could read me pretty well and I wasn't about to start lying to him after all this time. "Ain't fair."

"I know it ain't, but they're going to have chances we never did. Try and be happy for them, Mary. Can you do that?"

I wanted to be happy for them of course, but what about me? What about my feelings and my happiness? "I can try," I answered, but doubted it would ever happen like he wanted.

He kissed me on the head and smiled. "I think someone's had a long day," he said and ran a finger gently over Ali's cheek. She'd fallen asleep with her head resting on my shoulder. "Go lay her down and I'll help you clean up things."

I lay her down in the playpen out in the front room, touching her forehead that had grown warmer than usual. It was just another cold and she'd had a long, tiring day like the rest of us.

That night as Ali fussed in her crib ten feet away, Nigel comforted me in my bed for the second time. I loved him. I loved him so much. He and Ali was all I had left to love in the world.

Chapter 34

The Sugar Lady smiled at him, "C'mon in. Just getting the eggs on. Have a seat." As both of her hands were occupied, she motioned towards the table with the wave of an elbow and a tip of her head.

"I want to go home," Brandon said even as his stomach growled.

"Sounds to me like you want some breakfast."

"I can go home after we eat?"

The woman smiled without answering.

Ginny handed him a bundle of forks instead, "Here, you can help, too." It was the closest Brandon had ever been to her. He looked into her unsmiling eyes. Reluctant, he took the forks and turned to put one at each of the place settings. Maybe he was dreaming. That had to be it. He'd fallen asleep in that box.

Allan was filling mismatched cups with apple juice. He didn't seem quite as sad at Ginny, but this sure didn't feel like Saturday morning breakfast at his house. Nobody was joking. No one was laughing. There wasn't even a radio on. It was all very gray, like in the Wizard of Oz before Dorothy crushed the witch, only not quite. There were colors, but they were drab and muted, as if looking through a dirty window. Brandon looked towards the kitchen door and bit his lip with thought. The glass, at least from this side, looked freshly washed and nearly crystal clear.

"How'd I get in here?" he asked.

Brandon didn't miss the silent looks Ginny and Allan gave each other.

"BOO!" the little girl suddenly yelled and giggled. "It's a boo!"

The Sugar Lady turned around with the pan full of scrambled eggs and starting scooping equal portions onto each plate. "You're silly," she said to the smallest of the children. "Get up in your chair. Everyone, sit. Brandon you can go right over there by Allan."

He sat. Ginny put a plate full of bacon in the middle of the table beside the one loaded with buttered toast that was probably already cold. The eggs on his plate were flat and gray, not fluffy yellow like Mommy made. As the others dug in, his appetite dwindled. He should eat something. He'd not had anything since the trick-or-treat candy from the night before. Brandon filled his fork and took a bite. The texture of soggy, mushed tissues filled his mouth. It tasted as good as it felt and looked. He chewed slowly, working hard not to gag. The sip he took of apple juice was flavorless, but at least it was liquid and cold. Maybe the bacon would be better? Brandon selected a piece from the plate, studied it and took a careful bite. Thin, brittle tree bark crunched between his teeth. The toast was little more than a dried out, crumbling dish sponge. More apple juice washed all of these down before he wiped his mouth and pushed the plate slightly away.

The Sugar Lady watched with a growing frown of disapproval. "You should eat more than that," she said.

"I'm not really hungry," he said, though he really was deep, down inside.

323

Her face grew stern. "Don't be asking for a snack before lunchtime." She said and went back to her own plate.

"You said I could go home after we ate breakfast," Brandon protested.

"I said no such thing," The Sugar Lady replied. "Besides, you ain't eaten your breakfast, so even if I had said that, it wouldn't count."

"I'm not going to eat it. It's gross!" Brandon pushed himself way from the table. "I'm going home. You can't make me stay here." Now that is was daylight, he was feeling a lot braver. He darted towards the kitchen door, grabbed the knob, twisted, and pulled. It was locked, that's all. Just locked. "Unlock this door! I want to go home! Let me go home!"

The Sugar Lady's cold hand wrapped around his upper arm and pulled him back. "Y'ain't going home until I get what I want," she hissed and when Brandon looked up at her face he instantly wished he hadn't. It was the witch from the Spook Barn, only this one had hold of him and was pulling him back into the room. Her fingers gripped like iron. "You need to be put in the cellar."

"Mary, don't," Ginny burst out.

One look from the woman snapped the girl's mouth shut. Her eyes grew round with fear and somehow Brandon understood she didn't want to be here, either. Allan looked just as petrified. Only the littlest one didn't seem to notice or care as she gnawed happily on a piece of bacon.

Brandon tried to dig in his heels, reaching for chairs and door frames as he was pulled into the darker parts of the house. They went out into the hallway, then into a side room with a fireplace where he saw another door. The Sugar Lady dragged Brandon behind her like he was nothing more than an empty sack of clothes. How could she be so strong? She was so skinny and old-looking.

Once they reached the bottom, Mary adjusted the grip she had on the collar of his robe and hoisted him into another box. This was bigger than the first one, but as black inside as the coal it stank of. A heavy wooden lid slammed down and Brandon heard something slide into place, locking him inside.

"And there you'll stay until I decide you've suffered enough," she growled. "Nobody gave a damn about my suffering. All they done was take, take, take from me until they got me good and crazy. Then they took some more! I'm done being taken from. They need to give me what I want."

The door at the top of the stairs slammed shut.

Sam's hand had barely reached the screen door when the inner door swung open, releasing a waft of what had likely been dinner not so long ago. Lee Yagar had changed into clean clothes, but judging by the scowl on his face, his mood had not improved much. "C'mon in," he mumbled, giving the screen a slight push without actually opening it much.

Renee stepped inside first, smiling at the cozy feeling she got from the place. The wall on the right-hand-side of the entry hall was covered with pictures, mostly children, several teens, weddings, group shots, and the like.

"Ladies've gone to church. We have about an hour and a half. Got coffee on if you're partial to it?" He waved a hand towards the half-empty pot. Two clean cups sat nearby.

Renee declined. "I'll be up all night if I drink coffee this late, but thank you."

"Suit yourself," Lee shrugged, yanked out a chair, and sat down.

Sam pulled off her jacket and hung it on the back of the chair beside where Renee was just settling in. "You have a nice place here, Mr. Yagar," Sam said.

"Thank ya." He picked up the cup of black coffee that looked as if he'd poured it fresh just before coming to the door and took a sip. "So," he looked across the table at the two of them. "Ya want to know about that house, do ya?"

Renee leaned forward, the palms of both hands flat on the table, "Mr. Yagar, does that house have anything to do with my son being missing?"

The old man stared across the room at the opposite wall for so long Renee thought he wasn't going to answer. Then he nodded ever so slightly. "Ain't so much the house, as Mary."

"Mary Brown? I thought she was dead."

"Well," he rubbed the back of his neck before running his hand over the day's worth of white stubble that covered his jaw and chin, making a sound like it was being run over rough sandpaper.

"Mr. Yagar, is she dead or not?" Sam pressed.

"I reckon she is, yeah."

Sam scoffed. "You reckon she is? What's that mean? A person either is or isn't dead. There's no in between."

Lee actually smiled a bit, "Now, there's where you're wrong, young man." He looked at Sam, unsure, "or, whatever the hell ya are. There is an in between."

When Renee and Sam had first met, Sam would have climbed over the table and strangled the man. But in the few years they'd been together, she'd seen her partner handle the situation with growing ease. Yes, she did look rather butch, but Sam had always embraced the term 'dyke' with pride. She wasn't ashamed of who she was and, considering the huge generation gap between Mr. Yagar and them, Sam only clenched her jaw. "I'm female."

"Well, whatever ya are, I tell ya there's an in between place. Just like I reckon where ya come from, ya know, being queer and all. Not a fella, not a lady, somewhere in the middle."

Renee reached over and took Sam's hand, squeezing it. "We get the idea, but if Mary's not dead and she's not alive, what is she? A ghost?"

Lee tipped his head and grimaced, rubbing the nape of his neck again, "Well, I don't know if that's the right word for it either. And, mind ya, I ain't so sure I really understand it myself, but your boy, he ain't the first one she's took a liking to."

"Other children have gone missing?"

"Yeah. The first one would have been in 1982, just a couple years after the Martin boys bought the place. Little girl, only three years old. She was playing in their yard one minute, and I mean the same yard that's now yours, and gone the next." Lee snapped his fingers. "Poof. The dad was out front washing the car. Mom was laying out back with the girl sunning herself. They had a sandbox. The mother said she was playing in it and talking to herself like little kids do. All of a sudden she realized she didn't hear the girl talking no more. Sure enough, she was gone. Never seen alive again."

Renee felt all the color drain from her face. "They found her though? A body, I mean?"

Lee nodded, "Yeah. Sorry to upset ya like this, but ya wanted to know. I'm telling ya like it is."

"I know. It's alright." She braced herself. "Go on. What happened to her?"

"Well, that's where it gets peculiar." Lee took a longer sip of coffee this time. "The police came, done just like they been doing looking for yours. Nothing come of it until nearly a month later. She was found out in that chicken coop out back."

"Oh, Jesus," Renee covered her mouth with her hand.

"We know it," Sam said. "We were over there with Mr. Martin a few weeks ago. I wanted to get some pictures and he was showing me around. While I was with him, Brandon ran off. We found him hiding in the chicken coop. Said he was playing Hide-and-Seek with some other kids. We never heard or saw any other kids though."

"A boy and two girls?" Lee asked.

Renee scowled, pulling her hand away. "I don't think he ever said, did he, Sam?"

Sam shook her head. "I know there was at least one boy, Allan."

Lee Yagar rubbed at his facial stubble again. "Damn."

"Do you know who Allan is?"

"I might, but let me get back to the girl. They found her in the coop. Remember, they searched that whole place up and down, inside and out. She wasn't in that coop then, but then she was and she'd been dead quite awhile. They figured about three weeks."

"Someone dumped her there, maybe?"

Lee nodded. "Yeah, what else could they figure? But, when they got her out of there, they found a handful of marbles in one of her pockets, 'cept they weren't hers. The mother said they'd found them one day while out on a walk. They'd walk down past the dead end sign and go play in the creek. Found the marbles on their first trip, all in a little pile in the dirt where the road met with the driveway. They'd been there a long time, she guessed. But the girl liked them. So they'd brought them home, washed them off, and she played with them."

Sam leaned back and crossed her arms in thought, "You said something about not taking anything from the place. Brandon never took anything from the house, in fact, it was The Sugar Lady who took something from him."

"The Sugar Lady?"

Renee relayed the experiences with the woman Brandon had seen which left Lee scratching his head. "She actually left a canning jar behind and took a coloring book?"

"Yes. The coloring book was at the house the first time we went back, on the hatch doors to the basement," Sam confirmed.

"Has to be Mary," Lee concluded.

"Then she's alive. Ghosts can't do stuff like that, can they?"

"I'd not think so, but this is Mary we're talking about. Some folks say there's witch blood in the family from way back. I don't know about that. Either of ya ever see her?"

They shook their heads.

"What about the other child you mentioned?" Renee asked.

Lee pulled himself from whatever deep thoughts he was having. "That'd of been around fifteen years ago. Twelve-year-old boy named Paul. Blonde hair, blue eyes, bit of a smartass from what I remember of him."

Renee braced herself for the worst.

"Paul was a curious one. Lived in the very same house as you and the other. Paul went over to the house a number of times on his bike looking for things. His dad said they found an old suitcase under the boy's bed full of things and the only place he could figure they come from was the house, including the suitcase. There were some old wire hangers, an empty can of shaving cream, a kid's shoe, that sort of thing. Useless junk, really.

"Well, one day Paul didn't come home from one of his bike rides. First place his folks looked was the house. They knew he snooped around over there. They brought in the police and dogs all over again. Like before, nothing was found of him, but Paul's bike was leaning up against the mail box.

"One night, 'bout week later, they hear something moving around on the front porch. He's out there, on his knees trying to crawl his way to the front door, pale as a fresh hospital bed sheet and covered in dirt head to toe. They rushed him to the hospital, but ..."

"He died?" Renee whispered.

"No, but he never talked after that, at least not to any of them. Seemed he was seeing and hearing things no one else was. Answering questions no one had asked. Eyes as dull and sightless as old Ray Charles.

Folks ended up sending him to some kind of special psychiatric hospital downstate and moved away. Don't know if he ever got better." He took up the cup of coffee again, gave the contents a couple of swirls, and took two swallows. "And now, your boy."

Renee suddenly felt very cold and tired. She rubbed her temples trying to keep calm and think clearly despite the headache that had been crawling up between her shoulder blades and now rested comfortably at the crown of her head. "And you think Mary is the cause of all this? How? Why? Where do the kids go? If she's, like you say, between worlds or whatever, how can this happen? And what about the children Brandon says he was playing Hide-and-Seek with. Who are they? You said you thought you knew who the one was? Allan?"

"Allan," Mr.Yagar blew out a long breath and slumped. He looked from Renee to Sam and back to Renee again. "You say ya been in the house?"

Renee shook her head. "No, I refused to go in."

"Smart girl."

"I went in with Doug Martin," Sam said.

"Did he take ya to the cellar?"

Sam nodded.

"Did he tell ya about the grave?"

Chapter 35

Come morning, Ali was looking and sounding worse. She was coughing and feverish, wanting little more than to be held and rocked. I got her to drink some water and apple juice, but she didn't want nothing to do with food. By the end of the day she was filling her diaper with a bad case of the runs and had started throwing up.

It was a sleepless night. Wearing nothing but a diaper, Alice lay on my chest while I sat in the rocking chair in the living room downstairs. She'd doze off now and then, only to wake, fuss, and cry ten minutes later.

"We need to get her to the doctor. You don't look so good, either." Nigel said and I wasn't about to argue, but then a terrible thought crossed my mind.

What if this was all they needed to prove me an unfit mother? "What about we go to Mrs. Yagar first instead? She might know what to do." We knew Mrs. Yagar wouldn't hesitate to help no matter what. I didn't even bother to call ahead and let her know we was coming

We found the midwife standing in her side yard tossing cracked corn down for the chickens. Her face broke into a smile when we first pulled up then fell in

Dark Hollow Road

alarm when she must have seen the frantic and weary expression on my face. "Ali's real sick, Mrs. Yagar," I told her all the details as she took my baby into her arms.

"Oh, she's burning up," the older woman gasped. "Let's get inside. I got a little tub we can put her in with some cool, wet towels. You done the right thing coming here."

Nigel opted to stay outside and talk to Mrs. Yagar's youngest son, Lee.

Mrs. Yagar wasn't a real doctor, or even a registered nurse, but she was still the best and only thing we had close by. She handed me a bunch of towels and told me to get them good and wet then put them in a big plastic tub while she took Ali's temperature, listened to her chest, looked into her ears, and down her throat. Once done, she put Ali in the tub and covered her with a dry towel.

"We need to get the fever down," she told me. "It gets up too high for too long it could cause brain damage."

I watched my little one shiver in her nest of towels while her face was still beet red with fever.

"You got plenty of baby aspirin?"

"I got a whole bottle."

"Good." There was the sudden sound of Ali's bowels letting go into her diaper, followed almost instantly by the wail of her crying. "How's her cough? Dry or wet? Does it sound like a seal pup barking to be nursed?"

I had no idea what a seal pup sounded like so answered, "It's kind of phlegmy, but not like a bark."

"Isn't the Croup then, More likely the flu. That isn't so good, neither. There isn't much that can be done for, either. They just have to run their course. Our job is to keep them as comfortable as we can so their little bodies can rest and get through it. Get her to drink as much as you can as often as you can. She gets dehydrated and that will kill her."

My top teeth worried against my bottom lip. "She ain't eaten since yesterday afternoon. Got some applesauce into her."

"That's good. Applesauce is good, but more important is the liquids. A body can go a good long spell without food, but it only takes three days to die of dehydration." She must have seen the utter terror in my eyes. Mrs. Yagar stepped away from Ali's little cooling tub and came to me with a big hug. "She's going to be alright. You did the right thing bringing her to me." She pulled back and held me at arm's length. "I won't let no harm come to that little one. She's as dear to me as my own, just like you are." She gave me another quick hug then drew back again. "You stay here with her and I'll get some coffee made. You look like you could use a cup. You feeling alright, hon? You're looking a little peaked."

I attempted a smile, "Things ain't been easy lately."

She shook her head. "I know they haven't, hon. I know they haven't. I'll go get the coffee on."

As soon as she was gone, I slumped into the chair next to the table Ali's tub was perched on. Her sweet face, normally always so happy, was lax and unsmiling. There were traces of dark circles under her closed eyes. Her mouth hung open as it almost always did and she was perfectly motionless. Cold panic slapped me. My hand shot out and touched her cheek. It was warmer than it should be, but it wasn't burning as much as it had been before. The wet towels must be working.

I dared close my own eyes just for a second, just long enough to take a few deep breaths and let my brain and body know it was going to be alright. Mrs. Yagar had saved the day again.

I dreamed about Mama, me, and Katie working in the garden. No babies had been made by mistake then. No other babies had died. It was just us three girls pulling up weeds in the hot, summer sun.

Mama was singing. "It's a-long John, he's a-long gone. Like a turkey through the corn, through the long corn."

Kate and me would laugh and repeat after her. "It's a-long John, he's a-long gone. Like a turkey through the corn, through the long corn."

On and on it went through the afternoon, that sun beating down and making us all hot and sweaty. Mama said it was a song her mama had taught her and her mother before her.

"I'm thirsty," I straightened up and stretched my back.

"Yes, it sure is hot. I'll give you that."

A hand come down on my shoulder. For a second I thought it was Daddy home early from work looking for some Loving Time. My body jerked away.

Except, I wasn't standing in Mama's garden no more. I was sitting in Mrs. Yagar's little clinic room and it was her hand on my shoulder. I could smell the coffee she'd made. Confused, the dream still lingering in a steamy fog around my head, I stammered. "I'm thirsty. Sure is hot." Not in the garden. Mama's dead. Katie's gone away, a-long gone.

Mrs. Yagar, who had put the coffee down on the table before trying to wake me, frowned and placed the back of her cool hand on my forehead and cheeks.

"Mary Alice, I think you come down with the flu, too. You're hot as toast."

My hand rose to touch my warm face. "It's just a cold." A chill shuddered through me. Mrs. Yagar was pulling me to my feet and walking me over to a narrow cot along the back wall of the room. "Nothing to worry about."

It didn't take any effort at all on her part to get me to lie down. "You rest. I'll be right back."

"Ali ..."

"She's sleeping. You get some sleep, too. It will do the both of you a world of good."

The clinic door clicked shut. Sleep sucked me under like quicksand, back to the garden, back to Mama's singing, and back into that steaming, hot August day of weeding and sweating and working until my muscles ached.

The room was long with shadows when I opened my eyes again. I was soaked through with sweat. I had to get up. I didn't have time to rest. Garden needed weeding. Daddy would be home from work and there'd be no supper on the table. Mama had a sick baby to take care of. I'd have to be the lady of the house for awhile. I sat up too fast, sending the room into a slow, dipping spin. My stomach coiled, making itself ready to spew its contents. I swallowed hard on a dry, sore throat. So thirsty.

"Alice?" Where was my baby? Reality came back. I was at the Yagar farm. They'd taken Alice. They'd taken my baby and left me here to die. No. That wasn't right. Nigel and I had brought her here, sick. Now I was sick, too. God, I so wanted a drink.

Dark Hollow Road

Poising myself to stand, I called out for Mrs. Yagar. On shaky knees across a tipping, swaying floor, I made it as far as the table before the door opened and she came in. "Mary Alice, you get back to that bed." She swooped over to me, turning me around, walking me back to the cot and blankets damp with sweat. "You aren't going anywhere today and maybe not tomorrow, you hear?"

"Ali?" The word burned at the back of my throat.

"I got Ali in the other room with me. You don't worry about her." She got me to lie down again.

"Can I get some water?"

"Of course." The rim of a cold glass pressed to my lips as Mrs. Yagar helped to keep my head up so I could drink. Every swallow hurt and refreshed at the same time. "Take these aspirins." I took them, gagging on the second briefly before feeling my head lowered down onto a pillow and a sheet drawn up over me.

"Nigel?"

Her cool hand petted the hair off my face. "I fed Nigel a nice big supper and he went home. I'll feed him breakfast in the morning when he stops on his way to work. You rest." Something clicked, a motor started, then a gentle, cool breeze began blowing on my face.

Things got all fuzzy after that. I didn't want to sleep, but the sheet might as well have been made of lead, the way it held me down so I couldn't move. The fan turned back and forth, rattling slightly at some point in its cycle. Sleep would have its way with me no matter how hard I tried to fight it.

The windows and the room was pitch black and thirst ragged hard at the back of my throat, when I woke again with the urge to pee. The bathroom wasn't far away. I was sure I could make it that far without help.

Sitting up became my first trouble. Every ounce of strength seemed to have left my body. Turning back and forth in the dark, the fan's breeze sent chills through me many times over as I sat on the edge of the bed fighting the nausea and trying to focus on obstacle number two, standing. I tried to remember the layout of the room. Was the table or one of its chairs close enough for me to grope my way to? I didn't think so. The nightstand wouldn't be of any help, either. I was on my own. I leaned forward, found a place of balance, and got about halfway up before my knees turned to gelatin and I had to sit down again. My bladder ached.

I tried again, made it to my feet that time, held out my hands, and shuffled in the direction I knew the door into the hallway to be. My hands hit the door then slipped down to find the cool, ceramic knob. What if it was locked? Fresh beads of sweat broke out all over my body. Still clutching the knob with both hands, I rested my forehead on the door to collect myself. *There's no reason for it to be locked, Mary Alice. Stop thinking crazy things.*

After swallowing what felt like pieces of broken glass, I straightened and turned the knob. The latched clicked and the door opened. Not locked. Not locked at all. I went across the hall, closed the bathroom door and found the light switch. The flood of light I'd expected never came. Instead, the single bulb hanging from a cord in the middle of the room glowed a dim, nearly-useless, brown. Toggling the switch up and down didn't help and I was afraid if I did it more, I'd end up with no light at all. At least I could see the toilet. It wasn't any more than three steps away.

I opened the lid and all that twisting, tipping, and gurgling my stomach had been doing before came heaving up and splashing down into a porcelain bowl thick with human waste. There was no time to aim and I couldn't imagine getting closer to the already nasty contents of the soiled bowl and seat. Even worse, the violent surge of my vomiting had also released my bladder. I staggered towards, then into, the bathtub, tripped over the side, thudded against the opposite wall and sank to my knees in all my delirious, fever-induced glory. The overhead bulb dimmed, buzzed, and flickered.

"Mary Alice?"

Clutching my stomach as I rocked and moaned in the tub, I barely heard the voice. It was a soft voice, a deep voice, not the voice of Mrs. Yagar. What was left in my stomach lurched upwards as I puked towards the drain hole.

"Mary Alice?" It was a man's voice.

I tried to answer, but my throat was filled with molten glass. Whoever it was opened the door and stepped in. The breeze the act generated sent a wave of familiar scents over me. The stench of coal, mud, motor oil, manure, and my father's aftershave settled around my curled and aching body.

"Mary Alice," he said for the third time.

Even over my screams I could hear the sound of his belt being undone and the zipper on his pants coming down.

Chapter 36

Brandon pulled his knees up to his chest in a close hug. Kicking, screaming, and pounding on the black, wooden walls of his prison had done no good. Thrashing around had kicked up what remained of the coal dust inside the box which had got him coughing instead of screaming and now his eyes burned, too.

Mommy was right. They never should have come over here at all. This was a very bad place. He wanted to go home so bad.

"Brandon!"

The boy lifted his head. "Mommy?" he whispered. It had sounded just like his mother's voice. Of course! How dumb was he? They'd come to look for him! They'd not found him in his bed and they'd come looking. Mama Sam had a key to the house and the basement lock and they were here searching. Brandon howled with joy and shifted to his knees to better pound on the box walls.

"Down here!" he shouted. "I'm in the cellar, Mommy! DOWN HERE! I'M HERE! MOMMY!"

He stopped to listen again.

"Brandon, are you over here? Answer me, baby!"

Someone pounded on something overhead.

"MOMMY!" Brandon screamed as loud as he could, pounding his fists on the walls. "HELP ME!" Breathing in to catch his breath filled his lungs with more coal dust, sending him into another coughing fit.

"Hello? Is there anyone in there? Brandon?" That was Mama Sam from somewhere nearby. Not the same direction as Mommy's voice had come from. Closer.

"I'm here," he choked out the words, coughed and shouted again. "DOWN HERE, MAMA SAM! DOWN IN THE CELLAR! COME GET ME!"

Brandon sat very still trying to hear where they might be and then something strange occurred to him. Why didn't he hear The Sugar Lady or the kids? Why didn't Mommy or Mama Sam see them in the kitchen? Were they hiding? They had to be. They must have heard Mommy and Mama Sam drive up and they'd run to hide. What about the food? They couldn't have hidden all that stuff that fast, could they? And they sure as heck couldn't hide the smell of bacon.

"Hold up, Babe," Mama Sam called. The words were followed quickly by the thunk-thunk-thunk of someone going down a short flight of stairs. "Watch out for woodchuck holes!"

Why didn't they come into the house? Don't worry about that. They'll be back. They were looking. If they didn't find him right away, they'd call the police and Mr. Martin. The Sugar Lady and Allan and Ginny would be sorry. It wouldn't be long now. Help was on the way. He was sure of it. He just had to sit tight and wait.

"The grave?" Renee's jaw dropped

Lee drew in a breath, exhaling it with a low, soft groan. "Yeah. There was a grave in the cellar. A small one in the corner."

Renee probably really didn't want to know but she asked anyway, "How small?"

The old man sucked air through his teeth. "Infant sized going by Butch Martin's story."

"Jesus Christ," Sam said in a stunned whisper.

Lee cleared his throat and shifted in the wooden chair. "Two possibilities," he went on. "Mrs. Brown gave birth to a stillborn around 1950. May have been '51. No matter which. My mother was the midwife to that birth. She told us it was a girl and that Mr. Brown had wrapped it up and taken it away in a carpet bag. Mrs. Brown, Mary's mother, didn't last no more than half an hour after. Clay Brown refused to let her call anyone about it, but she insisted on filing the death certificates herself. What was done with either body no one but the Brown family knows, but I don't think it's the same child."

Renee nodded in agreement. Something in her gut, call it Mother's Intuition, twisted. "I get the impression this family was pretty tight. They'd have buried the mother and child together."

Lee nodded, "I'm convinced there's another grave on that property."

"What's the other option?" Sam asked.

Lee covered his mouth with one gnarled hand, rubbing at his cheeks slowly. His old eyes had softened considerably since their arrival. His hand dropped back to the table. "I think it was Mary's."

"Mary's?"

He rocked a bit in the chair, lips puckered in thought. "I had an older brother, Larry," he started and stopped, took a sip from his nearly empty cup of coffee, and shook his head. "Larry used to pal around with a couple boys back in the day, Richard and Elmer. In '65 Larry was in a bad car wreck. Lived through it,

but not for long. We was real close, me and Larry."
Lee stopped again, gathering his thoughts and maybe
even his courage. He cleared his throat again before
continuing. "A nurse called me to his hospital room
when it was close. Said he wanted to talk to me alone.
It was a terrible thing, a terrible thing."

"You don't have to tell us, Mr. Yagar," Renee
reached out. The old man actually let her put her hand
on top of his for a moment of comfort.

But, he shook his head. "No, I do have to tell ya."
His hand withdrew. "Larry had a confession to make.
He told me about a night some ten or eleven years
before when he and Richard and Elmer had met up
with Mary coming out of the theatre. Richard wanted
to treat her to a burger at Kelley's."

"Seems nice of him."

"No," Lee scowled. "No, it wasn't nice of him.
Richard had other ideas only Larry didn't know it right
away. After they left Kelley's, Richard offered to give
Mary a ride home. They didn't take Mary home.
Richard went down some other road, pulled over, and,
well, he and Elmer raped Mary in a ditch. Larry
refused. They called him a pansy or something similar,
and left the both of them there alongside the road in the
middle of the night."

"Oh, God," Renee moaned. "That poor girl and
your brother. Oh, Mr. Yagar, I'm so sorry."

He grunted, "Nothing to be sorry about. Ain't
nothing we can do anything about now."

"And you think Mary got pregnant as a result?"
Sam asked.

"Don't see why not. She would have been fifteen
or sixteen, near the same age as Larry."

Renee considered it for a minute. "Wouldn't someone have noticed she was pregnant? She must have gone into town now and then."

"The Browns kept to themselves for the most part. Months would pass without anyone seeing anyone but Clay in town."

"What about school?"

"The two boys and the littlest girl, Kate, yeah, they went to school, but Clay kept Mary to home after the mother died. Said she needed to take care of things and be the woman of the house after that." He finished the cup of coffee. "That brings up a third possibility."

"Dear, God," Renee's heart sank. "The father."

Lee nodded. "Plenty of rumors about that, too, yeah." He picked up his coffee cup and shoved the chair back as if the conversation was suddenly over. It was the action of a man who didn't really want to talk about it anymore. He headed to the counter where the coffee pot sat half empty. "Sure ya don't want some coffee? Maybe some tea? Maggie's got more tea than Carter's got pills. I can heat up a cup of water for ya in the microwave."

Renee's surrendered to the man's kindness and the knowledge that if he was offering more to drink, he still had plenty to say. "Tea would be nice. What do you have?"

Lee nodded, turning to Sam. "What about you? Still not thirsty? You a beer drinker, maybe? Got some PBR."

Relief sparked in Sam's eyes at the mention of beer even though Renee knew her partner loathed Pabst Blue Ribbon, calling it piss water. "Yeah, a beer sounds great. Thank you."

Five minutes later, Renee was dunking her teabag up and down in a cup of hot water and Sam was sipping from a beer can. Lee glanced at the kitchen clock, "Girls will be home in about half an hour. We need to cut to the chase here."

"Mr. Yagar, what does the grave of a stillborn have to do with the boy my son says he's seen. It's an older boy, maybe ten or so, not an infant."

"Right, that. My father bought up all the land except the half acre the house, barn, and that little apple orchard out back. Didn't want nothing to do with owning those. He kept any eye on it for the family, he said. Making sure it wasn't broken into and all that until it went up for auction. When my father passed, I got the land for farming."

"So, the cornfield around us is all yours?"

"Yep, sure is." He smiled. "Use to own that little spot your place sits on, too, until someone got interested in building there."

"The baby, Mr. Yagar," Sam interrupted. "What about the baby in the grave? What connection is it to the boy Brandon has told us about?"

"Doug and Ed were cleaning out in the cellar. There was a ton of old tools down there. Ed said there was some sort of workbench down there?" Sam nodded and said there was. "Well, from where that bench sits, ya got the stairs going up behind ya to the left, that corner of the house, nearest the barn, that's where they found it. Looked like just a pile of rocks. They got to poking around and found a big flat stone, maybe a foot square and an inch thick. He flipped it over and there it was. The name 'Allan' painted on it. They dug around a bit more and found another one that said 'Baby'. Course, one thing led to another and before they knew it, they found themselves looking at a pile of tiny bones topped with a tiny skull."

Cold shock rippled through Renee's arms.

"Called in the police and they sent over someone to take care of it. Folks at the morgue said it was too young to determine the sex. Not sure what they did with the remains after that."

Sam looked as confused as Renee felt. "But, that's a baby, not a ten-year-old boy. If I believed in ghosts, which I don't, how could the boy Brandon has seen be the same person as the Allan found in the cellar?"

"Really don't know," Lee confessed.

"And what about the other two children, the two girls? Who are they? Where do they come from?"

"Don't know that either," Lee went on. "Mrs. Brown gave birth to a stillborn baby girl, we know that for certain. Chances are high it's buried around there somewhere along with the mother. Maybe that's something to do with it."

"Unless dead babies grow up into ghost children, this doesn't make sense. Not that any of this makes any sense, anyway."

"I'm only telling ya what I know," Lee said. "And what I know is this. After they found that grave and after those remains were removed from that house, something changed around that place. It had never been a pleasant place to be before that, but after, it was downright eerie. Always felt like ya was being watched. Always felt like ya was going to turn around and see someone standing right there. Nearest I get is when I'm plowing and harvesting the fields and even then, that's too damn close."

"You think it's Mary," Renee said.

"Has to be. I think they got her riled up when they dug up and took away that baby. That's why I think it was hers and that's why I think she's going after other kids. They took her baby away. Now, if some other kid comes along and takes anything from the place, she figures it's her right to take the kid. Ya sure your boy didn't take anything from the property?"

Renee nodded. "He never went into the house, Mr. Yagar. He couldn't have."

"But I did," Sam said as if waking from a deep sleep. "I went into the house and I took something from it, the basement even, compliments of Doug Martin."

Light dawned on Renee as well, "The crate of lamp parts."

"Damn," Lee muttered, scrubbing at his stubble-covered face again. "Ya still got 'em?"

Sam nodded, "Yeah, in the garage. I was going take them to a friend of mine down in Jersey who has a little shop and a lamp restoration business."

"They should be put back where ya got them." Lee said.

Sam's frowned. "There was something else, too." She twisted in the seat, reaching into the pocket of her jacket draped over the back of the kitchen chair. "This." Sam pulled out the long, narrow ribbon of pale blue fabric dotted with flowers. "Brandon noticed it."

She held it out towards Lee who recoiled as if being presented with a venomous snake. "Where did he get it?"

"It was in snagged on one of the corner nails of the crate."

Lee had gone ashen white and mute.

"Mr. Yagar, do you know what that's from?"

His hands and voice trembled. "Mary's dress."

Sam's eyes grew wide, "That's what Brandon said."

"It needs to all be put back," Lee said in earnest. "Ya understand? All of it. Ya didn't take anything else out of that crate, did ya?"

"No, nothing."

"It needs to go back, right back where ya found it."

"But it's just a box of ..."

"Don't matter," Lee cut Sam off, "Don't matter what it was. It was just a bunch of old marbles in the driveway the first time. It was just a bunch of junk and a suitcase the second time. Mary ain't particular. If it's on that property and she thinks it belongs to her, she doesn't care what it is. All the other things, the furniture and what-not, was removed before they found that grave. The Martins took her baby from that grave and that was the last straw. Ya need to put all them things back as soon as ya can."

Renee's mind was in turmoil. How was this possible? What madness had they stumbled on? "Mr. Yagar, what happened to Mary? Do you know? Do you think she's dead, I mean, is her body dead? Did she move away? When was the last time you or anyone actually saw her alive?"

Lee Yagar was visibly shaken. It took him awhile to answer as the clock ticked down the minutes until his wife and sister returned.

"1977," he said quietly.

"What happened in 1977, Mr. Yagar?"

The old man stared at some distant point over Renee's shoulder, lost in thoughts and memories kept buried for decades. "Her brother Nigel died," he said in a whisper.

Chapter 37

They told me it was just a fever dream. I wasn't fooled. They'd done something to me. Maybe it hadn't been Daddy Clay who showed up in that bathroom, but it was a man. It was too dark to really tell, but whoever he was, he pulled me from that bathtub like I weighed nothing. I clawed at the tile floor and done my best to scramble away on hands and knees, but it done no good. He was stronger and he just kept pulling me back easy as you please. My screams and cries for help fell on deaf ears.

When he was done, he put me back in the tub, turned the shower on, and flicked off what little dim light there was.

Mrs. Yagar came in a short time after still in her nightclothes. The room flooded with light. Why hadn't it worked for me? He must have changed the light bulb. That had to be it. "Mary Alice, what are you doing? It's the middle of the night, sweetheart." She pretended like she didn't know. I had a feeling it had been her husband and they were in it together.

The shower shut off and I felt her trying to pull me back out of the ball I'd curled up into. "Mary, sit back. Let me run you a bath instead."

I yanked away from her. "Don't touch me. He already touched me enough."

"Who, honey? Who touched you?"

My head hurt as I tried to think. It had been real dark in there and the man hadn't said anything but my name. "Daddy Clay," I blurted out. "It was Daddy Clay." It was as close as I ever come to telling anyone about the things my father had done to us.

Mrs. Yagar's movements stopped. "Mary, your father's gone. He's dead."

She was right. Who had it been? Maybe it was just a dream. No. It had been too real to be a dream. Not a dream. Mr. Yagar. Daddy Clay. Richard Barrows. Nigel. Daddy Clay. Daddy Clay's dead. You fed him to the pigs, remember? "I don't know," I heard myself say. "A man came in and he, he did his man business."

Water started running again. It was cold like ice and it was soon filling up the tub. "Mary, sit back, honey. Sit back and relax. You're sick. You've got a terribly bad fever. You're imagining things."

I didn't want to sit in that cold tub, but I uncurled myself because the water was almost to my nose. I could feel the steam of it against my skin. It was funny. I ain't never seen cold water steam like that before, unless it was mist rising from a pond on a chilly morning. Mrs. Yagar knelt beside the tub holding a washcloth, looking at me with worried and weary eyes. My gaze darted towards the toilet. It wasn't full of shit no more. There was lots of puke on the seat and on the floor where I'd missed, but it wasn't dirty like I'd seen it at all. Someone had flushed it.

I looked at the floor, to where I'd tried to get away expecting to see something, anything that would show I'd passed that way covered in vomit. It was all clean. Even the towels were all neat and tidy. My shaking hands rose to cover my face. "I want to go home." All I wanted was to take my little Ali and go home to my own house, my own bed, to my brother. I needed Nigel. I needed him to love me. "Nigel loves me," I said.

"Of course he does," Mrs. Yagar was running the cool washcloth over my back. "Let me wipe off your face, Mary." While I sat there shivering, she cleaned me off then wrapped me up in a big pink towel before we went back across the hallway to the clinic.

I'd just gotten the fresh nightgown on when Mr. Yagar tapped on the door. "Everything alright?"

His wife nodded, "We're fine. Just a fever dream." She picked up the brush she'd brought with us from the bathroom. "Go on back to bed. It's all over with."

His smile gave me the heebie-jeebies. I'd never noticed how it was all lopsided before. "Need me to do anything?"

The brush began to get worked through the wet tangles of my hair. "Not unless you want to clean the puke up in the bathroom for me," Mrs. Yagar smiled. She knew. God, she knew it was him who'd come in earlier. I could see it in her eyes.

I was put to bed and even though my brain kept telling me to get up and find Ali and run home, my body wouldn't let me. Two days passed before the fever broke and I come to my senses. By then, Ali was well on the mend, too. Mrs. Yagar made us both stay another day just to make sure I was well enough to take care of the both of us. Nigel drove us home after we'd all had a big supper.

Angry, dark clouds hung over us all the way home. Other than the rumbles of thunder that drew closer and the sound of the truck's engine, the ride was quiet. Ali clung to me as tightly as I to her. We were both still tired and not completely well, but the idea of going home done my heart good. Just as we turned down Dark Hollow Road, a blinding flash of lightening turned everything around us pure white. The crack of thunder that came right on top of it sent Ali to screaming.

"That was close." Nigel flipped on the wipers, leaned towards the windshield, and looked up towards the blackening sky. "Here comes the rain."

The moment I stepped into the front entry, the familiar warm smells soothed and calmed me. Home. Nothing was better than home. I'd only been away for three days. It felt like it three years. Ali must have felt it, too. Her head came to rest on my shoulder as the two middle fingers of her right hand slid into her mouth to be sucked on.

I planted a kiss on her forehead, "We're home, sweetie." She didn't seem to hear me, but that was okay. "Nothing's gonna hurt you. Mama's here."

Another flash of close lightning and thunder rippled through the house and shook the old glass in the windows. Ali turned her head as if trying to figure out where all this racket was coming from.

"You want some tea or something? I can make it," Nigel offered.

"Tea would be nice." I followed my brother into the kitchen and sat at the table, tucking Ali half on my lap, half on my shoulder where she clung. "Is it supposed to storm all night?"

"On and off, I think."

My heart sank a bit, "Would you sleep with us tonight, then?"

Nigel paused half a second as he was pulling cups from the shelf. "Sure," he said, reaching for the tea bags. "I'm glad you're back, Mary. It's been real quiet and lonely without you."

I couldn't even begin to imagine what this house must feel like empty. I'd never spent a night alone here my entire life. "I'm glad to be back, too." I saw a trace of Mama in his eyes when he smiled.

We drank our tea as the storm raged on. The tin roof clattered like a crazy, metal drum. Rainwater rushed and shot past the gutters like they wasn't even there. Ali eventually nodded off in my arms. What a wonderful night it was. Nigel and I put Ali between us on the bed before pulling the covers over us all.

Over her sleeping figure he reached out, stroked my cheek, and smiled again. He didn't kiss me, but I could tell he wanted to. I wanted him to, too, but it was more important to sleep than have our Loving Time.

September came to an end and I realized I hadn't got my lady time yet that month. I'd heard somewhere that when you're sick that sometimes makes you run late, so I waited. October came and went, too.

When Nigel found me standing at the stove making supper and crying when he come home from work, it was almost too much for me to say the words. Folks were going to talk. They didn't know about the man who raped me while I was with the Yagar's. They'd automatically assume it was Nigel's and that me and Nigel had been living like man and wife. Truth was, I didn't know whose baby it was. Truth was, I wanted it to be Nigel's. I wanted it so bad that I worked to convince myself that it was just like Mrs. Yagar had said, all a fever dream.

I was God-awful sick this time around, but I didn't dare call anyone. Hiding my growing belly through the winter was easy enough. Come spring, I stayed home as much as possible. When I did go into town, I made sure it was on a rainy day so I had an excuse to wear my big raincoat.

On April nineteenth while I was making me and Ali some lunch, a pain like searing metal doubled me over with a scream. Ali was sitting under the table playing with rubber animals and stacking rings when I cried out. She looked up and stuck the butt end of the hippo into her mouth and watched without concern. It was two months too early for labor pains. No sooner did I get myself standing upright again when another wave of pain lanced through me. My vision blurred as nausea soured the back of my throat. I needed to get to the phone. I'd call Nigel.

With the room going tipsy-turvy, I groped my way towards the kitchen door holding onto anything within reach, a chair here, a wall there, the edge of the stove, the doorframe, all kept me upright until I felt something warm seeping down the insides of my legs. The phone seemed miles away.

The third pain brought me to my knees. The blood went from a trickle to a gush. The little hallway where all the downstairs room met, tipped on its side and grew longer. A steady woosh-woosh-woosh throbbed in my head just before all the air was sucked from the room and things went black and silent.

It was over. They knew. The choking smell of antiseptic woke me with a cough. A hand that felt like someone had tied a five-pound bag of sugar to it, slid across the neatly pressed sheets and came to rest on my flat, empty stomach. Gone. There was nothing left but the hollow, aching pain of what could have been.

A pair of shoes whispered across the floor from the hallway, bringing a nurse into the room. She smiled faintly. "You're awake," she said. "Let me get the doctor."

An older man with short gray hair and a kind face came in shortly. The gold badge on his pocket said he was Dr. James. I didn't want to look at him. I didn't want to hear what he had to say.

"Miss Brown," he said, stepping closer. "I'm Dr. James. I'm afraid ..."

"I know," I said with a voice that sounded like dry corn husks rubbing together.

"The nurse is calling your brother," he added. "You lost a lot of blood. We were afraid we were going to lose you, too."

I wished I had been lost. At least being dead would make the pain stop. I closed my eyes and wished for him to just go away and leave me alone. I must have fallen back to sleep, because Nigel was sitting where the doctor had been standing when I opened my eyes again. He looked pale and tired.

"Mary," he whispered with relief, seeing my eyes open.

I tried to squeeze his hand. I don't know if I succeeded. "Alice?" I didn't think it possible for him to get any paler, but he did. His eyes flashed wider just before looking away towards the window where the curtains were drawn tight. My heart skipped a beat. "Is she safe?"

Nigel barely nodded. "Mr. and Mrs. Yagar are taking care of her," he said and swallowed.

"When can you take me home?"

"Couple of days," he said. "They said your body needs a couple more days to build your blood back up again." He frowned. "I thought you were dead, Mary. I was sure you was dead. Doctor said you probably would have been if I'd been another couple hours later."

"You saved my life." I wished he'd smile. I'd have felt so much better if he'd smiled.

Nigel finally looked at me and I knew right away there wasn't nothing close to a smile coming my way. "They called Mrs. Hayes," he said.

My heart went cold. "Who? Why?"

"The hospital." He looked out the window again and repeated that old line we'd both heard dozens of times before. "In the best interests of the child."

Chapter 38

Somewhere in the jumbled layers of half sleep, Brandon heard a scratching sound. Chish-chish-chish it clawed at a piece of wood. His eyes snapped open to the pitch black; cold sweat broke out along the entire length of his body. Brandon tried to lick his dry lips, but his tongue felt like it was made of sandpaper. Chish-chish, the sound came again. Chish-chish-chish. Down at the other end of the box. He knew what it had to be, a rat. It only sounded like one, but that was more than enough.

Chish-chizzle-chizzle. Its claws were replaced by teeth, chewing on the wood, chewing and scratching and trying to get in. Silence. Maybe it had gone away. Then the click-click of its tiny feet skittering across the floor, moving closer to his safe corner. For one terrifying second, the idea that the rat was inside the box instead of outside flashed through his head. It was going to crawl on him. Its toenails would jab like needles into his bare legs. Its razor sharp teeth would eat him alive.

Brandon yelped, kicked out, and shifted to the left to dodge the rat-sized bullet. It passed by, inches way. Not in the box. No, it wasn't in the box; it was outside trying to find a way in because it could smell him and it was hungry.

Chizzle-chizzle-chizzle-chish. It was right beside him, only as far away as the wall was thick. Brandon slammed his body back to the other side, screaming. "GO AWAY!"

It only needed a little hole to get through. Once it found or made one that would be the end of him. He'd never be able to stand it.

"GO AWAY! GO AWAY!" he pleaded, kicking at the wall.

That horrible dust came sucking into his lungs again, making him retch and cough.

Chish-chizzle-chish.

Why didn't it just go away?! There were lots of things to eat in other places! It didn't need to get in here. It really didn't.

Squeaking sounds whispered through the layer of wood, thumps, tip-tack-tip-tack went the tiny claws back and forth, searching for a way in. Chizzle-chizzle down at the other end again. Chish-chish to his right. Tip-tack back and forth. More than one! All around, all of them trying to get in.

Brandon got to his knees and pushed on the top of the box. It shifted, but held fast by whatever lock The Sugar Lady had put in place. "Let me out of here!" He shrieked, banging on the lid with his fists. "Please let me out! I'll stay with you for as long as you want if you just let me out and make the rats go away! PLEASE! LET ME OUT!"

He collapsed to his butt again, hugging his knees up tight to his chest, listening, shaking, sweating, and crying as the rats went round and round, digging, biting, scratching, gnawing and getting closer one sliver of wood at a time.

Brandon buried his face into his drawn-up knees, whimpering, and waiting to be eaten alive.

"Nigel was only thirty-five. He and Mary had been keeping house alone for, oh, six or seven years, I think."

"Wait, what?" Sam held up her hand. "Alone? What about the rest of the family? Mr. Martin said there was quite a few of them."

"There were four of them. Mary was the oldest, then Nigel, then Seth and the youngest one was Kate. Seth and Kate had been gone a good long time by the time Nigel passed."

"Where did they go?"

"Last I knew they were in Scranton. They'd been living with their uncle since they were young teens, after the father went missing. They were in town after Nigel's death but only stayed a couple days," Lee explained. "There'd been some sort of falling out with Mary over the years and they stayed away." He shook his head. "It was a real shame, that whole family used to be so close, then one tragedy after another eventually ripped it apart at the seams."

Renee felt her heart softening for Mary. At least it was starting to make a little bit of sense. "What happened to Nigel? How'd he die?"

"Had some sort of seizure, or a stroke, or one of those aneurism things. He was out plowing when it happened. Mary went out looking for him when he didn't come in for supper. I believe she had him cremated."

"Didn't you go to the funeral?" Renee asked.

Lee shook his head. "Mary wouldn't have it. I don't even think there was a proper funeral home or church service. I imagine she just took the remains home from wherever they were cremated and," he gave a weary shrug. "Another set of remains on that property probably."

"And what about Mary? What became of her?"

Again, Lee seemed at a loss. "Gone."

"Dead?"

He shook his head. "I don't know. I can't shake the feeling that she's still around somehow, somewhere, watching over that house and everything in it."

"If she's alive, she has to come out some time," Sam said. "She'd have to get food and water, right? And she can't be in the house. That place has been searched half a dozen times. I don't see how she can possibly be staying there."

Lee was nodding in agreement. "I know what I'm saying don't make a lick of sense and that's one reason I don't talk much about it. All I can tell ya is that as far as I know, nobody has seen her since after Nigel died and her family went back to Scranton."

Renee nibbled thoughtfully on the inside of her bottom lip. "What did she look like, Mr. Yagar? Tall, thin? Short, fat?"

"Oh, the Brown kids were all thin, thin but strong as the Devil. Nigel was close to six foot tall and Mary," he paused as if visualizing the woman in his head, "Mary, she was probably about five-five, five-six. Always kept her hair long. She pulled it back in a ponytail now and then. She had brown hair, like the rest of them, though God help me, she was looking about twice her age last time I saw her, I tell ya."

"How old would she be if she's still alive?" Sam asked.

Lee hmm'd. "Well, I reckon she was a year or two younger than Larry, so that would put her around seventy-four or seventy-five now."

"So, she really could still be alive," Renee's thoughts and words trailed off.

"Oh, yeah. The Browns were a hearty, stubborn lot. Their parents taught them to do for themselves. For the most part ya never saw them in town except to get those few odds and ends they couldn't make themselves like picking up toilet paper and sugar and the like."

Renee stopped breathing, her hands suddenly cold and damp. "Sugar?"

"I heard Mary was quite a baker and loved to make pies. I'm told she made one of the best apple pies in these parts. They had a little orchard out back of the house, half a dozen trees."

She felt like she was going to pass out until Sam's warm hand covered the one Renee had resting on the table, "You okay?"

She wasn't sure that she was. Her mouth opened and closed a few times before she could get the air in and the words out, "The Sugar Lady." Renee looked at her partner. "Mary Brown, it has to be the same person."

"Then she has to be alive if Brandon saw her." Sam turned a desperate, questioning eye to Mr. Yagar. "She must have a place nearby. Something in the woods, an old shack or, or something. No one is living in that house, Mr. Yagar. I guarantee that. There were cobwebs in the stove. If she was there, wouldn't she at least use the stove for heat and cooking?"

The old man's expression remained unreadable. "Police searched the woods, right?"

"Of course," Sam said.

"Did they find anything?"

"No."

Lee's gaze flicked towards the golden sunburst of a clock hung over the kitchen sink. "They didn't find anything the other two times, either. There ain't no shack. There ain't no place on God's green earth that Mary Brown would be but her own property. She's there, somewhere. I feel it every time I'm out that way on the tractor. She's watching and she knows exactly who I am. She remembers me and she ain't too fond."

Renee scowled. "Oh? Why not?"

Lee grunted and all the friendliness he'd shown them for over an hour was swiped away with the sound. "She just ain't," he said and stood up abruptly. "Now, I think it's time ya headed on back home. I told ya all I can about the place. Ladies'll be home soon."

Renee remained stubbornly seated. "Why doesn't Mary like you?"

His brow grew even more creased. "That's personal, family business and none of your concern. I told ya all I know about the house and Mary that matters to your missing boy. That's what ya come here for. That's all you're getting."

Sam stood and reached for her jacket, giving Renee a gentle pat on the shoulder, "Come on, babe. Let's not push our welcome."

"Listen to her," Mr. Yagar gave a curt nod. "I know none of it is what ya probably wanted to hear, but it's all I got to tell ya."

Renee stood, the pit of her stomach sour and knotted. None of this had made her feel any better. She'd hoped Mr. Yagar would know so much more, but all he'd really done was make it all more confusing and impossible to believe. They followed their host to the front door and stood on the stoop in the cold, November air. "Mr. Yagar," puffs of mist drifted from her mouth as she spoke, "can I ask just one more question?"

He nodded, holding the door, clearly eager to close them and the cold out.

"Do you know how to get in touch with the other two kids, I mean, Mary's brother and sister? Even a hint of an address or phone number, anything?"

He shook his head, inching the door closed. Renee set her palm flat on the wood, hoping the desperation she felt shown in her eyes. "No," he said, "not really. Their uncle was named Eli and his wife, Lily, but they're long dead by now. They lived in Scranton. That's all I know."

The door nudged against Renee's hand but she pushed back just as hard. "Eli Brown or was he the mother's brother?" She needed to know more.

"Gunderman," he said. "Eli and Lily Gunderman."

The moment Renee's arm relaxed and her hand dropped to her side, the door slammed shut.

"Any luck?"

Renee leaned back in the office chair, eyes still on the glowing computer monitor. "Any guess how many Browns there are in Pennsylvania?"

Sam chuckled, "A lot. What about Facebook?"

"I stopped counting after a hundred and that was just the ones named Seth."

"Did you try and narrow it down to just Scranton?"

She rubbed her eyes and moaned. "Yeah. It's just too common a name."

"What about Gunderman?"

"There are fewer, but still, there are a lot of Pennsylvania Dutch and Germans around, too many to just call at random and hope we have the right family and, of course, no Eli or Lily. And who's to say they even stayed in the area? It's been forty years since Lee saw any of them."

Sam's hand came to rest on Renee's shoulders, rubbing them gently. "We should try and get some sleep."

"I'm not tired," Renee lied. She was exhausted, but how could she hope for sleep when her baby was still out there somewhere? Doing this made her feel like she was helping. It was better than feeling useless and hopeless. It was better than the nightmares she feared waited for her if she closed her eyes. She checked the lower right hand corner of the monitor. It was almost midnight.

Sam kissed the top of her head, "Then come snuggle with me so I can sleep. I hate to do this, baby, but I have to go to work tomorrow for the lunch and dinner crowd."

Renee pulled her twitching fingers from the keyboard. She put a hand on top of Sam's and rubbed her own face with the other. "I'll try," she conceded.

"That's all I'm asking."

With a heavy sigh, Renee reached for the mouse, poising the cursor over the X in the upper right hand corner of the screen to close the search window.

"Something the matter?" Sam asked, watching over her shoulder.

"No, but I just had an idea." Renee said, pulled her hand away and typed a name into the search engine.

Behind her back, Sam drew in a sharp breath, "No, fucking, way."

Renee grinned and click on the name that had come up. "Looks to be the right age, too. 65-70."

"There are only three. And only one is the right age and in the right area. That's just a few miles east of Scranton."

Renee sat back in the chair, hope gushing into her heart as she gazed at the name on the screen, Katherine S. Gunderman.

Chapter 39

If I'd ever doubted her motives before that day, I couldn't do it now. Mrs. Hayes sat stiff-backed and tight-lipped as she pulled papers out of an envelope and put them on the desk that separated her from us. She topped them with a pen and gave a curt nod. "For everyone's sake, I'd suggest you sign the papers and have this over and done with, Miss Brown."

"But we didn't do nothing wrong," I protested. "It wasn't Nigel. I swear it."

She let out a frustrated sigh. "We have been over this one too many times already, Mary Alice. You," her eyes flicked to Nigel who sat beside me, "and your brother, have created an environment that the court does not find suitable for a child. An environment that well ... we don't really need to get into that again, do we?"

"It wasn't Nigel's!" I burst to my feet, fists clenched at my sides. "It was that other man. Nigel and me love each other, yeah, but he's my brother, course I love my brother, but we ain't done anything wrong together."

I could see Mrs. Hayes was doing her best to be calm during my outburst. "We've talked to Mr. and Mrs. Yagar about this already. You were ill and clearly hallucinating as a result of a very high fever. You were not raped in their bathroom by Mr. Yagar or anyone else for that matter."

"Were you there?" I shouted. "You wasn't! I was! I seen him! I felt him! That's when I got that baby put in me, not by my brother."

Nigel's hand wrapped around my clenched one. "Mary, please," he said in a calm, quiet voice. Why wasn't he standing up for me and for Ali and for himself? Didn't he understand what they were trying to do to our family? He had to deny it.

"Tell her, Nigel! Tell her."

Big, puppy dog eyes and a growing frown tugged at the corners of his full lips. "You sure you want me to? You really sure? I thought we was supposed to not tell anyone about that night. No need to call the police, you said." What was he talking about?

Mrs. Hayes waited.

I gave a nod and sat back down in the hard, wooden chair. "Tell her," I said.

It took him a minute to compose himself. "We had a burglar, Mrs. Hayes."

"Oh?" Her head tipped slightly back as her eyebrows rose.

"A few weeks after Mary come home from the Yagar's, he broke in. He snuck into Mary's room and that's where I found him. I heard her screaming for help and heard the man talking and being rough with her. I grabbed Daddy Clay's old shotgun and ran down the hall." The fear was plain as day on Nigel's face. "He was on top of her, ma'am, doing, well, having his way with her. I hollered out for him to stop or I'd shoot. He stopped, fell off the bed even, what with his trousers only pulled down to his knees like they was, and sat there on the floor looking up the barrel of the shotgun. I told him to get out or I'd shoot him right then and there, right between the legs."

A shiver passed through me. It was all a lie. Nigel was making it all up for us.

"Then what?"

"Well, he begged me not to shoot him, of course. He fumbled around with his pants and stumbled his way out of the house with me following right behind him. Then he run off."

"Did you recognize this man?"

Nigel licked his lips, "No, never seen him before. We figured it wouldn't do no good to call the police. What would they do about it? Wasn't nothing stolen and," he looked at me again, "well, it would have only made things harder for Mary, getting asked all sorts of personal questions about it. We decided to not tell anyone. It would be our secret and as long as he never come back, well, that was good enough for us. A couple months later, I come home from work and found her crying in the kitchen. That's when she told me she thought she was pregnant."

"And you've still kept it all a secret? Why?"

"Because it wasn't nobody's business but ours, like I told you. Daddy Clay taught us to take care of ourselves. That's what we were doing."

"Didn't you consider how odd it would look to people when all of a sudden they see Mary and you with a second baby?"

"We, we thought maybe we'd drop it off at a church or something," I piped up. "Some of them big churches got those doors you can put babies into, right? Or maybe sneak it into a bathroom at a hospital. Something like that, so someone would find it right off and it would get taken care of."

Dark Hollow Road

Mrs. Hayes tapped a long, lacquered fingernail on her desk, her face pinched in thought. "It's an interesting story," she finally said. "But do I have to I remind you that the court does not need you to sign the papers to remove Ali from your custody? They already have what they need, my statements, the statements of the Yagar's, and the statements of the hospital staff who attended you. Even if I were to retract my report, which I am not about to do, they still have enough." She reached out and tapped the papers twice with a single finger. "Sign."

I was halfway across the top of the desk before Nigel could grab me by the waist and pull me back. "I won't! I won't sign them! She's my baby! You won't take her from me! You won't!" I screamed and kicked and clawed against my brother's grip to get at the throat of the social worker. I didn't care how crazy I looked. I didn't care I was only making myself look even more unstable as a mother. They couldn't do this to me! They couldn't take away my little Ali, too. Nigel wrestled me to the floor and held me there until all I could do was sob and rock in despair. I'd get even. I'd show them all. I'd make them all pay for taking everything from me.

"Take her home, Mr. Brown," I heard Mrs. Hayes say along with the rustle of papers. "I would also suggest you look into getting her some sort of proper mental care." Her shoes click-clacked across the floor, the door opened, then was firmly shut at her exit.

She'd stay with the Yagars until we had our day in court, two weeks away. I didn't see the point of it. No one believed us. They believed Mrs. Hayes and the Yagars and the doctors and nurses, not me. Uncle Eli was sent word of what was going on. I assume Mrs.

Hayes called him, spewing her lies about everything. I half expected the checks to stop coming and to never hear from my brother or sister again. Soon, my baby would be off living with strangers. Mrs. Hayes said once she was adopted by someone, I'd never hear anything again until she was big enough to decide if she wanted to know me. She figured they'd put her in a foster home or orphanage in Scranton or Wilkes-Barre, someplace big like that, where more folks could see her like she was some sort of puppy up for grabs in a pet shop window.

White hot fury burned in my veins. I planned all sorts of ways to get her back. I could nab her from Mrs. Yagar in the grocery store or on the street. Maybe I'd wait outside their church. I even thought about pretending I was alright with the whole thing, get them to trust me so at least I could see my little girl then, when they least expected it, I'd be out of there. My and Nigel's favorite plan was to sneak over in the middle of the night and just take her, then run. Nigel and me could pack up the truck ahead of time, have it waiting, then like thieves in the night, get Ali and be hundreds of miles away before anyone knew we was even gone. I had other ideas, too, like poisoning them all somehow, but was afraid they might give Ali whatever concoction I come up with.

Nigel and me took to sleeping together all the time. I liked his company and needed him to hold and love me to get what little sleep there was to be had. Was during those times, I stopped being so sad. Even if it was just for a few minutes, that was enough. I'd forget everything else and open myself up and let him take me away from all the hurting.

Talk spreads like wildfire on a dry, summer day in small towns like Murphey Mills. Going to the Red and

White became a nightmare. Didn't talk to no one and no one seemed to want to talk to me. I heard them whispering, though. I ain't deaf after all. I bit my tongue, hurried my way through, and checked out as fast as I could without looking at anyone. Nigel heard things, too. They didn't seem to bother him as much as they did me. Maybe was just because he was a man and had a thicker skin, but eventually it all fell onto his boss's desk. Men don't gossip as much as women, but they do wag a tongue or two over their beer and whiskey on a Friday night.

The boss didn't know if what he heard was true or not, and he hoped to God it wasn't, but if things kept on like they were, he'd have to let Nigel go. He didn't want to do that. Nigel was a good, hard worker, but these were serious charges. He couldn't ignore them. They were causing distractions and even the slightest distraction down in the hole could lead to serious injuries.

Nigel tried to be positive while he was telling me all this, but I didn't hold out much hope. Why would we be given a break now? We'd never had one before. Just when we thought things was going to get better, we'd get struck down by the next thing. It was how our life was. You can only get kicked in the stomach so many times before you start listening to that big voice yelling at you to just stay down. "You ain't nothing but an old dog in the gutter," it roars. "Stay in the mud where you belong."

The next two weeks dragged on forever. I did my best to look nice on court day, wearing my best blue dress. It had been Mama's favorite and even if it was a little old-fashioned, it was still pretty and in good shape. The skirt had a sheer layer over top decorated with little white and yellow flowers and had fit Mama perfectly. On me it hung like an old flour sack. As I looked in the mirror that morning trying to do something nice with my hair, I didn't see the twenty-one-year-old woman I was at all. I saw a strange woman who was twice my age staring back at me with dull, sad eyes. I tried on a smile. It didn't fit either and fell from my face in the same way my dress hung from my bony shoulders.

Nigel waited downstairs, dressed in his best suit, and handed me my sweater. It helped to hide my protruding collar bones at least. I didn't have any hope of getting Ali back. At the very most, I just wanted to see her again.

We climbed into the truck just as the windshield started to become dappled with a light rain. A cold wind had been gusting all morning as dark clouds inched themselves up through the river valley. It suited me just fine. All the way to the courthouse in Tunkhannock, I stared out the window, watching the tiny rivulets of rainwater wiggle their way across the glass. I knew that frail, trembling, battered by the storm, cold feeling as well as they did. A great deluge greeted us outside the huge, white brick building where so many fates had been sealed.

Nigel found the closest parking spot he could and cut the engine. His warm hand reached out to cover and hold mine that had gone cold. "We'll get through this, Mary Alice." He knew better than to say everything was going to be alright. It never had been. Why believe things would miraculously turn in our favor?

As we walked up the stairs and into the courthouse, I may as well have been a shackled prisoner shuffling her way to the electric chair. No one prayed for me, though. Even the prayers I'd had for myself had dried up and withered away in the past two weeks.

Everyone was waiting in one of the smaller meeting rooms. Mr. and Mrs. Yagar were there with Mrs. Hayes and the regular doctor I'd been taking Alice to. There was no sign of Ali. Uncle Eli, Aunt Lily, Seth, and Katie sat on the other side. In the center, framed by the United States flag on one side and the state flag on the other, squatted a big desk and the somber, gray-haired judge seated behind it. He looked up as me and Nigel approached down the middle, taking seats at the table pointed out to us by some sort of court officer.

I sat and listened, numb and half-deaf to everything going on around me. I wasn't even able to cry. Like my prayers, my tears had turned to dust. I honestly can't tell you how long it took for them to go over all the statements against us. Eventually, the judge got around to asking me and Nigel questions. Nigel did most of the answering and it turned out that Uncle Eli was there to further confirm the financial support that he'd been sending us would continue for as long as it was needed. The judge had questions for Seth and Kate, too. There was even a letter from Nigel's boss detailing our income.

But, when it come right down to it, none of this was about how much money we had, not really. It was about the house and the environment and the relationship I had with Nigel and who, exactly, the father of the baby I'd lost really was. It was about my own mental and physical stability and how well I could take care of a child with mental retardation and a host of medical problems.

"Miss Brown, do you have anything to say in your own defense before I make my final decision?" the judge asked.

With Nigel's help, I stood up, my knees so weak and shaking I'm surprised I was able to get to my feet at all. "I love my baby, Your Honor. Ain't nobody going to love her as much as I do," I said with a dry, trembling voice. "I know I can take care of her like I been taking care of the rest of my family since our Mama died and since Daddy Clay went missing. We ain't struggling like we was before either and I'm real grateful for the help Uncle Eli and Mrs. Yagar been giving us. I know in my heart I can take care of Alice if folks would just give me the chance to prove it. She been fine this first year and I did everything the doctor told me to do with her. That's all I'm asking for, is for folks to believe in me. I guess that's all, Your Honor." I sat back down hoping I looked as confident as my words were meant to sound.

The judge studied me, drew in a breath, and looked down at his papers before closing up the folder he had on the desk. "There will be a one hour recess while I look over my notes. We are adjourned until eleven o'clock. Please do not leave the courthouse." His gavel hit the little wooden pad once, he rose, and left through a side door without another word to anyone.

Nigel took my hand and gave it a squeeze, "What you said was real good, Mary. Real good."

Kate and Seth come up to the table and gave me and Nigel hugs. "It's going to be okay, Mary," Katie said as she kissed me on the cheek. "You were a real good mother to Seth and me, to all of us. The judge has to see that."

"Not good enough for you to stay with me though, apparently." The venomous words spat from me faster than I could even think to stop them. "You couldn't get away from Dark Hollow Road fast enough. I maybe don't have all the book learning you got, but I ain't stupid."

My sister pulled back in shock. "We didn't have a choice, Mary Alice. You know that."

"Girls," Uncle Eli put a hand on each of our shoulders, "now is not the time to be arguing about this."

I still wasn't sure whose side my uncle was on. He'd done everything he'd promised to do, yet part of me was still full of hate and hurt. That part believed whole-heartedly that he'd worked to get Kate and Seth removed from the house. He'd done something behind my back, worked with or paid off Mrs. Hayes, convinced my brother and sister that they'd be happier and better off with him and his wife, something. The other side of me understood that my siblings really were better off and that the law was the law. I should be happy for them that they had a new and better life away from Dark Hollow Road.

I pulled away from Uncle Eli with a loathsome glare, but wasn't quite ready to be silenced. "I'm starting to think Daddy Clay was right about you. Your presents come with a price. I won't be bought, Uncle Eli. If you'd meant to do right by us, you'd have taken us all out of there right after Mama died. Instead, you vanished. You abandoned us to him."

He tried to put his hand on my shoulder again, but I jerked back, "Mary, I told you I tried to keep in touch. Your father ..."

"You're lying," I hissed back. "You could have come to the house while he was at work. You could have stopped him anytime you wanted."

It was his turn to back off, the nostrils of his narrow nose flaring as his jaw grew tight. He knew I was right. I could see I'd hit the truth right between the eyes. It was just like Daddy Clay had always said. Uncle Eli was a good for nothing city slicker and was just trying to buy us off.

He spun around and headed for the door, grabbing the arm of his wife as he marched out.

Seth and Kate stood like statues for a few more seconds before hurrying off after their legal guardians, erasing the question of whose side they were on, too.

Chapter 40

Rocking and humming blocked out most of the scritch-scritch-scritch, chizzle-chizzle, chish-chish-chish, tip-tack, pit-pat, tap-tap, scritch that surrounded the small, frightened boy in the coal bin. "Out, out, let me out," he rocked and sang to himself a repetitious, nursery rhyme-like tune to sing-song his fears away. Crazy, that's what he was going, crazy.

Brandon remembered the old homeless guy who hung around outside the laundry mat back in the city before they'd moved. While Mommy had moved their clean clothes from the washers to the dryers, the dirty, old guy with matted grey hair and the big stain on the front of his pants, sat himself down outside and started to eat slices of pizza from a greasy, paper bag.

"Who's that?" Brandon had asked when Mommy had come to get him.

"I don't know, buddy. Let's look at your book." She'd taken his hand and urged him away.

Mommy tugged a little harder as the man erupted into a long string of bad words, waved his arms around, then spoke in a language Brandon didn't understand. "What's he saying?"

"Don't worry about it. He's just some crazy, homeless man. Come sit with me."

"But what's he saying?"

"I don't know, buddy. I don't speak Spanish."

Brandon had a feeling Mommy did know what he as saying and that's why she didn't want Brandon to hear it. "He needs a bath."

Brandon wished he knew Spanish or had a piece of pizza and right now he'd not have turned down a bath, either. His stomach and head hurt real bad.

"Out, out, let me out. Somebody let me out," he sang and rocked side to side instead of back and forth now. "No pizza for me. No pizza for me."

Something big, warm, and solid suddenly landed on Brandon's shoulder, releasing a scream from his dry throat and sending him scrambling on hands and knees in the opposite direction before he even dared open his eyes to see what it was, because he knew what it was as sure as that homeless old man needed a bath. It was a rat. It had made its way through and dinner was on, Brandon Pizza.

"Quiet," a voice shushed him.

Brandon waited for the biting to start but it didn't and he cracked open his eyes.

The lid of the coal box was open. It wasn't a rat that peered down at him. Even though he couldn't see the face because it was still too dark and lit from the back, he knew it was Ginny by the long hair. "You thirsty?" she whispered.

Brandon nodded.

Her thin arm reached in and set a canning jar full of water next to him. "Thought you might be. Lid ain't tight so be careful." A floorboard creaked overhead and she turned to look, just enough for Brandon to see the frown on her face before she turned back. "Ain't supposed to be down here," she went on, apparently satisfied the coast was clear. "Brought you some apples, too. Ain't much, but it's the best I could do." A crumpled brown, paper lunch bag joined the jar of water.

Heavy footsteps thudded overhead. Brandon looked up, realizing now was his chance. "Get me out of here," he said, starting to stand.

"Can't!" Ginny shook her head and pushed him back down. "Need to hide." The coal bin lid slammed and was latched before Brandon could blink.

"You hear that thud?" It was a man's voice.

"Yeah. Sounded like something in the cellar," a different man than the first one answered.

It didn't matter who the men were, as long as it wasn't The Sugar Lady. Maybe it was the police. They'd search the whole house and they'd find him.

"Down here!" he hollered, banging on the wall of the dark prison. "I'm down here. They locked me in this box! I'm down here!"

A door opened. Footfall double-timed down the stairs then scraped on the dirt floor. "See anything?" Man Number One asked.

"Nothing to speak of."

"HERE!" Brandon screamed. "IN HERE!!!" The wooden wall throbbed under his tiny pounding fists.

"It's creepy as fuck down here," Man Number Two said.

The other one chuckled. "No shit. Hey, here. Look. I bet this is what we heard."

"Jesus Christ, that stinks."

One of them coughed.

"I'M OVER HERE! HEY!"

"What do you think it was?"

"I'm going to guess peaches." He coughed. "We probably spooked a rat or squirrel or something while we were thudding around upstairs and it knocked this off the shelf."

"Help me!" Brandon yelled. Why didn't they answer? Why didn't they hear him? They were right in the same room. They should at least look in the box in the corner. If they were looking for him, they'd look. Small boys fit into small places and look, look, look over there, it's a box! A big box for a small boy! "LET ME OUT!" His throat was starting to burn.

Their shoes scuffed as they searched. Then the dreaded sound of the stairs creaking again and the two men retreating back up them. What happened? The door latched shut. They'd been right there. Right there!

"Nooooooo," Brandon sniffled. "No, no. no." And the rocking started again, back and forth, back and forth.

From the bed, Renee looked towards the window at the ebony darkness outside. Stars peeked in and out of view through a partially overcast sky. Her thoughts were crowded and jumbled. Katherine Gunderman. Meddiah, Pennsylvania. Brandon. Mary Alice. Dark Hollow Road. Gunderman. Behind her Sam lay sprawled on her back snoring. It was almost four o'clock. Renee could call Katherine in another five hours. Nine o'clock seemed reasonable. Maybe eight. An hour could make a huge difference. Where was Brandon? A lump rose and choked a sob out of her throat.

The entire conversation they'd had with Lee Yagar repeated its endless loop as Renee reached over for the box of tissues she now kept religiously at her bedside. "Mary don't like when people take things from her house," Lee's warning echoed in her head.

Someone had to know what had become of Mary. And what if it turns out she's dead? If she was dead then Brandon couldn't possibly be with her, but he'd seen her. He'd seen her at least twice. Ghosts don't go around handing out canning jars for sugar or stealing coloring books. Renee needed the woman to be alive. But, the boy, Allan and the two girls. Who were they? Sam had heard someone yell, "Ready or not here I come!" while at the house.

Brandon hadn't taken anything from the house. Shouldn't Sam be the one Mary was after? Renee wiped her eyes then her nose, trying to be quiet so Sam could sleep. Renee didn't think she'd slept at all, but here it was four o'clock in the morning. Surely she'd not been staring at that window listening to Sam snore all this time. She closed her eyes.

"I'm here! Look! Look over here! Let me out!" Renee's eyes snapped open again.

"Brandon?" She sat up, ears straining into the darkness.

Renee slipped from bed and went to the window. It was too dark to see anything. Sam rolled over and stopped snoring as Renee grabbed her robe and headed downstairs and out onto the back deck. "Brandon?" she called in a half whispered shout.

She'd heard him. She knew it.

Her eyes went towards that infernal house. She couldn't see it from here, but she could feel it. "Where is he, you bitch?" she asked the tops of the shuddering cornstalks. All the pity she'd felt during Lee's story drained away. She hated Mary Brown. "I'm going to find you and when I do …" The thoughts and words fell flat. She'd do what? Kill her? Beat the living shit out of a seventy-five year old woman?

"Let me out. I'm in here."

Cold prickled down her arms and sent the hairs to stand on end.

"Brandon!" Renee stepped off the deck into the frosty grass, eyes wide and mouth gaping. Damn it, she'd heard him. "Brandon, where are you? Keep yelling, baby! Mommy hears you." Oblivious to the cold, Renee moved towards the fence, scanning the uncut rows of corn with a growing sense of urgency. He's out there. Somehow in all the searching, they'd missed him, but he was out there and he was alive and she could hear him.

Renee rushed around to the gate, let herself out, and ran to the edge of the cornfield, peering in, listening for any sound of movement or her son's voice again. "Brandon! Where are you?"

A soft whoosh rustled behind her. Moments later a confused Sam came through the open sliding glass door and stepped onto the back deck. "Renee, what are you doing?"

"He's out here," she called back. "I heard him."

Sam joined Renee at the cornfield's edge. "You sure? What did you hear? Maybe it was an owl or coyote or something."

It took all of Renee's strength not to run into the field and start screaming for her son. She shook her head, "No, it was his voice. He said, 'Let me out. I'm in here.'."

Sam scowled. "How far away? Which ..." The questions cut off as Sam looked at Renee's profile. "The house? You're positive you heard it? You weren't dreaming? Mr. Yagar told us some pretty wild things earlier."

She shook her head. "No, I wasn't dreaming. I'd not even gotten to sleep." But doubts had already started springing up in her mind. The words had not had the sound of being shouted, but spoken. Spoken in her head? Imagined? They'd been desperate and pleading and there was no doubt it had been her son's voice. She shoved this all aside. "We have to at least look. Just in case."

Sam started to say something, maybe a protest to it being the wee hours of the morning, but closed her mouth, appeared to change her mind and nodded instead. "Let's get some real clothes on and we'll go over."

Renee needed no further encouragement.

Sam parked the Jeep so the headlights shown directly at the front corner of the house. "Aren't the police supposed to be here?" she wondered aloud.

But, Renee was already grabbing the flashlight she'd brought and scrambling from the passenger's seat. "He's here," she said as she mounted the front porch steps.

Sam double-timed across the front yard while yanking the small bundle of house keys from her pants pocket. "Do you hear him?"

Her partner froze in place, cocking her head like a curious dog, giving an abrupt shush.

Holding the keys still, Sam listened. The air was heavy and still, tainted with the bitter tang of an approaching storm. Not a cricket chirruped. Not a leaf rustled.

Renee's face broke out into a joyous smile, "Yes! Did you hear it? Open the door, Sam. He's inside."

But Sam hadn't heard a thing. "What did you hear?"

"Brandon!" her partner insisted. "Hurry up and open the door."

Confused, but not wanting to waste any time in case Renee really had heard something, Sam unlocked the front door and led them both into the narrow entryway. Cold and damp radiated from the walls as if they'd just walked into a grocery store beer cooler. "Shit," she sputtered, her breath suddenly visible in what little light the Jeep's headlights and their bobbing, panning flashlights provided. It had to be at least ten degrees colder in here than it was outside.

"Brandon!" Renee called, heading deeper into the frigid gloom. "Where are you, baby? Answer me. Tell me where you are."

They quit moving again to listen. Nothing. All was just as quiet as before, at least to Sam's ears.

Renee apparently thought something completely different. "Over here," she shouted and darted forward, turning right into what Sam knew to be the dining room towards the back of the house. The headlights from outside barely slivered light between the layers of cardboard, but Renee's flashlight turned back and forth, aiming at the floor. "How do we get to the basement?"

"There's a staircase from the living room," Sam told her. As much as she hated to use the analogy, the place was as quiet as a tomb.

"Show me!"

Sam headed towards the door, pausing before she opened it. "What are you hearing?" she finally dared to ask.

"What do you mean, what am I hearing? It's Brandon calling out. You don't hear him?"

Sam studied Renee's face. "I haven't heard a thing, babe. Nothing."

"Then you need to get your ears checked," Renee nudged by and opened the door to the basement herself, releasing an icy-cold blast of air from below.

Chapter 41

It all came down to one person's opinion. They'll say it was in everyone's best interests and that it was what needed to be done. They'll tell you that Ali was better off going to be with a family who had the financial resources I lacked. They'd take good care of her and make sure she had every advantage that a girl of her disabilities could possibly have.

They might say it was too bad about the mother. Maybe. If anyone even remembered who the real mother was. I wondered what sorts of stories she'd be told about me. Maybe they'd never tell her she was adopted. From what I understood, that was up to the new parents to decide. I was out of the picture. If they wanted me never to exist, I didn't.

I didn't want to exist anyway. I'd never forgive the Yagars for their part in this. I'd never forgive Mrs. Hayes or the doctor. And even though my kin had stood up for me in their own way, I couldn't find it in myself to forgive or trust them, either. For all I knew, and strongly suspected, them being there at all was nothing but a picture show put on for my benefit. It would look a lot better in the years to come, if the records showed they'd been there and spoke up for me.

At the very least, they'd have something to pretend and lie to themselves about.

"We tried to help," I'd hear Katie say the last time I saw her.

Uncle Eli's checks kept coming month after month, year after year. He'd bought his own conscience off for two-hundred dollars a month.

Nigel was the only one who understood. He'd never abandoned me, not for one minute for as long as he went on to live. He was able to keep his job at the mine. I refused to go into town at all, afraid I'd see someone like the Yagars and be reminded about things I didn't need any reminding of.

Every now and then he'd surprise me with pretty things, flowers mostly, but sometimes he'd bring me new hair bands, or a pretty bottle of colored glass that's he'd seen in the window of the thrift store. One day in August, he came home with the best present ever.

He knew it was going to be a harder than usual day for me. It was Ali's fourth birthday. A day didn't go by that I didn't cry for her and miss her. I longed to hold her and kiss her and tell her how much I loved her, but she was gone, gone beyond anything I could give her or tell her.

Nigel was later than usual coming home from work, supper was starting to get cold, and I'd begun to worry that something had gone wrong when I heard the increasingly loud rumble of Daddy's truck that still hadn't given up on us. Nigel came in through the kitchen door, battered lunch pail in one hand and a box not much bigger than a Campbell's soup can wrapped in pink paper and curly–Q ribbons in the other. I knew better than to protest that he shouldn't be wasting money on presents. We'd played that 45 record one too many times already.

"You can open it after supper," he said with a smile before planting a playful kiss on my lips and heading over to wash his hands at the kitchen sink.

He ate extra slow that night then took extra helpings.

"Go on," he said as I sat back down after serving us both up a piece of peach pie. "Open it."

Resting inside a nest of tissue paper, a porcelain figurine peeked out at me. She wore a full skirt, a tiny halo painted gold and a little pair of wings. Draped across her chest was a pink sash on which was written, "August" in gold paint. She cradled a big pink rose in her right arm and held a small basket with more flowers in her left.

"Oh, Nigel. She's beautiful." I pulled the figurine out, turning it this way and that in the light.

Through his smile, I saw uncertainty in his eyes. "It reminded me of Ali, I guess," he said. "They got one for every month down at the drug store. Oh, don't cry," his whispered trembled. "I didn't mean for it to make you cry. I just thought it would be something those sons of bitches couldn't be taking away from you, from us."

I never was much for crying, but this time I couldn't be stopped. Nigel come over to where I sat, pulled me up, and held me tight against his broad chest. Everything, every hardship, every hurt, every injustice that was ever put down on my shoulders come sobbing out of me that night. It wasn't fair. Why had me and mine been damned our entire lives? We was good people. We never meant anyone any harm and just wanted to live our lives in our own simple, humble way.

Why was we being punished for the sins our father had committed against us?

Dark Hollow Road

Nigel walked me to the front room and we sat on the sofa, my head resting against his shoulder as I clutched the little porcelain angel against my chest as if it really were my lost baby girl. We sat a long while. My thoughts were dark and full of pain. Sorrow swelled time and time again to my eyes and spilled over. Anger and revenge squeezed in my chest and rose to stick in my throat. "I hate them," eventually pushed its way out between my tense vocal chords.

"I know," Nigel rubbed my shoulder. "I'm sorry the angel made you cry. I can take it back …"

"No." I clutched it closer, tighter. "No, it's beautiful." My hold on the figurine relaxed as I pulled it out to look at the round, Cherubic face with its pink-tinted lips, blue eyes, and tumble of brown hair held down by the gold halo. I kissed Ali's little porcelain face. I put her on the mantel where she could watch over us.

"What you think we should do?" I asked my brother as we were just finishing up our dinner that night in June of '72. It had been raining straight for three days. I kept the radio or television on all the time, listening to the weather reports and watching the horrible images brought to us. We'd both been keeping an eye on the creek as it inched its way higher and higher up the bank. If the rain kept coming, and the weatherman said that was exactly what it was supposed to do, there was no question it was going to crest overnight, but how high and how close would it get to us?

He gave a little shrug, "Let's clean up the basement at least. Everything we can bring up from there, we should bring up. All your canning we can put in the pantry up here. Water ain't gonna hurt the coal or my tools none."

"You sure that's as far as it'll go, the basement? I been watching the television and ..."

His comforting hand patted mine. "Ain't we always made our way through?"

I nodded, but something in my heart was sinking. "We should get started."

Nigel smiled. "Right after dessert. What kind of pie you have for us tonight?"

By the time we finished, I think we'd went up and down them cellar steps a million times, but the cellar was as cleaned out as we could get it. Nigel chuckled when I said I was going out to get an extra rocks to pile on top of Allan's little grave. The smile vanished when I come back and told him the water was no more than a foot from touching the underside of the bridge. When he scanned the kitchen, fear gripped me tight.

"It won't come all the way into the house, will it?"

"Don't know," he said, rubbing the back of his neck like I seen Daddy do hundreds of times. "Let's make sure everything's up as high as we can get it down here, too, just to be safe."

We worked until midnight putting anything that the water could harm on top of the tables and cupboards and bookcase and shelves. Lastly, Nigel unplugged the television and carried it upstairs to our bedroom.

Nigel moved the cows and pigs up to the top of the barn which was a good deal higher ground than the house. Yeah, they might glut themselves on hay, but at least they'd not drown. I wrangled the chickens, two by two, into the barn where they happily went to roost high in the rafters.

Dark Hollow Road

The sound of ceaseless rain coming down on the metal kitchen roof lulled me as I snuggled into the safety of Nigel's strong arms that night. It was going to be fine, just like he said.

The screaming of nails being ripped from their holes and the snap and crash of wood twisting and coming apart woke us at four in the morning. I sat bolt upright as Nigel leaped out of bed, yanking his trousers on and stuffing his feet into his muck boots. "What was that?" I made quick work of getting dressed myself.

"Think it was the bridge." That's all he said as he shot from the room, yanking a t-shirt over his head. The heavy thunk-thunk-thunk of his boots raced down the stairs. The kitchen door opened and slammed shut as I hurried my way into my sneakers.

I made it as far as the kitchen before the sound of water running stopped me dead center of the room. I listened and realized it was coming from below my feet. The cellar. I grabbed a flashlight from off the top of the fridge and went to the cellar door. I didn't dare turn on the light switch for fear of getting electrocuted.

The beam of light cut a line down to a layer of muddy, rippling water that now covered the floor. "Sugar tit," I cursed. I went down as far as I could, scanning the light across the field stone walls that now wept with seeping creek water. I guessed the three bottom steps were now underwater which put an easy eighteen inches between the sole of my shoe and the packed dirt floor.

I started a small fire in the stove and put coffee on before heading out to the kitchen porch to wait for my brother.

He came along about ten minutes later. "Bridge is

gone," he said. "Nothing left on this side but the big twelve-by-twelve uprights and they're leaning hard and twisted. Water's still rising."

I bit into my bottom lip. "I made coffee," I offered and waited until Nigel was settled at the table before telling him about the flooded basement.

"Maybe we should pack up the truck just in case things get real bad."

"We ain't leaving!" I snapped.

He frowned, "Just in case, Mary Alice."

"No," I insisted. "They done took everything else from me that I cared about. They ain't taking my house, too, unless I'm in it. I don't care if it come crashing down around my ears and I get washed away and drown. I'd rather die than leave. It's all I got left but you, Nige."

He really wanted to leave and I suppose if he'd really insisted, we'd have gone. Instead, we sat at the kitchen table drinking coffee as the water in the cellar rose to cover one step at a time. Nigel kept an eye on the progression of the river outside. Four hours after being woke up by the sound of the bridge being torn away, the river was running along the west foundation wall. By noon, we were surrounded and still it rose. First the floor of the kitchen porch, then into the kitchen.

"Mary, we need to leave," he dared to insist again, but I'd inherited a mean stubborn streak from Daddy that refused to let go.

Around two that afternoon it stopped raining. The sky that had been a dark, flat gray for at least a week, began to brighten. We'd retreated to the second floor, leaving behind two foot of water that rushed and whirled and sloshed on the first floor. The power'd gone out, but the battery radio was still able to tell us about the evacuations, closed roads, how the National Guard had been called in, and that the Red Cross had set up shelters for those in need. We were an island as the river slowly consumed half of Dark Hollow Road.

"Listen," Nigel hurried went to the window. "You hear that?"

I did. "Sounds like an engine."

I followed him down the hallway and into the road-facing bedroom that had once been his and Seth's. A wide, silver motorboat was heading our way from the main road. One man sat at the back steering, another sat at the front. Seth opened the window once they was in shouting distance. They wore military uniforms.

"You folks need to get to higher ground," the man in front yelled up with a megaphone to be heard over the engine and noise created by the raging of the river.

"We're fine," Nigel told him. "Bridge is out," he added, as if that was all the reason in the world we needed to stay. "We got a tub full of water and lots of food," he said.

Both men scowled and shook their heads before the one up front put the megaphone to his mouth again. "Come with us. It's not safe. We'll take you to the shelter in town."

My brother read the scowl on my face before responding. "We'll be alright. We'd rather stay."

They conferred with each other, both shrugging. "Can't make you leave. Anyone you need us to get in touch with for you? Most of the phones are out, but we can still radio someone."

Nigel didn't have to check with me before answering. "No," he shouted. "There's no one."

"Alright. There'll be another crew around before it gets dark in case you change your minds. Take care, folks."

And with that, they were gone, backing the small craft around and heading towards the large olive drab vehicle we could see parked at the water's edge halfway up the road. Another vehicle waited by the main road. Clearly they were going house to house checking on folks.

My brother closed the window. "We're on our own," he said, not looking at all pleased.

It wasn't easy, but we weathered it all. The water rose only another foot after that. The ring of muck that clung to the walls downstairs fell a few inches short of the fireplace mantel where my angel sat just as happy and dry as could be. We shoveled inches of mud out of every room of the house downstairs and found two good-sized fish beached in the corner of the kitchen porch. All the while I was cleaning, vehicles came and went to see what was left of Dark Hollow Bridge, which wasn't much of anything.

I was scraping the dried mud off the front porch with a snow shovel when the Yagar's familiar station wagon came down the road. It slowed to a crawl as I stared down the people inside. Mr. and Mrs. Yagar sat in the front. Lee sat in the back. Beside him, on the driver's side, a little girl craned her neck to see around his bulky form.

Chapter 42

The hair on Sam's arms went to full attention as her skin prickled into bumpy goose flesh. The cold and dark seemed to be sucking the life right out of her flashlight's dimming bulb. "Brandon?" Renee's son's name puffed into the air and evaporated. "Where are you?"

Renee jolted, snapping around to look behind her, under the stairs, but there was nothing.

"Did you hear him? Do you see anything?"

Sam shook her head, "No, neither." She smacked the side of her flashlight, returning the bulb to its normal brilliance. "You?"

"He said Mommy, but ..." Renee inched her way towards one of the cellar windows situated beneath the front porch. Sam followed her with the beam of light. There was nothing but an old stone wall and a dirt floor to see. "Brandon! Keep yelling. I can hear you. Help me find you, baby!" Renee pressed the palm of her hand against the stone wall only to snap around, panic etching a deep vertical line between her eyebrows and tightening her lips. "Hear that?"

Sam heard nothing. Renee moved away from the spot towards the other side of the cellar. Sam was about to say something when a flicker of movement tugged at the corner of her eye, back to the spot where Renee had just been standing. A mouse or rat, she thought, darting out of the way and back into hiding. It was so damn cold down here the flashlight batteries were rattling together. Renee prowled the basement wall, tipping her head, her ears likely pricked for the slightest of sounds. Sam stuffed her free hand into her pocket in hopes of thawing out at least five of her icy fingers.

The moment she did, he was there and yet, not there. The air sucked from Sam's lungs as an unreal, semi-transparent black and white image of Brandon crouched on the floor flashed in front of her eyes. The flashlight beam bounced so violently she had to grip it with both hands. "Shit!" she shrieked. The three dimensional picture vanished just as quickly as it had appeared.

"What?" Renee's light shined on Sam's face briefly.

"I saw ..." Sam couldn't begin to even fathom what she'd seen. Whatever it was it wasn't there now. Wishful thinking maybe? Mass hysteria?

"What did you see?" Renee rushed to her side.

"Brandon," Sam said in a whisper. "I saw him, but ... Jesus Christ. What the fuck did I just see?"

"Where?"

Renee trained her light against the stone wall beneath the window. "He was right there, crouching on the floor, but ..."

"Brandon!?" The name burst from Renee's lips. "Brandon, where are you? Please answer Mommy." As before, her hand pressed flat to the wall.

" ...it was like he was a black and white silent movie, all jittery, wavy." Sam's couldn't stop trembling. The cold was sinking deeper and deeper into her flesh, reaching with skeleton fingers towards her bones.

"But you saw him? You're sure?" Renee backed away from the wall.

Sam shook her head, not sure about anything right now other than she felt like hypothermia was setting in. Renee's chattering teeth made it clear Sam wasn't the only one feeling the cold. "I thought I did, but ... it wasn't solid. I didn't look real somehow. Fuck, it's cold down here. I can't even think. You hear anything?"

They both held their breath as Renee listened. "No," she said after a few seconds. "It's quiet." Uncertainty crossed her face, eyes filling then spilling over with tears. "Maybe, I didn't. I've been so tired. I'm not thinking straight anymore. Oh, Sam, but I did! I did hear him. I swear to you, I did. It was like he was behind the wall or something." Renee was suddenly in Sam's arms, wrapping herself close and sobbing the desperate tears of a mother whose only child had been taken from her.

Sam held her tight, still staring at the spot on the floor where Brandon's translucent form had been. "I believe you," she whispered, stroking her partner's hair. And she did. Something was wrong with this place, just like Lee Yagar had told them, and whatever that something was it had to do with Mary Brown being here and not here at the same time.

If Sam had just seen what she thought she'd seen, that could only mean one thing in her mind. She'd seen a ghost and Brandon was dead, but she'd be damned if she'd say that aloud, and certainly not in front of her partner.

"Let's go home and get warmed up, babe," Sam said, knowing Renee wouldn't want to leave any more than Sam did but they needed a clear place to think and this freezer of a cellar was not the place to do that. "We have phone calls to make."

Renee clung to her, giving a reluctant nod. "He's here. You believe he's here, too?"

"Yeah," she admitted. "I do."

"No!" Brandon shrieked as Mommy and Mama Sam turned away and headed towards the stairs. "Don't go! Get me out. Take me home!"

They stopped at the bottom of the stairs. Mommy turned around. Her face and eyes were red and puffy from crying. "Brandon?" she said. Mama Sam said something, too, but to Brandon it sounded like he was underwater whenever she spoke. And Mama Sam had seen him, he was almost sure of it though he didn't understand how that could be when he was inside this box or how, for that matter, he could see them. It was like the box was invisible from the inside out. For that half a second when he'd been looking right into Mama Sam's eyes.

"Please don't leave me, Mommy," he pleaded.

"We're going to get some help, little man," his mother was saying now. "We'll be back. Just hold tight. We know you're here." But she wasn't really looking at him, not like Mama Sam had. Mommy was looking through him towards the wall.

"Right here!" he pounded with both fists against the clear wall that was starting to fog over and darken. "I'm right here!"

Mama Sam took Mommy gently by the elbow. Her garbled words like something being played in warped slow motion. They turned their backs, growing darker and dimmer as they went up the steps, until all was silent blackness.

Dark Hollow Road

"Please hurry," the little boy whimpered, fresh tears clearing flesh-toned lines down his cheeks.

The lid banged open, sending a shower of black soot down into Brandon's head and into his eyes and up his nose. He burst into a fit of coughing. The cellar was lit by a single dim bulb somewhere, but it was enough to make him squint. He didn't like what he saw.

The Sugar Lady glared down at him. "I should have known better than to use the box," she hissed. "C'mon, get out," she added. "You're going in the Hole instead. The Hole is where you belong. That'll get the job done. And don't you be breaking anything in there, either."

Her arms may be no bigger around than a baseball bat and her fingers little more than paper thin skin stretched over a skeleton's claw, but she was strong and hauled Brandon out of the box like a ragdoll. God, she stank. Brandon tried to hold his breath even as he twisted and fought to get out of her iron hold.

The Sugar Lady dragged him across the room and past an old workbench. Brandon lunged for one of the wooden legs, nabbed it, and hung on as hard as he could. Splinters bit deep into his fingers, but he didn't care. This hole thing didn't sound good.

The spindly, spider fingers of The Sugar Lady wrapped hard around his, trying to pry them away from the bench leg. "Y'ain't getting away," she shrieked.

Screaming and twisting, Brandon kicked out. His feet hit nothing but thin air. "Let me go! Mommy's calling the police. They're going to find you and take you to jail! Let me go you mean, old bitch." Thanks to Mama Sam he knew some pretty good swear words and now seemed as good a time to use them as any.

He never saw the hand coming that sent a slap so hard and painful across his face that his grip on the leg evaporated. "You mind your language," she said. "You say them bad words again and I'll do with you what we done to Daddy." She threw him down, pain snapping in his knee caps as he sprawled to the packed earth floor. "Now, get in there." A foot pushed at his butt. "Crawl in there."

Through all the dirt and tears and pain, Brandon couldn't see a thing, but he figured he'd better do what she said and start crawling. He hit his head on something almost immediately and let out a yelp.

"On your belly," she snapped. "Put your head down." Her foot was on his back, forcing him to his stomach. Things made of dust and spider webs pulled and snapped across his face. He didn't dare open his eyes or mouth, and didn't really even want to breathe in the horrible smells. Brandon groped and wormed his way forward, reaching out like the blind until he found what seemed to be an opening in the wall right in front of him, a hole.

He moved towards it, tasting dirt. Rocks scraped and stabbed into his stomach while more dirt tumbling down from above. He didn't like this. It felt like a grave.

"There," she said from somewhere near his feet, "that's a better place for you. Won't take long now. Won't take long now at all."

Something scraped in the direction of the opening he'd crawled through, a piece of wood maybe, followed by the thud of something heavy being set into place.

On his belly, Brandon could do little more than cry. He was going to die soon. He knew that. This place felt like a grave because that's what it was meant to be.

The rest of the morning fell just this side of madness. While Renee made coffee, Sam debated the merits of calling the police. What could they possibly tell the authorities that would make sense? That Renee, and only Renee, had heard what sounded like Brandon's voice all the way across a cornfield only to find out that maybe it had actually come from behind a stone wall in the basement? Or maybe it was better to report Sam's, and only Sam's, silent movie version of Brandon kneeling on the basement floor? Let's just tell them what Lee Yagar had said about Mary Brown, who might or might not be dead and her role in the other two incidents involving children that had gone missing near the house.

They needed to stop and take a deep breath. Their heads had been filled with all sorts of things by Mr. Yagar, heads that had not slept worth a damn in over forty-eight hours. She'd call in for another day off work in a few hours. If she kept this up, there wasn't going to be a job to call into even though her boss had said to take whatever time was needed.

"What about Doug Martin?" Renee handed Sam a steaming mug of freshly-brewed coffee.

"What about him?"

"Wouldn't he know the house better than anyone, even Mr. Yagar? Lee knows about the Browns, and I still get this weird feeling there are things he's not telling us, but he doesn't know the house."

Sam took a few tentative sips of coffee. "Maybe, yeah, but didn't he say his father owned it or took care of it at some point?"

Renee nodded, settling down at the dining room table. "He said his father should have burned it down when he had the chance. I don't remember if he said he owned it or not."

"Now that you put it that way, completely different. If there's some sort of secret chamber in the basement, I'd think Doug would have mentioned it during our tour."

"Unless, no one knows about it. Mary could still manage to live there, undetected."

Sam wanted to believe it was as simple as that. "That doesn't explain what I saw," she said. "And certainly not what you heard."

Renee's shoulders sagged. "No, it doesn't."

"So, what can we do or say that won't have the fine folks of Murphey Mills introducing us to the men in white coats?"

"I don't know," Renee said. "I need to speak to Katherine Gunderman. She's got to know if her sister is still living or not, don't you think?"

Renee didn't wait until nine. It had taken everything in her to hold off calling Katherine until eight. Three rings later, Renee found herself listening to a recorded voice telling her to please leave her name, number, and a brief message and that she would be gotten back to as soon as possible.

"Hello," she did her best to remain and sound calm. "This is Renee Evenson in Murphey Mills. My family and I live down the road from Dark Hollow Road. My six-year-old son is missing. Lee Yagar gave us your name. I really need to talk to you about your family, about Mary, your sister. Please, please call me back as soon as you can." Renee left the home phone number and both her and Sam's cell numbers and hung up.

Sam called and told Doug Martin the bare bones of what had happened earlier that morning. The property owner agreed to meet them at the house within the next half hour.

"The crate," Renee burst out just as Sam was shifting the Jeep into reverse. They'd both showered and changed clothes by now.

Sam slammed on the brakes and put the vehicle into park. "Right, the crate!" She jogged back to the garage, retrieved the wooden crate of old lamp parts and tucked it into the back seat.

"What are we going to do, Sam?" Renee asked as they waited for Doug to arrive. Sam had already let them in and they stood in the basement with the Bilco doors wide open. Though the space was still very dimly lit, it was a hell of a lot better than earlier. Bits and pieces of their own footprints could be seen in the dirt floor. Renee had gone immediately to the stone wall, squatted down and put both hands on the cold foundation.

Sam carried the crate back to the uneven shelves. The drag lines from where she'd pulled it out from under were still clearly marked in the dirt. She set it on the floor and slid it back into place with her foot. "I don't know, babe," she replied as she stepped back. "But, that's put back at least." She turned, watching Renee who squatted in front of the other wall. "Have you noticed how much warmer it is down here now?" Coats were still needed, it was November after all, but it was much more tolerable. Despite the warmer temperature, Sam pulled out the gloves she'd stuffed into her coat pocket and slid them on. A pale blue streamer of fabric slipped to the floor. It didn't even disturb the bone dry dirt it landed in.

Renee must have seen the flutter of movement as she stood and turned. "You dropped something."

Sam scooped it up, rubbing the fragile piece of fabric thoughtfully between her gloved fingers. "This should be put back, too." She looked to Renee for confirmation. "Lee said it was from Mary's dress." Sam's words misted from her mouth.

"So did Brandon."

The silence in the basement shivered.

Renee's cell phone ringtone jolted both of them.

Dark Hollow Road

Chapter 43

Hatred screamed in my head as Mrs. Yagar rolled down the window. "You need any help, Mary Alice? Do you need us to get ahold of your uncle?"

It was like she was speaking to me through a thick layer of wool. I threw the shovel down, stormed to the open car window, and wrapped my hands around Ruth Yagar's throat. I wanted her dead, her and her husband, and all their children and grandchildren. The girl in the back seat started screaming as I worked to throttle the life out of Mrs. Yagar. Lee and Mr. Yagar jumped out. Lee was the first to grab hold of me and I like to think I put up a good fight. I got in a few good kicks and scratches at any rate, until he and his father were able to pry my hands from that woman's throat. Like the girl in the back, the one I know they called Lisa, I was screaming.

"You'll never be rid of me, you hear?" I swore. "I'll always be watching you and yours. And if the Devil will let me, I'll take what you stole from me. That girl, she ain't yours no more. I'll see to it she's mine if it's the last thing I ever do. If you know what's good for you, don't you ever come here again, never. Don't you dare take anything from this property. Anyone, anyone at all, takes anything from my

405

property, they'll have hell to pay. I'll take what they love the most, their kin, their children, just like you got mine taken from me. I swear to you on my Mama's grave, I'll have my revenge. Mark my words, you'll know when it happens and you'll only have yourselves to blame. You brought my revenge down on everyone who dares walk this road ever again. Their blood and pain and tears will all be your fault."

At some point during my ranting curse, Nigel came running from the barn. It was him that held me back from lunging at the Yagars until something resembling sense crept back into my brain.

There weren't too many other folks from town there at the time, just a few young stragglers who stood their gawking at the scene.

I turned my attention to them even before Mr. Yagar managed to put the car in gear and started to pull away, looking for a place to turn around. He knew better than to do it in my driveway. "That goes for you, too!" I growled at the bystanders with their bicycles. Kids, just kids, but it didn't matter. Let them spread the word that Mary Alice Brown was not about to take any more stealing and backstabbing from anyone.

I heard muttered, frantic words like, "She's crazy," as they jumped on their bikes and pedaled away as fast as they could back towards the main road.

Nigel got me to my feet and wrapped me in his arms, cooing and rocking the insanity from me. He kissed my cheeks and forehead. He promised he'd never let anyone hurt me again and he'd keep them all away, then he took me inside and made me a cup of tea until I could stop shaking from the inside out.

We never spoke of the incident again. Nigel and me had an understanding of what was what and how things were going to be. It's funny, but despite the hatred we had for the man, we was doing things just the way Daddy would have liked. Mama, on the other hand, may not have taken such a shine to it.

Time stretched out. It took weeks to make the house decent again and even then I was forever after finding mud and debris in strange places. The smell of dead fish and rot never quite left the cellar. I guess it had penetrated the timbers down there pretty good and being shut up most of the time, it never really got a proper airing out. I replanted my ruined garden and hoped for the best.

Then 1977 happened.

"See you at lunchtime," he said, giving me a peck on the cheek after breakfast. It was Saturday and he was off to do some plowing.

The sun was bright and the warmth of a beautiful spring day was upon us. I'd started the washing soon as I got up. By then we had one of those fully automatic machines sitting out on the back porch, and I was determined to get my clotheslines full right away.

I went about my busy day. Noon came and went. Nigel didn't show up. It wasn't all that unusual for him to work through lunch, so I didn't give too much thought to it. But when got within a couple hours of sunset and the dinner hour passed, my mind began some serious fretting. From the back porch I could hear the tractor running in the distance, but something about it didn't seem quite right. The engine was going, but the direction it was coming from didn't seem to change and the tone was one, long, constant drone instead of the ups and downs of going faster and slower as he made the corners.

Five minutes after heading out on foot across the freshly-plowed back field, I caught sight of the tractor.

It wasn't moving. It was wedged into a stand of trees and it didn't look like anyone was in the driver's seat. I burst into a run, fear and dread squeezing my pounding heart. The closer I got, the more horrible the situation before me became.

There was someone slumped forward in the seat. That someone was Nigel. And Nigel wasn't moving. I scrambled up next to him. The moment I touched his shoulder, I knew.

Dead.

Cold and dead a good many hours.

"Nigel?" I whispered to what I knew to be a corpse. "Nigel, please." I gave him a useless shake. "Nigel, please don't be dead. Please, please, don't be dead." I leaned over and kissed cold, lifeless lips and shook him a second time. "Please, oh, God, please, don't be dead." The tears came, the panic, the terror and I screamed at him.

"Nigel Clayton Brown, you stop this! You stop this right now!"

His wide, blank stare gazed up at the darkening sky.

I had to get him home. I couldn't leave him out there. I should call an ambulance. That's what I should do. Maybe he wasn't dead. Maybe he was just in a coma. I shut the tractor off and somehow managed to pull my brother down off the seat and propped him against the back tire.

"I'm going to call an ambulance," I told him, palming his cheek, staring at his face, his beautiful face that was now so cold and pale. I kissed him again on the lips then the forehead. "I'll be back. I'll bring help. Hold on, Nigel. Please, hold on. Don't die, oh, please, oh please, don't die."

And I ran. I ran until I thought my lungs were going to explode and I kept on running. I raced into the house, through kitchen, nearly pulling the phone off the wall as I grabbed the receiver and called the operator.

"Please tell them to hurry. They have to hurry."

The ambulance was coming. I was supposed to wait at the house for them, but Nigel was out there all alone and night was coming. I couldn't just leave him to think he'd been abandoned. She insisted I wait at the house. If I wasn't there, how would the men in the ambulance know where to find us? Yes, that was true. I waited what seemed like hours until the sound of sirens reached me and I saw the white ambulance with its flashing red lights. A police car followed.

Through the uneven ridges and clods of turned earth they dragged the stretcher. There was no easy way to get to where my brother sat waiting. He hadn't moved. He still stared as the one checked for a pulse at his wrists and throat. They used a stethoscope on his chest. They whispered a little and then they brought over the stretcher, put Nigel on it, and covered him, head and all, with a white sheet.

"What you doing?" I protested. "He ain't dead. How's he gonna breathe ..."

"He's gone, ma'am." The man spoke real soft and gentle to me. "He's been gone quite some time."

I collapsed to my knees in the mud.

"Is there someone we can call for you?" A voice said to me through a world that had gone cold and gray.

I didn't answer.

"I'll get her back to the house," another man said. I remember thinking it was alright. The paramedics were there and they were going to take care of things.

They'd just covered his face because it was getting a little colder. That's all it meant. God could not possibly be this cruel, not after everything else I'd been forced to endure.

But He was that cruel and I hated Him for it.

They told me it was a blood clot in his lungs and asked if Nigel had mentioned any pain. He hadn't, but my brother never was one to complain. Someone called Uncle Eli. I wasn't grateful for that either.

For the first time ever I slept alone on Dark Hollow Road.

Questions. So many questions were thrown at me. What I wanted done with the body seemed to be the biggest one. I realized at some point during the next day that Kate and Seth were there with Uncle Eli. Someone suggested cremation. I agreed through the fog.

Someone asked me about bills and a banking account. Nigel took care of all that, I told them.

Another asked where I'd live.

That snapped me back briefly. "Here, of course," I said, finding myself looking into Seth's eyes.

"You can't stay here. The place is too big. It's too much upkeep for one person. You should get something smaller in town." The gall that Kate would even dare to suggest any of that fired up my rage.

"How dare you." I spat the words at her like a cobra spitting venom. "Get out, all of you! Get out of my house and never come back! You're all dead to me. You're happier without me and I'd just as soon be alone."

More arguments followed. They insisted they only wanted to help. They wanted to make sure I was taken care of and that I'd be alright. I didn't believe a lick of it. They'd abandoned me once, what made this any different than then? They went away shortly after, leaving me with a fancy little box full of human ashes for company.

I thought about putting it on the mantel beside my little angel, but took them both upstairs to my room instead. It was important we all be together. Eventually, we'd all go down to the basement. That's where Allan was and I felt kind of guilty for leaving him down there alone for so long.

I put whatever I could find up over the windows on the inside to keep away prying eyes. Wasn't nobody's business what I did. I went and got what little mail still came and I answered the phone as it pleased me, which wasn't often.

I stopped keeping track of the days. I don't know how many years it's been since Nigel died. I think it's taken me a good long time to type all this up, too, but I can't tell you how long. Maybe a month, maybe two. Maybe longer. It don't matter. What matters is that someday folks know the truth and understand my side of the story. I never wanted things to be this way, but they are what they are. I can't change them.

I made myself a place to hide out in. It's nothing fancy, but it's a good hiding spot and I've made it as comfortable as I can. I even put down a rug. I'm going to use a couple of sleeping bags for a bed. I got a radio and an oil lamp and a stack of Daddy's Westerns, plus this old portable typewriter and a stack of paper for it. Ali's angel and Nigel's ashes keep me company. There's plenty of canned vegetables and the creek ain't far. I can go fishing. Squirrel and rabbit ain't too bad.

Real tired. Making that hiding place in the cellar has been hard work. It's still not done, but it's good enough for now.

It's late and time to put the lamp out.

Pamela Morris

People moving and talking nearby woke me. Why can't folks just stay out of other people's business? Why they always gotta be putting their noses where they don't belong? I stayed put and listened best as I could from my secret place. They eventually went away, whoever they were.

Once I knew they were gone, I crept out and, believe you me, I hadn't forgotten my promise to the Yagars or to those kids on the bikes. They all better pray I didn't find anything missing. I made my way from room to room. It all looked fine. Lucky for them.

While I was out, I grabbed something to drink and a jar or two of preserves. I didn't want to be there any longer than I had to be, but only because I didn't want anyone to see me. I'd love to have gone on living in the house just like always, but that might foil my plan. No, the best I could hope for was to keep an eye on the place.

Let them all think I was long gone. I had a great place to hide. I'd let the weeds grow up around the place. They'd all think I'd left. I bet some of them would even come to believe I'd gone to stay with my brother and sister in Scranton. That made me smile. It was perfect.

I'd hide and wait and bide my time until some idiot slipped up and took what didn't belong to them. It was just that easy.

I'd lost all track of time. The batteries in my little radio gave out a lot sooner than I expected and I couldn't get more. I could guess at the months based on the seasons passing and I could guess at the time of day based on it being light and dark, but that's about it. Leaving the property made me feel weird, like my insides was turning to jelly. I figured it was nerves and the fear of being caught. Folks would still know I

412

was alive and kicking if they saw me wandering around.

It was quiet for a good long while. I was just as happy to go about my daily business as I was to wait for intruders, and just when I thought nothing was going to happen, it did.

I never expected them to take what they did. They were worse than thieves, worse than vandals, worse than trespassers and common criminals. They were grave robbers. At first I didn't recognize him, but soon as I heard one of the other men say his name, oh, yes. Yes. It had been a long time indeed, longer than I'd realized that's for sure.

The two men, the Martin boys from my nearly forgotten school days, were in my cellar. They was taking out all of Daddy's old tools and clearing out this and that. I was a little afraid they'd spot me, but I stayed still, not breathing, just listening, waiting, and watching.

"That's no rock, Doug."

"Holy shit," Doug Martin grunted. "That's a skull! A baby's skull!"

"Damn," his brother, who some called Ed and others called Butch, the one who'd picked up Allan's little skull, swore.

More folks came. Policemen with their sniffing dogs, men in suits, men in lab coats who dug around and took every last bit of what was left of my son's earthly remains.

I went to the hole they'd filled back in. They'd even taken my rock marker away. "Allan," I whispered to the earth. "Allan Brown, they took your body, but they can't take your soul, ain't that right? That's mine for the keeping. I let you be all this time, but now it's time you kept me company. Your Mama wants you here, Allan. You come to your Mama right now. Straight away."

You need to know I never claimed no knowledge of witchcraft, but Grandma Gunderman, who I only met a handful of times, loved to tell the story of having a real witch for an ancestor in generations long past. True or not, there was some sort of deep down darkness had taken root inside me since Nigel's passing, maybe even before that. I don't know if it come about out of hatred for all the wrong that was done to me all my life, or from the loneliness, or maybe even from the love I had for my family once upon a time, or maybe all three.

It felt like a big old knot nestled between the bottom of my ribcage and the top of my stomach. Remembering Grandma Gunderman's stories, I started calling it my witch's knot. That knot was rock hard, but it had things that grew from it like a potato sprouting eyes that would grow into roots. When I dug my hands into that grave, them roots tingled like they was full of electricity. I think my hair may have even stood on end a little bit, but it was my hands that felt it the most. Each finger was like a root that pushed deep and pulsed hard, like when Nigel and me made love. It felt better than that.

I picked up handfuls of the grave dirt. I pressed it to my face. I smelled it and tasted it and filled it with tears. "Allan Clayton Brown, you do as your Mama says and you stop hiding."

At the sound of shuffling behind me, I looked. There was my boy, naked as the day he was put in the grave and the spitting image of Nigel when he was about ten. I don't know how it was done, but it sure made me smile. I wasn't going to be alone ever again. That's when my plan really started to take shape.

Chapter 44

"Is this Renee Evenson?" The voice was that of a mature women, soft and hesitant.

"Yes," Renee replied.

"This is Kathy Gunderman."

After half a second of confusion, Renee's heart skipped beat. Kathy. Kate! "Oh! Thank you so much for calling back, Kathy. I have so many questions."

Kathy cleared her throat. "I don't know if I can give many answers. I haven't heard from my sister in over thirty years."

The hope of seconds ago sank. "Oh," Renee replied. "Then you don't know if she's still alive?"

There was a long pause. "No, I don't. I'm sorry."

Now what? Renee thought to herself. "We spoke to Lee Yagar …"

"I'm surprised he cooperated."

"He refused at first, rather vehemently, but something made him change his mind. I think it was our asking how he'd feel if it was his little sister who was missing instead of our son. He told us about the other two children that had gone missing over the years. He thinks your sister has something to do with all that and now, with our son."

Another lengthy silence came from the other side of the line. "The house is empty," she finally said. "It's been empty a long time."

"Yes, I know, but ..."

"Mary Alice would never have left it. She loved that house. It was all she had left after Nigel died."

"That's what Mr. Yagar told us, but no one knows what became of her. I was hoping the rumors of her having gone to Scranton ..."

"She never came here." The nervous edge to Kathy's voice was fading. "What else did Mr. Yagar say?"

Renee told Kathy as much as she could of the conversation, including how Mr. Yagar refused to tell them why he felt Mary Alice held such an intense hatred for Lee and his family. She also told her where they were now and why. "It's crazy, but we're ..."

"Have you met his little sister ... Lisa?"

"Briefly, yes."

Kathy let out a long-winded sigh, paused and sighed again. "Maybe I shouldn't be telling you, but I'm tired of the secrets and maybe it matters in this case. Lisa isn't Lee's sister, at least not biologically," she said. "She's my niece. She's Mary's daughter, Alice."

"What? No one's said a thing about her having a daughter."

"Alice was taken from Mary by the court when she was just a year old. Initially Alice was to be placed in an orphanage, but because of her medical condition they didn't feel she'd be adopted. The Yagars stepped in and said they would foster her instead. The court agreed. Mary never forgave them, or us. She firmly believed, and maybe rightly so on a lesser level, that we, myself, Seth, our aunt and uncle, were somehow

416

conspiring against her. Eventually, the Yagers officially adopted Alice, renamed her Allison and started calling her Lisa."

"Wow," Renee half whispered. "Mr. Yagar never even hinted at that."

"It's a very well-guarded secret. I'd guess most of the people who were around at the time it happened are gone now. Mary could never have given Alice all the care she needed. My sister had problems, Mrs. Evenson. We all did, but Mary refused to face them. She was stuck and she kept Nigel stuck, too. They wouldn't budge. The two of them were a lot more like our father than either would ever admit, especially Mary."

"I've been told things were rough for you."

"Very. Mary was livid when Seth and I left to live with Uncle Eli, but I couldn't stand being there anymore. I hated that place. I hated being reminded every day and night what happened there. Uncle Eli offered an out. Seth and I took that out. I have no regrets other than it hastened Mary's crazy ways."

"Do you think she's still around, I mean, like Mr. Yagar does? Do you think she has something to do with the missing kids and my son?"

"I don't see how. If she were still alive, you'd not be standing where you are. She'd never have let anyone in the place. If she'd dead, I'd think her body would have been found years ago."

"Maybe she wandered off into the woods. I've heard of people doing that."

"No," Kathy insisted, sounding just as perplexed as Renee now felt. "She'd not have done that. The house was her life. She put all her heart and soul into that place. She'd not have left it to die in the woods. I know it doesn't make sense. I'm sorry I haven't been more helpful."

Renee laughed a little, "You've told me things I didn't know before. That's helpful and I appreciate you calling me back so much."

"Mrs. Evenson?"

"Yes?"

"I'll pray that you find your little boy very soon and promise me something," she sounded scared, truly and deeply frightened. "Promise me you'll be careful in that house."

"Of course. It's a little rundown, but it's ..."

"I don't mean in that way."

"How then?"

"It's my turn to sound crazy. That house isn't right. Seth and I made a trip out there shortly before Mr. Martin and his brother bought the place. We didn't tell anyone, mind you, but we had to see it. Closure, I guess they call it. We saw things. We heard things. We felt things, things that terrified us both so much we vowed never to return."

"Ghosts?"

Kathy's voice trembled, almost laughed. "Maybe. If you believe in that sort of stuff. We weren't welcome. It was the middle of August and it should have been hotter than blue blazes in there, but it wasn't. It was freezing cold. The longer we stayed, the colder it got. I was going to take a memento, but Seth insisted we not touch a thing. He felt watched. Like one false move and we'd spring some sort of booby trap. So, be careful. Don't take anything from the place, though I can't imagine there's anything there to take after all this time."

"That's what Mr. Yagar told us, too, not to take anything. He believes that why the children were abducted."

"He just might very well be right about that."

"We'll be careful," Renee told her. "Thank you, again."

"You're welcome. Take care and do be careful, very careful."

Renee cleared the call from her end, feeling numb and overwhelmed at what she'd learned.

He had to stop crying. It was making it even harder to breathe. His head was pounding and he felt like he was going to throw up except there wasn't anything in his stomach to throw up. From his prone position, flat on his stomach, Brandon stretched out his arms and lifted his head. Air moved past his face, drying and cooling the last of his tears. It wasn't the freshest air, but it was air and it was somewhere ahead of him. He had to find it. He couldn't go back. The Sugar Lady was back there.

He rose to his hands and knees. Once he'd calmed down, Brandon realized the hole wasn't quite as small and tight as he'd first thought, at least not for a kid or someone as skinny as The Sugar Lady. All he had to do was keep crawling towards the moving air. This, he decided, wasn't so much a hole as a tunnel.

Brandon took a deep breath and tried to swallow. There wasn't a lot of spit in him to spare. If it hadn't been for Ginny bringing him the water and apples, he'd probably be dead by now. Like the waft of air he now inched towards ever so slowly, those things hadn't tasted or smelled the best, but if they were keeping him alive, that was alright.

Inch by inch, foot by foot, Brandon crawled. How long was this thing and where did it go?

His arms really hurt and he was pretty sure his stomach had more than few cuts into it from some of the jagged rocks he'd felt under it before. He'd made the mistake of opening his eyes a little bit, but the feeling of being completely blind had been too scary. From then on, he'd kept them shut tight. Brandon rolled to his back and stretched out his body as long and straight as he could, his fingers brushing against what felt like a stick or tree root. If it was a root, he must not be under the house anymore.

What if it was more than just a single root though, his very tired and imaginative brain asked. What if the whole tunnel was blocked by a lot of roots, big roots, roots that covered his escape route like a cage? Brandon started to panic.

He flipped back to his stomach, hoisted himself back up and gave the matter some thought. He hadn't crawled that far. Maybe it wasn't too late to go back and try and kick his way out. No, he didn't want to go back. The idea of being under the house again or facing The Sugar Lady was too much to think about. He'd only go back if something blocked the way ahead.

Brandon moved on. His fingers found the root again. It broke easily enough away when he pulled at it. All dried out, like maybe the tree it belonged to had died a long, long time ago. His hand found another one, a little bit bigger, then something that felt more like a rock than a root. There was a pile of them, mostly dried up sticks, like the digger of the tunnel had just pushed these things aside instead of hauling them out. Some of the dried roots were pretty long, too.

In the pitch black, he groped forward and found something that wasn't a rock and didn't quite feel like a stick either. It felt more like a wooden plate. Broad and flat and just a little bit bigger than the palm of his hand, it was light enough that he could easily pull it from where it rested. His fingers explored the outer rounded rim of the thing, found that it dipped down, had something bumpy in the middle and then rounded out again on the other side. Two smaller dish-shaped things with big holes in them hung under the big ones. It was almost like a butterfly's wings, only it was a lot bigger than any butterfly he knew of.

Brandon set it aside and went a little further only to meet up with a bunch of very hard, very pokey rocks. Maybe part of the tunnel had caved in. He didn't pay too much attention to these and kept going. The fingers of his left hand suddenly became tangled in a series of firm roots. Brandon yanked his hand back at first, before reaching out again. The fear of his way out being blocked surfaced with even greater clarity. This was it. The end of the line. Sorry, Brandon. You're a goner.

On second feel, the obstacle wasn't roots. He scowled, using his imagination to try and figure out what it really was. They felt like carved, wooden bars of wood, but they didn't go up and down like a jail cell. These were tossed off to the side just like the rocks, roots, and sticks he'd already found. It reminded him of something, but he really wasn't thinking very well right now. His brain was getting all light and fuzzy, and his heart was pounding so hard behind his eyes it felt like they were going to shoot right out of his head.

He needed to rest. This was hard work. Every part of his body hurt. If only he had something to drink. God, that would feel so good on his dry, scratchy throat. Brandon rolled to his back a second time. Just a little rest, what Mama Sam called a cat's nap.

"Brandon?"

The sound of his name snapped his eyes open. Who had said it? He should answer. It could have been Mommy or Mama Sam. Or, it could be The Sugar Lady. Brandon let his eyes close again and listened, praying so hard that it was anyone but The Sugar Lady. Even creepy Allan or Ginny would be better.

"Brandon, my boy. It's time to come out. Your punishment is over."

His body quaked inside with dread at the sound of The Sugar Lady's voice. He bit his tongue to keep from crying out. He forced himself to remain perfectly still.

"Brandon, I know you can hear me. I have a big glass of lemonade for you and I made cookies."

He groaned before he could stop himself.

Her laugh was so much like the cackle of the witch in the Spook Barn, Brandon couldn't help what he did next. He flipped back to his belly and scrambled forward as fast as he could, deeper into the blind tunnel.

"I guess I'll have to come in after you. You really don't want me to have to do that, do you? Come out or I come in."

He kept going and with a sudden gush of realization, found himself more on his feet crouching than on his hands and knees with no dirt walls to his left or right, no dirt roof that he kept bashing his head into, and most of all, the surface under him didn't feel like dirt. It was soft. His hand ran over it. If he didn't know better, he'd think it was a carpet.

"Ready or not, here I come," The Sugar Lady chimed as if they were playing some twisted game of Hide-and-Seek.

Brandon panted in panic. Where was he and how did he get out of here before she arrived? The sound of her drawing closer and closer, dragging herself through the dirt and rocks and sticks made him scream like he'd never screamed before.

Pamela Morris

Chapter 45

The next day I went out back to where we'd buried Mama. There wasn't any hope of bringing Mama back. She was in Heaven. But, I remembered being told once that you had to be baptized to get to Heaven. I knew my baby sister hadn't had that done. She was probably just as lonely as Allan had been all those years under the ground.

So, I done what I did in the basement. I got down on my knees and I talked to Virginia. I told her who I was and I promised to look after her. I was going to be her Mama now. We was going to be a real family, her, and me as the Mama with her Uncle Allan. "You hear me, Virginia Brown? I know you're down there now you come up. I need you to get on up here and be with me and Allan because you belong to me."

I thought maybe it had been too long when nothing happened right away like it had for Allan, but then Allan really was my son. Ginny, as I started to call her, was my sister. Then I thought maybe I was wrong about the baptizing thing. We'd never been church going people. I kept trying though. Night and day for a whole month I kept at it, doing my best to believe in Grandma Gunderman's story about having witch's blood in my veins.

"Oh, bother!" I groaned, pulling myself up from the crouching position I'd been in for what seemed forever.

"Mary?"

I turned around. It had to be her. It had to be Virginia, because as much as Allan looked like Nigel, Ginny looked like Katie Sue.

My heart was about bursting with joy when she come over to me and gave me a hug. "You're staying with me and Allan now, alright?"

Everything was getting back to the way it should have been. We spent special occasions in the house, but we still all hid when other folks come by. Allan and Ginny helped make our hiding spot bigger and better. We were a happy, little family except there was something missing. There was only the three of us. There needed to be six to make it right.

I saw the little girl and her mother walk by the house a lot from the basement. She wasn't that old, maybe three or four. I'd have preferred a boy, but six was six and I figured it would be alright. They went down to the creek to play on hot days. I knew they must live in the new house that had gone up. I don't remember the place actually being built, just one day I realized it was there. From Daddy Clay's old bedroom I could see their back yard real good. I'd seen her playing over there on a swing set and in a sandbox.

One day when they was coming back from the creek, the little girl stopped right by my mailbox. She looked at the house and asked who lived there. The mother told her nobody had lived there for a long, long time. "Then who's the lady watching us?" the child asked.

That shocked me and I immediately darted back away from the basement window.

"What lady?" I heard the mother ask.

"Oh, she's gone now. She was watching us from under the porch."

"You're being silly."

"No, I'm not. I saw her."

"Come on, silly goose. Let's get you home and washed up. You look like a mud baby."

I was inching my way closer to the glass when the girl shouted, "Look!" The little girl was pointing at the side of the road this time. "What's them?"

The mother crouched down, dug around with her finger, and laughed, "Looks like an old set of marbles. I guess kids must have lived here." Light reflected from the tiny, glass orbs she'd pulled from the earth. My earth.

"They're pretty. Can I have them?"

She shrugged, "I don't see why not." She got a stick and dug more, pulling a handful of the marbles out. "If you think they're pretty now, wait until we get them home and cleaned up."

The knot at the bottom of my ribcage grew tight and painful, like something was being ripped from deep inside it. It reminded me of how I'd felt when told Alice was no longer my child to raise. My hate-filled, revenge-sharpened promise rose to the surface. She was just a little girl, the one who had so innocently removed something from my property, but so had been my Alice. I'd keep that promise. I had to. A promise is a promise, right?

Weeks of planning went into what finally happened. Allan and Ginny were reluctant to help, but they liked the alternative of being returned to the cold ground even less.

I sent them over to the house. I figured she'd not be so afraid of other kids. They talked to her, making secret, imaginary friends, and were sure not to be seen by her parents. It wasn't that hard. There comes a time when grown-ups just stop listening to their little ones. I knew the mom had already stopped listening when she'd said what she did about the girl seeing me in the window. Imagination. Make-believe. You're just being silly.

My Allan and Ginny worked their own kind of magic on her. They found out her name was Hannah and that she was three years old. Then, one day, while Hannah's mom was sunbathing, Ginny convinced Hannah to come play Hide-and-Seek with them in the cornfield. She and Hannah would count and Allan would hide. She took Ginny's hand and a few minutes later, they came walking up the kitchen steps where I stood waiting and enjoying some fresh air. It was just that simple.

She liked our hiding place until I told her it was going to be hers, too. She wanted to go home. I couldn't let her. She'd tell them where we were and that would be the end of it all.

I gave her food, but she didn't like it. I've got a feeling the food has something to do with the magic, too, like the fairytales about eating a candy house or drinking wine offered by the little people.

"It's yucky," she said, crinkling up her nose at the bowl of peaches I'd put in front of her. Like it or not, it only took one bite or sip and they were brought into to my world.

"What do you mean, it's yucky. I canned them myself and they be perfectly fine." To prove my point I took a big bite. They were sweet and delicious and perfect. "See, they're good."

Her face puckered even more as she watched. "They smell funny. I don't like them. I want my mommy and daddy."

"I'm your mommy now and there ain't no daddy here. Daddies are bad men. Daddies make you do things you don't want to do."

She shook her head, "My daddy's not bad. I want to go home."

"This is your home now."

Hannah wouldn't listen. She whined and cried instead. Kids who do that get punished, so I took her to the hiding place and put her there and told her she wasn't going to be allowed to come out until she stopped her crying. She cried more, but it had to be done.

It was the fault of all those policemen that things went the way they did. They come stomping in not long after, searching the whole house, attic to basement, looking all over the grounds and in the barn before finally moving on. We all had to hide, of course. It was a long time before I felt it was safe enough to come back out and by then, well, what was done was done. I tried to get her to eat and drink. I really did. She kept saying no. She didn't like my food.

Woke up one morning to find her body cold and gray.

I wasn't entirely without hope. After all, I'd brought Allan and Ginny back and they'd been dead ages longer than Hannah. So, right off I put my hands on her and closed my eyes and told her what was what, and who was who, and how things was going to be from now on out. It happened almost instantly. She opened her eyes and sat up, sort of. Her flesh and blood body was still the same, but the spirit that made her who she had come back to stay. She had the sweetest smile and, finally, after all my failed efforts, Hannah accepted one of my cookies and some milk. She said the cookie was better than what her last mommy had made.

We waited a while longer, making sure the coast was clear, before taking her earthly remains out of our hiding place and put it in the chicken coop. Someone eventually found it.

The boy was a lot harder. I almost didn't try, but he just kept taking and taking and taking. And the mother in me needed him. If I was going to be Mama, I needed my two boys and two girls.

That final time, he was in the cellar going through what few things was still left there. When he started poking around on my canning shelves, we made our move.

"Who's there?" he fanned his flashlight's beam around the room then towards the stairs.

"Go now," I whispered in Ginny's ear. "Walk slow and be sure to smile."

We'd dressed her up pretty in an old dress we'd found still hanging in my bedroom closet.

From the top of the stairs I listened and through Ginny's eyes I watched.

"Who's there?" the boy demanded, his voice full of false bravado.

"Just me," Ginny said as she made her way down step by step, in no rush at all.

The beam of light shined in her eyes. "Who're you?"

"Ginny," she said. "Ginny Brown. Who are you?"

"Paul," he lowered the flashlight but still kept it trained in Ginny's direction. "What you doing here?"

"I live here," she said.

"You're full of it," he laughed. "Nobody lives here. It's abandoned."

"That ain't true," Ginny insisted, calm as could be. "I live here with my family."

"Yeah, right. There isn't any electricity or running water and nothing in the cupboards but old junk and jars of rotting food. That bedroom upstairs hasn't had anyone sleeping in it for years. Everything's covered with dirt and cobwebs. Where do you really live?"

"I told you." She took a step forward. Paul took one back. "I live here."

"You live in this empty basement with three other people?"

Ginny smiled and gave a little shrug, "Well, not really, but sort of."

"Sort of, yeah, that's what I figured. You're making it all up." He was getting braver and much more comfortable with Ginny. Growing up with two brothers I had a hunch he'd be more willing to follow a girl than another boy. Paul probably figured this place as his turf. Another boy showing up claiming ownership could have easily gone the wrong way and ended in a fight.

"I can prove it?"

He succumbed. "Alright."

Ginny pointed towards the wall where all the shelves stood, the same shelves that Paul had just been standing at and nosing around a little too close for comfort. "Right behind there," she said, moving to show him. "Look underneath, right next to that wooden crate."

The boy gave her a doubtful look and rolled his eyes. "Seriously?"

"Uh-huh. Look."

He got down on all fours, looked and when he leaned back his jaw was slack with surprise. "It's a tunnel."

"Told you."

"It's kind of small."

"It's big enough once you go back farther. You'll see."

"I'm not crawling in there. That's just some old woodchuck hole."

"No, it ain't. I'll show you."

With that, Ginny lowered herself down and crawled in easy as you please.

Slack-jawed, Paul stood there looking at the opening as the sounds of Ginny's crawling grew more muffled and distant until she'd reached her destination and turned back to shout, "Come on, or are you chicken?"

Calling the boy a chicken worked like a charm, especially being called one by a girl. "No, I'm not chicken," he replied and followed her in. His passage was slow and clumsy. He was bigger than her and trying to use his flashlight to guide his way.

As soon as the soles of his shoes was out of sight, I finished my descent down the stairs, shoved the crate of lamp parts back into place, and slid a cinder block in front of that. If he tried to come back out that way, I'd be waiting.

"What the hell?!" I heard him holler from behind the barricade. "Someone just put something over the opening!"

Ginny spoke calmly, sweetly, urging him to keep going. She was waiting for him. She even lit one of the candles so he could see better.

"Holy crap!" he yelped again. "What is this place? What the hell is this place?"

I didn't care for his swearing and questioned whether he was the right one for the job. Even if he wasn't, I reckoned it was too late. He knew the secret place. We couldn't let him go or he'd tell.

"You need to calm down," Ginny said. "It's just where we hide when folks come around nosing into Mary's business. I thought you weren't chicken."

"I'm not, but this is wrong. Where is everyone else? Why aren't they hiding from me?"

"They got chores to do, that's all."

"What kind of chores?"

She gave an indifferent shrug. "Oh, hunting and fishing. Fetching things for this and that."

It's weird how I could almost hear his heart trying to thump its way out of his chest like a throbbing up through the floor and between the walls. He was desperately trying to keep it together, to be a man about it, but I could feel he was on the verge of losing it. "You really all live in here?"

"Sort of. We hide here. We do as much as we can in the house, but we can't mess up and have it looking like anyone is there. That would ruin Mary's plan."

"What's her plan?"

I moved in closer, curious as to what she'd say.

"She's making us a family again."

I smiled. That was right.

"Why do you have to hide in the cellar for her to make you a family again? Why would it matter if people knew you all lived here if this is her house?"

Ginny hesitated because she really didn't have those answers. Only I did. "I'm not sure," she finally replied. "I'm sure Mary has her reasons. She doesn't tell us everything, but we have to do as she says or she'll send us back. I don't want to go back. It was so cold and dark and lonely there even with my mama nearby. Mama wasn't really there, not like I was. Mama had been gone to Heaven a long, long time. Mary rescued me."

"Send you back? Back where?"

"You know that song, *Amazing Grace*?"

"Yeah."

As quietly as possible I removed the barrier and started to make my way into the crawl space.

"I once was lost but now am found, was blind but now I see."

"I don't get it."

"Can I see your flashlight for a second?"

He handed it over.

Up ahead I could see the glow of light, Paul's stronger flashlight against Ginny's flickering candle flame.

"Well," Ginny continued. "It's like that song." The steadier light flicked out with a click. "It was very dark where I was, dark and cold and lonely. I was lost. I couldn't find my way to the light. It was the same for Allan. Then Mary come and set us free."

"Where were you?"

I was seeing things partially through Ginny, partially through myself, but mostly through whatever connection I had with the house. It wasn't like mind reading, but there was definitely a link, a sort of understanding and we could communicate with a few simple words and feeling.

I had to stop crawling about six feet from where the tunnel opened up into the cave. Shadows danced and shimmed on the walls decorated with curtains that covered imaginary windows and a few pictures I'd manage to tack up with long metal spikes.

"Where were you, Ginny?" Paul asked again when she still hadn't answered after a full minute. She was looking at the candle, her face pale and sullen. When her gaze lifted to look at the boy, and she lifted their only source of light closer to her face, the dull, deadness in her eyes made even me shiver.

She smiled ever so slightly. "We were dead, Paul," she said and blew out the candle.

Chapter 46

Renee's skin prickled and crawled at the sound of the screaming. She spun around looking from one wall to the next, eyes wide with panic. "You can't tell me you didn't hear that, Sam."

Sam, who was watching her, calmly and quietly, shook her head. "I didn't hear anything, babe."

"God, damn it!" she shrieked. "God damn it, why can't you hear it? He's screaming. Brandon! Brandon, baby. I hear you. I'm right here, sweetheart. Mommy's here." Renee ran to the wall covered by feeble, teetering shelves that looked ready to collapse at the slightest touch. She grabbed the edge of one of them, meaning to yank the damn thing apart by hand if she had to, but looks were deceiving and the shelf held firm against the wall. "Damn it!" she screamed, feeling her mind go red with rage and black with fear. Her son was back there, somehow, her son was behind this cursed shelf and that fieldstone cellar wall. "Give him back, you old bitch. Give back my son. He didn't take anything from you." Renee pulled and jerked, kicked and screamed at the barrier until Sam came up from behind, wrapped her arms around her, and pulled her back.

"Renee, stop. Doug Martin is on his way. He's got a whole truck full of tools."

Renee resisted and snapped, yanking herself away from her partner's hold. "He better have a fucking jack hammer and a twenty pound sledge!" She was falling apart. The days without sleep or eating like she should, the anxiety over losing her son, and listening to the stories she'd heard were crashing down on her head, making her crazy. Her knees buckled just as Sam was starting to lead her towards the open Bilco doors. "I can't lose him, Sam. I can't lose my baby."

The sky had gone gray and overcast, spitting rain that wanted to be snow, in the short time they'd been underground. A chilly November wind rattled the barren tree branches. The cold, brisk air bringing Renee a little more back to her senses.

"We'll find him, but throwing yourself against a stone wall like that isn't going to help. Come on; sit on the step here. Doug can't be too far away. Sit and try to calm down."

Calm down? How could she calm down when she knew where Brandon was but couldn't get to him? Sam must think she was nuts, hearing him like she was but … "You saw him, Sam. You saw him like you say you did, didn't you?"

Sam settled down beside her on the top step, still holding her hand, rubbing it and gave a nod. "I saw him," she said.

Renee put her head on Sam's soft shoulder, too wired to close her eyes and too tired to think in a straight line. She had to keep believing it was going to be alright. She'd never been much of a church-goer, but Renee found herself praying a lot lately. She had to believe someone, or something, was watching over her little boy. Renee didn't care who or what that was, as long as they took care of him long enough for her to find him and do it herself.

Sam squeezed her hand then sat up a little straighter. "I think I hear Doug's truck."

Brandon's back pressed against the wall, too scared to even scream. Who would hear him anyway? He thought he'd heard his mommy, but he couldn't be sure. It was hard to hear over the pain in his head, the pounding of his heart, and the scuffing of The Sugar Lady as she crawled and dragged herself closer to him.

"Ready or not, here I come," she kept saying over and over.

Brandon buried his face into his drawn up knees and waited. Rocking. Whimpering. He'd run out of tears.

"Ready or not ..."

He held his breath. Any second she'd be on top of him, grabbing at him with her bony fingers, her stinky breath breathing against him, pulling him somewhere else even worse than this.

But she didn't.

Brandon lifted his head and listened. He listened very hard.

She was probably sitting there watching him with her crazy see-in-the-dark rat-like eyes. That had to be it. She'd made it out of the hole and just sat there waiting for him to get good and scared. The monsters like it when you scream. I'm not going to do it, Brandon told himself. She can't make me scream any more. He didn't know if he even could. His throat was too sore and dry.

He tried to swallow, ended up coughing instead, the sound echoed back, but that was the only thing he heard. Brandon held his breath and willed his heart to slow down so he could hear over its frantic thumpa-thumpa-thumpa.

Quiet. It was perfectly still and quiet. Something made his hair flutter, but he instantly knew it wasn't the monster. It was the movement of air. Brandon turned his face towards it, lifted his chin, and sniffed. He'd seen dogs do that. He figured it helped them smell things better somehow. It didn't stink like her. Where was it coming from? It couldn't be back the way he'd just come. Brandon had never wanted his Bob The Builder flashlight more, but at least he still had Army Guy to keep him company.

He shifted from his curled-up squat to rest solely on his knees and turned to face the direction of the cooler, fresher air. He didn't know what might be that way, but it had to be better than here. Brandon patted the pocket where Army Guy waited for his orders, "Attention, soldier," Brandon said in as strong a voice as he could muster. "Time to be brave and head out!"

But there was nothing in the pocket. And nothing in the other one, either. Army Guy was gone. A casualty of the tunnel, Brandon thought with a disheartened frown. Almost seven-year-old Brandon Evenson wanted very, very much to start crying again, because now he really and truly was very much alone.

Doug appeared around the back of the house empty-handed. Sam was already on her feet to greet him. "I'm sorry to call you out here, Doug, but ..."

"No need to apologize." He looked up at the back of the house, his jaw firmly set. "This place needs to go," he said.

"What do you mean?" Behind Sam, Renee had pulled herself together a little more and stood up.

"Lee Yagar's said it for years," Doug continued. "Burn it down and bulldoze it under. It's a good strong house though, I told myself. Someone might come along one day and have the money to fix her up."

Renee's hand slid into Sam's and gave it a squeeze. "Brandon's in there," she said quietly. "I heard him." Doug started to protest, but Renee shook her head and held up a hand. "I know it sounds crazy, but I heard him. Sam saw him. He's in there behind a wall in the basement."

Doug's gaze flicked back to Sam. "You saw him?"

Reluctantly, Sam nodded. Renee was right. This all seemed crazy, but she knew what she'd seen. "You seen Star Wars?" she began. Doug nodded. "Remember the scene were the hologram of Princess Leia keeps getting projectioned from R2-D2? It was like that and it only happened that one time."

"But she can't hear him like I can," Renee added.

Sam wouldn't blame the guy if he laughed and kicked them off his property right then and there. He diverted his gaze towards the open cellar doors and rubbed at the back of his neck slowly. "I don't know what's going on here anymore than you folks do, but I'm starting to think Lee's right. Let's have a look," he said, lowering his arm back to his side. "I've got shovels, a pickaxe, and a ten-pound sledge back in the truck if we need them."

Sam smiled as Renee's grip slipped from her hand and she rushed forward to hug Mr. Martin. "Thank you," she practically sobbed. "Thank you so much."

Mr. Martin gave her a fatherly hug in return. "We'll get your boy back if we have to take this place apart stone by stone and board by board."

Brandon scuttled ahead, suddenly running into a
dead end. He got onto his knees and placed his palms
flat against the dirt surface. He reached up as high as
he could, pulling himself to his feet as he stretched.
Soon he was standing. Brandon lifted his arms as high
as he could and still found no ceiling, his face turned
upward. The feeling of fresh air kept shifting, or so he
thought. Maybe he was just getting turned around in
this dark, black place. With shuffling feet he moved a
few more steps, always keeping one hand on the wall.

Brandon froze. What if he got back to that tunnel
and she grabbed his leg? Maybe that's what she was
waiting for. His ears strained against the darkness.
There'd not been a peep of sound in a long time. He
didn't think anyone could be that quiet and still for that
long. If she was as blind as he was, he might give
himself away. He didn't think she was blind though.
No. Brandon was positive she could see in the dark.
The monsters always could. They could also be very,
very quiet.

Brandon bit on his lip. He couldn't just stand here.
If she was there, she could see him. If she was there,
why hadn't she grabbed him already? Something else
must have taken her attention away from him. Hadn't
he thought he'd heard Mommy and Mama Sam? That's
where she probably was, watching them instead of
him. He took the chance and moved another few steps,
dragging his feet, his right foot nudging slightly ahead,
his fingertips crawling across the dirt and stones of the
wall.

His toe hit something, kicking it over with the
gentle ting of metal on rock. Brandon crouched and
reached out towards the end of his invisible foot. Cool,
thin metal touched his outstretched fingers. He scowled
as he pulled it closer. It reminded him of a cupcake

paper only one made of thin, inflexible metal. His touch bumped into something sticking out from it. It was flat and smooth and bent in a gentle, backwards, C-shaped curve like the handle on a coffee cup. In the center of the thing was a tiny cup. Brandon stuck his finger into it to find another substance, not as hard as the metal. A smile blossomed on his face. Of course. It was one of those old candle holders. If there was a holder there must be a candle.

Reaching down slowly a second time, he felt around his foot until his fingers wrapped around the unmistakably smooth and waxy taper. His heart sank. He didn't have any way to light the candle and even if he found matches or a lighter, Brandon wasn't sure he'd know how to light them. Mommy always kept those things in places he couldn't get to.

Reluctantly he returned to his hands and knees, keeping the candle tight in one hand while setting the holder aside for now. The holder didn't matter so much. Inching along, Brandon swept his free hand back and forth along the surface of what he still thought was a rug. "Ow!" he winced and drew back as his forehead smacked into something hard. He reached up, felt the inch-thick edge. "Table," he said out loud. It was low and longer than it was wide. A coffee table, he decided. His spread his palms out and felt along the smooth, wooden surface. In the center was as a bowl. He reached in, snapping his arm back when his fingers touched something. He was never going to find matches or a lighter if he kept this up. He needed to be brave. Brandon took a breath and felt in the bowl again. His nose crinkled. Whatever it was it wasn't any bigger than a golf ball and it wasn't going to help him light a candle. Its hard, dry surface was tightly wrinkled and it had three friends just like it.

Brandon withdrew from the bowl to creep his fingers along further and bumped into something else. It was cold, glass, and big and exactly like the jar Ginny had brought him with water in it and the one The Sugar Lady had with her that first day. Brandon's thirst became almost unbearable thinking there might be water inside. Trying to lift it proved there was something inside

His sandpaper tongue raked across dry lips. He needed a drink so bad. Brandon pulled the jar closer, hugging it against his aching chest and now pained and rumbling stomach. "Please open," he whispered, gripping the lid that his small hand could barely reach across. "Please open and be something good."

The lid miraculously yielded to the first part of his request.

The three of them plodded back into the cellar, only this time they had Doug Martin's kickass thousand-candle-power flashlight and an arsenal of heavy tools of destruction. The weather was not improving. A drop in temperature had turned annoying rain into sleet. Icy blasts of wind funneled into the basement, but closing the double doors against it would have made the place much too dark.

Doug propped the sledge up against the post at the bottom of the stairs and scanned the area. "Where did you see him, Sam?"

Sam pointed towards the part of the basement nearest to the road that was nothing but an empty corner. "He was crouching under the window," she said.

The owner hummed in thought. "There was an old coal box there when we bought the place. He turned to Renee. "You heard him behind that wall?"

"No, over here." She moved to the completely opposite corner of the area. Renee crossed her arms, glaring at the wooden shelves as if by sheer willpower she could dissolve the whole thing and get to Brandon.

Doug's high-powered light lit the corner up like the brightest of days. Every nook and cranny gave up its secret stash of silt-filled cobwebs. Black shadows swayed behind the uprights of the shelves as the glimmers of metal and glass from within the old crate Sam had returned sparkled back at them from between the rustic slats.

Sam had hoped for so much more, a visible door of some kind, a long straight crack in the wall, anything to indicate an easy access point. But maybe there was another entry point. The dogs had tracked Brandon's scent into the barn, not to the basement. Wishing for gloves, she stuffed her cold hands deep into her pockets with a frustrated sigh.

The woman glared back at her with squinted eyes. Bedraggled hair, which had not been washed or combed in a very long time, hung in uneven clumps around her gaunt face. Over her narrow, stooped shoulders clung a tattered off-white sweater over a dirty blue dress. She was looking right at Sam with an expression that was filled with nothing but pure hatred and evil. Without warning, the figure rushed forwards, her mouth open wide as if she were screaming.

"SHIT!" Sam stumbled backwards away from her, darting to the right to get out of the way, only barely able to catch herself on the wobbly work bench. "What the fuck was that?!" she panted, heart pounding loud and hard in her chest.

"Sam!" Renee shouted in the same moment that Sam's hands made contact with the bench. "What is it?"

Mr. Martin had only taken a few steps back and looked baffled. "What was what?"

Sam straightened, turning in place frantically looked for any sight of the woman. "You didn't see her? She was right there!" She pointed to the spot in front of the shelving. "Right there!"

Renee had gone very pale. "I didn't see anyone," she said.

"Neither did I."

"She was right there. She ran at me. It looked like she was screaming, but I didn't hear anything. You didn't hear it, Renee?"

Her partner shook her head and looked like she was about to be sick.

"What did she look like?" Doug asked, training his light back to the shelf-covered wall.

As Sam described her, Renee put out hands to lean on the bench. "It's like what Brandon said." Renee moaned. "That's exactly how Brandon described her to me. It's The Sugar Lady."

"It's Mary Alice Brown, is who it is." Doug spoke with amazing surety and resolve. His express was hard and grim. "Lee Yagar's right. I have no doubt about it now. This place is going down. "

"But Brandon ..." Blotches of color had returned to Renee's cheeks.

"We'll find your boy," Doug assured her. "But before that we need to get Yagar out here. He's got to know more than what he's saying, and I'll be damned if I let him keep some secret at the cost of a little boy's life."

"He won't come in," Sam didn't see the point of dragging Lee into this any deeper.

"We'll see about that. I won't let one more innocent kid's life be destroyed because of this place and that woman. It's high time Lee took some responsibility." Doug Martin marched towards the doors and the dim light of day to which they permitted entry. The sleet was heavy and miserable.

Chapter 47

"You're ghosts? But, I can touch you. You're as solid as I am."

"That's cuz you're in our world. That's what Mary does, somehow." Ginny gave a weak smile. "I don't know what we are, but you can't leave. If you do, something bad will happen. Best you just accept what's happened and stay here."

As she spoke, Paul's brow tightened and his lips puckered into a scowl. "I'm not staying," he said. "And I don't believe in ghosts."

"You don't have a choice," she said. I know she was trying to sound strong, but there was a quaver to her voice that sounded dangerously sympathetic to the boy's situation. "You can't leave the way you came in. Mary's got the tunnel blocked. She's a lot stronger than she looks."

I held my breath. Don't do it, I thought. Just hush up your mouth, little lady.

His next move surprised me. Paul reached out and took Ginny's hand ever so gently. After a moment of looking at it in his, his gaze lifted as he let out a sigh. "Alright," he said. "I guess I can stay to keep you company. Maybe it won't be so bad."

My heart swelled at the words he spoke. He'd make a fine addition to our little family and if him and

Ginny grew to be in love, maybe things would happen to make all of this even better than I'd thought.

Satisfied, I worked my way backwards out of the tunnel to give the two some privacy. Everything was going to be just fine.

Ginny came upstairs about five minutes later, that far away, he-loves-me look in her eyes. Maybe they was a little young for it, but that didn't matter none to me. As long as the boy stayed long enough for the earth to do its job so I could do mine, I was content. It wouldn't take more than a few of days, we just had to be strong and ignore it when the screaming and crying started. It would be the hardest on Ginny. I'd make sure she was locked away in the closet just to be safe. Wasn't no point in letting temptation get any sort of hold on her.

But when the begging never came, I turned a suspicious eye to my little sister. "Why ain't he yelling?" I asked.

She shrugged as she quietly went about the business of taking clothes off the line and folding them before dropping them into the wicker basket. "He said he wanted to stay. Maybe he don't see the point of it." Then she did it. She absentmindedly bit the corner of her bottom lip.

"You're lying."

"Nobody can lie to you, Mary. You know everything that goes on around here. Someone so much as puts a little toe on the property, you know about it." She looked across the yard towards the barn. Blue-black storm clouds were heading our way. "Winds kicking up. We better get these down fast."

I didn't care nothing about the rainstorm coming or the laundry. "What did you do?" I growled. "What did you tell him after I left?"

Ginny lifted her chin ever so slightly even as she worked the clothespins free and moved down the line, dropping shirts into the basket she kept kicking along with her foot. "I didn't tell him nothing." When I didn't so much as lift a finger to help her with the chore, her hands dropped down and became planted firmly on her hips. "You really think I could lie to you?"

Up until that moment I didn't think she or any of them could. She was right. I had a way of knowing the comings and goings of anyone and anything that set foot on or left my property. Maybe the boy was simply accepting his fate with no whining and complaining, maybe. "No," I said. "I don't think you could." Together we emptied the line and hurried inside just as the first big drops of rain began to fall.

The remainder of the day I went through the motions of our lives like nothing was on my mind, but when night came my eyes wouldn't close and my brain wouldn't rest. The sounds of the house cooling with little ticks and creaks and sighs as old houses do usually soothed me. I let myself drift up and out until the beams were my bone, the siding my skin, the windows and doors were my eyes and ears. In the warm attic, my mind normally would be lulled while my feet remained firmly planted in the strong, solid earth of the stone basement walls. All was safe and sound and right with the world.

This was not the case that night at all. There were angry hornets in the attic along with bats that squeaked and flapped. Someone had covered the windows so I couldn't see out and the doorknobs wouldn't turn. My feet and legs crawled restlessly. Pacing did no good. I had to check. It should be done by now, but it wasn't. Something had gone wrong.

I made my way to the cellar in complete darkness and silence. The piece of wood and the cinderblock were still in place. I crawled along the tunnel, pausing every couple of yards to listen. All quiet. Emerging into the large cave of a room, I got up to my knees, scanning the space through an odd sort of green-glowing inner light. There was the little table and the bowl of apples. There were the lamps and the candles. Along the back wall was the cot covered in blankets that I slept on when we had to hide; a suitcase was tucked neatly beneath the sagging canvas. Old posters hung, semi-curled and brittle, from two of the walls, held in place by long railroad spikes. A set of old curtains hung on another wall as if to cover a window. I'd put a flowerbox with plastic flowers planted into it and resting on a stack of carefully placed bricks in my attempt to make the place feel less like a cave.

There was no boy.

My gaze fell back to the apples. Food. Damn. That's what it was. He'd never so much as eaten a cookie or had a sip of water. That was my fault, but there was another who was even more to blame.

Ginny's scream woke up the whole house when I pulled her out of bed by the hair.

"You helped him!" I shrieked.

"What? Who?" she fumbled on the floor, but I would not be fooled by any of it.

"You showed him the way out!"

"I didn't …"

I twisted her hair around into a rope and yanked on it harder. "Don't lie! You helped him, didn't you? Didn't you?!"

Ginny let out a pitiful, "Yes."

"Why'd you do that? Don't you know we need him? He was to be one of us." Crouching down next to her I gave her hair another tug until her head was nearly to the floor.

"Don't send me back, Mary. Please don't. He promised he'd not tell about us. He said if I loved him I'd let him go."

Anger had seared itself deep into my heart, the same anger I'd felt so long ago towards my father and all the other people who had taken things from me and denied me a happy life. "I should put you back in that grave with Mama," I hissed at her, knowing the others was watching and knowing I had to make an example of Ginny. Turning my head only slightly in Allan's direction, I gave the order, "Go get the shovel. She's going back. She can't be trusted."

Allan sat on his bed, unmoving and wide-eyed.

"Get the shovel," I screamed. "Or you'll be going back with her."

"Mama, you can't ..."

"Do as you're told, boy!" My father's voice came from my mouth. It was the anger and hatred he must have felt towards us, the pain he'd let build and build after Mama's death, and all those other confused and resentful feelings that had driven him to drink and to insanity and to his eventual suicide. And instantly, I hated myself.

Ginny's body slumped to the floor as I opened my fist from around the rope of her hair.

"Get," I said. "I don't want to see you for a good, long time." Sending her back would accomplish nothing.

"Where ...?" Ginny got cautiously to her feet.

"I don't care where, just go."

And she was gone like a wisp of smoke, out the door, down the stairs, and to parts unknown. Let her fend for herself for a while. She'd learn soon enough what it meant to not have me or the house to protect her.

I sent Allan over to the neighbors the next day. Paul wasn't there either. No one was there the rest of the day and when someone did show up, they looked haggard and pale. After a few more days we figured out Paul had made it back home, but something in him had snapped. He wasn't talking. I guess the house made sure he kept his promise not to talk. He wasn't doing nothing but staring off into space. Not too long after that the moving van showed up and the house was empty again.

Lee Yagar had taken over working the fields around my house for a good many years by then. Watching Lee's comings and goings and having no power to stop him infuriated me. It wanted my revenge on him more than anyone else, but I couldn't think of a way to get my payment. He stayed on his tractor all the time and lived beyond my powers to reach him.

He wasn't a child. He couldn't be lured in like the innocent, trusting ones. He knew better than to park his car out front, than to get out, than to walk the grounds and peer into the windows, than to take even so much as a blade of grass or a pebble from me. Lee was wise to how I watched and waited. Maybe his father told him something. Maybe it was because of the bond he had with my Ali, his Lisa.

I'd not seen her since the day he and his family had stopped during Hurricane Agnes, and even then I'd not seen her well. She's a full-grown woman now, and I've been aching for her all this time just as much now as I did that first night she'd been taken from me.

When the house across the field became someone's home again, I couldn't help but crave the child they brought with them. He wasn't Ali, none of them would ever really replace her, but that anyone lived there at all was the fault of the Yagars, and Lee's directly. He'd brought this all on himself knowing what he knew and going ahead and doing it, anyway.

Course, I wasn't the least bit surprised when the police and their dogs come looking for the boy. They'll never find him until I let go and I ain't about to do that, at least not until he crosses over. I'm keeping a good eye on this one. Not trusting anyone but myself to make sure it's done right. He's pretty near the end now and probably would have made the change if Ginny hadn't given him that water. I'm not happy with my baby sister.

And here come the two women with Doug Martin again, snooping around, threatening to tear down my house, threatening to rip apart everything I've worked so hard to build. I can't allow that. I'll stand here and guard what is mine. After I'm done with them they'll wish they never stepped foot on Dark Hollow Road.

Chapter 48

Lee pulled his truck to a stop in front of the house. He wasn't angry, anymore. He was terrified. "Ya stay in this truck. Ya lock these doors and ya keep the windows shut up tight, and no matter who comes along telling ya it's okay to step one foot on that property, unless it's me, ya stay put!" He finally dragged his attention away from the house's closed front door to look at her. She was staring out her own window at the place. "Ya hear me!?" He grabbed Lisa's arm and gave it a firm shake.

"Ow!" Lisa snapped back, giving him an annoyed scowl as she pulled her arm out of his hold. "I hear you. I'm not deaf. Why can't I go with you?"

"I told ya already. Pay attention! It's not safe. It's just not safe. Not for you, not for anyone to be in there. I need to get these idiots out. Last thing I need is to have to fish you out, too." The tension of the white-knuckled drive over here wasn't even close to easing. It was worse. Of all the days for his wife to be off visiting friends, forcing him to bring Lisa along. "You'll stay put?"

She rolled her eyes and sighed. "I'll stay put, Lee. God. You're so annoying sometimes. Why didn't you just leave me at the farm to work? I could have puttered with something."

Why indeed? The week after Halloween was a dead zone on the farm. Kids were back in school, parents went back to work. Jack-o'-lantern carving season was over. Things would pick up a little bit just before Thanksgiving for the few people who made pumpkin pies from scratch, but for the most part, the season was over. It was Monday and Lisa's normal day off. He'd panicked. This was the last place he wanted her to be, but something in his gut had twisted so hard that he'd brought her anyway. All he wanted now was for her to stay safe. "Promise me," he insisted. She didn't understand the dangers. None of them did. He wouldn't either, if his father hadn't shown him and explained all those years ago.

Lisa's eyes widened, her partially open mouth letting out a vague growl of annoyance. "I promise. Hurry up and just go. I'll read my book."

His sweat-slicked palm slipped on the door handle as he got out. "Lock the doors," he repeated and slammed the driver's side one harder than necessary. Lisa hit the interior button that locked both doors in one satisfying click. "Don't leave the truck."

Lisa made a face and opened her book.

"He's here." At the sound of a car door slamming, Doug headed for the front of the house with Sam and Renee following quickly behind. Lee stood in the middle of what had once been the dirt and gravel driveway, gawking at the house, his face as pale as paper. His truck was parked on the far side of the road. "Lee, thanks for coming."

Lee's slack-jawed stare towards the upstairs windows didn't shift. "Don't thank me for nothing," he said. "We need to get the hell out of here. She's watching and she's pissed."

"We need to find the boy first," Doug insisted.

The old man's shoulders sagged, suddenly looking twice his age as his drooping eyes pulled from the house to the people standing in front of him. "Once she's got them, it's too late. Don't ya get it? He's in Mary's world now. Can't get him back. Least not how ya think we can."

The tears that Renee had only recently quit shedding, started to flow again. "The others were found, the one boy ..."

"One was dead. The other lost his mind. That what ya want for your boy?" Lee snapped. "It's too late, I tell ya! I brought two full gas cans with me. We can pour it and torch the place and be done with it today."

Renee shrieked, tore herself from her partner's side, and lunged at Lee, nearly pushing him to the ground. "My son is in there, you heartless bastard! I heard him! Sam saw him!"

Sam yanked her back, trying to be comforting to her partner while at the same time, looking as tough as nails at the man who was proving of no help at all. "He's in there," she said.

Lee's expression shifted from determined grouch to shocked curiosity. "Ya seen him? Where? The basement?"

"Yes," Doug stepped up, trying to put a barrier between the understandably distraught parents and Lee. "How do you know that?"

"Maybe it ain't too late." Lee looked towards the couple instead, "You put everything back how you found it? That box you told me about and that piece of fabric?"

Renee, her breathing coming in ragged sobs as she clung to her partner was unable to speak, but Sam nodded. "I put it back." Then her face drew into a somber frown. "No," she said, reaching into her jacket pocket. "No, I still have the fabric." This she pulled into view as if drawing out a long, writhing snake. It fluttered in the gentle breeze, harmless it seemed. It was only a piece of thin, pale blue fabric with little flowers on it.

Sam's eyes grew wide and round. "Shit," she hissed, eyes riveted to the other side of the road where Lee had parked his truck and Lisa had already been sucked into the world of her story.

Lee turned around, fists raised as if expecting someone to be creeping up on him with a baseball bat. Doug saw nothing out of place and Renee was giving her partner the oddest look. Sam pulled away and took a tentative step forward. "She's there," the words were barely above a whisper. "I see her."

"Who?" Renee asked.

"The Sugar Lady," Sam replied. "Mary."

"What?" Lee growled. "Where?"

As if transfixed, Sam had only managed to move a few paces before coming to a helpless halt, the ribbon of fabric held tight in her fist. Her lips were parted, but she wouldn't, or possibly couldn't, answer.

"What are you seeing, Sam?" Doug asked. "Give me the fabric."

Lee Yagar rushed forward to snatch at the dangling, fragile cloth. It ripped in two, the larger piece in Lee's burly hand. "No!" He lunged several strides towards the truck, back into the middle of the dead end road, no more than ten feet from Lisa, and also froze in place. It was as if both he and Sam had laid eyes on the mythical gorgon Medusa with her hair of serpents and a gaze that could turn the strongest of men to stone.

Lisa looked up from her book.

The vague look of boredom was swept away by one of horror. Her hands flew up to cover her mouth to hold back the scream that erupted from her all the same. In the next instant, the scream was cut off and Lisa's hand dropped down to her throat as if she were choking on something.

"What's going on?" Renee screamed, grabbing at Sam's empty hand. "What are they looking at? Do you see anything, Doug?"

"Nothing," he called back. "But I think we need to get Lisa out of the truck. She's choking on something!" He darted forward, slid against the door, and yanked at the handle. Locked. "Open the door!" he yelled through the glass. "Lisa! Unlock the door!"

Her eyes were bulging, her lips turning blue, as one hand dropped, fingers fumbling for the button to release the locks.

"NO!" Lee's baritone shout broke out in the same second his whole body surged forward as if released like a pebble from a slingshot. "Don't open the door!"

"She's choking!" Doug insisted half a second before being bowled over by the rugged farmer.

"Get away from her!" Lee swung around. Doug braced himself to be pummeled by Lee's massive fists, but instead Yagar took a huge stride over the fallen man and began grappling with some unseen foe, wrestling it back towards the house, falling headlong into the tall weeds, and rolling over and over until he hit the porch and could go no further.

Sam, too, became animated again. The blank stare snapped into recognition and she turned, racing towards Lee. "We've got her!" Sam shouted, wrapping her arms around something Doug still could not see. In the truck behind him, Lisa sobbed and coughed.

"Hold on to her!" Lee shouted from the ground.

Whatever Sam held in a bear hug, she held very tight. "I've got her!"

"What the hell is going on!?" Renee yelled.

Sam's body fell backwards. The hold had broken and she hit the ground hard.

"No, God damn it! No!" At first Lee, panting and red-faced, acted as if he wanted to stand. "No, no, no," but gave up just as quickly and sank back to his knees with his hands over his face.

"Sam?" Renee knelt down beside her partner who was slowly sitting back up. "You okay? What the hell were the two of you doing?"

"Talk to me, Lee," Doug crouched down. "What just happened?"

"Lisa?!" Lee's tear-stained face jerked up.

"Lisa's fine," Doug assured him.

"She didn't get out of the truck, did she?" The old man strained to rise, to see for himself that his little sister was alright. Doug grabbed hold of Lee's hand, helping to heave him to his feet.

Once upright Lee hurried over to her. "Roll down the window," he instructed.

Lisa was a mess, but very much alive. "Who was that? She tried to choke me! Why'd she try to choke me?"

"Mommy?"

Doug Martin spun around at the voice, no louder than the mew of a newborn kitten.

Pale and shivering, a little boy covered head to toe in dirt, the knees of his pajamas ripped and bloodied, stood at the back corner of the house.

Renee let out a strangled sob of disbelief. "Brandon!?"

Her arms were wrapped around him in seconds, holding him tight in trembling arms. Renee kissed his cheeks and his gashed forehead. The boy's gaze was a distant and hollow glaze. His arms hung lifelessly at his side. He didn't hug his mother back, but he had spoken. That was more than the previous kidnapped child had ever done.

Pulling back, Renee looked at her son's dull, blank expression with growing concern. "Brandon, baby? It's okay. You're going to be okay."

He seemed to look through her, just before his eyes rolled up into his head and he collapsed.

Chapter 49

I couldn't hold on. Lord, how I tried. I almost had her! I almost had my baby girl back in my arms, but it was too much. My head kept screeching at me, "The boy! The boy is getting away!" and then my brain split in half and shrieked, "Alice! My baby! Don't let go of my baby!" I need them both, I wanted them both. I had to have them both. But I couldn't. Oh, dear God, why couldn't I have held on for just a few more minutes?

Oh, but I saw her. I touched her. I know the sort of woman she's grown up to become. She's so beautiful, my little Alice. I didn't mean to scare her. That was wrong of me. I should have sweet talked her out of the truck after I'd told her who I was. "I'm your real mama," I said. "I'm your real, flesh and blood Mama that them horrible Yagars stole you away from." At least I'd been able to tell her that much before they'd pounced.

I should have sent Allan to coax her out like I had sent Ginny on the other boy. I really should have done it that way. But, I wasn't thinking clearly, was I? No. For a minute or two I wasn't right in the head.

My baby was sitting right there, all grown up and reading, right there, so close. I had to touch her. I had to have her that minute. There's only one way I can have her with me for always. I would have but for that damned, fat cow who still had a piece of my dress! She ruined everything, her and that cursed Lee Yagar! Damn every last one of them.

I have to think what my next step will be. There's still a chance. I can hold my hands up to my nose and breath in deep and I can smell my Alice. I'll keep it with me forever. They can't take that from me.

I'm real tired, though. It's a lot of work to step off the properly like that. I need some resting time but hate to go. When I wake up, they'll have taken Alice away. I know that. They're all gathered around the mother and the boy. They're gathering him up and going to the car and Lee is getting back into his truck. Alice is watching out the window, looking at me as I look back at her through the house's eyes. I don't know if she really sees me like this. Maybe. Maybe not, but I bet she knows I'm watching. I'm her mother. That's what we do. We watch after our children.

We watch them get taken away from us knowing there ain't a thing we can do about it. Even when they are long gone down the road and out of sight, we keep watching. Eventually, we sink to our knees and crawl into the dark, dirty tunnels of our own making to wait.

I've gotten real good at waiting.

Chapter 50

"How's he doing?"

Sam plopped down in the plastic chair at the table in the hospital's cafeteria and leaned back with her eyes closed. "He's going to be okay. They're keeping him overnight, but mostly he's just dehydrated." She opened her eyes to see the concerned faces of Lee and Doug looking back at her. "Renee is sitting with him until he falls asleep."

Lee rotated the Styrofoam cup half filled with tepid coffee slowly on the table. "Has he said what happened?"

"A little, something about a tunnel in the cellar, an underground room, and that a girl named Ginny helped him get out."

"Damn," Doug muttered.

"He mostly just wanted Renee to hold him."

"I'm sorry I didn't warn ya better." Lee's voice was low and weary.

Sam managed a half smile. "How would anyone explain that? Even if you'd tried, who would have believed you?"

"My dad used to talk about tunnels around the place. Guess I should have listened more, but after a while, folks stop listening when ya go on so much about a place." Lee gave them a half smile before his shoulders sagged. He looked deeper into the black coffee in front of him. "We have to go back, ya know? It's time to put this all to rest." He dared a glance at Doug. "We on the same page now?"

"We are."

Lee's head lifted ever so slightly to look towards Sam. "You want to help?"

"Let me light the match, Mr. Yagar."

The old man permitted himself a brief chuckle. "We got some digging to do first, then we can light that place up like the Fourth of July."

"Has Lisa said anything to you?"

Lee's head hung down again as he shook it side to side. "No, not a word. She's shut up tight as a fresh clam."

"Damn. I'm sorry, Lee. I shouldn't have called you."

He grumbled. "I haven't been exactly an open book on the subject, at least not in the way I ought to have been. Lisa will be alright. She's a lot smarter than most folks give her credit for. We'll sit down with her tomorrow and have a good long chat. Her adoption should never have been kept a secret."

Doug drained the last of his coffee and crushed the cup. "You both free Wednesday? I want to get this over and done with as soon as possible."

Renee stayed home with a very clingy Brandon who wanted nothing more than to be held and rocked by his mother. Renee was more than happy to oblige. Physically he was going to make a full recovery, but the doctors had no way of knowing at this point how much psychological damage had been done, and

Brandon still had yet to tell them much of anything about his escape.

Under a cloudy, gray sky that dribbled rain, a small backhoe waited in the backyard of the house on Dark Hollow Road. In the cellar, now thicker than usual with dirt and dust, a pile of ripped-up timbers that had once been canning shelves lay in the middle of the floor, giving Sam, Doug, and Lee easy access to the hole near the floor. Of the three of them, only Doug was able to get in much at all and he wasn't willing to do any more than poke his head in. "It goes back a good twenty or thirty feet," he calculated from his position on the floor, aiming his strongest flashlight down the length of the rough-cut dirt tube. "Looks like it opens up into a room of some sort." He leaned in until his head vanished into the space. "Shit," he hissed and backed out much faster than he'd gone in.

"What ya got?" Lee, who had been crouched with his hands on his knees trying to see anything at all, straightened.

"I think your dad was right."

Lee's eyebrows arched. "Yeah?"

Doug's grim expression said it all.

"She's watching," Lee tossed another shovelful of dirt onto the rapidly growing mound in the back yard.

Sam's spine had been tingling with that feeling for the past ten minutes. "Yeah, I feel it, too."

Pausing, Doug looked up at the house. His eyes shifted from one window to the next. If he saw or felt anything, he didn't say.

Twenty minutes later Sam's shovel went out from under her and sank half way up the handle before she could find her balance enough to pull it back out. "Got something," she announced.

The blind, accusing, black eye of a hole as big around as a bowling ball glared up at her. Doug got down on his belly and shined his flashlight into the abyss. "Yeah, that's it. There's a big, open space down there. Keep digging, but be careful. We don't want this thing collapsing in on us. Last thing we need is another dead body to take off the property."

For the next hour, they dug, stretching the single hole into a trough, revealing the long, narrow confines of the tunnel below.

"Ah, shit!" Lee moaned. "Shit ..."

"What you got?"

The old man stepped back, his face gone slightly white.

Sam peered in. "Fuck."

Stretched out below them was the unmistakable site of human remains. Both arms were extended out, reaching for the end of the tunnel furthest from the house with the fingertips pressed deeply into the surrounding soil. Sam took a wary step back, half expecting the thing to suddenly come to life and finish its last desperate claw towards freedom. The skeleton, for that's really all it was, anymore, wore a ragged, knit sweater over a tattered blue dress dotted with white and yellow flowers. Part of the hem was missing, torn away, a piece the exact same size and shape of a ribbon of fabric that now lay in two pieces somewhere in the overgrown front yard.

"We should call the police," Doug said quietly as if afraid to wake the corpse.

The others nodded but no one made the move to do so. "Let's keep digging this way," Lee finally suggested. "Let's see where she was trying to get to. Once the cops get here, they'll take over the whole damn place. No need for anyone but us to know which way we was digging before we found her."

The three of them hoisted their shovels and went back to work.

Three o'clock was pushing down on them and it had started to rain an hour before. By the time they'd made a big enough hole to see into the cavern, a steady drizzle had replaced the light misting and with the temperature slipping lower, they wouldn't have been surprised to see sleet. Doug jumped down into the trench, squatted a bit and looked into the darkness. "This is amazing," he said, not looking up at Sam or Lee who waited anxiously topside.

"How big?"

Doug took a moment, "Oh, probably ten or twelve feet across, I'd guess."

"Damn. Ya realize how much work all this was?"

"I'm going in," and without any more warning than that, Doug Martin ducked his head and vanished under the thick rim of crumbling earth.

Dark Hollow Road

Chapter 51

How dare them sons of bitches!? They torn it all to pieces. I couldn't do nothing but stand by and watch helplessly as they dug into our hiding spot. I tried, but after that torn piece of me fell from their hands and fluttered back to the ground, I just ain't got the strength no more. They jumped down into the hole they made with shovels and that was the beginning of the end.

One item at a time they lifted out, my little table, a chair, my bowl of apples, my blankets and books, the portable typewriter I'd been using to write everything down with and the stack of writing I'd done on it. Even the rug and one of Seth's little, green Army men that the boy had found in the chicken coop while playing Hide-and-Seek, and later lost in the tunnel, was tossed out.

"Well, we know what happened to Nigel now," Doug Martin pulled my brother's boxed ashes out from the cubby hole I'd dug into the wall to house them. Slightly stooped, he carried it back to the gaping hole and handed it up to Lee who brushed the dirt off in slow, gentle strokes and read the name plate.

After a moment, he handed it off to the husky woman whose relationship with the boy Brandon I still wasn't clear on. "Set that over on the porch stoop, will ya, Sam? We'll tend to it later."

467

She bowed her head against the cold rain, looking curiously at the typed pages of my manuscript more than where she was going with the box of ashes and sat it down practically at my feet. Though I remained unseen, something made her look up a bit more quickly than normal. She took a step back, pupils shifting left and right, searching. Her mouth opened as she took in a breath, preparing to say something, but she didn't speak. Instead, she put my pages down and moved Nigel's remains on top of them for a paper weight. I was alright with her taking the papers. I'd written them hoping someone might one day read them after all.

I watched in silent fury as Lee rose up holding my most precious of treasures, a little China angel with a pink sash holding a basket of roses. Unlike the other things, he didn't just toss it into the heap nor did he hand it off to anyone else. He rubbed his thumb over the ribbon and read what was written on it before looking up at the house. Lee licked his lips, hauled himself out of the hole using his shovel as a crutch, and looked not through, but at me.

"What you got there, Lee?" Doug asked from below. Yagar didn't answer.

He held the dirt-covered angel like a rock and headed towards me.

"Mr. Yagar? You alright?" the woman Sam asked.

He ignored her, too, making his way towards the back porch with heavy, firm strides in a matter of seconds. With his jaw set and his eyes narrowed in what could not be mistaken for anything other than what it was, fury, he stopped his march and met me square in the eye. "Yes, I can see ya," he snorted.

I admit, I was dumbstruck. I'd not been addressed by anyone so directly in a very long time.

468

Dark Hollow Road

"Ya want this?" he held the angel out at arm's length.

With a nod I stammered, "Yes." Was he really going to let me keep it? My cold hands moved out, hesitant, afraid, and trembling. "Please," I pleaded.

My fingers were only inches from her when Lee's hand retracted. His whole arm drew back then he swung it forward like a baseball player on the pitcher's mound. It only took a matter of seconds for the hollow, tinkling sound of shattering porcelain to reach me. It was met with a scream as the pieces slid down the siding and scattered to the ground.

"Tough shit," Lee said, grinning. "I know two other mothers that would like their children back, too. At least yours is still alive and well."

I fell to my knees as Lee walked back to his stunned and watchful friends. My soul was as broken as Ali's little angel. No one came to comfort me. I don't know what became of Allan and Hannah. I'd not seen them since Brandon got away. Maybe Ginny had helped them escape, too.

In the darkening fog, I heard Lee say, "Go ahead and call the police now, Doug."

Chapter 52

The pit was turning into a sloppy mess by the time the sheriff, ambulance, and medical examiner arrived. The ME slid down into the mud that instantly added a heavy layer of tread to his work boots. As he looked down at what little he could see of the remains, he snapped on a pair of pale-blue latex gloves.

With the end of a short, stainless steel rod, the medical man pushed aside the thick clump of dark hair that covered the front of the skull. The jaw hung open, giving the face a wide, tooth-filled smile. Sam stared at the empty eye sockets, knowing all too well what they had looked like in life.

"She's been here a long time," the examiner noted. Crouching, he looked into the dark, root-choked tunnel that led back into the house's basement. "Looks like her ankle got snagged up on a mess of tree roots somehow." He pulled out a digital camera to document as much as he could from this angle.

"Someone get a body bag down here."

Sam, mute and numb, paid no attention to the steady rain that fell around her. How much of this should she pass on to Renee? How was any of this even possible? There was no doubt in her mind that the bones and skull they were now loading with the greatest of care into a black body bag had belonged to Mary Alice Brown, The Sugar Lady.

"How ya doing?" Lee Yagar shifted beside her.

Sam let out an unsteady breath. "Not sure. This is ... I don't know what this is."

"It's over," Lee sounded sure and steady. "That's what it is. As soon as we burn this place to the ground and I till as much rock salt into the plot as I can, this nightmare will be over and done."

"I hope you're right, Mr. Yagar."

"Your boy's going to be okay," the old man added. "Might not be a bad idea to put that place of yours up for sale. I'll give ya a fair price for it, if you're interested."

"Yeah," Sam was disheartened at the idea, but Lee was probably right. A lot would depend on Brandon's recovery and how Renee felt living on a piece of land that had also once been part of Clay Brown's property.

"Your boy said anything more since he's been home?

Sam couldn't take her eyes off the mud-covered skull as it was placed into the bag, then zipped away out of sight. "No, not really. Ginny saved him, that's what he says. It was Ginny who showed him the way out."

"All the way to the chicken coop," Lee added. "I bet that's how that other boy, Paul, got out, too, all those years back."

Sam listened with the hope that these grounds had seen the last of their painful days. "Yeah."

Rain dripping from the bill of his baseball cap, Doug Martin made his way to where they stood by the kitchen stoop. He'd spent the past forty-five minutes talking to the police. He offered Sam and Lee a wan smile. "Soon as they clear out, and we can get a small fire crew on hand to keep from setting Lee's field on fire, we can light her up."

"You're still going to let me light the match, right?"

"By all means," Doug replied.

Chapter 53

The smell of smoke and wet rot clung to my dress, hair, and skin like a humid layer of sour sweat. The air dripped with the residue left behind by the work of four firemen and the rain. All now gone. The drip-drip-drip reminded me of a rainy, summer night and wasn't entirely unpleasant. As I stood in the front doorway and leaned against the scorched frame, I couldn't help but smile. It had been a good try. It really had. But nothing had changed for me.

I had my hiding places. They were places they'd never find. They were my secrets. No one would ever be able to find me. In the years after Nigel's death, I hadn't sat idle. I'd worked hard in the dark of night with a pickaxe and shovel. With a bucket and wheelbarrow, load after load of dirt and rocks had been hauled from the basement to the riverbank. Once I had my tunnels and chambers complete, all that remained was to wait, watch, and listen.

My body'd been carried away now, along with Nigel's remains, but that didn't matter none. I chalked it up as just two more thing that had been taken away. Them thoughts only add to my hatred of anyone who dares step foot on my property.

Behind me, the sounds of groaning wood hung low and deep against the ground before growing taller, as if I were listening to trees reaching out one limb, one beam, one truss, and one wall at a time. The air creaked. Shards of shattered glass tinkled like a wind chime in the soft night breeze. The scrape of bricks sliding over mud grew into the clunk of them being stacked one by one, to loom high and chimney straight above the metallic snap and screech of metal roofing being bent back into shape.

I pulled in a deep breath to savor the crisp, fresh autumn air and looked at the starry sky. The air was ripe and starting to get musty with corn, sweet apples turning sour, rotting pumpkins, and late season wildflowers that swayed in the tall grass of my dark front yard. It didn't matter if they couldn't see me. It mattered even less if they believed the place where my house stood was empty. Remnants of old homesteads like this never entirely go away. There's always something to be found just below the dirt's surface. Let them see and believe what they wanted. I know the truth.

Eventually, someone would come down to the dead end of Dark Hollow Road. They'd see the empty plot and figure out that once upon a time a house had stood here, still stands here as far as I'm concerned. Curiosity will get the best of them.

I felt myself smiling, knowing what curiosity had done to the cat, and I turned from the view of the cornfield and went back into my house. I closed the door, but left it unlocked. Why make things more difficult for them? Let them come in. Let them trespass and steal. I'll be ready and waiting to take care of things. That's what we Browns do, after all. We keep to ourselves and we take care of things on our own.

Dark Hollow Road

Six Months Later

Deep rows of black soil churned up beneath the heavy, steel furrowing blades. Half-cocked around in the tractor's seat, Lee Yagar kept a practiced eye on where he was going and where he'd been, pleased at the sight of the thick salt layer he'd spread by hand being plowed under.

All of it was gone; the house, the barn, and the chicken coop were wiped out of existence. They'd even ripped up the gnarled, old apple trees, burning the sweet wood right along with the barn timbers. He and Doug Martin had agreed that nothing, not one scrap of wood from any structure, would be salvaged despite a handful of people telling them that timber was worth good money. Peace of mind was much more valuable as far as the two men were concerned.

If there were any other bodies buried on the homestead plot, they hadn't been found. Lee was okay with that. Let them folks rest in peace right where they were. Mary Alice's remains were gone and so, he prayed, was she. He'd dreamed about that last sight of her on the kitchen porch, as over and over again he saw that look in her eyes, a broken and hopeful sadness that morphed into the hate and vengeful glare just before she'd vanished. That was tough. He'd carry that vision to the grave. The link between her and Lisa needed to be broken completely, shattered. He and Mary needed to move on from the past. Maybe now they could. He hoped so, for both their sakes.

The ladies had taken him up on the offer of buying their house, but hadn't left Murphey Mills. They'd moved closer to town and from what Lee had seen and heard, the little boy was doing alright. There were the occasional nightmares, but given enough time they were hopeful those would become less frequent.

Renee's antique shop hadn't opened in time for the holiday season of the previous year, but it was doing business now and with any luck at all, would be turning a profit once the summer tourists started passing through on their way to and from the bigger cities nearby.

Sam had taken the typed pages they'd found, promising to burn them when she was done. Lee wanted nothing to do with that. It was the past. It needed to be buried and forgotten.

The hardest part of this whole mess had been coming clean to Lisa. He'd told her what he believed to be the truth, what his parents had told him, but part of him knew there was probably a lot more to it than they'd said.

He may never know if what he'd done this warm spring day with a tractor, a plow, and two-hundred pounds of rock salt would make a difference and accomplish what his father had told him it would.

Lee plowed the final row, lifted the blades, and made his way back to the hard-packed surface of the dead end road. He paused only long enough to glance over his shoulder at the turned soil he left behind before shifting the tractor into high gear and heading back to the fields he'd dared plant with corn.

Dark Hollow Road

He never saw the frail-looking figure of a woman wearing a tattered knit sweater and a light blue dress with tiny white and yellow flowers on it step out from behind one of the maple trees at the end of Dark Hollow Road.

Samantha Whalen stood at the dining room table staring at the crumpled, water-warped, and mud-soiled pages. In the madness of selling their place to Lee, moving to another house closer to town, and helping Renee get her shop up and running, the papers Sam had found had been tucked away and slightly forgotten. Now, alone, she sat, took a sip from her fresh cup of coffee, and began to read.

I was eight years old in 1948 the night Daddy Clay came into my room and pulled the blankets down for the first time.

Acknowledgements & Thanks –

Despite my writing space being in the living room, creating there remains a solitary act. Most writers I know work best when alone and I am no exception. However, this doesn't mean we're complete hermits. You can't write believable characters or scenarios if you never go out and experience real people and places.

With that, I'd like to acknowledge and thank those out there who have inspired, motivated and assisted me over the years. Of course, at the top of the list is fellow Horror author, Hunter Shea, to whom this book is dedicated. Our various conversations via Facebook have made a world of difference to how I view my work and efforts. His willingness to dispense advice and the encouragement he's given over the past few years deserve more than just a mere thank you.

Devon and Aurora: Thank you for choosing me to be your mom.

Jim: Thank you for being such a huge part of making my childhood dreams come true.

Thanks go out to Thomas S. Gunther and Jason J. Nugent, for the friendship, for urging me to never give up, for their advice and for sharing their work with me even before they deemed it worthy for the eyes of the world. I appreciate that level of trust.

Big thanks to Isaac Thorne and Israel Finn who are retweeting mad men!

The Final Guys Cult Crew: This small group of people give me at least an hour every week to just kick back, relax, listen, drink a little, and chat with fellow fans of Horror and followers of The Final Guys podcast hosted by Jason Brant, Jack Campisi, and Hunter Shea. A big, gushy, heartfelt CHEERS to W. Sheridan Bradford, Audra Stinson, Spencer (Scoops) Dunning, Tim Meyer, Jim Herbert, and Steve Barnard. We've never met in the flesh, and we may never, but damn that would be a hell of a party if we could! You all are the reason I have to go back and watch the recorded version of the show because you're so distracting in the chat room.

For my returning readers: You haven't just bought the first book, but continue to lay down cold, hard cash for all of those that have followed. That's a huge boost to my confidence and so very much appreciated. Specifically, Roger C., Pat C., Cynthia L., James S., Susan S., Kaye W., Kathryn H., Debbie C., Johanna W., Sherry S., Katharine H.M., Jack R., Jackie & Bill M., Lorraine S., Diana B., Gene C., Candy O., Cheryl S., Jean K., Irene M., Sarah A., Linda P., Amber I., Josh L., and Kat. A.

To all of you who have liked and are following my author page on Facebook: I love your comments and your company. It makes me so happy to have you all there to share this dream of mine with!

About The Author

Raised in the Finger Lakes region of Upstate New York, but forever longing for the white sands of New Mexico, Pamela has always loved mysteries and the macabre. Combining the two in her own writing, along with her love for historical research and genealogy, came naturally. Hours spent watching 'Monster Movie Matinee', 'Twilight Zone', 'Carl Kolchak: The Night Stalker', along with a myriad of Hammer Films, and devouring the works of Wilkie Collins, Shirley Jackson, Richard Matheson, Rod Serling, Stephen King, and Tanith Lee only added fuel to the fire.

Outside of her work as a novelist, Pamela enjoys the challenges of genealogy research for family and friends. She loves watching bad B-Movies just as much as amazing horror films, taking road trips with her husband, and is hoping to one day convince the crows that frequent their back yard that she honestly wants to be their friend.

pamelamorrisbooks.com

Also by Pamela Morris

The Barnesville Chronicles
Secrets Of The Scarecrow Moon
That's What Shadows Are Made Of
The Witch's Backbone 1: The Curse
Coming soon:
The Witch's Backbone 2: The Murder

Psychological Horror
Dark Hollow Road

HELLBOUND BOOKS PUBLISHING
No Rest For The Wicked
Beautiful Tragedies – Dark Poetry Anthropology

Pink Flamingo Media
THE GREENBRIER TRILOGY:
ROMANTIC-EROTICA AS VICTORIA MORRIS
The Virgin of Greenbrier
The Mistress of Greenbrier
Mistress For Sale